To Jo!

The Secret *of* Jackdaws

Merry Christmas

Tony

Tony Jackson

Grosvenor House
Publishing Limited

This book is published by
Grosvenor House Publishing Ltd
Link House
140 The Broadway, Tolworth, Surrey, KT6 7HT.
www.grosvenorhousepublishing.co.uk

A CIP record for this book
is available from the British Library

ISBN 978-1-83975-344-2

ACKNOWLEDGEMENTS

I would like to acknowledge the following people for the help they have given me in the making of this book.

Ken & Val Graham
Dave & Anne Coulthard
Dulcie Hind

Who helped with editing the book

Also Subscription Bowling Club. Carlisle

Not forgetting
My wife Pat

Who put up with me during the months I sat at the computer writing this novel

FOREWORD

"The Secret of Jackdaws"

This is the third book to feature DS Benedict (Bene) Douglas of Levensbridge Police Force

London – May – 1940
A secret letter is taken by courier for onward transmission to an unknown destination

Ballydonal - Ireland – June – 2012
A dishonest bank manager is forced into desperate measures to save himself and safeguard his future

Levensbridge – South Cumbria – 2018
DS Bene Douglas is called upon to investigate as members of the Bowling Club become targets of a homicidal maniac. The race is on to discover the identity of an unidentified body from 2012 and recover a secret package and stolen money hidden in the village of Longbarrow.
Can he do all this and unmask the killer before he becomes the final victim?

Chapter 1

London May 7th 1940

A Secret Packet

The night was much colder than usual and the man sitting stationary astride his motorcycle was shivering. He pulled his leather jacket tightly around him in a desperate bid to keep warm. But the biting wind was still finding the gaps, working its way through his clothing to chill his very bones. Now May had arrived it should be getting warmer, but ever since this ghastly war had started everything seemed to be that much colder. "Please let it be over soon" he thought "and we can all get back to normal."

He stamped his feet down hard on the road trying to get some feeling back into them, how much longer would he have to wait. He looked up again to the window on the second floor in the building opposite him; although there were many windows in that building he knew he had the right one. Earlier he'd watched as five men entered the building and climbed the stairs, two minutes later a small dim shaft of light appeared below the blackout blind in that window. It should have been blacked out entirely as were all the others, not only in

London but all over the country. But if any German bombers were about that night they'd never spot it from above and that was all that mattered.

He looked at his watch which showed ten minutes to nine, it was only five minutes since he'd last checked but it seemed much longer than that. Southampton Row was a broad street with high buildings on either side, most of which were offices or hotels. There was little traffic at this time of night as the blackout was in operation; most of the city workers had left for the day and were now sitting warm and comfortable in their own homes. Morosely he looked along the long empty stretch of road which tonight was acting like a wind tunnel; the strong wind and patchy rain blowing straight down it.

The long wait was becoming exceedingly boring so he turned his thoughts to more pleasant things. In two weeks' time he'd be celebrating his fortieth birthday and a party had been arranged. It should have been a secret, and it would have been if his big-mouthed sister hadn't blurted it out the day before. He was upstairs in the bathroom at the time, and with the door slightly open he could hear her discussing the arrangements with his wife down in the kitchen. Tactfully when he came downstairs he gave no indication he'd overheard the conversation and was pleased to see the relief on their faces believing the secret was still safe.

All the family would be there, his wife Margaret, two children James and Catherine, his sister along with her husband, and also his brother and his wife. He'd have to practise a look of surprise, it wouldn't do to disappoint them after all the trouble they'd gone to. He was looking forward to his party and he was going to enjoy it. A cold draught of wind caught him and he quickly snapped back to reality and the reason he was in this part of London tonight. He looked up to the window again and was just in time to catch sight of the light being switched off. "Right my son this is it, get ready".

He pressed his foot down hard on the kick start and 1,000 cc of raw power roared into life. The Brough Superior SS100 was his pride and joy; he'd saved long and hard for this machine and tonight it would have the chance to pay him back. The engine settled down to a steady and powerful rhythm as he waited for the messenger to arrive. In the next few hours he'd need to call on all the power of his machine and his riding skills if he were to succeed in his mission tonight.

Earlier five men had entered the building across the road, but only one of them came out. Standing on the opposite pavement the man looked nervously up and down the road before crossing over to meet him. The messenger wore a large leather overcoat with the collar turned up and a trilby hat pulled down to conceal his face. He held out a small packet wrapped in oilskin and tied with string, it had a red seal across the knots. It bore no name or address, just a plain ordinary packet with no outward indication as to where it was going or for whom it was intended.

The rider took possession of the packet, making sure he kept his head down and his eyes averted; he didn't want to be remembered, and if asked he certainly didn't want to be in a position of having to describe the messenger. As far as he was concerned the less he knew about the packet and the person who gave it to him the better. He knew where he had to take it and what he had to do with it, and that was all he wanted to know. The packet was handed over without acknowledgement and the sooner it started its journey the better. In less than twenty four hours it would reach its final destination, and when it was opened and the contents revealed the course of the war would change dramatically.

He placed the packet in the side pannier of his bike and started off immediately down Southampton Row passing Russell Square and Tavistock Square along the way. He needed to use the network of smaller roads before making his way across to Edgware Road and out of London altogether. He'd just turned onto George Street when he first became aware of the vehicle behind him; it was about a hundred yards behind with dimmed headlights which were compulsory during war time. At this point he wasn't unduly alarmed it could be anyone. The roads at this time of night were usually quiet but never entirely free of traffic. Keeping both eyes on his route he changed direction and took a left onto Baker Street then right down Portman Close. A glance behind told him the car was still there, this no longer looked to be coincidence he was definitely being followed. There was no need to panic it was something he considered might happen and he was prepared for it; his knowledge of London's roads and his powerful motorbike would keep him safe.

Feeling a little anxious he took a right into Gloucester Place and opened up the throttle. He raced along this road until he came again to George Street, without looking back he turned into it and sped off down to the junction with Edgware Road.

Once there he stopped for a few seconds to check the road behind him, sure enough the dimmed lights of what appeared to be the same vehicle were still there, he hadn't been able to shake it off. Now he was on the main road leading out of the capital it was time to see what the bike was really capable of and get rid of the pursuing car. Twisting the throttle back he accelerated along the road, certain that his machine had a top speed that was far superior to the vehicle following him.

It would be a long ride up to Liverpool and he'd be tired when he got there so it was just as well he'd booked into a hotel for the night. There was no need to travel back to London right away he could stay in Liverpool and return home the following day, or maybe the day after if he fancied a bit of the night life; he'd heard it was pretty lively up there so maybe he'd take advantage of it. No-one would know, not even his wife, he'd told her he may be away for a couple of days so she had no need to worry.

It was not only a long ride to Liverpool but also a very boring one so he was thankful when at last he came across the outskirts of the metropolis. He knew that RAF Speke was situated within the city itself on the Mersey estuary and that was where he would hand over the packet. He'd never been this far up country before but he had no doubt he'd find the airport without much trouble; in fact he didn't think he could be too far from it now.

There was little traffic on the road and it was starting to get misty so he assumed he must be close to the river. A little further ahead a sign came into view, and when he got closer he read the directions.

<<Diversion ahead – Turn left and follow the route indicated by the arrows>>

"That's good." he thought. "I'm sure the airport will be along there somewhere." Turning onto the new road he found the surface to be in poor condition and he had to ride carefully, there was no lighting and the surface was peppered with potholes.

"Why the hell do they send travellers along here to a city airport for God's sake? It beggars belief; there has to be a better route than this."

He was cursing and muttering because he had to slow right down to avoid the potholes; it needed all his concentration just to keep the bike on a level course.

With his eyes fixed firmly on the road he made his way cautiously along the diversion. Suddenly out of the gloom a man in police uniform appeared right in front of him signalling him to stop, he had to brake hard and only just managed to pull up before colliding with the officer, he cursed loudly belittling the shocking state of the road.

The policeman came around to his side and apologised profusely for the diversion and asked him to pull over onto the grass verge at the side of the road. He followed the policeman's instruction but kept the engine running ready to resume his journey. Suddenly and without warning the policeman was joined by another man, a much bigger man who'd crept up behind and grabbed hold of him around the waist; together the two men dragged the rider from his machine. The bigger man held him down while the other wrenched open the pannier and removed the packet. Now the rider was worried, not so much for losing the packet but for what they intended to do with him. Hopefully they'd be satisfied with getting the packet and leave him unharmed so he could return home. If that was the case he'd consider himself lucky because there was no way he was going to tell anyone what had happened. As far as they were concerned he'd carried out his part of the deal. He'd handed over the packet to some person at the airport who'd given him the right password, and whatever happened to it after that he couldn't care less, he'd done his job and that was that.

However he wasn't kept waiting long, for the man in uniform suddenly pulled out a gun.

"Christ I know this is wartime, but what the hell is this all about?"

The policemen didn't speak but signalled him to move further onto the grass verge, prodding him with the gun until he was standing right on the edge. Looking down to his left the rider saw a shaft of moonlight reflected on the surface of water far below. It looked like a disused quarry that had filled up with rain water over the years and had the appearance of a small lake. The sight of the gun put the fear of God into him and his legs buckled as he struggled to keep his balance on the grass verge, he was terrified of falling over the edge.

But he needn't have worried for when the bullet entered his skull it deadened all sense of consciousness. With eyes wide open and a look of total surprise on his face he slumped forward and toppled over the edge, falling down towards the dark waters below. When his body hit the water the splash was barely audible to the two men watching above.

Unfortunately the rider hadn't brought any ID with him. Everything that could have identified him had been left down in London. Up here in Liverpool there'd be nothing to say who he was, what he was doing there or where he'd come from. He'd been so careful not to tell anyone where he was going that night. His family would miss him of course, and it was a great shame he wouldn't be with them to enjoy his birthday party.

The two men on the road above were discussing what to do about the motorbike.

"It's a bloody good bike and too good to waste." said the man in uniform.

"When the governor gets here we'll see if he'll let us keep it" replied the other.

"The sound of the shot hasn't brought anyone here so he should be putting in an appearance any time now"

No sooner had he spoken than a car which had been crawling silently up the road suddenly pulled up alongside them, the door opened and the governor got out.

"OK lads, job well done, now rip the plates off that bike and chuck it into the quarry."

"Oh hell boss," said one of the men, "it's too good to throw away, we could sell it."

"Just do it!" the governor spat out "or you'll be joining it." He held out his hand.

"And the packet if you please." The packet was duly handed over.

"The gun as well guys." Begrudgingly the gun was also handed over.

"What's in the packet that makes it worth killing that guy?" asked the uniformed man.

"It's something that's going to make me a very rich man when this war is over."

The governor said grinning.

"And what's in it for us then?" asked the other "We killed him didn't we? So we want our share" He pointed a finger at his governor.

"Remember we know who you are, so don't think you can rip us off; we're going to need plenty of dough for what we've done tonight"

The governor smiled. He was enjoying himself.

"OK guys, now the van I gave you to come over in, did you check it out?"

"What do you mean?" said the man in uniform.

"Well if you'd looked in the back you'd have seen your reward because that's where I put it. If you'd checked it out first you'd have found it and saved me the trouble of coming all the way over here."

The two men smiled, but the bigger one had a question.

"How do you know we wouldn't just take the money and not do the job?"

"I trust you guys don't I?" said the governor with a laugh, "And don't forget, I know you as well as you know me."

All three were laughing now; the two men went over to the van and climbed into the back to get their reward. They looked all around inside the vehicle but could see nothing apart from a few sacks and some tins of paint.

"There's bugger all in here," said one, "what the hell's going on, is this some kind of joke?" The governor stuck his head into the back of the van.

"Aw guys, I'm sorry about that, I must have left it back in the office."

The two men were not amused.

The Governor swept his arm around the inside of the van as though admiring the quality.

"I picked a great van though didn't I; the soundproofing in the back is so good. And I want you to believe me guys because I'm going to hate doing this." He stood back and smiled.

"It's been great knowing you, and thanks for making it nice and easy for me."

Abruptly his mood changed and a nasty smirk crept across his face.

"Now I'm a busy man guys and I've got lots to do so let's not prolong this any longer eh."

He fired off several shots into the back of the van, then stood back and listened quietly for a full minute watching and listening for any sound or movement from inside. When he was satisfied there was no life left in the two men, he removed the key from the ignition and closed and locked the back doors. Putting the key back into the ignition he started the engine and drove the van slowly to the edge of the grass verge. He got out and walked around to the back and gave it a little push, and standing back he watched as it rolled over the edge and down into the quarry. It didn't take long to sink but he waited patiently until it was completely submerged and the bubbles had stopped rising; slowly the clear reflection returned to the surface of the water. He returned to his car and started the engine.

"Yes I knew you guys too well," he chuckled. "But if I'd let you live you'd just have spoiled it all. Anyway I can't hang around here all night I have to get to Dublin. So long guys."

Chapter 2

Ballydonal - Ireland June 27th, 2012.

A Manager's dilemma

Ballydonal is a small town and fishing port on the east coast of Ireland, in reality more a large village than a small town. There was nothing special about it, just an ordinary town. Nothing of any significance had ever happened there, nor could it lay claim to anyone famous, past or present who had any connection with the place. Although it was roughly half way between Dublin and Dundalk, it was not on the main route so very few people passed through there. It was a place which in the past would probably have kept its population constant with a few newcomers moving in and some selective inbreeding. With little work in the town most of the younger generation had left and moved to the larger towns and cities to find work. The present population consisted of people who were either working the land, employed in the small shops and businesses, or were otherwise retired. A number of houses had been taken over as second homes by city people buying them up as bolt holes to escape the madness of Dublin.

There was only one bank in the town, a small branch of the Southern Irish Bank where the manager Finnian

Brennan and his two clerks Dermot Laughlin and Roisin Corrigan were employed. Finnian was sitting alone in his small private office hunched over his desk and deep in thought, the lines of worry showing clearly on his face. He was a man of small stature and pale complexion, the result of too many hours spent sitting in his office and his rented accommodation in the town. The narrow rimmed glasses that hung precariously on the end of his nose and barely touching his ears gave the impression of someone who wasn't too happy with his present life and hoping for something much better in the future.

The news he'd received that morning had done nothing to alleviate his misery; in fact it was the worst possible news he could have been given. He stared blankly at the letter which was lying open on the desk in front of him; it had arrived along with the mornings post from the head office in Dublin. He'd read it over and over again but still found it difficult to take in the full impact of its contents. Whichever way he looked at it the message was the same, brief, clear and to the point. The branch in Ballydonal would close for business on the week-end following the next quarter day and would not re-open for business again. When Finnian checked his calendar he saw the next quarter day was Wednesday the first of August, and with the branch not open on Saturday's the bank in Ballydonal would close on Friday the third, a little over five weeks from now.

The letter informed him that The Southern Irish Bank was still coming to terms with the effects of bad debts and investments which it had accrued over the years, leading to millions of euros paid out in compensation.

The letter went on to emphasise that the banking business in general had been through a long and protracted difficult period, but as he was a long serving and highly respected employee of the bank there would be a position for him in Dublin, but unfortunately not as a manager.

Finnian realised that moving to Dublin was never going to be an option for him and there was an obvious reason for this. Once the small branch had closed down and the business and strong-room contents transferred to Dublin it wouldn't be too long before his little indiscretions would come to light. Very soon the bank would discover what had been happening in this little backwater town, and their solicitors would be instructed to instigate legal proceedings against him. For him this would mean a long custodial sentence, and did he want that, of course he didn't.

Five weeks, it didn't afford him much time! However it may be long enough to put in place certain arrangements that would guarantee his safety. He should be able to get out of the country within the next week or two and find a safe haven somewhere in England, or Scotland maybe. He had a cousin in Cumbria and that may be a possible refuge on a temporary basis, but he couldn't stay there too long for it would only be a matter of time before the authorities tracked him down. A week with his cousin was about as long as he could stay. He would have to find somewhere else to live on a more permanent basis; somewhere he could live in safety without having to look over his shoulder waiting for his crimes to catch up with him.

Over the last few years he'd been able to secrete away several hundred thousand euros; money which had been coming into the bank on a regular basis and paid into an account in the name of EMR UK. The names of the directors of this company meant nothing to Finnian; he'd never met them and they'd never once visited the bank. The payments were always deposited in cash, usually in quite substantial amounts and on no fixed dates or times. They were paid in by the same man who on arrival would always ask for him by name. It had been agreed from the start that the source of this money or the amounts deposited would not be questioned, and for this Finnian would receive small amounts in the form of inducements.

After the first year and with no sign of any money being withdrawn from the account greed had tempted him to dip into it, and as time went on he began to take more and more for himself. He understood that the account was for someone who was in prison and when released would be coming to collect it. A few innocuous questions revealed it would be at least another year or so before this was likely to happen.

It wasn't the only account that Finnian had been tempted to tap into; he'd begun to dip his greedy fingers into others as well. There were three accounts for recently deceased customers whose relations were patiently waiting for solicitors to free up the money. This could often take months before it was released, and one of them would take a little longer as the will was being contested. In the short term it may mean robbing Peter to pay Paul, but even so he'd have to get out sooner rather than later before it all came crashing down on him.

It had always been his intention to leave the bank well before his retirement, his pension alone was never going to provide him with the lifestyle he craved in his middle age; EMR UK was going to take care of that! As for the miserly pension from the bank, well they know what they could do with that. Over time he had created two false accounts with the bank and managed to move most of the money over to London. Flying over there recently he'd withdrawn it and invested in a safety deposit box with one of the private banks; it could lay there until such time as he needed it. He could and maybe should have stayed in England but greed had got the better of him. Flying back to Dublin he reckoned he could carry on for another few months before raising any suspicions, and in that time he'd be able to add a few thousand more to his account.

His brother Stuart who had relocated to Scotland several years earlier had recently died. After the funeral Finnian had looked for and found his passport. Stuart had been a year older than Finnian and was very similar in looks, so the passport could easily be used to establish his new identity. The two brothers had never been close and this had been reflected in Stuart's will which had been made out in favour of his cousin.

He looked up at the clock to see it was almost closing time. There was no sound coming from the main part of the bank. There'd be no customers in there now, only the two clerks getting ready to leave and hoping for no late comers to keep them back. A nice hot meal and an evening watching television was what they were looking forward to. They hadn't been informed of the banks closure, Finnian would keep that little bit of news to himself for the time being. Although the bank had guaranteed him a place in Dublin they'd failed to mention if Dermot and Roisin would be given the same guarantee. If head office were to contact them directly then he may have to act a little faster than he'd have liked, but any correspondence regarding himself or his staff usually came to him first so it shouldn't be a problem.

The Southern Irish Bank was the only bank left in Ballydonal after two of the original banks in the town had closed down. Finnian naively believed his bank would always be there providing a service for the good people of the town. But now he was thinking more deeply about it, he began to understand the significance of what he should have been aware of but had carelessly ignored. All the signs had been there and they were pretty clear as to which way the banking industry had been going. He should have realised that overall there had been a slow and steady decline over the last few years due in part to the internet as an alternative means of banking. There were also changes that had taken place in the town itself. Most of the younger generation had moved away to work in the city and the houses they'd left behind had been taken over and used as second homes. The new weekend only occupants had no need for a local bank so it was hardly surprising that head office wanted to close it. He should have seen it coming of course, but it had crept up on him unawares and he hadn't spotted the danger.

Dermot knocked on the door and entered Finnian's office. "OK if we get away Mr Brennan, everything's put away and the balance has been done for the day."

"Yes, that's fine Dermot off you go, leave the main bunch of keys on the counter and lock up with your own, I'll be here for a while yet I just need to check the safe. I'll see you both in the morning."

"Goodnight Mr Brennan."

"Goodnight Dermot."

Alone again Finnian began to plan his escape.

Old Isaac would be the man to help him and he could be found down at the harbour in Dundalk, more than likely in one of the bars along the harbour side. He would go and see him tonight or maybe tomorrow, because not a moment had to be lost if he was to get away safely. Isaac had been a good friend in the past taking him out in his boat when he was a young lad, he knew the old boy would do anything for money and not be too fussy whether it was legal or not.

The manager was the only one allowed into the bank's vaults on his own. On occasion Dermot would accompany him, but before he took Dermot in he made sure anything incriminating was kept safely out of sight.

Switching on the light he made his way down the stairs to the vaults below; the metal railed entrance was the same as had been installed many years ago. For such a small bank the vaults were exceptionally large and occupied an area much the same as the main office above it. The key slid into the well-oiled lock and the gate opened easily and silently. There was a large wooden cabinet which ran the entire length of one wall and this held most of the valuables which had been entrusted to the banks safekeeping. He wouldn't remove anything tonight; most of the money he could safely get away with, he'd already taken, but there were a few little extras he'd take with him when the time came. He ran his hand along the high centre shelf until it came into contact with a small dusty packet wrapped in oilskin; it was tied with string and sealed with red wax. He'd seen this many times and wondered just what it was; a card had been tied to it with the message

"Paid for in Dublin, to be left until such time as Mr J.S. O'Halloran will call to collect"

He'd no idea how long the packet had been there but knew it had lain undisturbed for several years at least. Maybe he'd take it with him it could be something of value, and if it hadn't been collected before now it was unlikely it was ever going to be collected. He checked around the items he would take with him, there was quite a wad of cash and he could take some of that. But most of the money he'd stolen had already been converted into bonds which could easily be cashed in the future. He could take a small amount, but he didn't want to arouse suspicion from Isaac so better not be too greedy at this late stage, he'd take just enough to pay Isaac for the trip and sufficient to keep himself in England for a few days.

He removed one or two items from the shelf and locked the vaults behind him as he left. He'd just got back to his office and sat down when he heard a loud knock on the outside door. He rose and went over to the intercom to speak to the person outside.

"I'm sorry but the bank is now closed we'll be open again at nine in the morning."

There was a short pause before the person outside spoke.

"I'm here on behalf of EMR UK Mr Brennan, and I need to talk to you about our account here. I believe this branch is about to close so we'll have to discuss what we do to close the account down. We can't afford to have it transferred to Dublin for obvious reasons. I'll be back on Monday and we can arrange a series of cash withdrawals over the next ten days or so, are you OK with that."

The bank manager was stunned into silence and there was a long pause.

"Are you still there Mr. Brennan?"

"Yes, yes I'm still here, Monday you say, that's not really a good day could we not make it later in the week?"

Finnian was struggling with the enormity of what this could mean; he needed time, and somehow he must delay seeing this man for as long as possible, but the man outside was getting impatient.

"I'm sorry, but it has to be Monday Mr Brennan and I'll be with you shortly after nine. Now don't start messing with us Mr Brennan, we've been very generous with you but all good things must come to an end and you should appreciate that. Monday it is then Mr Brennan, and make sure you're free to talk." The intercom went silent.

Chapter 3

Ballydonal – Ireland June 27th and 28th 2012

A Manager's decision

Finnian was a single man with no children and few close relations or friends. Born in Dundalk he'd kept his house there and rented one in Ballydonal for his term in the town. His intention had been to move back to Dundalk when he retired. But this wouldn't be possible now, as when his crimes came to light the bank, the police and his victims would soon hunt him down and come looking for their money. He needed to leave the country altogether and find a new home. The longer he thought about it he realised the decision would not be such a painful one. Leaving Ballydonal and Dundalk wouldn't be too much of a wrench.

It was a pity he couldn't continue with his scheme a little longer, but the best part of a million euros should provide him with a very comfortable retirement, somewhere with a warmer climate would be most satisfying. What to do first though that was the problem. There wasn't much time to arrange everything and he needed to act fast. He must get back to his house in Dundalk where he kept his brother's passport and a few other articles, then make plans to get out of the country at the weekend. It was more than likely he'd be a hunted man, and leaving through the normal channels via ports or airports wouldn't be an option. Could he go over to Scotland and stay at his brother's old house. No, that would be one of the first places they'd look for him. His cousin in England would be a safer bet as no-one in Ireland knew about him. He could stay there for a while, news of his transgressions wouldn't reach England for some time at least, if ever. His old fisherman friend Isaac would ferry him across for a price and he did have access to funds to pay him for the trip. Yes old Isaac would do it no problem; he wasn't afraid to take a bit of a risk.

He closed the bank and made his way over the road to the car park, checking all the time that neither he nor the car was being watched. It was possible that the man who called at the bank may know more about his private life than he'd have liked. Finally he plucked up courage and walked swiftly but not rushing over to his car, quickly unlocking it he slid into the driver's seat and drove away without delay.

Once in Dundalk he left the car some way from his house and walked slowly to the corner of the street. He watched intently, focusing on the house which was half way down the terrace, there was just enough light to convince him it wasn't being watched. Carefully and without hurrying he made his way to the front door and let himself in. Once inside he stood back from the window and checked the road and pavement outside. Satisfied there was no-one around he went to the kitchen and checked the back of the property; again he could see no-one. He'd used the house occasionally at weekends so the electricity and water supply were still connected. Making himself a cup of coffee he settled down in the armchair to plan his next move.

He didn't want to give any indication the house was occupied so he'd leave the lights off and spend the night there. It was too late to go looking for Isaac that could wait until the morning; he knew where he could find him. What he needed to do now or at least sometime before midnight was withdraw the daily limit from his two bank accounts, then just after midnight he could draw on them again. That would give him enough cash to pay Isaac, and leave some over to keep him in England for a few days until he started to draw on his capital over there.

He took the piece of paper showing the details of the bank and box number where his money was stored in London and wrote it down inside an envelope which he sealed; the piece of paper was destroyed. At half eleven he left the house and drove to the two banks and withdrew his cash limit from the ATM's. Waiting until just after midnight he duplicated the task. With all the trauma of the day his mind had given no thought to food, he hadn't eaten anything since breakfast and now he was decidedly hungry. There was an all-night McDonalds in the town so he bought a couple of burgers and some French fries and took them back to the house with him.

Rising early the next morning he checked again that the house wasn't being watched. Dressed in more suitable clothes he left by the back entrance and headed to the quayside where he should find Isaac. It didn't take long as Isaac could be seen talking to a fellow fisherman. The two men were very similar in appearance, both of medium height with slim wiry figures; both had grey hair and short straggly beards stained with tobacco, they could easily have been mistaken for brothers, one in all blue denims and Isaac in a dark blue boiler suit. Finnian waited until the conversation was over and the other man had left before approaching Isaac who greeted him warmly. It had been a while since the two had last met, and although Isaac was pleased to see his old friend he could sense there was something troubling him.

Finnian had intended to return to Ballydonal that morning and carry on working until the weekend but all that changed when Isaac threw a spanner in the works. When Finnian told him of his plan Isaac pulled a long face.

"Sorry Finnian but I've let the boat out to a group of men for a fishing trip at the weekend it will have to be sometime later next week, I'm afraid that's all I can offer you."

Finnian's hopes had been dashed; he knew he couldn't afford to be in the country even for a few more days. His mind went numb; he'd been so sure he could rely on Isaac to get him out of the country. He fell silent for a few moments and Isaac could feel the tension. Then Finnian brightened up, he had another proposition; it was desperate but worth a chance.

"How about tonight then, you could get me over there and be back in good time for the fishing trip at the weekend." There was a long pause before he got his answer but eventually Isaac was in agreement; a deal was struck and money changed hands.

In the meantime Isaac would buy extra fuel for the long trip over to England and they would meet up just after dark that night to begin their journey. Finnian phoned Dermot at the bank explaining some problem with his house, and he needed him to provide cover until the following day.

Due to the boat being relatively small and the distance they would have to travel Isaac insisted on doing the trip in two stages.

"Don't forget," he said, "the ferry from Dublin to Liverpool takes eight hours, and the distance is about the same as we'll be taking if not a bit further, and this is a much smaller boat so it'll take us a lot longer than that. We'll have to do it in two stages, first to the Isle of Man, then over to Cumbria."

"We can't get there any quicker than that?"

"Relax man, I don't know why you need to get over there in such a damned hurry and neither do I care, but whatever your reason I've got to make it look like a normal trip. I take scallops over to my brother sometimes, and it's a while since I was over there so he'll be pleased to see me, and even more pleased to get some fresh scallops and that'll be our reason for going there. It might look a bit odd me leaving him in the early evening but I'll tell him I'm going to try some new fishing grounds while I'm in the area. Hopefully no-one will notice which direction we take when we leave, because that's the risky bit getting over to the UK mainland and back to the Isle of Man again. After I've dropped you off I'll go down the coast a bit and put in at a little place I know and get a few hours' sleep. I'll try the waters for scallops or crabs and call at my brothers again before coming back to Ireland."

Finnian had been taking all this in and reckoned the trip was going to cost him a lot more than he previously thought. Isaac had been thinking as well, and he knew that whatever the reason Finnian wanted to go with him, it was anything but a normal trip. Why all the secrecy? There must be a damned good reason for not taking the easier option as there were numerous ferry's travelling over to the UK several times daily. Something very dodgy was afoot, but Isaac wasn't going to worry about that so long as the price was right. Yes, old friend or not he'd make sure he was paid a bit more than the going rate, a hell of a lot more. Old Isaac grinned; this was going to be a nice little earner.

Chapter 4

Cumbria - July 4th 2012

Finnian arrives in England

The crossing from Dundalk to the Isle of Man had taken much longer than the two men expected, and once there Isaac took a panic attack and refused to carry on with the final part of the trip.

"It's too bloody risky Finnian; if I get caught on this last lap with no reason to be in these waters they'll bloody well lock me up."

Now it was Finnian who was panicking.

"Well I've come this far and I can't bloody well go back, I have to get to the mainland. And if I don't I'll be locked up as well, and for a bloody lot longer than you."

"Calm down man it's OK, I've spoken to my brother and he'll take you over. He's a resident here so he has fishing rights and a legitimate reason for being in these waters so don't you worry. The only problem is you'll have to stay here with him for a few days before he can take you over. But he knows the coast much better than I do and he'll be able to drop you off exactly where you want to be."

Finnian was left with no choice, there was no way back he couldn't return to Ireland. It was morning back there and when he didn't arrive for work at the bank they'd start looking for him, and when they couldn't find him another manager would be called in and probably an audit team as well. When all his wrongdoings came to light the hunt to find him would be on.

Four long days he waited in the Isle of Man, all the time knowing there'd be a nationwide search going on for him back in Ireland; his picture would be on TV and in the newspapers. When eventually they did leave the Isle of Man the relief was overwhelming. The journey was easily taken and the wind had been favourable, but it had been much colder than the forecast predicted. Finnian took the torch from his pocket and shielding the light with his hand checked the time on his watch; it was almost three o'clock. It would be some time before daylight broke and he was thankful for the darkness which would protect him over the next few precious hours. The rain had stopped almost an hour ago but the dark clouds still hung menacingly overhead. The small boat with its engine now switched off drifted slowly towards the isolated West Cumbrian coast at the northern end of Morecambe Bay.

Finnian waited until the boat had ground to a halt on the shingle beach before slowly rising from his cramped position on the coarse wooden seat; he stepped ashore and in silence handed over an envelope to the man who'd brought him there. As soon as the payment had been checked Finnian pushed the boat back into the water. He waited until it had turned round and the engine re-started, then Isaac's brother slowly disappeared into the darkness to begin his journey back home.

He turned round to face the awesome backdrop of the South Lakeland hills. Standing there quietly he waited for his eyes to fully adjust to his new surroundings. Satisfying himself he had a reasonable idea of just where he was he began to make his way to higher ground. He needed to put distance between himself and the coast as quickly as possible. He was a little apprehensive as he'd never been in a situation quite like this before, alone in the dark in a strange place. It was doubtful if anyone had witnessed the landing, and he hoped he wouldn't be seen or challenged at least until he was far away from here. It would be much better all-round if his arrival in the country was to go completely unnoticed.

He was faced with a long journey and all of it on foot until he reached the farm where his cousin lived. He felt inside the large pocket of his jacket to make sure the packet was still there containing his money, bank envelope, passport and the small packet he'd been so careful to protect. Two hours later he got the first sight of the farm which was on the outskirts of Longbarrow village. It had been a few years since he'd last been there but the walks he took on previous visits now proved useful to him. Although the years had passed his memory of the surrounding countryside hadn't diminished; strangely enough he found himself more at home here than back in Ireland. Thinking back to his house in Dundalk which had been his home for many years he realised it would never be worth very much, and it would be quite easy to forget all about it. He had enough money to live comfortably somewhere much nicer. Maybe in years to come he might want to go back there but he doubted it, it would be much better to cut all ties with Ireland completely and leave the house to rot.

At last he approached the farm, there were no lights showing in the house as it was still early morning and his cousin wouldn't be out of bed for another hour at least. Although he was sure he hadn't been followed there were little things that kept niggling away at him, odd noises as though someone was closer to him than he'd have liked, someone trying not to give their position away or arouse suspicion. But realistically there was no way anyone could know he was here or the purpose of his visit; surely it was just the dark and his imagination playing tricks on him. He took a small tour of the farm buildings and found they were just as he remembered cold and depressing, and containing much of what he'd seen on earlier visits. He was still feeling a little uneasy and couldn't shake off the irritating feeling that something was not quite right, and it was praying on his mind. He was still cursing the four days he had to spend on the Isle of Man; if only he could have got away from there when he should have done he'd be feeling a whole lot better. Suddenly he remembered there was a place where he'd be safe and out of sight, and he could wait there until daylight. It wasn't too far away and in a matter of minutes he found it. Once there he concealed himself and settled down and prepared to wait. Then another thought came to him, he knew exactly where he could leave his valuables, somewhere they'd be safe and he could retrieve them just before he left. That would be much better than carrying them around all the time, and they'd be safe from his cousin as well. Finnian didn't want him to accidently find them as it could lead to some very awkward questions, questions he'd find difficult to answer.

He glanced outside to make sure no-one was around and then walked over and placed the package neatly into a place where he knew it wouldn't be found, even by his cousin. Feeling bored he decided not to wait for his cousin to get up; he would take steps to allay his fears however unfounded they may be, and satisfy himself he was alone and completely safe. There was a strip of open land between him and the village and he broke out into a sprint to cover the distance as quickly as possible. He reached the small village and ran past the pub and down a narrow lane into the saw mill where he could smell the contents of a large creosote tank. The smell was quite overpowering, when he looked inside there were some wooden gates that had been soaking up the liquid overnight. A shortcut over to the left took him back to his cousin's farm; he stopped to check if he'd been followed but there was no indication that anyone else was there. He sat down and considered what to do. It wouldn't be long until dawn and the village folk would soon be getting up to go about their daily business.

He walked back to the saw mill and wandered around, looking to see if there was anything familiar he could remember from his visits there as a child. The smell from the tank was particularly strong; it was one of those smells that had never changed over the years. He smiled to himself as he looked over to see the contents which took him back to long ago and his childhood visits to the farm and the village. The wind was gathering strength and the leaves on the trees began to rustle; these natural little noises comforted him as he stood there, his thoughts wafting aimlessly towards the future he was just about to enjoy.

Maybe he'd relaxed a little too early for slowly but quietly a dark shadow had been looming up behind him. Suddenly a pair of strong hands grabbed him round the neck, pushing him forwards and forcing his head over the side of the tank, his attacker plunged his head down into the pungent liquid. Finnian gasped, and in doing so inhaled some of the creosote; he coughed frantically trying to get it out of his system.

"Right you bugger where is it?" a deep voice with a strong Irish accent demanded. Finnian couldn't have spoken even if he wanted to as the creosote was scolding his throat. The man not realising the effect it was having on his victim again demanded an answer, and not getting one plunged Finnian's head back down into the revolting liquid. Desperately trying to breathe Finnian tried to reach the man's arms that were holding him in a vice-like grip, but the action only resulted in him taking more of the viscous liquid into his lungs. He slowly drifted out of consciousness, went limp and slumped over the edge of the tank unable to right himself. Voices coming up from the lane finally put an end to the man's torment as his assailant relaxed his hold on him and disappeared down the lane without getting the answer he wanted. Finnian slowly slipped off the edge of the tank and slithered down onto the sodden floor of dirt and sawdust below. The village was starting to come to life and people were moving around but no-one seemed to notice the poor man lying prostrate behind the creosote tank.

Slowly Finnian drifted back into a semiconscious state; he dragged himself around the tank where he thought he'd be safe from another attack, little knowing that his assailant had fled. There'd been too many people around for the Irishman to take another chance. Finnian lay unnoticed for the next few hours unable to cope with the nauseating liquid which was slowly poisoning him; there was no way he was going to enjoy the fruits of his crime now. He'd gladly have given the information to his assailant if only he could, but was given no chance to do so the creosote had put paid to that. It had rendered his throat incapable of any form of coherent speech. It had almost cleared from his mouth and throat but the damage had already been done, the toxic liquid was working away deep down inside him and slowly destroying his organs. What a sad end to his well laid plans, and it was no consolation that he'd never be prosecuted for his crimes.

It was the school holidays and the local children were out playing 'hounds and hares' around the village. Two of the boys ran down towards the saw mill and thought the giant tank would be a good place to hide behind. When they reached it they were shocked to find this strange man lying on his side with his face covered in a black substance. Their first instinct was to run away, but the man seemed harmless enough just lying there and unable to get up; he was trying to signal them to come over as if he wanted to speak to them. They hesitated in case it was some sort of trap, but as the man seemed incapable of movement they cautiously crept nearer keeping a safe distance in case he should attempt to grab hold of them. He motioned them closer, and in a hoarse whisper and a strange accent which was difficult to understand he spoke to them. He was trying to tell his story and explain what he'd done with the package, but his words were slurred and the boys couldn't understand. Eventually the effort proved too much for the man and moments later he slumped over and went completely limp. The frightened boys ran off, too scared to tell anyone what they'd seen and heard; they decided it would be best not to tell anyone about what they'd witnessed in case they got into trouble, and be blamed for being there.

Later that day young Stephen Dawes thought he'd understood a little of what the dying man had said, but it made no sense to him.

"Judge Alice has it" he'd said, but Stephen didn't know any judge's, and the only Alice he knew was his old aunt but she wasn't a judge. And what else did he say "Wollocks" or something like that, well he had no idea what or where Wollocks was, maybe it was bollocks." The poor man must have been gaga.

Chapter 5

Levensbridge August 2018

Incident in the Car Wash

It had been a good day so far, and for Arnold Bainbridge the journey home from work was a pleasant one. He sat relaxed at the wheel of his car looking forward to a nice quiet weekend at home; it was Friday and he'd managed to complete his day's work earlier than expected. Thankfully the rep he should have seen late that afternoon had called off at the last minute. This suited Arnold fine because his diary was nowhere near full the following week and he'd have no trouble fitting an extra appointment in then.

The weather was good and the sun high in the sky, with the temperature in the low twenties and forecast to stay that way for the next few days the weekend looked inviting, just waiting for him to enjoy it. The sign ahead told him he was approaching the outskirts of Levensbridge, the small south Cumbrian town where he lived with his wife Laura. It would be her fiftieth birthday next month and as yet he hadn't been able to think of a suitable present to mark the occasion. He'd reached the same milestone himself two years earlier and they'd taken a cruise in the Mediterranean to celebrate. It was the first time either of them had been on a cruise and they'd enjoyed it immensely. Maybe they could do something similar this year, or better still somewhere different, somewhere they hadn't been before. "Australia maybe?" he mused, "No that would take too long, he couldn't afford to take that much time off work. It would have to be somewhere a bit closer. New York possibly, yes that would be better, Times Square, The Empire State Building and Central Park, take in a couple of shows, yes that would be a holiday they'd treasure for a long time."

Just up ahead was a car wash, the one he often used on his way home from work on Fridays. He'd stop off there and run his car through, it would only take a few minutes and it would save him precious time at home where other jobs might be waiting for him. Laura would expect him to cut the grass but that wouldn't take long, he could do that in the morning, and then he'd be free to do whatever he liked for the remainder of the weekend. He indicated and turned into the wash there were only two cars waiting so he pulled in behind them. It wouldn't be long before it was his turn; he wound down the window to let some fresh air into the car as it was getting stuffy.

A few minutes later and it was Arnold's turn, paying the attendant for a wash and wax he wound the window back up. The attendant pumped up the pressure on the spray and walked round the car spraying the wheels; taking out a large soapy brush he roughly lathered the windscreen and both sides of the vehicle. With this done he motioned Arnold to bring the car forward onto the conveyor which would take it through the wash; the car was now lined up and in position to begin its journey. Arnold found the sound of water gushing over the car pleasant and relaxing; moving slowly through the wash the brushes swept along the sides of the car and up over the bonnet onto the windscreen. For a while the large brush fully covered the screen and blocked his vision completely; then as it moved onto the roof it allowed a little light to come back into the car, although the windscreen was still blurred by running water.

It was at this point his attention was drawn to a shadow partially blocking out the light ahead, what on earth was it? He tried hard to focus his eyes, there was definitely something there just beyond the dryer but he couldn't make out what it was. As the windscreen cleared the shadow became a little clearer it looked as though someone was standing inside the exit.

"What the hell is he doing there the silly bugger; some bloody kid I suppose," it was only a trivial matter but never the less it irked him. As the dryer started to rise up over the windscreen his vision again became blocked.

"Oh well, no doubt he'll run off before I get that far."

Settling back into the comfort of his seat he waited until the dryer crept slowly up and over the windscreen. It always amazed him how close it came to touching the vehicle. As it disappeared onto the roof he could see it wasn't a kid after all who was standing there. It was a fully grown adult, someone dressed in a light grey tracksuit with the hood covering most of their face. The car continued slowly forward propelled by the roller conveyor to the final part of the wash, the furry drying belts dragged slowly across the bonnet and onto the windscreen before continuing up and over the roof. As they did so the man appeared again in full vision right in front of the car.

As he got closer Arnold was able to see more of the man's face, and it was the face of someone vaguely familiar to him. He thought he knew who this person was. It was the clothes that had confused him because this man never dressed like that; he was always well turned out and would never be seen in anything resembling the cheap jogging gear he was wearing now. The man remained stationary just a yard or so in front of the car. Arnold's eyes were transfixed; there must be some reason for this and no doubt he'd find out soon enough.

As the car approached the exit Arnold wound down the window, the man leaned forward and bent his head close to it smiling as his recognition of the driver was confirmed.

"Well Arnold, we meet again at long last, I've been a bit worried about you lately and I believe it's time we found a solution to our little problem don't you?" At this point the stranger bent his head further down to within inches of Arnold's face, his next words were whispered quietly "You remember that night.................?" The man went on to explain his problem and also the solution he'd come up with. The effect on Arnold was devastating; he went to speak but the words coming from his mouth made no sense at all, it was gibberish. The man who previously had his hands in his pockets now withdrew one of them, and that hand held a gun.

The realisation of how suddenly the situation had changed hit Arnold hard for the gun was pointed directly at him. He froze completely, he couldn't move any part of his body whatsoever, nor was he able to speak; somehow his mind had become detached from his physical body and all his senses paralyzed.

"Why the hell is this happening to me," he thought "is it just to scare me," if so it was certainly working. He felt a strange sensation down below as wetness started to seep slowly into the groin area of his trousers; it was this that helped bring him back to the reality of what was happening. At last he found his voice.

"Jesus man, this is unreal! For Christ's sake put that bloody thing away I'm not the man you want, you're making a big mistake."

But the man was unmoved.

"There's no mistake Arnold, I've got the right man alright."

Slowly he brought the gun level with the car window, and looking directly into Arnold's eyes and without wavering he gently squeezed the trigger.

The gun made only the slightest noise, a loud pop was all that came from the silencer, not enough to alert anyone or to suggest that anything was amiss inside the car wash. Arnold slumped forward over the steering wheel and a thin red line of blood slowly trickled down from his motionless head to form a small pool on the dashboard clock. The man turned away replacing the gun in his pocket as he did so. He walked calmly out of the car wash passing the sign which read 'Drive away when your windscreen reaches this point' It would be some time before Arnold's car would pass through there. The man crossed the road to the car park and climbed into a silver Toyota hatchback. He drove casually out onto the main road and out of town, his mission for the day complete. One down, four to go.

By this time the driver immediately behind Arnold's car was getting annoyed. He began beeping his horn to get the car in front to move on, this alerted the attendant who came round to see why Arnold's car hadn't driven off as expected. Looking through the open window he saw the figure of the driver slouched over the wheel. He reached in and touched the man on the shoulder; the drivers head rolled to the side and revealed the dashboard splashed with blood. He didn't want to see any more, he spun round and ran out from the wash and vomited heavily at the side of the bay.

Chapter 6

Levensbridge Police Station

Bene is stung into action

Levensbridge police station could be found a short distance from the town centre; situated at the end of a row of terraced houses on a narrow street. Built in the Victorian era it had never changed its outward appearance, but inside the building had undergone several alterations and was now fully equipped and computerised to deal with all modern police operations.

It was late in the afternoon and the station was unusually quiet, the desk sergeant had taken a few calls since lunchtime but nothing of a serious nature, and none that required a police presence. Val the admin clerk was up-to-date with her work and could afford to sit back and relax, but as a precaution she made sure there was paperwork in her in-tray, although this had been dealt with there was good reason for it to be there. If Inspector Sowerby should deem it necessary to check on what was happening in the outer office she could pull out one of the files and go through the motions of working on it; heaven forbid if he thought she had nothing to do for he would soon find her something.

Val was nobody's fool and a month earlier she'd seized on an opportunity that presented itself during the office re-organisation. The rest of her colleagues had failed to see it, or if they had they hadn't reacted to it early enough. She'd strategically placed her desk where she could sit with her back against the only blank wall in the office, and this gave her a definite advantage as she had a clear view of the office and all the doors leading into it; most importantly the door which led to Inspector Sowerby's office. In this position she had first warning of anyone coming into the office, especially the Inspector. This particular afternoon she sat half hidden behind her computer screen concentrating on something much more important than police work, a final polishing of her nails. Looking at them proudly she admired each one in turn, all sporting different colours and designs and all finished off with dazzling glitter.

The thoughts of DS Bene Douglas of the CID were also directed away from police work, his mind was very much elsewhere, pondering over a difficult decision he would soon have to make. He'd been living with his wife Alex and her mother Dot for the last year, and although the arrangement suited him well enough Alex was anxious to leave her Mother's house and move to a home that Bene and she could call their own. Bene's broad brow creased up as he mulled over the problem.

"I suppose Alex's wishes must come first, and if that was what she wanted then that's what they must do." They'd always got on well with Dot and it would be a wrench to leave, and of course if they did it would have to be somewhere not too far away. Luckily he was warming to the idea, and as he liked the area it shouldn't be too difficult to find somewhere suitable. A lot of people on the estate were business people and frequently moving around with their jobs so there was never a shortage of houses for sale. They'd been saving hard for this but it was coming just a bit sooner than he'd planned for. A sergeant's salary wasn't that good and he'd been hoping to get his promotion through first before taking on a mortgage. Alex was bringing in a wage as well so they should be able to finance it, but they'd also been planning a family so how would that impact on everything. He gave a long drawn out sigh which didn't go unnoticed by Val and the other officers who silently exchanged smiles and a shake of heads.

It wasn't the only thing on Bene's mind today; he was still waiting for his DC, Emlyn Thomas to return from his honeymoon. Emlyn who was more commonly known as ET had been his DC for the past year; together they made a good team even though they differed in many ways. Bene was a local man and looked exactly that. His full name was Benedict Douglas but to everyone who knew him he was just Bene; he wasn't good looking but made up for this with his charm and friendly nature. He was just over six feet tall with an athletic build; his face displayed a full range of rustic features and on top was a mop of thick curly brown hair. Bene had learned his trade from DI Adam Firth who was now retired from the force. Adam and he had enjoyed a good relationship in CID, and with Adam taking the lead it was a relationship that had worked well.

ET was about three inches shorter than Bene but much broader. He was Welsh, and not unsurprisingly a Rugby man, his face showing all the classic signs of being involved in that unforgiving sport, the squat nose, deep set eyes under the broad forehead, and ears welded to the side of his head. His hair was cut short which only helped to emphasise his facial characteristics, but behind this mask was a hard-working, honest and intelligent man.

The Senior Police officer at Levensbridge was Inspector Gordon Sowerby, a strict man and strong on discipline, a firm believer in doing everything by the book. Sowerby was one of the old school types who had come up through the ranks. He stood tall, well over six feet with a slim figure to match; his upright posture was a relic of his army past and his angular bony features tended to disguise any feelings he had. No one could take him for anything other than what he was, a well-respected, efficient, and no nonsense officer of the law.

Suddenly there was a loud crash and everyone in the office jumped as Sowerby's door flew open, Val cursed, and not too quietly either as she smudged one of her nails. Bene dropped the file he'd been holding and the papers spilled all over the floor; the plastic coffee cup that had sat on his desk got knocked over and the remaining cold liquid splashed all over his desk.

"Bloody hell" he swore as he promptly dropped onto his knees to try and retrieve the situation.

"Bene," Sowerby shouted, "get off the floor and in my office right away!" before storming back into his office and slamming the door behind him.

"What the hell's the matter with him this afternoon?" said Bene.

"I wouldn't hang about Bene," said Val, "if you don't get in there pretty quick he'll be in an even worse mood, you know what he's like."

Bene quickly gathered up the papers and dumped them on the only dry part of his desk. "Clean that up for me someone please," he asked of no-one in particular as he dashed over to Sowerby's office. He gave a swift rap on the door and went straight in. Sowerby was waiting there drumming his fingers on the desk.

"We have an incident up at the car wash on Windermere Road Bene. I've just had a phone call from the attendant and it seems that someone's been attacked, possibly shot. I don't have much information but you should get up there ASAP. It might be some sort of accident but you'll have to check it out, the lad wasn't too coherent. You can pick up Devlin on the way he's waiting for you at Tesco's. I haven't anyone else just now but your DC should be back sometime today, so give him a call when you get over there and tell him not to come here but meet you at the car wash. That's all I have for you at the moment so find out what's happened and let me know as soon as you have a bit more information."

"Better not grab another coffee before I go," Bene thought, "Sowerby will be watching from his office window to make sure I leave right away." It took him less than ten minutes to pick up PC Devlin and get to the car wash, and when he arrived he found the attendant and the ambulance men waiting for them.

"OK Devlin, all I need you to do at the moment is stop anyone coming into the wash. It's important that we seal the place off and we have the site to ourselves," then pointing over to two cars at the far side whose drivers were looking to see what was going on,

"And get rid of them as well; don't tell them anything other than the place is now closed for the day." PC Devlin went off to do his duty and Bene went over to the ambulance men who were attending someone in the driver's seat of the silver VW. Bene walked over and looked in through the driver's window which was open.

"How is he?" he asked, "dead or alive?"

"Dead," replied one of the ambulance men "looks as if he was shot right between the eyes, death would have been instantaneous."

"Oh it's true then, he was shot?"

"No doubt about it. And it wasn't an accident either it was a deliberate act, whoever did it meant to kill him. The pathologist is on his way we're just waiting for him to get here."

Bene shook his head.

"Christ! Right here in broad daylight in the middle of the day, I can't believe it. Don't move anything until forensics get here OK? Does anybody know who he is?"

"No, but the attendant says he comes in regularly so he must live somewhere in the town."

"No problem then, the car has a local registration so I'll give DVLA a call and they can tell me. Bullet right in the middle of the forehead eh, and at close range as well. The poor bugger wouldn't have stood a chance." Bene was finding it hard to take in.

"Did it happen in the car wash? It seems a bit strange doesn't it a busy place like this, someone must have seen or heard something."

He went over to the attendant and showed his warrant card.

"Are you going to be OK, you look a bit shaken? Let's go over to your office and get a drink and you can tell me what happened." Just then the pathologist arrived, Bene needed to speak to him.

"OK, you go and sit down; I'll be with you in a minute I need to see this guy first." Bene left the lad and went back to the car to hear what the pathologist could tell him.

"Looks a straight forward case to me, but I'll have to get him back to the morgue and on the slab before committing myself." Then he turned to the ambulance men. "Bring him over as soon as you've finished here."

Bene told him that photos and forensics had to be done first. The pathologist brought out his camera and took the photos he needed, and in a matter of minutes he had everything he wanted and left.

Bene went over to the office to see the attendant.

"How do you feel now, it's been quite a shock for you hasn't it?" The attendant looked pale and distraught and his hands were still shaking, but Bene needed information.

"Now, first of all tell me what you saw, I mean did you actually see what happened when this guy drove his car through the wash?"

"No, I didn't know anything about it until this car horn started blaring away and I went round to see what the problem was." The attendant pointed a rather shaky finger over to the car. "I haven't touched anything apart from helping to push the car out of the wash, and that was just to let the guy behind get his car out. I phoned for an ambulance and you lot first, then I closed the place down."

"Did you know what had happened to him?"

"I'm not sure but it was one hell of a shock finding him like that. Is it right that he was actually shot?" he asked in a quite unbelieving way.

"We don't know how he died just yet, and we won't know for certain until they've had a better look at him, but don't go spreading any rumours because we have to let the pathologist do his work, and it will be him who tells us what the cause of death was." Bene didn't want to give out too much information as God knows what the attendant might start telling people.

Luckily he spotted his colleague ET who'd just arrived and was showing his warrant card to the constable at the entrance. ET drove in and immediately came over to the office to be greeted by Bene.

Bene needed someone to communicate with Inspector Sowerby while he continued interviewing the attendant. He took ET out of the office and brought him up to speed with what he'd discovered which wasn't much at all.

"Get Sowerby on your mobile and tell him what's happening. I don't know if he wants to come up here himself but let him know what we're doing anyway. Oh and get forensics up here as well for photos and any prints. Then I want you to go to the car park across the road and catch anyone coming in for their cars, see if any of them saw anything unusual, like someone running away or anyone or anything that looked suspicious. We're looking at some time in the last hour to an hour and a half. Then again whoever it was might have been here earlier and lying in wait for the fellow to arrive, so it could be any time in the last two or three hours. It's possible it was a random shooting of course but I think this fellow was the intended target, and whoever did it knew the victim and knew he'd find him here at this particular time." Benny pointed over the road. "There aren't many houses around here so get a couple of extra bodies and do a house-to-house check to see if anyone saw anything, but leave Devlin here to keep the site secure."

"Anything else boss?" asked ET.

"We still don't know who the victim is, so take the registration and find out from DVLA"

Bene went back to see the attendant.

"If you're ready now, I'd like to ask you a few more questions."

"Yeah sure, I'll tell you what I know but it's not much. I've been going over it in my mind ever since, and however much I've thought about it the truth is I didn't see or hear anything."

"OK, just tell me everything, and start from before the guy came in. Did you notice anyone hanging around looking as if they might be waiting for someone, or did you notice anyone here you hadn't seen before?"

"Not really, I mean I'd been busy all afternoon because there were plenty of cars coming in for the pre-weekend wash, most of them were regulars and I know a lot of them, and the other ones you don't take much notice of. Once the car goes into the wash you forget about it and concentrate on the next one. I don't remember seeing anyone that wasn't in a car."

"How about outside the wash, was there anything that looked suspicious?"

"I didn't notice anything unusual, not until that guy started blowing his horn and I had to go round to see what had happened."

"And then what?"

The attendant started to shake a little

"I walked round to the front and saw the car was out of the wash but hadn't been driven away. The driver's window was down which looked a bit odd so I looked in and saw him, he was slumped over the wheel and I thought he'd had a heart attack or something. I shook his shoulder to see if I could rouse him but he was well out of it, then I saw all the blood so I called the ambulance and you lot as well."

"Did you move him at all?"

"No, not a chance, I switched off the machine and the guy in the car behind got out, together we pushed the front car out so he could get his car out of there, but he didn't want to hang around he drove off pretty quick."

"So when you were there did you see anyone or anything apart from the two car drivers?"

"No, not many people walk past here they're all in cars. There's a car park across the road and there's always people coming and going from there, but they're going the other way, into the town or back from it. I didn't look over there anyway, not after what I'd seen here."

Bene wondered why there was only one attendant at the car wash and asked why he was working alone.

"The lad who should have been here phoned in sick this morning. I asked my boss if he could send someone to help me but there wasn't anyone, he said I was to carry on by myself and he'd make it up to me. He wouldn't close for the day because it's always busy on Fridays and he didn't want to lose any money."

"It's against the law you know," said Bene "there should be at least two of you here."

"Yeah I know, but it's happened before and I can't afford to lose any money or my job, so I just get on with it."

"The lad who should have been here with you, how long has he worked here?"

"A few weeks that's all and he's not too reliable either, it's not the first time he's pulled a sickie."

"I'll need to speak to him, have you got an address or phone number for him?" The attendant supplied Bene with both.

"And the driver of the car behind, do you know who he was?"

"Yeah he's local, he lives up on the Edge, you'll find him in the Con club most nights; his name's Ferdy something; he'll be in there tonight if you want to see him."

"Good, well better let your boss know what's happened down here and then get yourself off home; we'll be here for a while yet. I'll need a statement from you but that can wait until tomorrow, can you come into the station in the morning and we'll go through it together. Before you go though, I need your name and address and a contact phone number."

"Sean Barton, 24 Broadacres and here's my mobile number."

It suddenly dawned on Bene.

"Sean of course, I thought I'd seen you before, you were a friend of Danny Mason the postman weren't you? It's a pity how that turned out. I'm sorry because you two were good pals weren't you?"

"Yeah we were good mates since school, but he got his head turned when he started dealing in drugs; it made him greedy and he changed. We were never as close again and we didn't see much of each other after that, but I was still gutted when he died."

Bene said again how sorry he was and left Sean to contact his boss. He began to reflect on the case of Danny Mason, the first case he'd worked on without the help of his old boss and mentor Adam Firth. He let out a huge sigh.

"Oh well, I'll have to forget all about that and get on with this one. I hope house-to-house enquiries or the car park turn up something because there doesn't seem to be anything here to shed any light on what happened, or who was responsible for it."

Chapter 7

The Fox and Pheasant

An odd assortment

Bene and ET walked into the Fox and Pheasant public house and bought a couple of beers, they chose a table at the far end of the room where it was much quieter. ET had discovered the victim's name was Arnold Bainbridge a resident of Levensbridge. Settling down they both took a long draft from their glasses before starting a conversation. ET leaned forward and placed his elbows on the table, his head supported by his large expansive hands. Taking the initiative he began by trying to make some sense out of the day's events.

"Looking at what we've got so far, which isn't much, I'm thinking along the same lines as you and I don't believe it was a random shooting. It doesn't look like someone has gone out there looking for the first guy he sees to kill, but we can't rule it out completely until we get more evidence. As I see it we're looking for someone Arnold knew. It looks like his killer was lying in wait for him and made quite sure of his identity before shooting him in cold blood." He looked over at Bene to gauge his reaction, Bene remained silent, his hands slowly turning round the pint glass in his hands with his eyes firmly fixed on that movement.

ET continued.

"As far as we know Arnold was just a normal run of the mill family guy, but something he's done or hasn't done has upset someone badly enough to want to kill him. Whatever the reason it's probably something that's happened recently. Again he looked over to Bene but there was a further lack of response, ET took this to mean he should continue with his observations. "I think we should start by looking closely at his private life. We need to talk to his wife again, because when I broke the news to her earlier she was far too upset and in no fit state to answer any of my questions. But we can't leave it too long before we speak to her again. I think we should go first thing in the morning and see if she can throw any light on why this has happened, and if she knows if he's made any enemies lately. Then we need to contact his friends and colleagues at work, one of them might be able to tell us if there's someone we should be looking for."

Bene remained quiet, seemingly reluctant to speak. ET thought he had gone far enough for the moment; anything more would be pure speculation and only confuse the few facts they did have. At last Bene broke his silence.

"Yes, you're right we've got absolutely nothing to go on. We've no witnesses and nothing from door-to-door enquiries or the car park, and no CCTV to look at either. The answer will be in what his wife, his friends and colleagues can tell us, although I expect we'll get more from his friends and colleagues than we will from his wife. Anything as serious as this he'd most certainly have kept well away from his home life. Still you're right about his wife, we'll go and see her first thing in the morning." There was a short pause before he continued.

"We know where he worked and this happened on his way home from there. The thing that's bothering me is how the killer knew he'd be at the car wash. The guy said Arnold did come in on Fridays, but he didn't come in every week. So was it just opportune? Did the killer take a chance that he might be there this particular Friday? It didn't look like a random shooting did it; it looks as if Arnold was definitely targeted, so maybe the killer had been there before just waiting for the time when Arnold turned up. If that's the case then the killing was certainly premeditated. But why the car wash? If he knew Arnold that well he'd know where he lived, his social habits and where he could be found at any given time; surely he could have chosen a better place to carry out the killing. So why choose such a public place to do it?"

There was a long silence while the two men pondered over this last question. The door to the bar opened and a strange old chap entered and went over to the bar to be greeted by Kris the owner of the public house.

"Now then Donald same as usual is it?"

"Aye and I'll have a wee malt to go with it as well."

The new arrival was dressed in country tweeds complete with cap, once served he picked out a table a little way from them and placed his drinks on it, putting his hat on the spare chair he sat down to read his newspaper. With his hat removed it revealed a ridiculously looking wig that didn't quite cover his natural hair which protruded from underneath on both sides. Purposely ignoring the other occupants in the bar he seemed happy and content to be left in his own company with his daily paper.

"Who the hell is that?" mouthed ET as he'd never seen the man before.

"Tell you later," Bene whispered, and then went back to the case in hand.

"We know that Arnold was the manager of a steel fabrication company in Kendal. I can't think there'd be any problem there, but we can't rule anything out at this stage. We'll go over there tomorrow after we've spoken to his wife and talk to everyone in the company. It's possible he may have sacked someone and they wanted revenge, or maybe he was having an affair with one of the workers wives and got found out. It's all conjecture of course but we need to be thorough. We'll have to find out if anything's happened there recently that could have led to his murder."

The door opened and two more men entered the bar. The first man was tall but his height disguised due to the severe curvature of his spine which obviously aggrieved him; he leaned heavily on his walking aid, a permanent pained expression etched across his face. The man who followed him was unmistakably related, he was also tall but without the disability. Aged about sixty their facial characteristics were similar; both had smooth black hair brushed well back and thin faces almost unnaturally so, sallow complexions and tight thin lips which created a rather sad but cruel appearance. Once they'd been served they took their drinks and joined the little Scotsman who had come in minutes earlier. The three had barely started their conversation when another man came into the room; he also bought a drink before joining the others at the table. The newcomer was different class altogether. Definitely not rural, nor was he local judging by his accent when indulging in polite conversation at the bar. This was a man probably in his late fifties, who looked as though he'd made the effort over the years to keep his body in good shape. His face was nicely rounded but pale, and the addition of spectacles told of years working indoors, most likely in an office. But he was no mere clerk; he was someone of much higher status, a manager perhaps, possibly a solicitor, undeniably something of that ilk. So what was his connection with the other three? There didn't appear to be any noticeable link.

ET had been distracted watching this odd bunch assemble across the room and shook his head in disbelief; Bene had to bring him back to the case.

"You'll have to ignore that lot for the moment, they're a queer bunch I know, but I'll fill you in on them later, now concentrate"

There were two lines of enquiry. Bene told ET what he'd heard from the attendant.

"I realised when I spoke to him that he looked familiar, his name is Sean Barton and he helped me in my first case when a friend of his was murdered. He's OK, but obviously a bit cut up about what's just happened. Anyway he'd been working on his own today as his colleague had phoned in sick; now I have this other guy's name and contact details so we urgently need to speak to him. He's only been working there for a few weeks so why phone in sick this Friday of all days? Does he know something and he's implicated in some way, or was he was warned off by someone, maybe he decided to stay well away because he knew something was going to happen. There may be nothing in it of course but we need to check him out."

"And the other line is what?" asked ET.

"The fellow in the car behind, according to Sean he didn't see or hear anything, but he didn't hang around either so we need to speak to him as well. He's called Ferdy something and evidently we can catch him in the Conservative club on any night. I suggest we finish our drinks and go up there, and let's see what he can tell us."

The drinks finished the two men got up and left the pub, ET giving the four newcomers a long searching look on passing. Once outside he questioned Bene about the men.

"That Scotsman, he's someone you know then?"

Bene smiled as the memory of his first encounter with the man came back to him.

"Yes that's old Donald Neves; he worked up at Grosvenor House a couple of miles out of Kendal, for years he was manservant and general dogsbody to Andrew McLean the self styed laird up there. Andrew had no wife or children to leave his big house to, his only relations were a couple of nephews who he described as complete wasters. He said he wouldn't leave them anything; they only came when they needed him to bail them out of whatever predicament they'd got into. With great delight he'd tell everyone.

"When I die everything here goes to Donald, and I'd love to be able to see their faces when they realise they're getting nothing and old Donald here walks away with the lot."

Bene chuckled to himself.

"The funniest thing was that every time Andrew had visitors he'd find something trivial to berate Donald with, and then follow it up by bellowing at him. "And by the way Neves you're fired, you're no bloody use to me anymore, now get out!"

Donald would hesitate for a moment, then bow to his employer and respond in his broadest Scottish accent. "Thank you my lord, will that be all?"

I was up there once to witness this daft affair and one of the other guests was a bit quick to reprimand Andrew.

"That was a bit callous wasn't it; you really should go easy on the little fellow."

"Bah!" said Andrew "take no notice of that, he gets fired every week sometimes daily, it's a standing joke between us. But believe me you'll enjoy the meal he'll serve up for us"

"We were relieved to see the funny side of this charade. It pleased us to know it was just an ongoing bit of theatre between the two men, who for different reasons appeared to be totally dependent on one another. Sure enough a few minutes later Donald returned to say dinner would be served. When we sat down at the table and saw the spread he'd laid out before us it left us quite in awe of the rather timid but wonderfully efficient servant; he'd served up a meal which endeared him to us all. So that's old Donald for you, and when Andrew died he was true to his word and left everything to Donald just as he said he would. But it was a big house and with Donald now on his own and not getting any younger he sold up and moved down here where he lives in a comfortable little cottage; just him and his old dog Bella."

"And the other three who the hell are they? An odd looking bunch for sure, I'm positive I've never seen any of them before."

"No you probably haven't, well the tall fellow with the stick who looks as if he could fall over at any time that's Alfie Brooks, an ex-bookmaker, and I believe he's been like that for years. Something happened long ago, an accident or something but he was convinced it was deliberate. He reckons one of his so called friends pushed him over a bridge; his back was so badly damaged the doctors couldn't repair it. There was a girl involved and Alfie and another guy were competing for her, Alfie reckons it was him she wanted, but after the accident she shied away and he lost her to the other fellow. He still carries a grudge and swears he'll get even with him, even though the couple married and moved away shortly afterwards."

"So the fellow who came in with him must be his brother, neither of them looks as if they would have any friends."

"You're right they don't. I'm not sure what little Donald sees in them they're certainly not his type at all. You must have noticed something about the brother though and how the others tried to distance themselves from him; he smells to high heaven and everyone I know treats him like a leper. I think the others try to avoid him but he always finds them and follows them around like a little dog. It's a wonder he hasn't got the message by now because they go to great lengths not to include him in anything. I mean the man must have no nous at all anyone else would have taken the hint long ago."

"And that last fellow, he doesn't seem to fit in with any of them, but they looked as though they were getting on quite well so they must have something in common."

Bene was racking his brains about the fourth member of the group; deep down there was something about the man, something he'd heard not long ago and it troubled him, but at the moment he couldn't put his finger on what it was. ET was puzzled by the long pause in Bene's description of the four but knew enough not to intrude on his thoughts. Bene was thinking hard but nothing was coming, he decided to give ET the little he did know.

"That last fellow is someone I should know more about but I can't remember what it is, it's filed away somewhere in the back of my memory. I know he's President of the local bowls club and has been for the last year or so. He's not local but he's lived here a number of years, I've no idea where he came from originally. I could ask my old boss I suppose because he's a member of the same club, I'll do that the next time I see him."

ET had to be satisfied with that.

"Right," said Bene, "let's make our way over to the Con club and have a word with this Ferdy fellow."

CHAPTER 8

The value of nothing

Friday and Saturday nights at the Conservative Club were arguably the only two nights in which the club would make a profit; on other nights the club was much quieter and there would only be a handful of customers on the premises. Tonight it was boy's night out and all the regulars were there, split into their tribal groups around their designated tables. Everyone knew everyone in there, and everyone knew everyone's business. Ferdy was easily identified by the barman who told them it was Fergy and not Ferdy and the man's real name was Robert Ferguson. Bene and ET approached the table and introduced themselves, Bene took the lead.

"Is there somewhere we can go Robert that's a bit quieter. I'd like to ask you a few questions about what happened earlier up at the car wash?"

"Of course, it's probably best if we go outside there's nowhere in here tonight where we can talk; there's only the one room open downstairs and there's a party going on upstairs so that's a no go; follow me." The three men left by the back entrance. Robert laughed

"Oh and before we go any further, it's Fergy. It's only Robert to my mother and my sisters."

"OK Fergy, what we want to know is what you saw at the car wash this afternoon. We know that you helped the operator push the car in front out of the wash but we need to know what happened in there just before that."

Fergy knew exactly what they wanted to know because he wanted to know himself.

"I knew you'd be looking for me and on second thoughts maybe I should have contacted you first instead of driving off. But to be honest there was nothing I could do as the poor guy was either seriously hurt, or dead. I didn't look too closely but I did see all the blood. I asked the attendant to phone for an ambulance, and I believe that's what he did."

"OK, now tell us about your journey through the car wash. I want to know if you could see the car in front at any time, and if so, did anyone approach it? And was there anyone else in or around the place that you noticed?"

There was a pause. Fergy had been thinking deeply about his time at the car wash, but as far as he knew there was nothing he could help them with.

"I'm sorry fella's but there was nothing out of the ordinary, when I drove into the wash the car in front looked as though he was finished; all you could see was the back end and even then only part of it was visible. Then the rollers came up on my car and blocked everything out, and when they cleared my car had moved forward but the car in front hadn't; it was stuck at the exit. I wasn't bothered at first because I still had to go through the driers. But as I was going through there I knew the car would have to move or I'd run into it, I blew my horn to get him to drive off but he never moved. I kept hooting because the conveyor was taking me right up to the back of the car. Eventually the attendant came round to see what I was hooting at, and after looking in the car in front he stopped the machine and went off to be sick. I got out and helped the guy push the car out of the wash so that I could get out as well."

"Did you notice anything unusual about the place or anything that didn't seem just right?" Bene paused for a moment to let the man think about it, but he was taking too long.

"Maybe you heard someone talking or shouting, do you remember anything like that?"

"No just the sound of the wash that's all."

"And you didn't see anyone inside the wash or at the exit?"

"No, there was nobody inside the wash, but I couldn't see the exit so if there was anyone there I didn't see them. To be honest there was nothing to see and nothing to hear except the water and the rollers. Until I came up to the back of that car everything was normal. If I'd seen or heard anyone, or noticed anything different I would tell you, I mean I wish there was something, but there wasn't."

"OK" said a dejected Bene. "But I'll need you to make a statement, if you can come down to the station tomorrow morning and do that for me that should be all, and leave your contact details in case we need to talk to you again. In the meantime if you do remember anything, however trivial you might think it is give me a call." Bene handed over his card.

"Yeah of course that's no problem but tell me this, what was wrong with the guy, I guess he must be dead and that's why you're here right?"

"Yes he's dead alright but that's all I can tell you, we're still waiting for the path report." Bene and ET left the club.

"What now?" asked ET.

"Home for both of us I think I've had enough for today. Sowerby will want answers in the morning but God knows what mood he'll be in when he finds we've got nothing for him."

Bene went home and was not in a good mood. Neither was Dot, she was furious.

"Where have you been Bene, dinner finished over an hour ago, you know you should have phoned if you were going to be this late." Bene had never seen Dot this angry before. She was clearly annoyed with him and with good reason. The pleasant face he usually saw, the one which belied her age was looking much older now as she scowled angrily at him. Let no-one be in any doubt that although she was much shorter than him, this slim and attractive lady had full command of her house and any situation within it. Her natural blonde hair curled up around the top of her head and usually immaculate, now looked a little untidy and dishevelled owing to the temper brewing inside her.

"Sorry Dot, but it's been a really crap day and I'm whacked, but if there're any scraps left I'd love them; I'm almost past hunger. Where's Alex by the way?"

"She was hoping to show you a house she'd seen on the internet; she was so excited about it and wanted you to see it with her, but when you didn't come home and hadn't phoned she got herself all upset and went to bed. If I were you I'd leave her for a while, let her get to sleep and you can talk in the morning."

Bene had a late dinner and watched TV until such time as Alex would be asleep; he didn't want any arguments tonight, he wasn't in the mood.

The following morning Inspector Sowerby was waiting for the two detectives to arrive, he was expecting a report from the previous night's interview. Bene and ET arrived together, strategically and pre-arranged at exactly the same time as neither wanted to face Sowerby alone, not in the mood he'd undoubtedly be in when he found out they had nothing to give him. The Inspector met them "Anything from the man you went to see last night?"

"I'm afraid not Sir." said Bene "He never saw or heard anything. He said everything was normal until he came up behind the car in front which was stationary at the exit, he had to blow his horn to get the attendant to stop the machine otherwise he'd have run into the back of it, he helped the lad push it out of the way, but apart from seeing the blood on the dashboard he didn't notice anything that could help us." Bene looked away and waited for the Inspector to kick off, but instead he went quiet. He knew the two detectives well enough to know they'd have asked all the right questions, and if the answers weren't forthcoming then obviously there was nothing to be got from the interview.

"So what other lines have we got to follow, please tell me there are some?"

"We're going to see his widow again this morning, she was in a bit of a state last night and ET didn't get anything from her. I don't suppose she'll have slept much, but after the shock of losing her husband she might now be wondering why someone would want to kill him. Hopefully this morning she'll be able to give us some idea who it could be. When we're finished up there I'm going to see the lad who should have been at the car wash but phoned in sick, and ET is going to Kendal to interview his boss and his colleagues, hopefully we'll have something for you later."

"OK then, report back to me as soon as you've finished these enquiries, somebody out there knows something and we need to find out what they know."

Bene and ET called at the home of Laura Bainbridge. They'd been expected and were let into the house by Laura's son-in-law. Laura was sitting quietly on the sofa in her front room, her eldest daughter beside her with an arm around to comfort her. The small and rather delicate woman looked even more so as she sat hunched up on the sofa. It was obvious there'd been a lot of tears but very little sleep. Her face was pale and showing signs of exhaustion and sadness which was only to be expected with the sudden loss of her husband.

The two men took up the offer to sit down and ET began the interview.

"We're really sorry to intrude again Laura but we do need to ask you some questions. I know it was difficult for you last night but we're trying our hardest to find out why Arnold was killed, and up to now we don't have any clues as to why he was the target."

Laura wanted to help the two men because she also wanted to know why her husband had been shot.

"I've been thinking of nothing else ever since it happened and believe me I can't come up with anything. In my mind I'm sure it was a case of mistaken identity, I mean Arnold had no enemies at all he was friends with everyone."

"Did he ever talk about any problems he was having at work, maybe a disagreement with his boss or one of his colleagues?"

"No, nothing at all, Arnold always came home from work happy; he loved his work and all the people he worked with. It wasn't like work to him it was more like spending time with his friends. If there'd been anything wrong I would have noticed it, I know I would."

"And what about his social life; was everything OK with that? Tell us about his interests and what he liked to do when he wasn't working."

"Well he was just happy being at home with me, and he loved doing his garden. We liked the same TV programs and we'd go out for the odd meal now and again, sometimes with friends and sometimes just the two of us. Apart from that his main passion was his bowls, he loved it down there. And he didn't always go to play bowls you know, him and his pals would often go there and just sit and have a pint or two; they got just as much enjoyment watching a game as they did playing it. Arnold had lots of friends down there, and sometimes after a game they'd go to the pub for a drink and a bit of a natter."

ET wasn't getting anything from this, dare he push harder.

"Laura this may sound a bit harsh but we need to know if everything was alright between you and Arnold?"

"Yes of course it was, and if you think there was another woman involved then you're wrong. But if you want proof of that you can ask anyone who knew him and they'll all tell you the same, Arnold was the best husband and father you could ask for. If there'd been anything untoward you can be sure it would be all round the town. Levensbridge isn't a big place and nothing stays a secret here for long, you should know that."

"Just one last thing Laura, did Arnold have any money problems that you were aware of, any debts for instance, did he speak of someone he might have owed money to?"

"Absolutely not, we only have a bit left on the mortgage, the car's paid for and we have money in the bank, so we don't need to take out loans or borrow from anyone. We've always been satisfied with what we have, and if we couldn't afford something we were quite prepared to wait until we could afford it."

"How about gambling then, did Arnold like the odd flutter on the horses or dogs maybe?"

"No never, we both did the lotto on Saturday but that's it. There's absolutely nothing else I can assure you, and as for betting Arnold wouldn't know Red Rum from a donkey."

There didn't seem to be any point in staying longer as Laura couldn't give them any idea as to why her husband had been shot. Bene couldn't think of anything else to ask because ET had covered everything. It would seem that Arnold was just an ordinary man who led a normal life both at home and at work. They had nowhere to look and no-one to look for. It was another dead end, and another dead end that Inspector Sowerby would not like.

It was still just short of midday and the two detectives would have to split up and go their separate ways to complete the day's investigations. Bene would go to interview the lad who should have been at the car wash, and ET would go to Kendal to interview Arnold's boss and his colleagues. Bene was aware that Sowerby desperately needed something to go on and everything now depended on what they could find out in the next few hours.

"Right ET, let's go out and get something. I mean this happened in the middle of the day for God's sake, there's got to be someone who saw or heard something. I don't believe it was a random shooting, this guy was definitely targeted and we've got to find out why. Something's happened at some point in his life that we know nothing about. It might have happened recently, or maybe it lies somewhere in the past, but whatever it is his wife doesn't know anything about it, we'll have to dig a lot deeper. OK let's go, keep your phone handy and keep me in touch."

The two men went their separate ways with fingers crossed that at least one of them would come back with some good news; any lead however slender or tenuous would do, but there had to be something they could take back to Sowerby.

After phoning Sean and finding the lad was still absent from work Bene went to his house where his Auntie Pat informed him Gary wasn't at home.

"Somewhere in town he'll be but I don't know where, he doesn't tell me anything."

Bene left the house to go and look for the truant car wash attendant, finally tracking him down in the local snooker hall.

There was only one table in use and Bene soon found the lad he was looking for.

"Gary isn't it?" Bene showed his warrant card as he addressed the lad.

"Maybe it is maybe it isn't, what's it about?"

"It's about the car wash; you work there don't you?"

"Sometimes, it depends what I feel like, it's a crap job with crap wages. I might go back, but after what happened up there yesterday I might not either."

"Got a minute then Gary just to answer a few questions?" The lad didn't object so Bene led him away from the table and his friends to a quiet corner of the room.

"Was there any reason why you didn't go in to work yesterday?"

"No, I just didn't fancy it, it was too hot and it's always busy on Fridays. Apart from that you get soaked to the skin with the spray, the hose has got a bloody leak in it and the boss won't spend money on a new one. When I get home my jeans are soaked and my feet are wet, and for what he pays me it's not worth it. In fact now I think about it I don't think I will go back."

"So was that the only reason you didn't go, you weren't approached by anyone telling you not to go in or anything like that?"

"No of course not, I told you why."

"Did you know something was going to happen yesterday, and that's why you stayed away?"

"How the hell would I know what was going to happen, are you trying to say I had something to do with it, I didn't know anything about it until last night when auntie Pat told me. I didn't even know the guy so how could I know anything about it."

"So what did you do yesterday if you weren't at work and you weren't at home?"

"Just messing around, I was in the town for a bit then I went down to the river to see if it was any good for fishing."

"And was it?"

"Nah, there's still too much flood water in it; it needs a few more days to let the level drop a bit before its fishable again."

During the conversation Bene could sense that the lad wasn't local.

"You don't sound as if you were born around here Gary?"

"No, I came up here to live with my auntie last year."

And that was all the information he was prepared to give. There was a silence where he sensed Bene was waiting for more, but Gary had given as much as he wanted to and declined to expand on the matter any further. Bene finally decided that the lad knew nothing about the events of the previous day and left him to finish his game. Hopefully ET would come up with something.

It was going to take ET a lot longer to do his interviews in Kendal so Bene decided to drive over there and give him a hand. When he arrived he found that ET had already interviewed Arnold's boss and five of his colleagues.

"There's nothing here so far and I've only got two left to see, they're all in shock and I can't find anybody who had a grudge against Arnold or even a bad word to say about him; he seems to have been popular with everyone here."

"OK, I'll take one of the last two and see what we get from them?"

"Yes let's get on with it it's our last chance, after that I don't know where we can look."

The last two men were interviewed, but like the others before them they could offer no reason for the attack on Arnold. The two detectives left the premises downhearted and utterly miserable. They drove back to Levensbridge separately trying to think of what they could tell Sowerby. Meeting up again in the town they went for a coffee to try and come up with some new lines to follow. Bene had one bit of information, but it probably meant very little.

"You know when we were in the pub last night and that last fella came in and sat down at the table with the other three. I said I should know something about him but couldn't remember what it was?"

"Yeah, you said he was president of the bowls club?"

"That's right, well Arnold was a member of the same club wasn't he, so do you think there could be a connection there?"

"You still can't remember anything about him though?"

"No, I can't."

"Why don't we go down there and speak to some of them it might be worthwhile, I mean we've got nothing else to go on."

The two left with no great hopes of finding out anything, but they needed to do something rather than return to the station empty handed.

On arrival at the bowls club they found to their dismay it had closed for the day. Bene sighed.

"It'll have to wait until tomorrow, maybe we'll find someone here then," and for the two detectives that completed what had been an absolutely useless and fruitless day's work. There was nothing for it but to go back to the station and face the music.

Sowerby was waiting for them and he sighed heavily when told the day's interviews had yielded nothing.

"So it's another blank then. I think we need more manpower to help speed things up a bit. I've given one of our uniform staff a temporary promotion to DC, and they'll be with you first thing tomorrow. If needed I may be able to spare another officer, but see how you get on with this one for now." Sowerby didn't say as much but it was obvious he was finding it hard to conceal his disappointment.

"Anyway that's it for today, go home and get some sleep, we'll make an early start in the morning and hopefully we'll have a bit more luck then."

CHAPTER 9

Hils joins the team

The two detectives met at 7.30 prompt at the station. ET asked the question they were both dying to know.

"OK boss, who do you think it's going to be?"

"I'm going for that new lad Jamil, he's young and he seems keen, and I think he'd be useful to us, how about you?"

"I'm going for Devlin, he was with us on the first day and he seemed to do alright; he did everything we asked him and I think Sowerby will let us have him."

"You're not going for Fisher on the desk then? I thought you and him were pally?"

"Fisher would have been alright but I can't see Sowerby letting him go can you, no I'm sure it'll be Devlin."

The two didn't have long to wait before they were joined by their new partner, and when she arrived she took them both by surprise. Much desired by the male uniformed officers the attractive and shapely form of PC Hilary Taylor suddenly appeared before them as if from nowhere. They'd never seen her out of uniform and here she was dressed in civvies. In uniform she was always a good looker, but in plain clothes she was a stunner. Only an inch short of six feet tall she had a beautiful if slightly cheeky face. Normally her auburn hair would be tied back, but now it hung loose across the full spread of her shoulders. She had a full but pleasing figure and a reputation for being a good sport and always up for a laugh; she was quite capable of giving a bit of ribbing, but she could take it as well.

"Where are you off to?" asked ET "don't let Sowerby see you dressed like that or he'll blow a fuse." Hilary laughed.

"Didn't he tell you, I'm your new DC for the next week or so, and he's sent me here to help you two losers."

"Bugger me" shouted ET "so Hilary Taylor wants to be a real live detective does she?"

"Yes and you can forget the Hilary bit, I only ever answer to Hils."

She looked at them both quizzically. "I hope that's OK with you both?"

"Hils it is then" they said in unison. "Let's get started".

A plan was drawn up for the morning at least. It was too early to go back to the bowls club, there'd be no-one there until lunch time at the earliest. Bene told them where he was going.

"I'm off to call on Adam Firth and see if there's anything he can tell me, he's a member of the bowls club and would have known Arnold pretty well. He might know something about him that we haven't been able to find out. Hils, you go with ET and try another house-to-house across from the car wash. Maybe now the news is out about the shooting it may have jogged someone's memory. Try the car park as well, anyone coming in or going out of there, it's a long shot but we don't have anything else to go on. It was busy there yesterday with the Saturday market but the two officers on duty didn't turn up anything new. Give it another go this morning and make it thorough, and let me know if you have any luck."

Adam was still enjoying his breakfast when his wife Ellen opened the door to greet him; they were always pleased to see him when he called.

"He's in the kitchen Bene just go through."

Bene walked through to the kitchen to see his old mentor and governor.

"We were wondering how long it would be before you came to see us again. Come on through to the front room and we'll have coffee." Adam rose from the breakfast table and directed Bene through to the lounge where the two men settled down to talk. Bene glanced over to his former governor and saw that nothing had changed. He was exactly the same man he'd served under during his first three years as a detective.

Adam had retired from the force the previous year. A heart attack had made the decision easy for him and he was now enjoying the full benefits of life outside the force. His appearance was deceptive on first meeting him you would never guess his former career, more suited to an old-fashioned small town doctor or solicitor perhaps, much preferring his old checked jacket with the leather patches on the sleeves to a suit. His face was long and mostly without expression, languid would probably describe it best. But those who know him or had worked with him knew that underneath it all there was someone with a razor sharp mind and an uncanny knack of being able to sense when something wasn't just right, it was this that had served him well during his time in the force.

Bene's eyes were focusing on the surrounding family photos he'd seen many times before on his visits to the house whilst waiting patiently for the interrogation he knew was coming.

"So you've got another murder on your hands Bene, tell me all about it and what you've got so far." Bene was looking a bit sheepish because he knew it would be embarrassing.

"Yeah, you're right about the murder Adam, it's a puzzler and no mistake. I can't make head or tail of it. I mean no-one saw or heard anything even though it happened in broad daylight. We've interviewed everyone who was there, done a complete house-to-house check, we've spoken to his wife, his boss and colleagues at his workplace and still come up with nothing. On top of that I don't know where to look next, the bowls club is the only place left that I can think of" He looked over to Adam. "I know he was a member of the club so maybe someone down there knows something."

Ellen brought in two coffees and placed them on the side table. She was a bubbly woman and much shorter than Adam, about five foot five with short curly mousey-coloured hair. Her rounded face and stout body fitted her profile exactly, a wife and mother, a homely type who fussed constantly over her husband. Not wishing to distract them she tidied the table and discretely left the room leaving the two men to continue their tête-à-tête.

Bene didn't want his visit to look as if his only reason for calling on Adam was to ask for his help, but nevertheless he did need to do that.

"You're a member of the bowls club Adam, so you'll have known Arnold pretty well with him being a member there too. What I'd like to know is how well you knew him and what was he like? I wondered if you knew much about his private life outside of bowls. The thing is someone or something he's been involved with has led to him being killed. I don't know if it has anything to do with the bowls club or it's in his private life. Up to now I've no idea what it is, but it has to be something damned serious if he was killed for it."

Adam nodded in approval; he'd been expecting Bene to ask these questions.

"Yes you're right Bene, there has to be a reason for it. On the face of it Arnold was just as his persona would have you believe, a man who was happy and content with his life and where it was taking him. He was a good member of the club and he had many friends there. I didn't see a great deal of him as he was still working, and as you know I'm retired. We tend to have two different groups within the club; my fellow retirees and I spend most of our time there in the afternoons, whereas the ones who are still working generally go down in the evenings. At the weekend of course it's different, we all mix in together and that's when we get to know each other a bit better."

Adam paused for a second as if unsure he should continue, he finally decided that what he could tell Bene might be helpful and could give him a bit of a lead.

"I don't know if what I'm going to tell you will help Bene because it's just my own suspicions, so don't take it as gospel you'll have to carry out your own enquiries and make up your own mind."

"Anything you can give me Adam would be helpful, even if it is only suspicions."

"Right, well don't repeat any of this and make sure you keep me right out of it, OK?"

"It goes without saying Adam, just tell me."

"I know something must have happened to Arnold in the last week or so because I could see a change in him last weekend when we were playing together; something was certainly bothering him. There was nothing conspicuous about it and maybe no-one else noticed, but all my years in the force has taught me to recognise these little signs. It's the way people's appearance or expression changes, sometimes you notice it in their speech, sometimes it's their body language or their facial expressions. But I'm not mistaken Bene the signs were there alright, the man was scared. I could tell he was trying to conceal it, but it was obvious to me that he was frightened of someone or something. Who or what I have no idea, but it must have happened in the last week or so because up until then he was perfectly normal."

Bene had been listening intently to this and wondered if it could be the lead he was looking for, the one he desperately needed.

"Do you think it had anything to do with the club Adam? Maybe one of the other bowlers had it in for him, or do you think it was something completely different and nothing to do with the club?" Adam sighed, he wanted to help Bene as much as he could but he didn't want him to go off and act solely on what he'd just told him.

"I don't want any of this to get back to the club Bene so be careful how you go about it; you have to realise that what I've told you is just my personal observations; there's no evidence to show it had any bearing on what happened to Arnold, so don't you go down there and repeat any of it."

He paused again for a moment to make sure Bene fully understood before continuing.

"But to answer your question, no I don't think anyone at the club had it in for him; in fact I'm sure they hadn't. If that had been the case then everyone would have known about it; it's a closely knit club and no-one down there is a stranger."

There was another short pause before he continued.

"What you might want to do is talk to some of the lads down there, I'll give you names of one or two who may know something, but for heaven's sake make it look casual, don't let them think they've been picked out deliberately."

"That's not a problem Adam I can handle that, and rest assured I'll not let it slip that you've had anything to do with it."

"Good because from what I've noticed it wasn't just Arnold who was affected. I detected similar signs in one or two of the others who I thought were looking a bit out of sorts. They were good friends with Arnold, and apart from the bowls they socialised together as well. If you were to approach them carefully they may be able to tell you something. But to be honest I don't think it's got anything to do with the club, I think it's something else altogether."

Bene took out his notebook.

"OK, give me some names Adam?" Adam obliged and Bene jotted them down in his book.

They continued talking for another ten minutes about more personal matters before Bene took his leave, fond farewells were exchanged and he left the house to catch up with ET and Hils. He'd just reached his car when his mobile rang, flipping it open he was surprised to see it was Inspector Sowerby calling and not ET.

"Yes sir?"

"Bene we've just received a call from a woman who says she saw someone running from the direction of the car wash on Friday afternoon about the time we're interested in, I want you to go and see her and hear what she has to say."

"Right sir, I'm on my way now, what's the lady's name and address?"

"She lives in Longbarrow village about seven miles away near the coast. Her name is Alison Dawes and she lives in Smithy Cottage, you should be able to find it alright it's not a big village. Get over there right away and let me know what you come up with."

"Very good sir, let's hope she can give us something useful. She lives a bit far out of town though; I guess she must have been there to do her shopping. I'll get back to you as soon as I've seen her."

He'd travelled about a mile down the road when suddenly he jumped up from his seat and thumped his hands down hard on the steering wheel.

"Damn it! I've only just left Adam and I forgot to ask him about Bernard Liversedge; there's something not just right about that fellow and Adam would be the man to tell me what it is."

He checked the time on his watch. "I haven't got time to go back. I could phone him I suppose, but it's not that important I'll check this lady out first and call him when I've finished in Longbarrow." Bene continued his journey with high expectations that something good would come from his visit to the village, the matter of the bowls club President was pushed to the back of his mind again.

11

It was Sunday and the car park opposite the car wash was quiet. It had been much busier the previous day when checks were done by uniform officers. It had been market day in the town and they'd interviewed all the folk who'd been parked there the day before, even so they'd hit a blank and come back with nothing. Most of people they spoke to had finished their shopping and gone home before the shooting took place. The market place was about 150 yards away, so parking was ideal for the market, not so ideal for the town centre shops, but people wanting to visit the larger shops would normally drive into the town centre to park.

ET and Hils had split up to cover the main entry and exit gates and interview everyone going into and out of the park. Earlier that morning the second house-to-house enquiries had produced the same outcome as the previous day; it appeared that no-one had seen or heard anything unusual. At noon the car park was almost empty, most of the people had finished their shopping and were on their way back home; one or two last minute stragglers had come in, and in another hour or so it would be completely empty, ET was getting hungry.

"Right, I'm off to get something to eat before the fast food van packs up. I'll bring you something back if you want, is there anything you'd like?"

"Oh yes please, a cheeseburger and a can of something would be good."

"OK, I won't be long but make sure you don't miss anybody; most of the folk have gone or will be leaving soon but keep an eye on the other gate as well, OK?"

"Yeah, no problem but hurry up I'm starving."

ET went off to get the foodstuff and in his absence Hils had little to do, only four cars were leaving and none of the occupants could give her any information regarding Friday afternoon as none of them had been in the town. It was turning out to be a frustrating and wasteful day for the two of them. No more cars had come in to the park so when ET returned Hils had nothing to report.

The burgers and drinks were quickly consumed and both were getting bored with inactivity. "It isn't going to take two of us to finish off here." said ET. "We'll spin for it, one of us will stay here until 5.00pm to cover the time the shooting happened, and the other can meet up with Bene and do something more useful, what do you say?"

"Yeah suits me, but be warned I always win a toss-up."

ET produced a coin and flipped it, only to confirm Hils prediction.

"Told you so." she laughed "You better phone Bene and see where I've to meet him."

ET made the call only to discover Bene was at Longbarrow village following up a lead.

"He says to wait here and he'll pick you up in about half an hour, I don't know where he's going but it'll be better than hanging around here all day. And another thing, remind me never to spin a coin with you again."

The drive to Longbarrow village was a pleasant one, the surrounding countryside and the views along the way were typical of this part of the county, exquisitely rural and very easy on the eye. Odd farms were dotted along the route and the fields and hedges were all well maintained. There were scattered houses of different shapes, sizes and design and most were built with the local sandstone. On arrival in the village it was just as he expected; a working village and similar to many others in the county. Longbarrow village was owned mostly by the wealthy Harwood family who for many generations had lived in the large estate house of Brackenhill. Most of the population had at one time worked for the estate and lived in the tied houses in the village. Over the years and due to ongoing family disputes and some hefty death duties the fortunes of the estate had declined. To keep it sustainable they'd been forced into selling off some measures of land for development; and also some of the outlying farms which were now in the ownership of private hands. But none of this had affected the actual village itself.

Smithy Cottage was easily found as it sat right in the centre of the village, with the Globe Inn on one side and a couple of small cottages and the old, but now unused reading room on the other side. Matthew Dawes the tenant of Smithy Cottage was one of the few men still employed by the estate. Primarily he was the estate's joiner and carpenter although his duties now embraced many other aspects of estate work. The forestry side which in better times had employed about a dozen workers was now under the control of a private agency and any work required in the woods was carried out by them. Labour costs had risen sharply in recent years but the estate had to remain viable, so to offset these costs it was decided that when workers retired or died they would simply not be replaced. Apart from a young apprentice Matthew was on his own in the joiners shop, and also the sole operator down at the saw mill.

Alison received Bene into her home and offered him a cup of tea which he gratefully accepted along with a slice of cake. Bene put her age at about thirty six or maybe slightly older; she was a slim woman with a warm disposition, dark brown hair tied back in a ponytail and her face devoid of any make-up. She was wearing a short sleeved light blue shirt hanging loose over dark blue jeans. Bene was a bit nervous because time was not on his side; he desperately needed something concrete to work with. He was hoping that what she told him would make his journey there worthwhile. He didn't have long to wait, Alison gave him a full account of what she'd seen on Friday afternoon.

"I'd left the car in the park opposite the car wash to do a bit of shopping; it's not as busy at that time on Friday so it's easy to park there and get the shopping done. I don't go into the centre very often I much prefer the smaller shops at this end of town. It was when I got back to the car about an hour later that I noticed something unusual. I didn't think too much about it at the time, but it did seem a bit odd and it stuck in my mind."

"So what exactly did you see? Was it someone at the car wash?"

"Well not actually at the wash but I did see someone running away from it, or running away from what I thought must be the wash, I mean there's nothing on the other side of it so he must have come from there."

"Did you see enough of this person to get a description?"

"Yes, he was a young man about average height I'd say, quite slim and athletic looking, he was wearing a grey tracksuit which looked a bit faded so you could tell it wasn't new, and the top was the hooded sort you see all the kids wearing now."

"And did he have the hood up or down? I mean did you get a chance to see his face?"

"Yes, I saw his face alright but there was nothing unusual about it, he had a normal boy's face. He was probably in his late teens or early twenties with sandy coloured hair, definitely a white man. As he was running he kept looking back as though someone was chasing him, but there wasn't anyone behind him, I looked"

Bene had been busy writing this down and was relieved that at last he had what promised to be a definite lead; someone he could now say was a person of interest.

"Is there anything else you can tell me about him, or where he was running to?"

"I don't know where he went because I only watched him for a few seconds, I was putting the shopping in the back of the car at the time and when I looked up again he was gone. He might have gone off somewhere down the other side of the road, or he might have come over to the side I was on and into the car park at the bottom end. I don't know, but wherever he went I didn't see him again."

Alison couldn't give him any more information so he had to be satisfied with what he had. At least he now had a description of the man he was looking for, and he'd have to use all his resources in his efforts to find him.

He was just finishing his tea and writing up his notes when Alison's husband came in. Matthew was a man of average height and muscular build, a ruddy complexion with smiling eyes and tousled brown hair. He wore a dusty checked shirt and jeans, and a pair of well-worn brown boots. Bene thought he may be a year or two younger than his wife.

"Ah, you two still at it then, I hope your journey hasn't been wasted lad?"

"No it's been very worthwhile, your good lady here has been very helpful and I think I have a good idea now where we can start looking."

"That's good then, and I hope you catch this one, I mean we don't want two murderers running around loose in the county do we?"

Bene was puzzled.

"Two murderers you say?"

"Yeah, well you lot never caught the first one did you"

Bene was further confused.

"You've got me with that I've no idea what you're talking about, you'll have to tell me."

"Well that fella who drowned in the creosote tank here about six years ago. The police said it was either suicide or an accident but nothing ever came of it; they never found out who he was, where he came from or what he was doing here, and they never arrested anyone for it."

"Why do you think it was murder if the police were satisfied with the outcome?"

"Oh come on now, no buggers going to commit suicide that way are they? I mean if you're that way inclined there's got to be better ways of doing away with yourself, and there's no way it was an accident either, that fella was murdered for sure."

"I seem to remember reading something about it, but I wasn't in the force back then so I didn't take much notice of it, but you think it was murder do you?"

"I'm convinced of it and I'll tell you why."

Bene was reluctant to stay much longer as he badly wanted to get started on the hunt for the man Alison had seen running away from the car wash. But he was interested in what Matthew had been telling him about this other death in the village, and his inquisitive nature demanded to know more about it.

"Well I really need to get going and start acting on this new information, but I would like to know more about what happened here back then, and why you think it was murder. Do you think we could keep it brief and I'll let you know what I think?"

Just then Matthew's son arrived home from school and without a word to his parents and completely ignoring Bene he dumped his bag by the door and promptly went upstairs to his bedroom.

"Kids eh," Matthew said. "Who'd have em?"

Bene smiled to himself as there was nothing that Alex and he wanted more than a child of their own.

"Right." said Matthew "Just the bare facts then and you can make your own mind up. Well this fella was found early one morning lying beside the old creosote tank at the saw mill. His head was covered in creosote and his lungs were full of the stuff. I mean if he was going to commit suicide he wouldn't have put his head over the side and drunk it in would he? If he was going to kill himself that way he'd have dived into it, but I can't for one minute believe he'd do anything so stupid. And it couldn't have been an accident either because he'd have been found inside the tank and not outside it. You see only his head and shoulders had been in the creosote not the rest of his body, because his clothes were still fairly clean apart from the top half of them. No, someone pushed him over the edge and held his head down until he suffocated on the stuff that's what's happened. But why would anyone do that? No-one ever found out who he was or how he came to be here. The police never found out anything about him, he had no ID on him to say who he was, and no-one in the village recognised him. So what was it that attracted him to this village in particular, and who else was here at the time to do something like that? Do you think he came here to meet someone and it all went wrong, you tell me?"

This was all new to Bene and he'd have liked nothing better than to look into it more closely. But time was not on his side, and whatever the real facts or reason behind this incident long ago it would have to wait until his present case was finished.

"It certainly raises a few questions and I wish I had time to look into it a bit further Matthew, but I've got to concentrate on this recent murder first. How would it be, if when I get this one sorted and out of the way I'll come back and we'll look into it, how would that do?"

"Yes, I'd be pleased to do that, I've always known something wasn't right about it and I'd like to know who the fellow was, where he came from and what he was doing here. You might be the right man to get the answers."

With that agreement in place Bene left the Dawes household with a lot more questions than he had answers for. Although one thing did stand out, he now had a pretty good idea who it was he was looking for. The description Alison had given him of the man she had seen running away from the car wash fitted almost exactly with that of Gary Maitland.

CHAPTER 10

The hunt is on

It was getting late in the afternoon when Bene met up with the other two officers at the car park, and after hearing there was no new information he decided they should call it a day. ET and Hils had established that the only vehicles remaining in the park belonged to local people, and they'd be parked there overnight.

The three returned to the station to bring Inspector Sowerby up to date with the day's events.

Bene told the inspector of his visit to Longbarrow and his interview with Alison Dawes.

"From the description she gave me it matches that of Gary Maitland the lad who cried off sick yesterday. So if it was him, what was he doing there and why did he tell me he wasn't anywhere near the place yesterday."

Sowerby was quick to answer. "Well whatever he was up to, if it was him of course, we need to bring him in for an interview. I suggest that's done right away and see what we can get out of him. ET you can do that and I'll let you take Devlin with you. Go and pick the lad up and bring him back here. Hils you can go with Bene and speak to those bowlers down at the club and see what they can tell you about Arnold Bainbridge. I want you all back here tonight, and Bene you can sit in with me on the interview with Gary Maitland. We'll have a team briefing immediately afterwards to see where we are with it, alright off you go."

Bene phoned Alex to tell her what he was doing and not to expect him home until late, and not to worry about dinner as he'd grab a snack somewhere on the way. He left the station with Hils, leaving ET to bring Gary into the station for interview.

It had just turned six thirty when they arrived at the bowls club and found a game in full swing. Bene looked around to see if Adam was there, but as he hadn't spotted his car in the car park he wasn't surprised when he didn't see him on the green or sitting on any of the surrounding benches. He didn't have a description of the men whose names Adam had supplied him with so they'd have to make one or two discreet enquiries. There were a few members sitting on benches watching the game and Bene thought they could ask them. They walked over and one of the men invited them to join him on the bench.

"It's a bit late for you two to be working isn't it?" said the cheerful fellow. "I expect you've come about poor old Arnold have you?"

"I'm afraid we have, we wondered if anyone here knew Arnold well enough to give us some idea why he was targeted. I was told that one of your members Gordon Finchley or was it Dessie Milburn was a good friend of Arnold's"

"Ah well you're in luck lad because this fella next to me is Dessie and Gordon is the one over there on rink four, the one with the tank top on. If you want to speak to Dessie here privately I'll leave you to it, and if you want a word with Gordon I'll let him know you're here. But it'll be a good hour yet before he's finished his game, you'll have to sit here and wait for him." With that the cheery fellow got up and left him with Dessie.

There was a short silence before Dessie decided to speak.

"So you want to know about Arnold do you, well I'll tell you what I know but it isn't much; we weren't best friends you know, only friends down here at the bowls."

Bene didn't think Dessie was going to be much help. When he sat down he was sure he'd deliberately looked away as if deciding he wanted nothing to do with him, and his body language was telling him the same. He thought Dessie would gladly have got up and left if it wasn't for the fact the other man had given Bene his name and left them alone together.

"You don't know much about his private life then?"

"Not really, I knew where he lived of course and he was married. I mean we spoke often enough, but it was only about the bowls, politics or sport, you know the usual stuff. We didn't see each other outside of the bowls so I can't tell you anything about his private life. I'm sorry about what's happened of course because he was a good bloke and a good bowler as well, he'll be sadly missed."

There was another pause in which Dessie purposely looked away; it was obvious Bene would get nothing more from him. He had the feeling Dessie had prepared a little speech in his head before talking to him, just enough to give him a glimpse of his relationship with Arnold, but not enough to suggest that their friendship through bowls was anything more than that.

"Did he talk about anything that might have been worrying him, or could you tell if there was anything that had upset him recently?" Dessie didn't bother to face Bene but spoke instead to someone who might have been sitting on the roof of the bower.

"No, he was his usual self, if there was anything wrong he never told me about it. I'm sorry but that's about it, I don't think I can tell you anymore."

Dessie rose from the bench and walked over and sat down on the bench behind rink four; he was waiting for a word with Gordon Finchley who was bowling from the far end. Bene thought that Adam had been right, there was something not quite right here, Dessie had been careful not to give too much away but he certainly knew more than he was telling. Hils joined him on the bench and Bene told her how his conversation with Dessie had gone.

"I suppose we'll just have to wait to speak to the other guy when he's finished his game, although it looks as if your pal Dessie is going to warn him about the questions he'll be asked." Bene had a better idea.

"Rather than wait here for the next half hour or so which will probably be a waste of time let's find somebody else to talk to, I fancy a chat with that other guy who was sitting here." They found him sitting alone not far away and approached him in a casual manner.

"Thanks for that back there; it was considerate of you to let me speak to him alone."

"Hey, no problem lad, did it help at all?"

"He gave me a bit of information about Arnold but seemingly he didn't know him very well."

"Rubbish, Dessie and Arnold were good mates they did lots of things together, but I guess he didn't tell you very much eh?"

"No, he did seem a bit reluctant to talk. But you must have known Arnold well enough what can you tell me about him?"

"What exactly do you want to know?"

"I'd like to know if there was anything worrying him recently; there must have been something because whoever shot him had good reason to do it; you don't shoot someone just because you don't like them do you?"

The bowler who Bene discovered was called Simon Overton looked around to make sure he wouldn't be overheard, before answering.

"Arnold isn't the only one whose been looking troubled lately; you've probably guessed that Dessie is another." Then Simon pointed over to rink four.

"You can include his pal Gordon over there as well and I suspect there might be one or two others. It's affected them all but none of them are saying anything, whatever it is they're keeping it to themselves."

"And you've no idea what it is?"

"No, but I think it has something to do with the Fox and Pheasant. A group of them are regulars and I think something must have happened the last time they were in there because they haven't been back since. You should have a word with Kris; he might be able to tell you something."

Bene and Hils were at last getting one or two leads to work with. Simon continued.

"I'll tell you one thing though I'm getting a bit nervous myself. I mean if Arnold was murdered for something that involves the club do you think one of them could be next?"

"I don't know, but if we don't get to the bottom of it pretty quickly it has to be a possibility."

Simon gave him the names of two more bowlers he thought might be able to help. Bene didn't think it would be worthwhile waiting for Gordon to finish his game as he'd noticed Dessie speaking to him when he came down the rink to play his bowls. Their conversation only lasted a few seconds but during that time both men glanced over to the bench where Bene and Simon were sitting. Bene would get nothing more out of Gordon other than what Dessie had already told him, he decided they might as well leave. He was about to thank Simon for his help, but when he rose from the bench Simon tapped his arm, he insisted that the information he'd given and the suspicions he had were kept to himself; he didn't want to fall out with his friends at the club. Bene agreed that it would go no further and he'd speak to one or two of the others on his way out, telling them how he'd enjoyed watching the game with Simon who'd been explaining the rules of the game to him.

Hils hadn't taken part in the conversation but she'd been listening quietly and taking in everything that had been said. "What now then?" she asked.

"I know it's getting late and there's nothing more we can do here, but we have to get back to the station and interview the car wash lad. I know it's been a long day but that's the way it is I'm afraid. It's going to be like this until we find out who killed Arnold Bainbridge. If it was Gary Maitland then that's it case closed, but if not then we keep on looking."

Back at the station they were in for a disappointment, ET had returned without Gary. The lad wasn't at home and hadn't been there since Saturday. Gary's Auntie Pat hadn't seen him since he came back for his dinner that night, and when he finished his meal he went straight out again. He hadn't come home to sleep so she thought he must be staying with friends. She had no idea who they were as Gary was always very secretive about his friends and what they got up to. ET asked if she could check his bedroom to see if he'd taken anything with him, clothes maybe. This made her suspicious and she wasn't keen to do it, she wanted to know what it was all about.

"That other policeman came to see him yesterday down at the snooker club and Gary answered all his questions so why do you want to see him again, he was nowhere near the place when the shooting happened. He told that policeman what he'd been doing and he was satisfied. In fact Gary told me he wasn't going to work on Friday, so there you are."

"We just need to talk to him again. I know he told my colleague he knew nothing about what happened, but we think there might have been something unusual that occurred at the car wash in the day or so leading up to the incident, and if there was then it might have a bearing on the shooting. He may have noticed something but not thought it important at the time, but if there was anything it could be significant to our enquiries, we just need to speak to him again to be sure. If he comes home later that's fine; we'll come back and see him, but if he's going to be away for any longer then we need to get out there and find him."

She went upstairs to check his room and returned a few minutes later.

"Gary's room is always a mess; he just throws off his clothes and leaves them lying around on the floor waiting for me to pick them up, but most of his stuff seems to be there. If he's taken anything it can't be much, an old sweater or a pair of jeans maybe, but when he's staying over at friends you don't know whose clothes he's coming back in. I'm sorry but I can't tell you any more than that, Gary hasn't lived with me that long so he doesn't have many friends here." She was certain of one thing though. "Gary didn't know the man who was killed and I know he had nothing to do with what happened to him either."

ET gave her his card and one of Bene's.

"OK, well if he comes back or phones I want you to contact one of us immediately, it really is important that we speak to him."

"I'll tell him." She took the cards and dropped them on the telephone table.

ET and Devlin left the house and set off to trawl Gary's known haunts in the town, but at each one they visited the result was the same, no-one had seen Gary since the day before. There was nothing else they could do so ET dropped Devlin off at his home and returned to the station to report back to Inspector Sowerby. As far as ET was concerned there was one thing for sure, guilty or not Gary Maitland had done a runner.

When Bene and Hils got back to the station ET and Sowerby were waiting, the Inspector quickly gave them the news of Gary's disappearance. As soon as Sowerby had got ET's report he'd wasted no time, calls had been put out to all police stations with a description of the wanted man and the need to find him as soon as possible. He'd also drafted in extra men from around the district to conduct a thorough search of the town for the wanted man the following day. Bene briefly gave the Inspector his own news and although it didn't amount to much it might lead to something more substantial if it was followed up.

It was getting late in the evening and the three officers had been chasing shadows all day. The Inspector could see they were weary and had nothing more to give him. He wanted them back in the morning bright and fresh so the decision was made to wrap it up for the day. "I'll have a few more officers here to help with the search in the morning. ET I want you to take Hils with you and co-ordinate the search. I don't think the lad's left town; I think he's hiding out here somewhere. Put the word out in all the shops and clubs and anywhere else he might frequent; if it is him then we need him caught before he has the opportunity to carry out any more shootings. Bene I want you to do a lot more digging and get to the bottom of what it is that's got those bowlers so scared. I don't think Gary's the only one we're looking for; from what you've told me I don't think he's capable of carrying out something like this on his own. There must be someone else behind it. Maybe Gary's just the man who pulls the trigger, and if he is then I'd like to know how he got the gun and where it came from. Right, off you go, get a good night's sleep and I'll see you back here in the morning."

CHAPTER 11

More enquiries

Bene trudged down the path fully expecting another cold welcome as he went through the door; he was dreadfully late of course and dinner again would have to be warmed up for him. Things hadn't gone to plan that day, but none of it was his fault or his making. He was a detective and Alex knew his job would never be a nine to five one; sometimes he was required to work excessively long and unsociable hours in order to get a result. The last two days had been like that and it would stay that way until the murderer was caught and in custody. Of course this was unfair on Alex and Dot as it threw them out of their daily routine. He'd have to be firm and explain that it was all part of his job and they'd just have to accept it. Like Sowerby he didn't think Gary had left the town, with a bit of luck a thorough search tomorrow would flush him out. But of course he wasn't a local lad so it's possible he might go back to his home town wherever that was. He'd have to check that out in the morning.

Bracing himself for a cool reception he walked through the door and was immediately struck by a rich aroma coming from the kitchen. He glanced into the lounge on passing but saw no-one there so he followed his nose towards the source of those delicious smells; in the kitchen he found Dot and Alex busy dishing up a casserole.

"Just in time." said Dot. "Alex said you might be a bit late so we thought we'd wait for you and we could all sit down together and eat." She waved him over to the table.

"Come on then it's ready, sit yourself down and we'll dish it up."

This wasn't at all what Bene had expected but he was extremely relieved. He didn't want to spoil it by asking why he was getting this unexpected warm reception; he thought it best to remain silent and wait for his dinner to come to him, any explanations could wait until later.

The meal was excellent and exactly what he needed after a long and tiresome day. There was nothing much in the way of conversation at the table, but he was suspiciously aware of some knowing looks and smiles between Alex and her mother. "Something's up" he thought "I wonder what they've been up to." The house was nice and warm and he was beginning to feel a bit more relaxed when suddenly and without warning he felt a cold shiver shoot down his spine. It had just clicked and he knew exactly why they were looking so smug and happy. They'd been out to view a house and Alex has fallen in love with it, and to make matters worse he knew exactly which one it was. It was one they'd looked at on the internet just a couple of streets away, the one that was far too expensive and way above their budget. Alex had tried to convince him that by making a few cuts here and there and doing without

certain things they might just be able to manage it. But Bene had been more realistic, he knew there was no way they could afford it. Why on earth couldn't she have waited a few more days and they could have looked for one together, and find one they could realistically afford.
"So that's what all this is about; I knew it was too good to be true."

When the meal was finished Dot rose to clear the plates from the table, Bene rose with her intending to quiz her in the kitchen but Dot placed a hand on his shoulder.

"No, you sit there Bene, you and Alex need to talk."

Bene was sitting across the table from his wife. Looking over he saw the same girl he'd met and fallen in love with in this very house just over a year ago. The girl with short dark hair who was sitting on a stool at the breakfast bar watching television, she'd turned to face him when he entered the kitchen and smiled briefly before switching her attention back to the TV. He had a few brief moments in which to observe and appreciate the girl's natural good looks. She was attractive, not beautiful but certainly pretty, sitting there with one leg on the foot rest and the other stretched out to the floor. She had a delightful figure that suited her height which he judged at the time to be around five foot six or seven. Dot had smiled seeing the interest in his face. "This is my daughter Alex" she'd said as she introduced the girl to Bene, he'd walked around to try and catch a better glimpse of the girl and she smiled again, this time engaging his eyes for a few moments longer. It was love at first sight and he was hooked.

He had to dismiss these thoughts from his mind and concentrate on how he was going to deal with the problem. Dot had left the room and he could sense an atmosphere developing. He continued to look at Alex and saw the same sparkle in her eyes that had first attracted him in what seemed a lifetime ago, that devilish and mischievous smile of hers that could always win him over. He had to drag his eyes away because there was no way he wanted to see that smile turn to tears when he dashed her hopes of buying a house she'd set her heart on. She had that look in her eye and Bene was afraid. He was going to hate this and it would break her heart, but nevertheless he had to do it, she had to be told.

But it was Alex who broke the silence.

"Look Bene I know you've had to work long hours these last couple of days and you haven't been here much, but mam and I have been busy."

Bene held up his hand, there was no way he was going to let her go any further.

"You're right Alex, it's not my fault I haven't been here much these last few days, and I haven't had time to go with you and your mam to look at houses. But I know the one you're going to tell me about; it's the one we looked at on the internet, and yes we all loved it and wished we could have it. But let's not get carried away because we haven't actually been to see it, so we don't know if it's as good in reality as it looks on the internet. I know you had your heart set on it, but honestly Alex we can't afford it."

Alex tried to butt in, but Bene was having none of it he had to be firm. She was going to be disappointed and there were bound to be tears, but nevertheless it had to be done.

"Now you're going to hate me for this but it has to stop here." He smacked his hand down hard on the table and looked directly into her eyes, but to his surprise she was still smiling and he couldn't understand why. Did she think she just had to turn on the charm and he'd give in, admittedly he usually did? Many times in the past he'd been so sure of himself when they'd had a difference of opinion, but it was always Alex who came out on top and got her own way; this time he had to make sure it was him who came out on top.

"Darling, we just can't afford it, you'll have to wait a bit longer."

There was no way he could let her down lightly, but neither did he want to destroy her dream altogether. He was feeling dreadful about the whole bloody house thing and his head slumped forward and banged on the table. He reached out for her hands and took them in his.

Addressing the table top he gave her the only assurance he could offer.

"I promise we will find a house that we like just as much as that one, but honestly Alex it's got to be within our budget."

There was a long silence before he dared look up from the table, expecting a cold and hostile stare and maybe tears. He was surprised to see she was still smiling.

"Why on earth are you rabbiting on about houses?" she said.

This was too much for Bene. He had no idea what was going on or why she was acting so strangely. She should have been crying or shouting at him; he would have understood that, but not this.

"That's what you and your mam have been doing isn't it, looking at that house?"

Alex laughed.

"Don't be daft we wouldn't go without you, you silly sod, we know you're in the middle of a murder case and we're quite prepared to wait until that's done before we start looking again."

"Well what the hell is this all about, you and your mother smirking away at each other and not letting me in on it, I thought you'd been to see that house and put an offer in for it."

Alex was still laughing. Bene gave up; he couldn't understand what was going on, if it wasn't the house then what was it?

"It's got nothing to do with the house silly boy." Then she changed the subject.

"How's your case going anyway? Are you any nearer to finding out who did it?"

"Never mind about the case, I want to know what's going on with you and your mam?"

"Oh that, oh it's nothing really you probably wouldn't be interested." She still had that stupid grin on her face. He'd never seen her like this before. This was a different Alex, an Alex he didn't recognise and couldn't understand.

"Well try me anyway; I might be interested you never know."

"Well it's nothing much, but…….. There was a slight hesitation before she continued.

"I'm having a baby silly; you're going to be a father Bene."

Bene's jaw dropped; he sat there looking at her open mouthed and speechless, trying to take in what she'd just told him. Eventually finding some words he blurted out.

"How did that happen?"

"Oh come on Bene, how do you think, you're such a dope sometimes."

At last the penny dropped and he jumped up and grabbed hold of her, clutching her tightly he kissed her face all over.

"Oh you clever girl when will this happen?"

"Well I only found out today, but I'm ten weeks pregnant so you can work it out for yourself." Dot came back into the room to congratulate the pair.

"Well now that's out of the way we can start looking for a house again."

All three burst into laughter.

The Bene who got out of bed the next morning was a completely different man to the one who had risen the previous day. This new one was full of hope and enthusiasm for the coming day and the future, he was still on a high from the news Alex's had given him the night before. A good breakfast had set him up perfectly and he was confident that today there'd be some good news which would hopefully end in an arrest. And then he really could relax a bit and devote more of his time to Alex and their search for a new home.

At the station the team from the previous day had been expanded and now included an extra five uniformed officers drawn from the surrounding districts. Inspector Sowerby was holding the morning brief; he gave them details of the man they were looking for and then left it to ET to allot each of the men an area of the town to concentrate on. A few minutes later the search for Gary Maitland was underway with ET in charge of co-ordination.

The Inspector waited until the search party had left before taking Bene into his office.

"Right that's them out of the way, let's hope they find this fella soon and bring him back here, and then we can all relax."

Bene was in full agreement and conveyed his confidence to the Inspector.

"Well Levensbridge isn't a big town so Gary's probably hiding out at a friend's house. If that's the case it shouldn't take them long to track him down and bring him in. So how do you want me to approach these men at the bowls club?"

"You said you'd spoken to Adam Firth about it, and as he's a member at the club I suggest you talk to him again, then get the addresses of those other men and go and talk to them. You can be quite blunt about it, tell them we're concerned for the safety of all the members, and emphasise that you think the murder may be linked to the club. Hopefully they'll open up a bit and give us an idea as to what's behind it. After you've seen them go over to the Fox and Pheasant and have a word with the landlord and see what you can get out of him. We need a name or names Bene, so be a bit more brutal in your approach. OK I'll not keep you any longer, let's make it a good day. The last thing we want is for this to drag on much longer, because if it does I'll be forced to hand it over to division."

Bene didn't hang around and went straight over to Adam's house where he found him in the kitchen reading the morning paper. He'd finished his breakfast and was in good spirits. Bene started by telling Adam and Ellen his good news; they were delighted and shook his hand warmly. The visit was serving two purposes, bringing the good news to his friends and giving him the chance to talk to Adam again.

"Well done lad" said Adam, "come on through if you've got time and tell us all about it."

Bene was only too pleased to tell them. "She's only just found out; she's ten weeks pregnant so we've plenty of time to prepare for it."

"You must be very proud Bene," said Ellen I'm so pleased for you both; you must bring her round and we can do a bit of a celebrating."

Adam wanted to know how the investigation was going and asked Bene to fill him in on his visit to the bowls club.

"Yeah, it was quite useful but I didn't get much out of Dessie, it was obvious he didn't want to talk about it, and I didn't get the chance to speak to Gordon, Dessie got to him first. But I did have a good chat with Simon Overton and he was more helpful. He confirmed what you told me about some of the members getting jittery but he couldn't tell me why. I need to speak to them Adam, and I need you to tell me where I can get hold of them because they could be in danger. We do have a suspect and we're out looking for him at the moment, but we think there may be someone else involved and we desperately need to find them."

Bene called at the first address Adam had given him and found Gordon Finchley at home in his garden. His wife answered the door, she looked a little worried when he showed his warrant card but she didn't query the nature of his visit. She took him straight through the house and showed him into the rear garden, after introducing him to her husband she left them to talk. "She knows something" thought Bene as he greeted Gordon.

"Hi Gordon I don't know if you saw me but I came down to the bowls club last night to have a word with you, I didn't get the chance to speak because you were in the middle of a game and I didn't want to interrupt it. How did you get on by the way?"

Bene had the impression his visit was not exactly unexpected.

"Ah, we were well beaten, but they're a good pair so there was no shame in it, we've beaten them before and we can do it again. It all depends on the day and which way the luck runs. Anyway what was it you wanted to speak to me about?"

"To be honest it's about that business with Arnold. We haven't been able to catch the fellow who shot him yet and we're a bit worried that it could have something to do with the bowls club. We're concerned that other members of the club could be on the killers list as well."

Gordon was leaning on his hoe looking down at the trench he'd just made, deliberately avoiding eye contact with Bene.

"And what makes you think that?"

"Well we know in the days leading up to his murder Arnold was worried about something, and we're sure it was something to do with the club or the club members. We're concerned for all of you down there and we need to find out what's behind it all." He paused for a moment to try and judge Gordon's reaction. There was no immediate response, Gordon was thinking and mulling over in his mind what he would say.

"Have you any idea what was troubling him Gordon? Because if you do, you need to tell me, we have to put a stop to it before there're any more tragedies." Gordon sighed and slowly looked up, he'd reached his decision but it was not the one Bene wanted.

"There's nothing I can think of, Arnold seemed OK to me but then I don't know much about his private life it must have something to do with that. I'm sure it's got nothing to do with the club." And with that he stared directly at Bene with a look that said "that's all you're getting from me pal, you'll have to look elsewhere for your answers."

"Think carefully Gordon, if there is anything now's the time to tell me, this isn't going away and I'm afraid that if we don't catch this fellow quickly there could be another murder. Are you absolutely sure there's nothing you want to tell me?"

Gordon looked at him blankly, he was definitely worried because it was written all over his face, but Bene could get nothing more out of him Gordon remained silent. Bene could tell the man was aware of the danger he could be exposed to, but he'd made up his mind that he'd take his own chances in dealing with it.

Bene's next port of call was to the house of Brian Featherstone, but unlike his visit to Gordon Finchley it was obvious that Brian hadn't been expecting a visit from the police, he was most surprised and intrigued.

"Come on in lad, but if it's about that car I had stolen last month, the one that ended up in the river, you needn't have bothered because the insurance paid up without any bother."

"No, it's nothing to do with that Brian, we're talking to all Arnold's pals at the bowls club, to find out if anyone can tell us if they'd noticed anything different about him this last week or so, more specifically what he was so worried about. We think there's a connection between his murder and the bowls club, we don't know what it is but we desperately need to find out."

"Aye well I don't think I can help you with that lad. I mean he was a good sort Arnold was, but him and me never really spent much time together, just the odd game of bowls of course. But we never met socially, Arnold had a different circle of friends to me, so it's them you should be talking to, aye you have a word with them lad."

Several minutes later and Bene was making no headway at all; it was obvious Brian wasn't lying or trying to conceal anything. He genuinely didn't know Arnold that well and he'd no idea what could have been worrying him, even if there had been something. Bene decided not to waste any more time and try elsewhere.

"OK Brian thanks anyway, I'll go and talk to some of the others."

He prepared to leave and Brian rose from his chair.

"No doubt you'll be speaking to all the others, but try Dessie Milburn first; he was a good friend of Arnold's."

"I've already spoken to Dessie and he couldn't help, but thanks anyway."

"Well try Willie Jameson you might have better luck with him; he lives a fair way out mind but you should find him at home, he's never far from it."

"Where does he live Brian, out of town you say?"

"Yeah that's right, he's out at Longbarrow village if you know where that is; you go there lad, you'll find him easily enough."

Bene thought about Longbarrow village; "now why has that place come up again."

Chapter 12

A Second Death

The Fox and Pheasant wasn't open for business when Bene arrived, but on catching sight of Kris through the window he managed to attract his attention and gain access to the pub.

"Can't serve you a drink Bene you know that, we won't be open for another hour yet."

"Don't be daft you know that's not what I've come about. I need your help and I'm hoping you can give me some information."

Bene had been good friends with Kris and his wife Ebony for the past few years. Kris was a tall man; well over six feet with a figure that suggested more than a few pints had passed through his lips over the years. He had a rustic face with a permanent smile etched upon it and a good head of thick sandy-coloured hair. Ebony by contrast, was a few inches shorter than her husband, but where Kris had let his figure spread outwardly she had retained hers and was proud of it. Her auburn hair was swept up into a bun, and this allowed her face to be shown to its best advantage; a happy face with nice clear rounded lines which required merely the minimum of makeup.

"Go on then, what's this about?" Kris asked.

"It's about the murder up at the car wash on Friday I think some of your customers might be able to help me. Not that we think any of them were involved in it but I want to ask you a few questions. It's really the bowlers I'm interested in, the ones who come in for a drink after the game on Thursday nights."

"Oh that lot, well there's only a few of them come in, and as you say it's only on Thursday after their league match. They don't come in any other time, well not together they don't; one or two of them come in with their wives occasionally but as a group it's only Thursdays. Sometimes there're four of them, sometimes a couple more. What do you want to know about them?"

"I believe they haven't been in the last week or so is that right?" Kris thought about it.

"Yes I think you're right, come to mention it I don't remember seeing them for the last two or three weeks, and with old Arnold going the way he did it might put them off coming back for a while yet. Arnold was the star turn of that group alright; he always had a good story or a joke to tell, everything seemed to revolve around him. He was good for business was Arnold and I'm going to miss him."

"Can you cast your mind back to the last time they were in here Kris, because I think it may be something that happened then, and possibly the reason they haven't been back since?"

"Aye I see what you mean." Kris cupped his hands to his face trying to remember.

"Well they certainly weren't in last week and that was the day before Arnold was shot wasn't it, and I'm not sure if they were in the week before either, let me think now."

The room was quiet; Bene didn't want to disturb Kris's concentration for if he did remember something, it might be important.

"Right, well Thursday nights are fairly quiet, and apart from the bowlers I don't usually get many others in. Come to think of it they haven't been in the last two Thursdays, but the week before that I remember it was a bit busier than usual. The room wasn't full you understand, but there were a few in that night that I don't normally see. I'm trying to think who was here." There was another long silence while Kris racked his brains trying to recall the faces and names of the people who were in that night. Eventually the images came back to him.

"I think I've got it, yes, there were certainly four of the bowlers here, Arnold, Dessie, Gordon and Willie for sure and maybe one or two of the others but I'm not sure which ones. Then there was old Donald and he was joined by Alfie Brooks and his brother, now they don't usually come in on a Thursday night, I always see them on Friday's. A couple of young lads came in for a while but I'm not sure who they were. I might have seen one of them in here before, I think they're local but they're not regulars. They didn't stay long anyway I got them a pint each and then I had to go down to the cellar to change a barrel and when I came back they'd gone. Then there were a couple of fellows sitting behind Alfie and his brother and they were in for about an hour. Scottish they were, on their way down to the Midlands for a wedding. Apart from them there were a couple of reps sitting over there, but they're OK I've seen them in here a few times. And then there were two other fellows sitting over there." He pointed to a table by the window. "I've no idea who they were. Two smartly dressed fellows, but definitely not from round here they had southern accents, well-spoken and very polite they were. They took their drinks over to the table but there didn't seem to be much conversation between them, quiet and watchful I thought. But there was no problem with them so I didn't take much notice, they seemed alright. If anyone else came in later Ebony would have served them, I had to go to the kitchen and do an order for the brewery"

Bene took a photo of Gary Maitland from his pocket and showed it to Kris.

"Was this one of the lads who came in that night?"

Kris took the photo and looked at it.

"Yep, I think that could have been one of them, is he the lad you're looking for?"

"Yes, we've got a search party out now looking for him, I'm sure he's still local so we should have him soon. Now you say they weren't in very long, but did you notice if either of them spoke to any of the bowlers during that time?"

"Not while I was in here, but they may have done when I went to the cellar; you'll have to ask some of the group."

"So when you came back did you notice anything different?"

"No, the two lads had gone and one of the bowlers had gone as well but I forget which one it was, I only noticed because when they bought another round of drinks they ordered one less pint. Oh yes and Alfie's brother had gone as well, I remember the relief from the others as the smell went out with him."

"OK thanks for that, if you remember anything else you'll let me know yeah. I'll go and have a word with the other bowlers and see if Gary had spoken to them."

A quick phone call to ET told him the search was well underway but so far there was no sign of Gary. Bene decided he would drive over to Longbarrow village again, this time to speak to Willie Jameson.

It was his second visit to the village in two days and this time there was a bit more activity around the place. The weekend was over and the working week was in full swing again. Willie Jameson's cottage was easily found and only a few houses away from The Dawes household. There was a car parked outside the cottage which Bene assumed belonged to the tenant of the house. He knocked on the door and stood back waiting for it to be opened but no-one came. He knocked again harder and a bit longer this time, but still there was no reply. He moved over to one of the windows and glanced through into what appeared to be the kitchen, but the room was empty apart from the units and appliances, there was no sign of Willie Jameson. He moved to the next window and looked through into the lounge, but apart from the usual furniture there was no sign of life there either. Bene thought he was probably in the garden so he went around the side of the house to the back of the property. A quick scan of the area told him Willie wasn't there either.

"So if he never goes far I should be able to find him somewhere around here." Bene left the property and walked over to Smithy Cottage and knocked on the door. It was early afternoon and Matthew was home having a late lunch.

"Come in lad, I didn't expect to see you again so soon, have you caught your man yet?"

"No, but I think we'll have him before too long, we've got more officers out looking for him so there's a good chance we'll have him in custody by the end of the day. I haven't forgotten what you told me yesterday and I'll get back to you on that, but at the moment I'm looking for Willie Jameson who lives along the road from you, have you any idea where he is?"

"I haven't seen him today but have a look around the back of his house he's probably there."

"I've done that but he's not in the garden and he doesn't seem to be in the house either. Is that his car out there?" Bene pointed to the car in front of Willie's cottage.

"Aye that's Willie's car alright, so he must be at home. Was it about that bowler fellow that got killed the other day; is that what you want to see him about?"

"Yeah, somebody gave me his name and thought he might know something?"

"Well I'll come with you and we'll see what he's up to."

The two men walked over to Willie's cottage, while Bene was busy checking through the windows again, Matthew went around to the rear of the house. A minute later he came back with a blank face, Willie was nowhere to be seen and Matthew looked worried.

"Do you think it'll be alright if I let myself into the house I'm just a bit bothered that he's taken ill or something, because if his car's here then Willie should be here as well?"

Bene gave his consent and Matthew opened the door. He turned to Bene.

"He never locks it you know."

Matthew entered the cottage.

"Are you there Willie?" he shouted, but there was no answering call.

"He's certainly not down here. I'll have a quick look upstairs and check there."

With that he climbed the narrow staircase that led to the rooms above. Bene heard one door open and close again and then another door open. This was followed by a short silence before he heard a stumbling sound as if Matthew had fallen against something. It went quiet again and a few seconds later he saw Matthew appear at the top of the stairs. There was a startled look on his face and his hand was clamped tightly over his mouth.

"What is it then, is he up there?" Bene asked.

Matthew didn't or couldn't respond: he clattered down the stairs and pushed roughly passed him in the hall, running out of the house and onto the lawn he vomited on the grass.

Bene didn't ask again, something Matthew had seen in one of the upstairs rooms had upset him to such an extent that it had caused him to act in the way he did. Whatever it was the poor man hadn't been prepared for it. Something horrible had happened, and Bene was certain that when he went into that room he would find a body, and that body would not be a pretty sight.

He walked over to Matthew who was slumped over the back of a wooden bench next to the flower beds.

He helped him to sit down and told him to stay there until he'd been into the house. Satisfied that Matthew would be alright he went back to the cottage. Putting on his gloves and shoe protectors he climbed the stairs. The body of Willie Jameson was lying sprawled across the bed, arms outstretched with one leg hanging over the side almost touching the floor. Thankfully there was very little blood, only a small patch that had soaked into the duvet under the victims head. He touched the body and found it cold, death must have occurred several hours earlier, probably sometime during the previous night. At first glance the cause of death appeared to be a single bullet entry wound in the centre of the forehead, the similarity between the body he was looking at and that of Arnold Bainbridge was telling. The method used in both killings matched exactly, and there was no doubt in his mind that the killer in both cases was the same person.

Bene immediately called his Inspector to give him the bad news, and then called out the doctor, the pathologist and the forensics team. There was nothing to do now but wait, one or two people had stopped at the cottage gate, and seeing Matthew sitting there looking distressed enquired if he was alright. Bene told them there'd been an incident and Matthew had had a shock but he was OK; it would be better if they moved on. Matthew was beginning to get his colour back and looked up at Bene hoping for some answers.

"Why would anyone want to shoot my pal Willie? I don't understand, he was such a lovely man and never harmed anyone, I can't believe it."

Bene knew it wouldn't be too long before Matthew came to realise that Willie's death and that of Arnold Bainbridge were connected but at the moment his mind was still full of the horror of what he'd seen to make the connection.

Bene phoned Inspector Sowerby again to explain what had happened, and what he'd seen in the cottage.

"It's definitely murder, and the MO is exactly the same as Arnold Bainbridge, a bullet in the middle of the forehead. I've ruled out robbery as nothing seems to have been disturbed or taken. It looks like he was shot by the same Person who killed Arnold."

The Inspector had a little news. The forensic tests carried out on the bullet extracted from the body of Arnold Bainbridge had come back, and it was a 9mm bullet from an old Walther P38, a gun used by the Nazis in the last war. Forensics hadn't been able to get the results any earlier due to the weekend. On hearing of the resemblance between the two murders the Inspector told Bene to get forensics to check if the bullet used in this latest murder matched the first one. There was still no news of Gary Maitland, he hadn't returned home and the search so far hadn't revealed his whereabouts.

The news from the search had Bene thinking, for when he'd been speaking to Gary he hadn't got the impression he was the type of person who could carry out something as callous as this. Sometimes of course his instincts were wrong, but not often, and in Gary's case he was pretty sure the lad wasn't responsible for the murders. There were a few things that bothered him about the killings and he needed to get them straight in his mind.

"I know Gary hasn't got a car and I'm pretty sure he can't drive either, so if it was him then how did he get over here last night and shoot Willie Jameson?" Another thing that puzzled him was the fact that the lad had gone missing.

"He must know we're out looking for him, so if he's innocent why has he gone into hiding?" The description of the man Alison Dawes had seen was a good match for Gary and when he disappeared it just seemed to confirm his guilt. It looked like an open-and-shut case against him, find the lad, bring him in and charge him, case closed. But Bene wasn't sure it was that simple. He was beginning to think that these murders were going to prove a lot more complicated, and if Gary wasn't responsible for them they were back to square one with no idea where to look. The thought depressed him; he desperately needed help from somewhere.

"Those bloody bowlers, maybe now with another murder at their precious club they'll open up a bit, because if they insist on keeping their secrets to themselves they'll all end up dead." Then a terrible thought came to him. God I hope Adam isn't in any danger, I'll go and see him again and warn him, and maybe he'll come up with something that will help."

The doctor arrived along with the forensics team and Bene thought it best to leave them to get on with their jobs, so after a quick briefing he left them. The local constable was outside and Bene told him to secure the premises and keep the public away. He'd be joined shortly by more officers and they had orders to do a complete check on all the houses in the village. To get as much information as possible about anything unusual they'd seen or heard during the previous twenty four hours, and ask specifically if anyone had heard the shooting.

Bene took Matthew back to his cottage and sat him down whilst he went into the kitchen to make him a big mug of hot tea.

"Get that down you it'll do you good, or maybe you'd like something a bit stronger?"

"No, I don't touch the hard stuff this'll do fine. I can't help thinking about poor Willie lying there. He's gone to bed and some bastard's come into the house and shot him; why for God's sake? His door is always open like most of the houses around here and we've never have any trouble. Most of us keep them locked at night of course but Willie never locks his house at all. He's lived on his own since his wife died a few years back and his house is always open day and night." This seemed a bit strange to Bene.

Just then the door opened and Alison came in looking worried; she immediately went over to the settee and sat down beside Matthew and put her arm around to comfort him. She'd been at her cleaning job in the village pub when the news came about Willie Jameson. Bene gave them a minute or two together before asking Matthew some questions.

"So you reckon he leaves his door open all the time, I can understand him leaving it open through the day, but surely not at night?"

"I know but Willie had a bad turn a few months back and as he doesn't have a phone he couldn't let anybody know that he was ill or get any help in, so after that he always leaves the door open, one of us will pop in now and again to make sure he's alright; if you hadn't called today most likely I would have gone over a bit later to check on him."

"It looks as though he was woken up at some point through the night" said Bene "although he was dressed for bed he wasn't actually in it when he was shot was he? Whoever it was that came into the house either disturbed him and that made him get out of bed or he was made to get out of bed by the intruder before being shot. The sound of the gun going off must have made quite a noise, did neither of you hear it?"

"No nothing, I was asleep, and you didn't hear anything did you Alison? we were both sound asleep weren't we?" Alison nodded in agreement.

"Oh well there's a few more police here now and they'll be checking on the neighbours, maybe one of them heard the shot and can give us a time when the shooting happened. I mean it must be pretty quiet here at night someone must have heard it. Anyway, going back over the last day or so have you noticed anything unusual or suspicious in the village, any strangers hanging around or a car parked here that wasn't local or anything like that?"

"No nothing I can think of, Sunday is quiet here and we didn't go out except into the garden for an hour or so but we weren't aware of anything out of the ordinary."

"OK not to worry, let's talk about Willie. Have you seen much of him lately?"

"Yes I see him out and about in the village most days but there was nothing to suggest he was in any sort of trouble, and I'm sure he hadn't fallen out with anyone, he was just his normal self. I can't understand it, I mean he never kept much money in the house, and there was nothing of any value in there either, nothing worth stealing that's for sure. When I went in it didn't cross my mind to see if there was anything missing, but from what I remember it looked much the same as it always does, I didn't notice anything different. And if it was a burglary that had gone wrong they wouldn't have got away with much. I suppose that's another reason Willie never locked his door, there was bugger all in the house worth stealing."

Alison kept her arm around him because he was still shaking, still suffering from the shock of discovering Willie's body. Bene thought that further questions would be a waste of time. Maybe when he'd recovered a bit more and thought about it he might remember something that would help, but in the meantime it would have to wait.

He was about to leave when Matthew's son Stephen came in from school and wanted to know what all the fuss was about. Bene looked him over and thought the lad was about fourteen or fifteen years old, an exact replica of what his father would have been like at that age. Alison got up to greet him and to make sure he stayed in the house.

"There's been a bit of bother at Willie Jameson's place and the police are looking into it; it would be best if you go up to your room and get on with your homework son. I'll be making tea shortly so I'll do your favourite; off you go now and I'll give you a shout when it's ready."

Stephen didn't look as if he was going to be fobbed off that easily.

"What sort of bother mam? The place is swarming with police, something bad has happened hasn't it, is Willie dead?"

Stephen was going to find out sooner or later so his mother told him as much as her and her husband knew, and then told him to go to the kitchen and wash his hands before going up to his room. Stephen really wanted to go outside and find out what was happening, but he didn't want to annoy his parents so grudgingly he trudged off to the kitchen muttering.

"Maybe I could have helped them; I mean I could have helped them with the last one if they'd only asked me."

His dad was quick to put him down.

"What are you talking about lad, you didn't know anything about that last one you were only eight so how could you know anything?" Matthew looked angry and was dismissive of his son, but Bene had picked up on the boy's statement and he was curious.

"I'll have a word with the lad if you like and try and satisfy him without going into much detail." A nod from Matthew was good enough so Bene followed the boy into the kitchen and told him he'd like to hear what help he could have given the police about the last incident in the village. Stephen looked a bit sheepish, he wasn't sure if he should tell him or not. Bene wanted to reassure him.

"Let's go out the back into the garden; that'll be better won't it, and no-one needs to know what we're talking about, do they?" Stephen seemed to think that was a good idea and led the way outside. Bene wanted it to be friendly and informal, but if the boy gave him a tall story he'd have to chasten him.

"So what was the last one Stephen you'll have to tell me all about it, did something happen here in the village?"

Stephen's eyes lit up, he'd waited for years to tell someone his story about what had happened all those years ago but couldn't, but now he had the chance to tell a real detective, someone who would believe him.

"As my dad said I was only eight years old back then but I remember that day alright, I was playing in the village with the other kids." He stopped to check that Bene was listening and to see if he looked interested; satisfied with what he saw he continued.

"We were playing 'hounds and hares' and me and another lad ran off down to the saw mill because we thought it would be a good place to hide. When we got there we thought we'd hide behind the big creosote tank, although we really weren't supposed to go near it. But when we got there we saw this funny-looking man lying there covered in creosote. You couldn't see his face it was covered in the stuff. We thought he was dead and we were going to run away, but he reached out his arm as if he wanted to tell us something. At first we thought he was going to grab hold of us so we backed off, but he couldn't get up so we just stood there looking at him. It looked like he was trying to tell us something so we went a bit nearer, but what he said didn't make any sense."

"So what did he tell you?" asked Bene who was now very interested in the lad's story.

"Well I think it must have been all that stuff on his head; he must have swallowed some of it because his voice was really croaky and we couldn't make out what he was saying; it was just a load of rubbish." His eyes appealed to Bene. "But it's all true honestly; we did see him there that day." Again he looked up to Bene before continuing.

"Later on everyone said he was dead, but I know he wasn't dead when we saw him. We were really scared so we didn't dare tell anyone about it, and even if we had they wouldn't have believed us."

Bene believed it though and he wondered why the lad had kept it a secret all this time.

"Did you not think it would have been a good idea to tell your dad about it?"

"We thought we'd get into trouble because we're not supposed to go there, so we didn't tell anyone, and the longer it went on the harder it became. If I'd told dad the next day or the next week then he'd be angry and say why didn't I tell him back then so I thought it best to say nothing, but with what's happened to old Willie I'm pleased that at last I've told you."

"You said the man was talking rubbish, do you think he was foreign, or was it just his accent that was different?"

"I don't know, it sounded kind of English but what he said didn't make any sense."

"Go on then, have a go and see if you can remember any of it."

"Well he said "Wollocks or Bollocks" or something like that but I didn't know what he meant, and then he said "Judge Alice has it." Well I didn't know any judges. I've got an Auntie Alice but she isn't a judge so what was he talking about?"

"They never found out who the man was did they?" asked Bene

"I don't think so, there were police around for a bit but they soon gave up, and my dad wasn't happy with them he thinks the man was murdered. You won't tell him what I said will you?"

"No, your dad wanted me to come back and have a look into that incident because he wasn't satisfied with what the police had done, but I think it's best if we leave it like that for now eh? With what you've just told me I'll be happy to come back and help with it; maybe the three of us will crack it eh? Right, let's get you back inside"

Bene left Smithy Cottage and walked over to his car. He unlocked the door and was about to get in when he noticed a large black car stationary about twenty yards behind his own; he didn't give it much thought but the two well-dressed occupants in that vehicle were certainly taking an interest in him. As Bene drove away the black car remained stationary for a few seconds until Bene had turned the first corner, then the engine started and the big car silently moved off and followed him out of the village.

CHAPTER 13

An Anonymous Phone Call

Inspector Sowerby was waiting for an update. But this latest murder was still in the early stages and there wasn't much Bene could tell him that would add to what he already knew.

"As we speak, officers are busy questioning the villagers to see what they can tell us; until they've finished I don't know what else we can do. The bullet has been sent over to forensics to check if it came from the same gun, we should have the result back shortly but I expect the two bullets will match up. Is there any news on Gary Maitland?"

"No, and I'm beginning to think he may have slipped the net. Since the shooting last night he's had the best part of a day to get clear of the area, but there's a nationwide search in full swing so wherever he is we should soon have him."

Bene was having doubts and wanted to express them to the Inspector.

"Despite all the evidence that points to him I'm not totally convinced Gary is the one we should be looking for. I mean I've spoken to the lad and he just doesn't come across as someone who's capable of doing anything like this."

"Then why the hell has he gone into hiding if he's not guilty?"

"Yes I know it looks bad. I've no idea why he's disappeared it's just a feeling I have about the lad. If it is him then he's either a callous and cold blooded killer or a bloody good actor, or possibly both, but despite everything, my instinct is telling me he's neither of those. I may be wrong of course, because the description of the person seen running away from the car wash fits him alright. But the lad doesn't have a car and he can't drive, so if it was him last night how did he get out to Longbarrow, unless he had an accomplice of course, but that doesn't seem to fit with him either."

"OK Bene, I respect your views on the lad, but until we get him back here we'll never find out. Let's hope we catch him quickly and we can get this whole bloody mess cleared up."

"I'm going to see Adam Firth again. He's the only one at the club I can trust, and if he does know anything I know he'll tell me. He did give me one or two names to check out and I've already spoken to them, but there seems to be a code of silence operating down at the club and they just clam up, I couldn't get anything out of them. Hopefully Adam can give me another name."

"Right well after you've seen him I want you to go down to that club again, and this time spell it out in plain English that if none of them are going to help us there's a good chance this could escalate into a full-blown carnage, and some of them could end up as victims."

On arrival at the house he found that Adam was at the club playing in the weekly jumble.

"What time do you expect him back Ellen, should I wait here or go down to the club and catch him there?"

"The jumble finishes about four o'clock and then they go into the bower and have a cup of tea and pay out the winners, so he's usually back here about five o'clock."

She could see it wasn't a social call and suggested Bene didn't waste time at the house.

"If it's urgent Bene maybe you should go down and catch him there, the game will be finishing shortly so if you leave now you should just about make it before they go inside."

Bene didn't go into details about his need to see Adam, and Ellen was wise enough not to question it, he said his goodbye with a promise to call again soon.

It was just as Ellen told him. He drove into the car park and could see the players collecting their bowls and drifting off into the bower. Adam recognised Bene's car coming into the park and left his bowls beside the bower to walk over and speak to him.

"You look serious Bene, not having any luck with this case then?"

The two men sat down on a bench well away from the bower and Bene gave Adam the news of Willie Jameson's murder.

"Bloody hell Bene, this is getting serious! We wondered why we didn't see him this afternoon. Murdered you say, my God when did that happen? The lads will be devastated they still haven't come to terms with Arnold's death, and the poor fellow isn't in his grave yet." He gave Bene a knowing look, but already knew the answer to his next question before asking it.

"Willie's death is linked to Arnold's isn't it?" Bene nodded

"And the MO was that similar as well?"

"Almost exactly; he was shot in the head at close range last night in his bedroom. There was a bullet-hole right in the centre of his forehead the man didn't stand a chance. I'm worried about you Adam, I mean some of these bowlers are sure as hell going to be in danger, and I just hope you're not one of them. I'd like to think it stops with those two, but if not then everyone here is in danger. I don't like to think about it but I have a nasty feeling this isn't going to be the end of it, and if I'm honest I'm sure there's more to come."

There was a long silence as both men took in the full impact of the two deaths, which for some reason were connected to the bowls club. Adam was the first to speak. "The lads have all seen you come in Bene and they'll be wondering what all this is about, I think you should go in and tell them what's happened to Willie. You should ask if any of them can give you any idea or suspicions they have as to why those two men have been targeted. Personally I have no idea at all; apart from giving you the names of the ones I thought might know something. But it seems that whatever it is they're afraid of they're not willing to talk about it. But now with this second murder it's changed everything; someone in there knows what it's all about and if they've got any sense they'll have to come forward and tell you. Go in now while they're all in there and give it to them straight."

Bene had been looking at the bower which appeared to date from Victorian times. The two gables ends of half-timber construction faced the green with a long conservatory conversion in the centre where people could sit and watch the games in comfort. He knew from Adam that inside there was a large seated area decked with tables and chairs plus two changing rooms and a kitchen. He went in just as the winners had been announced and as he had their attention he took the opportunity to introduce himself. Firstly he broke the sad news of the second death of one of their fellow bowlers. There was deathly quiet in the room as Bene went on to explain that it looked very much like the two deaths were connected. He expressed the concern he had for the safety of the members of the club and the possibility that some of them could be future targets.

"I want you all to think very carefully about what's happened to your two friends and if you know anything or have any suspicions as to what could be behind their deaths then you need to tell me. If you do know something the worst thing you can do is keep it to yourself, because if you do that then I fear there could be more deaths. Someone in here must know something, so think hard about it and come and tell me what it is, don't put any more of your friend's lives in danger. We desperately need to catch the person or persons responsible for this outrage and bring it to an end. I'll be outside for the next fifteen minutes or so and if you want to speak to me there please do so, but if you want to keep it confidential then call me on this number any time at all, day or night."

He took out a few of his cards and placed them on the table.

"But don't hesitate because the longer this goes on the more chance there is of someone else falling victim, and it could be another member of your club."

The bower remained silent. He couldn't decide if this was because they genuinely didn't know anything and were too badly shaken by the news he'd given them, or the ones who did know something were too frightened to speak, whichever it was there was no way he could tell.

Bene could do no more; he went outside and sat on a bench on his own, hoping that one or two of the bowlers might come over and speak to him. Again he was out of luck as one by one they slowly departed the bower and made their way to the car park, got in their cars and drove home. When the last bowler had left Adam rose and picked up his bowling gear to take into the bower. A dejected Bene went with him, they entered the building and Bene waited patiently for Adam to put his bowling equipment away. Once this was done they walked back to the door and it was only when they were passing the table that Bene noticed something.

"I don't remember exactly how many cards I left here but I'm sure there were more than this, at least one or maybe two have been taken."

"That's good Bene, at least some of them have thought about what you said, and with a bit of luck you might get a call from them. Obviously they didn't want to talk to you while you were here with the others around; it looks as though they want to speak to you away from the club. That sounds promising and maybe you'll get a lead at last."

"God I hope so because this is getting me down, we've had no luck whatsoever with either murder, and Sowerby's worried that if we don't get something soon we'll have to hand it over to division, and he would absolutely hate that, and so would I."

It had been another long day and once again he had nothing to show for all his efforts, not one lead, and until a minute ago not even the whiff of one. It didn't look as if ET and his team were having any luck either; if they had he would certainly have heard about it by now. He should go home, but he knew he couldn't as others were still working hard on the case. ET with Hils and the other officers were still searching the town for Gary and Inspector Sowerby wouldn't leave the station until the search was completed and all the news collated. There was no way he could go home and leave everything to them. He made his way back to the station and found Inspector Sowerby with the phone glued to his ear and his hand drumming the desk with a pencil; he looked worried, drawn and dead beat. He must have been on the phone all day in constant contact with the search teams as they combed the town. It was getting late in the evening and the search was almost complete. Soon they would return to the station dejected and empty handed just as he had. His only hope now was for one of the bowlers to phone him, because at least one of them had picked up his card, and with two of their friends dead and both deaths connected to the club maybe that would be enough for someone to tell him what they knew, and what he desperately wanted to know.

It wasn't long before the search team arrived back at the station, and as the Inspector and Bene had feared there'd been no sign of the suspect. The team had carried out a thorough search and were certain that wherever Gary Maitland was he was certainly not in Levensbridge. Inspector Sowerby had no doubts the search had been conducted methodically and comprehensively and thanked the team for their efforts before standing them down for the day. That done he told the detectives to go home and he would see them again in the morning for another briefing.

Bene trooped off home for a well-earned meal and some rest. Physically he was OK, but mentally he was drained and his mind was threatening to implode and destroy him. He tried his best to join in with the conversation around the dinner table but was failing miserably. Both Dot and Alex could see through the feeble disguise to the torment that was raging inside him. What he needed was eight hours of uninterrupted sleep but he doubted very much his mind would allow that to happen. After they had eaten Alex took his arm and led him upstairs to settle down for the night, in the hope that a good night's sleep would help ease some of the pressure that was eating away at him. He submitted quietly, and allowed himself to be guided by his well-meaning and considerate wife.

Sleep did finally come but not the eight hours he'd been hoping for. The incessant ringing of his mobile woke him to tell him it was two-thirty in the morning; he tried to ignore it but the phone persisted with its ridiculous ringing tone. He thought if he picked it up and threw it out of the window it would be a bloody good idea. But the caller was not giving up easily, rather ungraciously he picked it up, and not recognising the number gave the caller a piece of his mind.

"Do you know what sodding time it is mate, half past bloody two, I'm trying very hard to get some sleep here and you should be doing the same, so bugger off and bother somebody else." A rather subdued but well-spoken voice answered.

"Is that Bene Douglas of the Levensbridge CID who came to the bowls club this afternoon?"

Bene jumped up in bed and was wide awake in a flash, could this be the call he was waiting for, if only half expectantly.

"Sorry about that, yes you have the right man, who am I talking to?"

The caller was reluctant to give his name.

"Well before I start I want to tell you that I'm not involved in any of this business, and because of that I'm not expecting any trouble either. But there was an incident which happened a few years ago, and I think it may be connected to what's been happening lately at the club."

Bene was desperate to discover which of the bowlers he was talking to.

"Is this Simon?"

"No, and by the way he's not involved either. I'm not giving you my name, but if you want to know what this is about I suggest you just listen?"

"OK, I'll not press further, just tell me what you know."

"It was before I joined the club, but back then the members enjoyed going on bowling tours, usually three or four days at a time, over to the North East sometimes but mainly up into Scotland. Well on one of these tours there was some sort of incident and after that the tours suddenly stopped. No-one said what had happened or why they didn't go away again, but there've been no tours for the last ten years or so."

Bene was no longer tired; he was intrigued with the story and he asked the obvious question.

"You say no-one talks about it, but you must have some idea what happened and you think it has something to do with Arnold and Willie's murders?"

"That's right, they were both on the tours at that time, but I'm not sure if they were on the last one. Gordon and Dessie usually went with them and of course there were others as well but I'm not sure which ones. But stories do have a habit of getting around no matter how hard people try concealing them. Now, some of what I'm going to tell you may be gossip, but I'll tell you what I know and what I've heard and you can make your own mind up."

Bene agreed and waited for the caller to continue.

"The last tour the club did was to Perth, and they played four or five games up there, some of them in Perth and some in the surrounding villages. After one of the village games some of the team went back for a night out in the pub where there was entertainment. I don't know exactly what happened, but at some point during the evening things seem to have got a bit out of hand and a young local girl ended up dead. They soon caught the man who did it and he went to prison for a long stretch, but down here for some reason it was hushed up and no-one talks about it. But I did hear recently that the man who went to prison might have finished his sentence and could be out again. I don't know his name, but it seems that he did live here in Levensbridge at the time and he was on the tour with them. I was thinking that some of our lads must have known about or even been involved in that girl's death, and this man has come back here looking for revenge. I think all this trouble we're having now stems from what happened up there, and I think if you went up to Perth you might find out what really did happen and if it has anything to do with the club, especially the people who went on the tour. There might be nothing in it of course, but I think you should go up there and find out."

Bene wanted as much information as he could get from the caller.

"You think it has something to do with the deaths of the two bowlers don't you?"

"Yes I do, so you go up there and find out." The line went dead.

CHAPTER 14

Barlinnie Prison – Glasgow

The treachery of friends

Alan Browning looked blankly at the wall facing him. Prison cells were designed to be like this, cramped, impersonal and depressingly soul destroying. His thoughts drifted back to his visit to the prison hospital two days ago and the news he'd been given there. What he'd been told had totally destroyed whatever hope he still retained of ever leaving this place. In simple terms it meant he wouldn't have to suffer this life much longer. So would that be a good or a bad thing? In some respects it might even be a blessing, who knows. At the moment it was still too raw in his mind and it would take more time for it to sink in completely. But of course time was not on his side anymore, so it was probably of no importance whether he came to terms with it or not.

He'd had his suspicions for a while that something wasn't quite right with his body, and this had been confirmed in an unemotional and matter of fact way by the prison doctor. What had he said, two months, possibly three at best? Any thoughts he'd harboured of seeing the outside world again had been cruelly dashed, it meant he would die in prison less than a year short of completing his fifteen year sentence. Still a fairly young man he was going to die in here all alone and without anyone on the outside knowing or even caring about his condition, or even his passing when it came. The only record to show he'd actually existed on this planet would be a death certificate signed by the prison doctor and a short entry in the governor's log book.

It hadn't always been this way. Up until that dreadful day when he'd been found guilty of a murder he hadn't committed he'd had a good life, a normal life with a loving wife and a beautiful son. He had a steady job which paid well and many friends with which to share his happiness. He'd realised only too late that it was these so-called friends who had betrayed and destroyed him, leaving him to spend the remainder of his life in prison while they continued theirs on the outside. They'd shown no remorse or guilt for what they'd done to ruin his life; it should have been them in here not him. Every single day he'd pleaded his innocence, but what good had that done because no-one believed him. According to the majority of his fellow inmates the prison would appear to be full of innocent men, everyone pleading wrongful arrest and internment for crimes they hadn't committed, so why should his case be any different.

Night-time came and the lights went out. Usually he could get off to sleep right away, but for some reason tonight sleep was eluding him. Something was nagging away at him something he should have done or be doing, but try as he could his fuzzed up brain couldn't get to grips with it. Then without warning and right out of the blue it hit him and he knew exactly what it was he had to do. He'd waited far too long and wasted too much time; it had to be done as soon as possible, tomorrow if he could. If he was lucky and his request successful he'd feel much better in himself and better prepared to meet his maker when the time came. If not, at least he could die in the knowledge that he'd tried to redeem himself in the eyes of the people who really mattered to him.

The mental energy he'd used in reaching this decision was now subsiding, leaving him with a feeling of slight elation but at the same time emotionally drained. At long last the sleep which had been eluding him for so long began to creep up on him and he drifted off into a long and peaceful slumber. He couldn't see it himself, but the tensed up muscles in his face and neck that had kept him awake for so long appeared to be a little more relaxed, a huge burden had been lifted ever so slightly from his shoulders.

Two days later Alan's ex-wife Maureen was surprised when she received a letter from the governor at Barlinnie prison. Many years had passed since there'd been any contact between the prison and her. With alarm and dismay she quickly did a mental check of the calendar and realised it must be to inform her of the date when her ex-husband would be released, it sent cold shivers down her spine.

The first few years into her husband's long sentence had been hard for her, not only had she been left bringing up a young son on her own but she also had to contend with the stigma of her husband's crime. Overnight she'd become an outcast in her home town, deserted by her family and friends and shunned by everyone else. After two years of humiliation the decision to move away to another town where no-one knew her or her past seemed the sensible thing to do. She began her new life in a town forty miles away. She'd divorced Alan, and two years after moving to her new home she found love again. She married a salesman called James Anderson and took her new husband's name. Her son David also changed his name to that of his stepfather. She'd been honest enough to tell James her real name and past history and he'd accepted it for what it was. As far as James was concerned she'd been an innocent party to a heinous crime of which she had no knowledge or involvement in. Together they'd lived in perfect idyll for the last ten years.

With trepidation she opened and read the contents of the letter. In it the prison governor explained Alan's condition and the fact he only had a few months to live. As there was no chance of him ever leaving prison he'd expressed a deeply emotional plea to see his son for one last time before he died. There was little else in the letter apart from the statutory condolence which he'd been duly obliged to include.

Her first husband's name and the memory of him had been absent from her thoughts for a long time, but now it was as if he were there in the room with her although the vision was slightly blurred, any photos of him had long been destroyed. Over the years she'd tried hard to wipe the memory and the image of him from her mind and in the main she'd succeeded, but this letter had thrown her back into the darkest days of her life.

At the time she had no doubts about her husband's guilt, all the evidence had pointed to him and no-one else. He hadn't been able to give an alibi for the time of the murder, only that he'd been concussed and had no recollection of what had happened that night, neither could he offer any explanation as to why his DNA was all over the victim. His defence team had little to work with and in the end the jury had no option but to go with the prosecution's case and find him guilty. The judge came down hard on Alan and imposed a life sentence with a recommendation that he serve at least fifteen years.

The question now was whether or not she should tell her son about the letter and its contents. A decision had to be made soon as time was not on her side, in another month or so Alan would be dead. In the end there was only one way to go, David would have to be told. If he were to find out about his father's request after he'd died and had wanted to see him he may not forgive her, David was a grown man now and would have to make his own decision.

That night the three sat down for dinner and discussed the letter. James and Maureen were in agreement that whatever David decided to do it would be alright with them. After much deliberation David thought he must go and see his father although he could only summon up vague memories of him. "I can barely remember him mum and you probably can't either, but after all he is my biological father."

He hesitated because he was worried he might upset his mum or James or both of them, and he was looking for support. It was James who came to his rescue.

"Listen David, I think you're right, he is your real father and if you decide that you want to see him again then yes, by all means go, and you'll go with our blessing. I've tried to be a good father to you and I hope I have, but I won't stand in your way or be offended if you want to go and see him; it could be the only chance you'll get before he dies."

It didn't take David long to make his decision. With the passing of years memories of his father had been pushed further and further back in his mind, but now this letter had brought it all back to him and to some of the happiest memories he had of his father when he'd been a child. So however difficult or painful it might be he owed his dad his last wish, any other decision would leave him with a lot of unanswered questions and most likely years of regret.

A date had been agreed for the visit and David set off to Glasgow to see his father. He was feeling apprehensive and a little frightened, but at the same time a little excited at the prospect of meeting him again. At the prison he underwent all the checks in the reception area and was escorted along several long corridors until at last he was shown into a room where his father was waiting for him. It was a large room but sparsely furnished; bare wooden tables and chairs were the only items in there. The police escort stood well back. David waited for a moment to compose himself before walking over to the only table that was occupied; the man sitting there had his back to him so he couldn't tell what he looked like, but this must be his father. His mother had taken down all the photos and destroyed those years ago.

He walked around the table and sat down on a chair opposite his father. After a few moments he slowly raised his head and looked up at him for the first time in many years. What he saw wasn't the beast that his mother had described, but a man looking a lot older than his age; his face was pale and gaunt and tired looking, but his eyes were just as he remembered them warm and friendly. He hadn't thought about how he would address his father and now faced with him he found himself tongue-tied. It remained that way for a full minute and the embarrassment of both men was clear to see.

Finally it was his father who broke the silence and when he spoke it was with a well-educated voice; it was soft and quiet and brought back more memories to his son. David listened as his father told him the reason why he wanted to see him. He explained that what he was about to tell him was the truth, and as he was so close to death there was no reason for him to lie. David understood and believed his father was sincere; he listened intently for several minutes as his father related his story. When the warder told them their time was up David and his father rose from their seats. David with tears streaming down his cheeks walked around the table and hugged his father tightly, although it was not strictly allowed. They stayed that way until the warder came and put his hand on Alan's shoulder, turned him away and led him back to his cell.

David left the prison determined to visit his father again before he died. At last he knew the real truth about the crime for which his father had been wrongly convicted and he was determined to make sure that justice was done and his father's name cleared.

On returning home he explained to his mother how the visit to his father had gone and how angry he was on hearing the real truth about the murder. "I'm sorry David, but whatever the real truth is I think we'll have to let it go. It's come far too late to do any good to anyone. If we pursue it it's just going to rake up the past again, and I don't think I could go through all that; it will destroy us all over again. It's not as if it's going to do your father any good either because he only has a month or so left to live, so any retrial will come too late to save him. I know you're angry, but promise me you won't take it any further." She put her arms around her son. "Remember we have a good life here and we're happy aren't we? Whatever happened back then and however unjust it was is now behind us and there's nothing to be gained by digging it all up. Go and see him again by all means, but please don't do anything stupid, just let it go."

Chapter 15

Two Bullets

Bene was in Inspector Sowerby's office first thing the next morning telling him about the late night call he'd received from the bowler, and the information he'd been given.

"It does sound possible," said the Inspector "and let's face it until we find that car wash lad we've nothing else to go on. I think you should go up there and dig out everything you can on that murder. If that fellow's out of prison I want to know who he is, where he is, and what his connection with Levensbridge is. Take Hils with you she seems bright enough, the two of you together might be able to find out if there's any connection with the murders down here. I can't let you have ET because I need him here, but make sure you don't miss anything, and don't take too long about it either. You'll have about a three hour drive ahead of you so grab some extra clothes in case you have to spend the night up there, tell Hils to do the same and then leave as soon as you can. You should get there about midday and I'll expect you back here later tonight, or early tomorrow at the latest. In the meantime I'll contact Perth and let them know you're coming and to have all the relevant information ready for when you get there. The actual place is somewhere outside Perth, so I'll ask for one of their men to go with you, someone who knows the area and the people there. He could be helpful so get everything you can from him; local knowledge, any witnesses or people who remember what happened there, even the gossip that was going around at the time. Get as much information as you can and phone me as soon as you have anything, worthwhile or not. Either way I need to know as soon as possible because time is running out for us."

Hils had offered to drive them up there and Bene was happy to let her. They'd driven about fifty miles with little meaningful conversation between them and Bene was feeling a bit of tension creeping in. Hils was concentrating on her driving and keeping her eyes glued to the road. The ice needed to be broken and he thought that as they were working together it would be good if they got to know each other a bit better. Hils had been in the force a little over two years and stationed at Levensbridge for the last year. But up until the last day or so he'd only had minimal contact with her, just a few friendly greetings and the odd mundane topic, usually the weather.

"I know you haven't been with us very long Hils, so tell me what it was that made you want to join the force?"

"Oh didn't you know. Well my dad was a policeman all his working life down in the Black Country, and when he retired he wanted to get away from the area and all the villains he'd been living and working among. Like most policemen mam and dad's friends were mainly other policemen and their families. They had a few other friends as well but most of them were in the force or retired from it, so leaving the area wasn't much of a wrench for them. They'd always taken holidays in the Lake District and they loved it. They had many happy memories of their time up here so they thought it would be the best place to come for their retirement. And I'm jolly pleased they did because when I finished college I came up here to live with them and I joined the force same as my dad had done."

"I knew by your accent you weren't local, but your accent isn't Brummie either so where does that come from?"

"From my college days, everyone loses their accent there, after a while everyone talks the same so it's difficult to pin anyone down by their accent once they've been to college."

"So outside of work what do you like to do. From what I've heard a bit of socialising is something you like, is there anything else?"

"Football, that's my biggest love, 'City Till I Die' that's me, I just love them."

"City, why's that? Surely you should be supporting Villa or Birmingham."

"Nah, I was at college in Manchester and one night we went out for a meal, four of the players were on the next table to us and we got talking to them. In the end they gave us a couple of complimentary tickets and that did it for me, I was hooked. Anyway, what about you, I know you're married and all that but why did you join up?"

Bene told her about his first years in the force working with Adam and how he'd been left on his own when Adam suffered a heart attack.

"For me that was the turning point; up until then I admit I was lazy and depended on Adam for everything. He'd cover for me when I was late, which happened far too often, and he always took the lead in everything we did, I was just coasting along with him doing all the work. Looking back it wasn't fair on him and I still feel guilty, if I'd taken a bit more responsibility and some of the weight off his shoulders he might not have had a heart attack. When it did happen it brought me to my senses and made me realise that I had to change my ways and pull myself together, work a lot harder, be more responsible and stand on my own two feet. Anyway from that moment on I tried my hardest to make a success of myself and my career, and in the end I think I became a much better person for it."

"Wow, that's something isn't it. No wonder you like Adam so much, and I can see how proud he is of you and how pleased he must be seeing his protégé come good. I mean look what you've achieved since then. I've heard so much about you but I had no idea about Adam and you. This is really good, I feel much more comfortable now. It's good to get to know a bit more about each other, especially as we're working together don't you think?"

"Much better, but don't go spreading any of this about, I had enough ribbing and sarcasm back then to last me a lifetime."

They were a few miles beyond Stirling on the A9 and had just left the roundabout with the turn off for Dunblane. Bene smiled because the next part of the journey he was going to enjoy. "I never think I'm properly in Scotland until I get here, but once we're over this hill it will feel like we're in Scotland at last, the real Scotland. I mean the border areas and even the central bit with Glasgow and Edinburgh doesn't feel right to me. I just love the highlands, and for me it all starts here and gets better the further up you go. I think I'll bring Alex up here for a holiday when this is all over."

"Yes, its lovely up there isn't it I've been a couple of times and it never disappoints, even if the weather's bad or the midges are out, it still makes you feel good."

The rest of the journey passed pleasantly, it had been a good opportunity for them to get a bit more personal. They spent the rest of the journey chatting away, exchanging bits of their life, likes and dislikes, favourite foods, films and social life in general. The journey as expected took a full three and a half hours and that was only because the road for some reason was quiet, which was unusual for a weekday when normally it would be busy with heavy wagons and holiday makers.

It was almost one o'clock when they pulled up outside the police station in Barrack Street. Sergeant MacBain was there to meet them and invited them into a room where he handed over all the material relating to the murder. He had one piece of news which straight away discounted one of the theories suggested by the late night caller.

"Alan Browning, the man jailed for the murder is still inside and not due to finish his sentence until next year. But when we contacted the prison they told us he's terminally ill and he won't finish his time; he's going to die in prison only a few months short of his release date." The two detectives showed their dismay.

"That rules him out then." said Bene. "He's not our man, have we got anything else?"

"Everything about the murder is in the file you have there. I read up on the case when I started here and I've looked through it again briefly this morning and it all seems quite straightforward just as it was back then, although it was before my time here. Nobody had any doubts at the time they'd got the right man. If you like I'll take you over to Glendargen village where it happened and you can ask around there. Most of the folk out there have lived in the village all their lives so some of them will remember what happened."

They left Bene's car at the station and jumped into the police car with the sergeant driving, as they drove out onto the road they almost collided with a large black saloon which was in the process of pulling up outside the station; the driver of the saloon reversed backwards swiftly thus avoiding eye contact with the officers in the police car. The sergeant tutted but didn't want to delay their journey for a harmless little incident. He continued to drive them down to the river and over the bridge towards the village of Glendargen; the black saloon with its two well-dressed occupants followed at a discreet distance.

The village of Glendargen was typical of the small rural villages in that area, a scattering of houses of all different shapes, sizes and designs set in a semi-circle around the large open green, the Church, a Public House and the Village Hall were clearly visible. MacBain suggested they do some house-to-house calls to find out which residents were at home, and if any of them remembered the events of that night all those years ago. It was Hils who struck lucky first and she called the other two over to hear what old Minnie McNair had to say. Hils asked her to relate to her colleagues what she had told her.

"Aye I remember that night alright, the pub was full to bursting with allsorts in there, the music had attracted a lot of folk from the villages round about and there were some who I'd never set eyes on before. I recognised some of them bowlers though as they'd been here in the afternoon playing the village team."

"So you were in the pub that night then?" asked Bene

"Aye that I was, and a good night it was an all, there was plenty of drink going down and the music was great; good old fashioned stuff from the fifties and sixties, rock and roll you ken. As far as I could see everything went well and everyone was enjoying themselves. When the music stopped Jamie and I went home and there were only a handful of the local lads left in there. Everyone else had gone including the bowlers. We didn't know what had happened until the next morning when the place was full of police, but my Jamie and me didn't see anything happen."

"You didn't see any trouble then, any fights or disagreements, or any falling out among the menfolk?"

"Nay, but some of them bowlers had a bit too much to drink; one of them could hardly stand up you ken. I don't think he was used to drinking our whisky, and he's the one who got arrested for the murder. Now if you ask me he could 'nay have done it; the man was staggering around the place all night, a danger to himself and a blooming nuisance to everybody else. Halfway through the night he had to be carried to a seat, and he stayed sitting in that chair for the rest of the night. I'm sure he'd have slept in it if he could; nay that lad was in nay fit state to murder anyone that night. One or two of the others now, I might have believed it of them. They were playing up to the lass something awful. Aye she might have been leading them on a bit because they were all buying her drink and she was taking advantage of it, but she was just enjoying herself. And when she left they all went oot with her, except the other fellow who was still sitting there dead drunk and nearly asleep. It was only later they came back for him and when they did they had to carry him oot, and they were mighty quick about it as well. They never stayed for another drink you ken they just wanted to get out of there. If you ask me they got the wrong fellow. I know he was found in the field next to her and with her DNA all over him, but to my mind he could 'nay have done it. I think it was one of the others who murdered the lassie and they put the blame on him; that's what I think."

She pointed at the officers as if to express herself more clearly.

"And believe you me there're a lot of others who will tell you the same, aye that there are."

Bene thanked her for her time

"Thanks for that Mrs McNair, what you've told us could be helpful, I'll go over your original statement just to check if there's anything new, if there is can I contact you again?"

"Aye, of course you can lad, you know where we are; we're never too far from hame."

The officers said goodbye and took their leave.

The next person they spoke to also remembered something from that night; she was a near neighbour of Mrs McNair. Mrs Paterson hadn't been in the pub that night but had witnessed some of the events leading up to the time when the girl was murdered.

"Yes I remember that night alright, we didn't fancy the pub on music night ourselves it's far too busy and noisy for us so we stayed in. We couldn't go to bed because it would have been a waste of time, we wouldn't get any sleep with that racket going on so we stayed up and watched a film on the TV instead. But we did see some of them leaving the pub. No-one round here bothers to close their curtains at night so we see all that goes on in the village day and night."

"Can you remember who you saw?" asked Bene

"Yes I think so, most of the locals left as soon as the music stopped and we watched them traipse by; we knew most of them of course. About five minutes later we heard some of the others leaving; there was a bit of banter going on so we looked out to see who it was. Now there were some of them bowlers that were here in the afternoon and they had that young lassie with them. They were pestering her a bit but she was laughing and joking with them, she seemed to be handling them alright so we didn't worry about it. It must have been about an hour later when they came back again, but just the men, the lassie wasn't with them. We thought they'd come back for more drink, but they were only in the pub a few minutes before they came out again. This time they had another man with them and he looked much the worse for wear, they had to half carry him back along the road to where they'd parked their car. And that was it, we didn't see them again. We thought they'd got in their car and gone back to wherever it was they were staying for the night."

Mrs Paterson couldn't tell them anymore.

"Thanks Mrs Paterson" said Bene "that was very helpful and it's given us something to think about. If we need to speak to you again would that be alright?"

"Yes of course lad."

"I haven't had time to look through all the witness statements yet but I'm sure yours will be among them. I'll have a read through to see if there's anything else in there, but you probably covered everything when you gave it to the officer."

Mrs Paterson looked surprised.

"Statement lad, I never gave a statement, none of your lot asked me for one. I think they took statements from the folk who were in the pub that night but they never bothered with anybody else. If you ask me they just wanted it done and dusted as quickly as possible. As far as they were concerned they'd got their man and they weren't looking for anyone else, nothing that would complicate things for them anyhow. No, they were happy with what they'd got and they didn't go looking any further into it. If you ask me they couldn't be bothered."

This latest piece of news worried Bene and he turned to Hils and MacBain.

"Surely as a matter of course the police would have carried out a more extensive and detailed investigation. I mean what that last woman told us throws up some disturbing and contentious points, especially relating to the fellow who's been banged up in jail this last decade. From what we've heard from these two women there's a good chance they did get the wrong man. It must have seemed like an open-and-shut case to the police at the time, so much so that they didn't bother to delve any deeper into it. If they'd taken a bit more time over it and taken statements from Mrs Paterson and some of the other villagers they'd have got a lot more evidence as to what had been witnessed that night. It would have given them good reason to look at some of the others who were in the village at the time and check to see if they had any involvement in the murder. No, I don't like it; the whole thing needs to be looked into again and much more closely. I'll put my concerns to your chief when we get back and see if he's willing to re-open the case, not that it will do that fellow in prison any good, but justice must be seen to be done and your Inspector should be the one to do it."

They continued looking for more witnesses and did find two more people who were in the pub that night, but neither could shed any more light on what they already knew. Both of them remembered the bowlers being in the pub and the girl being there as well but couldn't say when any of them left, according to them they might have left on their own or with the girl; either way they couldn't remember. Another old man only wanted to complain about the noise and asked the officers if they could have the music nights outlawed because he was only interested in listening to real music.

"They should be playing traditional Scottish music, not that bloody heathen stuff that comes blaring out of that damned pub." Bene left there with a promise that his complaint would be passed on to the local police. There was nothing more to be gained from the visit but it had proved a very worthwhile one. From what they'd heard at first hand it did look as if the murder up in Glendargen could have some connection with the murders in Levensbridge.

On their way back to Perth Bene was deep in thought. As soon as they reached the police station he would immediately ask to see the Inspector and put his suspicions about the murder on record. Although he had no authority to put pressure on him he would hope that the statements they'd taken from the villagers would be sufficient for the case to be re-opened. When that was done he'd call Inspector Sowerby and bring him up to date with the day's events. But long before they reached Perth and interrupting his thoughts his mobile rang, there was no need for him to phone the Inspector, he was already on the line.

"Do you have anything useful to bring back Bene or was it a waste of time?"

"I definitely think there's a link between what happened up here and the murders back in Levensbridge, but I'll explain better when I get back. Before we leave I need to speak to the Inspector in Perth and bring to his attention the statements we've taken today. I think there may be enough evidence to warrant another look at the case. Tomorrow I'll track down the address in Levensbridge where that fellow in prison lived and see where his family are now. There's nothing more we can do up here so we'll be leaving soon; we'll be back later tonight and I'll give you my full report then."

"OK, well I have some news for you, somethings happened down here that you should know about and I think it might keep you awake for a while tonight."

This was not something Bene wanted to hear.

"Go on sir, what is it?"

"I've had the lab reports back on the two bullets used in the murders."

"And?"

"Although the MO was the same in both murders, the bullets were from two different guns. The bullet that killed Arnold Bainbridge was from a Walther P38 9mm which is an old World War 11 gun, but the bullet used for the second murder came from a Glock 22, a handgun used by the police in America, now what do you make of that?"

The question was met with silence, the Inspector waited patiently for a reaction to this startling new piece of evidence. Bene was stunned; he was having difficulty taking in the implications of what he'd just been told. His reaction when finally it did come was to ask.

"Well how the hell can that be? The two men were connected alright, both members of the same bowls club and friends as well, and they were both shot in the same way. It must have been the same person who did it, but why two different guns?"

Inspector Sowerby had an explanation of his own.

"When you left this morning I contacted Willie's neighbour Matthew Dawes and he told me that Willie only went on the first two or three tours and then he stopped going. Now there were a few tours after that but Willie was definitely not on them. I also found out that it was Arnold who organised the tours and he'd been on all of them, so here's the problem. If this has anything to do with the murder up in Perth then that could tie in with Arnold's murder but not that of Willie Jameson; you see what I'm saying?"

"I think so, you're telling me the fact they were both shot in the same way was just a coincidence and the killer in each case was different, which would mean we're not looking for one killer, but two."

"Exactly, I think we're looking for two unrelated people who for whatever reason are targeting the same group of people but for different reasons. It's hard to believe but what other explanation can there be."

For Bene this was getting far too complicated, and the Inspector was right he'd get little sleep that night; somehow he had to get his head around this new information.

"I take it there's no news of Gary Maitland then?"

"No, he's still out there somewhere and he's still our number one suspect for Arnold Bainbridge's murder, but the reason for Willie Jameson's murder and whoever did that is far from clear. I think we need to have a more in-depth look into his private life, there has to be something there that we haven't come across yet."

"So the murder in Scotland could still tie in with Arnold's murder, if of course Gary Maitland didn't do it, but it would have nothing to do with that of Willie

Jameson. God what a complicated bloody mess, it just goes from bad to worse. How are division dealing with it, are they threatening to take it off us?"

"Not so far, I've managed to keep them at bay for the time being but I'm under no illusion that if we don't come up with something soon they'll be putting more pressure on us, we just need that break Bene."

There was another long silence as both men racked their brains trying to come up with something that might help, but nothing would materialise. The Inspector spoke again.

"Just get back here and we'll talk about it in the morning, don't bother coming into the station tonight it'll be too late, we'll both be a bit fresher in the morning. I still have a few officers out there looking for that lad but I'm not holding out much hope, if I'm honest I think he's long gone."

Bene switched off his mobile just as they were coming to the outskirts of Perth. Sergeant MacBain dropped them off at the police station and Bene told him to give the statements to his Inspector and express his doubts about the way the initial enquiry had been conducted.

"Tell him I'll speak to him in the morning."

Hils offered to drive back even though she'd driven all the way up there earlier in the day. Bene was happy to let her, and on the way back he remained a silent passenger for most of the journey thinking about the new developments. They arrived back in town just after eight o'clock and Bene asked her to drop him off at home.

"Take the car home with you Hils and pick me up in the morning, no later than seven thirty." He left Hils and walked wearily down the path and into the house.

Chapter 16

An offer of help

Bene received a warm welcome home and was directed straight over to the dinner table where a good hot meal awaited him. Alex sat down next to him and couldn't help but notice the anxiety in his face. She'd been aware of the change in him over the last few days as the stress of the case took its toll. It was eating away at him and draining his energy. How much more he could take she wasn't sure, but his health and wellbeing were becoming a serious worry for her.

"Want to talk about it then?" She asked.

Bene gave her a weak smile.

"Yes of course, it will be good to talk to someone who isn't connected to the case and you've always been a good listener. Let's finish dinner first and then we can sit down and I'll tell you what I can."

Half an hour later and with dinner finished Dot cleared away the dishes and took them to the kitchen to wash, leaving the two of them alone to talk. Sitting close together Alex pressed him to tell her what it was about the case he was finding so difficult to deal with.

"You know I did help you with your first case when Adam was ill and you were left alone to deal with it; we did alright then didn't we? Maybe I can help you with this one if I know what the problem is."

"Yes, you were brilliant back then."

Bene smiled as he thought back to the first case he'd worked on alone, and with Alex's help he'd succeeded in bringing it to a successful conclusion.

"Even though I got a real soaking when I fell over in that icy cold river and you just stood there laughing your socks off."

For Alex this was a good start she could see he was a bit more relaxed; now was a good time to tell him what she planned to do.

"So let me help you with this one as well, but I have to warn you I've already started on it."

Bene gave her an anxious look.

"What do you mean you've already started?"

"Now I know it's got something to do with the bowls club so I'm going there tomorrow."

Bene was speechless wondering what was coming next. Alex never failed to surprise him; she was always ready to jump headlong into the unknown, unaware or oblivious to any danger that might be waiting for her. Undeterred she continued.

"They've been advertising for new members, and they're giving free coaching lessons every Wednesday at four o'clock, so I thought I'd go down there after work and give it a go."

"Steady on Alex, you're right about the bowls club, it's connected to the case alright and that's why I don't want you getting involved in it. It's a dangerous place right now and we don't know what could happen next. Hopefully it stops with those two deaths, but then again maybe it won't, there might be another one just waiting to happen. I'm not going to risk you being anywhere near the place so you can put that idea right out of your head, and that's final."

From past experience he knew it wouldn't be final; she had an uncanny knack of making him feel far too sensitive and over protective of her, and she would use this as an opportunity to convince him otherwise. He had that familiar and uneasy feeling that nothing he could say or do was going to deter her. He waited for her response which wasn't long in coming. Alex sidled up closer on the sofa and cupped both his hands in hers.

"Don't be daft Bene I'll be alright, Adam will be there and he'll look after me."

"What, Adam's in on this as well is he; well he should bloody well know better."

"Look I'll be perfectly safe and I promise I won't be a nuisance, and I won't put myself in danger either. I mean they don't know me or the fact that I'm married to you, and anyway I won't be on my own because there are three other ladies going and I know one of them quite well. I'll just do a bit of snooping around and talk to some of the men, and let's face it they'll probably tell me a lot more than they'd tell you, men always respond better to an attractive girl don't you think?"

Now Bene was really worried, but he knew it was no good protesting because she'd already won the battle. She had that silly grin on her face and that look in her eye that told him there was no point trying to stop her. And of course she may be right, men did open up more to a younger woman than they would to another man, maybe she would be able to dig out something that he couldn't.

He sat in silence trying to weigh up the odds of her finding out anything useful against the possible danger she might find herself in, but it was a waste of time because she'd already made her decision, reluctantly he relented.

"OK I'll phone Adam, but I'll tell him he's not to leave you on your own, I'll see if he can help with the coaching, and as long as you stay with or around him you should be OK. But of course if you're with him all the time you probably won't find out anything. You'll have to tread carefully, don't barge in there asking too many questions or they'll clam up and you'll get nothing out of them. Let them believe you're interested in the club and you want to find out all about it, how it was formed and how old it is, how many members they have and things like that, ask if they have any well-known players there. But be very careful with any questions about the two men who were murdered. If it does come up in conversation say you don't think it could have anything to do with the club, it must be something to do with their private lives. But don't push or pry or they'll view you with suspicion and keep their mouths shut. But who knows, if you're lucky you might get something."

Alex gave him a big hug and a long sloppy kiss.

"Oh Bene you are wonderful, thank you, I'll start making plans straight away as to how I'm going to do this. It'll be just like that first case we solved, and I just know I'm going to find out what's behind it all and who killed those two men, boy isn't it exciting?"

Bene didn't look excited, he was dreading it, but he knew there was no turning back because Alex was already hyped up about it.

"Now look Alex remember what I've told you so don't go overboard about it. Whoever is doing this is a dangerous individual and they won't mind who gets in their way. They'll have no hesitation in killing again if they think someone is a threat to them, even a slip of a girl like you. So don't be too enthusiastic, keep calm and go about it with kid gloves on alright?"

"Yeah yeah I know, but I will find out something you just wait and see, I have a knack of getting information out of people without them realising it, and you know it's true so give me credit for it. I won't let you down and I'll steer clear of any danger so don't worry."

Dot joined them in the lounge; she'd been listening to the conversation from the kitchen.

"You really should be careful Alex, Bene's right, because whoever is doing this won't stop from killing again if they think someone suspects them, I agree with Bene and I don't think it's a good idea."

"It's alright mam I promise I won't try too hard. I'll just show an interest in the club and maybe ask how many women members there are, I'll say that I'm looking for another interest and want to find out if I could make some new friends there that's all, there's absolutely nothing to worry about I'll be safe as houses with Adam."

Wednesday morning and it was now five days since the first murder. Bene rose from his slumber and wondered what the day would hold for him and the other officers.

With a bit of luck they'd get a breakthrough, something significant would happen and give them the opportunity to prove they could handle even the most baffling cases. Then he had to pinch himself, maybe he was still dreaming for the likelihood of that happening seemed as remote now as ever it was. He wondered if Alex would find out anything at the bowls club. God he must be desperate to let her con him into going there. But at least she'd be with Adam and he was the most dependable man he knew, he would look after Alex as if she were his own daughter; even so he was still nervous. One thing was clear, Alex could go there today but that was all; any further visits or lessons at the club were out of the question, today would be her only chance. Then a voice in his head was telling him. "Yeah, you believe that if you like pal, fat chance."

He looked over at the clock to find it was only six thirty; he could have another half hour in bed before getting up. He glanced over at Alex who was fast asleep, so beautiful and peaceful without a care in the world. He found it hard to avert his eyes from her face, she was the best thing that had ever happened to him and he still couldn't believe his luck in finding her. If he were ever to lose her; well the mere thought of life without her was unthinkable and something he hoped he'd never have to contemplate.

She was right in her belief that sometimes he was a little over protective, but she was always so full on confidence and sure she could take care of herself in any situation. And when she had her mind set on something there was nothing he or anyone else could do to change it. Alex was very much a free spirit and that was what had attracted him to her the first time they'd met. Bene knew there were times when he just had to set her free, she was a beautiful butterfly with its newly discovered wings drying out in the sun, ready to take off on a voyage of discovery.

Chapter 17

Stainbeck Village

Freddie's secret

The small crowd standing outside the village church were waiting patiently for the funeral cortege to arrive. The sun shone bright in the sky to the south east giving the people waiting there the promise of a more pleasant end to a summer which by and large had been a disappointing one. Whatever the weather it was in no way to blame for the poor turnout, for the deceased had been one of the wealthiest and well known residents in the village and should have been accorded the very best of send-offs.

Of the twenty odd people gathered outside the church most were relations of the deceased. The few who weren't family members had only turned up to make sure he really was dead and they weren't the victims of some cruel hoax. It was probably true to say that none of the mourners, including most of his family were sorry to see him depart this life. He'd not been a nice man, nor a good husband or father. There would be no-one shedding tears for him or rushing to lay flowers on his grave. It was true to say that apart from one small boy the entire village thought it would be a much better place without him in it.

At last the funeral carriage could be heard approaching; the sound of the four black Silesian horses tramping the tarmac road in unison could be heard long before they were seen. Over the hill the tall purple ostrich plumes finally came into view followed by the horses themselves, the coachman and groom in their black Victorian livery sat motionless on the front box seat as the carriage neared the church gate. As it came to a halt the bearers moved quietly but with purpose to the rear of the carriage and began the sombre duty of unloading the coffin and conveying it into the church. The operation was completed silently and efficiently without a hitch. The people followed at a discrete distance behind the coffin and filed into the front rows of pews.

Ten year old Freddie Pearson scowled and curled up his bottom lip. Begrudgingly he followed his parents into the church, audibly showing his dissent by dragging his feet along the way. He didn't want to be there of course, he wanted to be out playing instead. But he'd been in enough trouble this week with his mam and dad, and if he didn't behave himself it would mean the rest of the day shut up in his bedroom. Why did they want him there anyway, none of the other boys in the village had to be there, just him, it was so unfair. He ruffled up his blonde hair and pulled his tie to one side; he hated having to dress up in his best clothes because his mam would always tell him off if she spotted even the tiniest bit of dirt on them. He wouldn't get them dirty today but he could easily rough them up a bit just to let her know he was there against his will.

It was his grandfather who was being buried and grandad had been good to him, but he was very old so how could anyone that old play the games that ten year old boys liked to play. At least his grandad had let him play up at his big house, and when he got into trouble he would stick up for him and make excuses for him. Even at that tender age Freddie knew that his grandad wasn't liked by anyone in the village, even his mam and dad hated him. But Freddie had liked his grandad and his grandad had liked him, they'd been good pals. The more Freddie thought about him the more he realised just how much he would miss him. He could tell grandad secrets that he wouldn't dare share with his parents, and together they would tell stories of the great adventures they'd both had.

"Yes." he thought "If grandad was still alive I could have told him about my latest adventure."

It had happened only a few hours ago while he'd been playing alone down by the river. Freddie had been picking up stones to throw in the water and was on his hands and knees looking for more stones behind some bushes. While he was crouched there a man had come down to the river bank. Freddie hadn't heard him coming and when he looked up and saw him he didn't recognise who it was so he thought it best to stay hidden and keep quiet. The man stood there for a while looking all around as if he was looking for something that he couldn't quite see, or maybe what he was looking for wasn't even there. Maybe he was expecting to meet someone. Freddie thought it was very suspicious. The man had a hoodie to cover his head but each time he turned Freddie got a glimpse of the man's face, and it wasn't a nice face. Suddenly the man seemed to come to a decision and brought something from his coat pocket wrapped in what looked like a scarf. Looking around quickly and for the last time he tossed the object into the middle of the river; it made a loud splash which told Freddie it must be something heavy. The man turned and left the river bank and walked up towards the road. As he disappeared from sight Freddie heard a loud voice which must have come from the man; he was shouting at someone. Freddie didn't dare move; he was scared because the man sounded angry and he didn't want him to come back and see him. He waited for a few seconds until the shouting stopped then came out from his hiding place and went to see where the man had gone. He heard an engine start, so he crept up the bank to be nearer the road, keeping his head down he crawled up to the edge and peered over the bank just in time to see the silver grey hatchback heading off towards the main road. What was it he'd thrown into the river?

It was too late now to try and retrieve it and he couldn't afford to get his clothes and shoes wet. He would have to leave it for the time being because he had to go home and change for the funeral. He made up his mind to return the next day and find out just what it was the man had thrown in the river. It was a pity because now his grandad was dead he had no-one to share his story with, he couldn't tell his parents because they wouldn't believe him and he would end up in more trouble. But tomorrow he would come back to the river and find out what it was. It must be something important he thought, maybe something valuable that he could sell, better still maybe he could swap it for that old bike his pal Darren had, he'd always wanted a one like that.

The next day and with the funeral out of the way it promised to be a good one for Freddie, at last he would be free to put on his old clothes after school and go back to the river. Then all of a sudden his plans were dealt a crushing blow with his parents insisting he go with them to visit the solicitors for the reading of his grandfather's will.

"Why is it grown-ups are only interested in money, money was alright for buying sweets and things but that was all, he didn't need any money so why did they always want more of it. With a bit of luck grandad would leave all his money to him and he'd keep it to himself and not give them any that would teach them."

The solicitor was the most boring man Freddie had ever met in his life and the day dragged on and on. He was completely fed up and wanted to go back home. His parents seemed happy with whatever the solicitor had told them and when it was all over and they left his office they kept smiling at him and giving him hugs. Yuk! He didn't want hugs, he wanted to go back home and find out what was in the river. The three of them went back to the car and Freddie's hopes started to rise, maybe there was still time for him to continue his adventure. But just when his hopes had been raised they were suddenly dashed again. They'd only been travelling a few minutes when the car pulled up outside a restaurant. Freddie was getting very angry, not only with his mam and dad but with that stupid solicitor and everybody and everything else; between them all they were completely ruining his day.

"What's happening dad why have we stopped? Why are we not going home? I want to go home."

"We're celebrating son." said his father.

"Grandad has left us quite a lot of money so we can enjoy ourselves a bit more now, we can have a few days out and some holidays by the seaside, what do you think about that eh?"

Well, even Freddie could see something good in that.

"Can we go somewhere soon dad, its ages since we went to the seaside and you know I love it there?"

"Yes, I think we can probably manage a week away before the summer ends, in a week or two's time maybe, I'll tell you what I'll fix it up tomorrow."

He put his arm around the boy's shoulder and bent over to whisper.

"If you like we could take your pal with us, and then you'll have someone your own age to play with, how about that?"

Freddie was excited with the news, he loved the seaside and this time he'd have Darren with him to make it even better; the river could wait until another day, maybe he would go there tomorrow.

CHAPTER 18

What is it with Longbarrow Village?

Bene jumped up in bed as his mobile spat out its ridiculous ringing tone, he would have to change that tone it really was annoying. Had he slept in? It only seemed a minute or so since he'd turned over; he checked the clock as he reached over to press the receive button. No it was only six forty five. He hadn't overslept so who the hell was it, could it not wait. Alex awoke at the same time and muttered something quite unladylike, which he hoped the caller didn't catch.

"Yes, what is it?"

The caller's voice was trembling and he found it difficult to understand the message.

"Take your time and calm down a little, then I'll be able to hear you better, OK."

Bene waited a few seconds listening to the laboured breathing coming through the phone; the caller seemed to accept his advice and waited a little longer until the breathing eased before speaking again.

"Is that DS Douglas?"

"Yes, you have the right number; can you give me your name?"

There was a slight pause where the caller seemed to be considering the question and wondering whether to continue. Eventually the lady caller spoke again.

"It's Gary Maitland's auntie."

"Oh right, have you heard from him?"

"Yes, he's here with me now but he's in bits the poor lad and doesn't know what to do; he's scared stiff about what's happened and he knows you've been looking for him. He's worried that you're going to arrest him for that murder and he swears he didn't do it."

"Right listen to me, can you keep him there and I'll come over and speak to him; if he had nothing to do with the murder and he can prove it then he has nothing to worry about."

"But that's the problem, he doesn't have an alibi and he thinks he's going to be arrested. But I believe him and I'm sure when you speak to him you'll believe him as well. His mind is all over the place with worry so can you get over here quickly, I don't want him to run off again because it will only make matters that much worse for him."

"I'm on my way now."

Bene phoned Inspector Sowerby to give him the news and he agreed that Bene should get over there quickly and bring the lad in for questioning. He kissed Alex and reminded her about her visit to the bowls club, and to stick close to Adam and not pry too much. She smiled that smile the one he knew only too well, and that did nothing to ease his discomfort. It looked as though his day was going to be a busy one and he would have to concentrate on that. There'd be no time to worry about

Alex and Adam; he'd taken all the precautions he could and he'd have to leave the rest to Adam.

Gary's auntie was waiting for him and Bene was relieved to hear that Gary was still with her.

"I've no idea where he's been these last few days and I've been worried out of my mind. Thankfully he doesn't seem to have come to any harm, not physically anyway but mentally he's a wreck, anyway come on in and have a word with him."

"When did he get back, was it this morning?"

"Yes but it was very early. He woke me up about five o'clock and I came down to let him in. I don't usually answer the door at that time of night but he shouted through the letter box to let me know it was him; he hadn't taken a key with him so I had to let him in. I didn't phone right away because I wanted to find out if he'd been involved in the murder, but he convinced me he hadn't and I believe him. He's not a bad lad you know, a bit moody and awkward sometimes but basically he's a good kid.

Bene entered the lounge where he found Gary sitting quietly on the sofa. He wanted to put the lad at ease so he went over and took a seat next to him.

"You don't look too good Gary, have you been sleeping rough? We thought we'd covered everywhere in the town but no-one could find any sign of you, where've you been the last few days?" Gary shrugged his shoulders.

"I stayed with a pal over in Kendal for a couple of days, but when he saw my picture on the TV and you were looking for me in connection with that murder he put me out. He said he wouldn't tell anyone but I couldn't stay there any longer. After that I dossed down in an old barn somewhere a few miles out but I can't remember where. Then I got sick of it all. I could only find scraps of food and it was getting too cold at nights. I knew it was only a matter of time before you caught up with me so I decided to come back to aunties and try to clear my name."

"That was a good decision Gary and a brave one. Now why don't we go down to the station and you can give me your version of events and where you were at the time. I'll put it all down in a statement and you can sign it for me, how would that be?"

Bene knew that when they got back to the station Gary was in for a thorough grilling; there'd be no favours for him, and if he couldn't come up with a solid and reliable alibi to satisfy the Inspector he'd be detained at the station while further investigations into his background and whereabouts could be established. There was no easy way this could be done, Inspector Sowerby would see to that. Bene's duty was to get him back to the station, and he couldn't tell the lad how hard it was going to be in case he got scared and ran off again. "All you have to do Gary is to tell the truth, and if you had nothing to do with it you've absolutely nothing to worry about."

It was almost nine o'clock when they arrived at the station and just as Bene was thinking his day had already been mapped out for him another shock awaited. Inspector Sowerby and ET were together in the Inspectors office waiting for them. The Inspector came out and led them down to the interview room where ET took Gary inside. The Inspector kept Bene outside in the corridor.

"We'll take over now Bene; ET can sit in on this with me and if Gary's our lad then we'll soon have it wrapped up. ET is more than capable of doing this on his own and I think it's time we gave him a bit of loose and let him take the lead in this."

At first Bene thought differently, that the interview with Gary would go much better if he was to lead it, but Sowerby was insistent.

"Have a think about it Bene."

Bene did think about it, and on reflection he had to agree with the Inspector. In hindsight maybe he should have given ET more of a chance to show what he was capable of. He'd never once complained about how things were conducted, and Bene hadn't realised until now that it was always him taking the lead and all the responsibility that went with it.

"You're right of course, I guess I've been far too involved in the case and I've not given him much of a chance have I, yes I'm pleased, it will do him good."

Even so it left Bene wondering what the Inspector had in mind for him this morning, but he wasn't kept waiting long for the answer.

"I've got something else for you Bene, there's another matter I want looked into."

"Is it connected to the case?"

"I don't know, but I'm sending you over to check it out."

"What's it about then?"

"That village where the last murder happened, there's something suspicious going on there."

"In what way suspicious sir?"

"There've been a couple of men going around asking all sorts of questions of the local village folk, it's got them a bit worked up and they're worried. These men are not from around here, and they're asking people about what they remember of an incident back in 2012 when there were two deaths in the village. It was before I took over here so I knew nothing about it, but the case file should still be here and I think you should have a look at it. Then go out there and find out what they're looking for. And when you find out, get rid of them, I don't want them hanging around our patch any longer. The local bobby is having a rough time of it at the moment, what with the murder in the village and then all this going on as well. He seems to have lost the confidence and respect of the village folk as it appears he's never in the area when these men are around."

"It does seem strange I suppose. I did hear a story about this old case when I was out there the last time, but I didn't think it could have any bearing on what's happening now, I mean it was years ago so how could it? But anyway I'll check out the file first and then go and make a few enquiries."

"Take Hils with you Bene, and give her some loose as well, let's see how she performs."

The Inspector left him and went to join ET in the interview room. Bene picked up Hils, and together they went down to the records office in the basement to dig out the file on the incident in Longbarrow.

The file when at last they did find it was not exactly what they were expecting. Usually a record of death, even a simple one such as suicide where a note had been left would still generate quite a large file, but this one was thin by comparison. It had been tucked away inside a row of much larger files, and hadn't been placed in either alphabetical or chronological order as the others were; it looked as though whoever put it there would prefer it remained unnoticed and undisturbed. Inside the file the record of the event was vague and concise stating only the basic details of the man's death. Bene quickly skimmed through it. There was the pathologist's report attached, which testified the cause of death as asphyxiation due to the lungs being flooded with a toxic fluid namely creosote. Added to this there were several photos showing the man lying prostrate on the ground where he'd been found, and some taken of the naked body in the mortuary. The man's name was not disclosed as there had been no means of identification on the body, neither was he known to any of the local people. It appeared that little if any effort had been made to try and find out who he was, or what he was doing there. An inquest had been carried out, but with no witnesses and no evidence submitted the coroner had no alternative but to make a ruling of death, either by suicide, misadventure or murder by person or persons unknown. After two weeks the body had been cremated and as far as the case went that seemed to be the end of it. No further investigation had been requested or carried out, and although the case remained open and unsolved it was clear that as far as the police were concerned it was as good as closed.

"Bloody hell Hils, what on earth do you make of this?"

"As far as I can see there's little or nothing in there to go on is there; no effort seems to have been made to find out who he was and the death wasn't reported in the local paper, no media coverage or appeal or anything like that; it's as if they didn't want to find out who he was or what he was doing there. If I didn't know better I'd say it was a cover-up."

"Yes my thoughts exactly." said Bene. "Have a look and see who the investigating officer was?"

Hils opened the file again and looked for the signature at the bottom of the report; rather than tell him who it was she handed the open file over to him. Bene looked for himself.

"Bloody hell I can't believe it." He shook his head in disbelief, at the bottom of the page was a signature he knew only too well and there was no doubt about it. The name glaring out at him from the bottom of the sheet was none other than his friend and old governor Adam Firth. The revelation stunned Bene, a myriad of suspicious thoughts swirled round in his head; surely Adam couldn't be responsible for this, there must be some other explanation. But one thing was clear, he would have to speak to Adam before they went to Longbarrow and get his version of the report, which to say the least was grossly under-investigated. Hils was aware of Bene's relationship with Adam and was wary of suggesting anything that might upset him. Bene would have to deal with this on his own. But Bene had other ideas.

"We need to speak to him Hils, and I think it might be better if you take part in it as well; you've read the report and you know it's not good enough. Forget he's a former officer and go about it as you would with anyone else. You have no obligation towards him or the fact he was once my boss, so put all that out of your mind and don't let it cloud your judgement OK?" There was silence as the two thought of how the interview would best be done. Hils was a bit uneasy as to how she would approach the matter as it appeared Bene was going to back off and let her take the lead. How could she bring the subject up? At the same time Bene knew he'd have to speak to Adam first, the fact he'd be looking after Alex at the bowls club later that afternoon would be a good opener, then he could introduce Hils and let her do the probing.

They pulled up outside Adam's house and the two officers approached the door, Adam had seen the car and came out to welcome them.

"Didn't expect to see you today Bene; have you come to give me some last minute instructions of how to keep all those virile seventy something miscreants at the bowls club away from your wife?"

"No, nothing like that I know she'll be perfectly safe with you, it's something else we want to speak to you about." He introduced him to Hils. "She's helping me with a new case and something's come up that we can't quite figure out, I'll let her explain."

This was Hils chance to show Bene how much she'd learned from him, and how she would conduct this rather tricky interview.

"To be honest we're not sure if it's connected to the two murders we've had here recently but it's possible, if it is then we need to check it out, and we think you might be able to help us clear up a few points we're concerned about."

She paused just long enough to let Adam take this in; she knew he'd be wondering what she was going to spring on him. He'd be on the defensive and maybe put up barriers, but Hils knew she'd recognise those signs if they were there.

Adam looked quizzical, but responded just as she thought he would.

"You think I might know something about the murders?"

"Not these latest ones but cast your mind back to 2012 and the village of Longbarrow."

Even Bene could see the shockwave as it hit Adam's face and it worried him, but he remained silent as Hils continued.

"You obviously know the case we're talking about because you were the investigating officer, that's right isn't it?"

Adam took a deep breath before speaking, Bene also drew a long and anguished breath because he'd no idea what was coming. Had Adam been concealing something from him all the time they'd worked together, and been friends, what had he been hiding. And had he been more involved in what happened back then than he was prepared to acknowledge.

The tone of Adam's voice changed, and when it came it was quiet and sombre.

"I think we should go inside."

He turned and led them into the house where Ellen was waiting to greet them.

"Hiya Bene, I thought you were going to stop out there all day and not bother to come in and see me." She smiled at Hils.

"And who's this then? You'll have to introduce me."

As soon as the introduction was made Adam took them through to the rear room.

"I just need a few minutes with these two love then we'll be back, alright?"

Ellen knew to leave them to it, whatever it was it was no concern of hers.

Once they were seated Bene and Hils waited for Adam to speak.

"Longbarrow, yes that takes me back." It brought back memories which he'd rather have left in the past. "You've read the report then?" he said. Hils replied.

"If that's what it is then yes, but it doesn't cover much does it, a man died either accidentally or was murdered and that just about sums the report up. No name, no witnesses, no evidence, no-one arrested and no follow up, surely the man deserved better than that. What went wrong? Could the police not be bothered to try and find out who the man was or what he was doing there? What about his poor wife and family, talk about slap-dash that doesn't even begin to describe it?"

Bene was pained to see Adam sitting there accepting the criticism without offering any explanation as to why the report was so brief and vague. The Adam he knew would have jumped up and defended himself instantly, but instead he shrunk back into the settee and remained quiet. Hils was not letting it go and pushed him for an explanation.

"Is that it then, you've got nothing more to add to what little there is in the report, I mean come on there must be something else, something you left out, just tell us what it was?"

There was a prolonged silence as none of them knew where to go next. Bene was sitting uncomfortably and wished he could say something, but what could he say, Adam had been caught out and it was embarrassing for both of them. Hils was still waiting for a response to her question. Adam sighed and decided now was probably a good time to share the secret he'd been keeping for far too long. After a brief pause he began to relate just what had happened back in 2012.

"Most of the officers at Levensbridge back then have either died, moved on, or retired, the ones who are still there know nothing about what happened back in 2012, not even Sowerby who came to us the year after." He looked a little more relaxed now and sat back into a more comfortable position.

"It was a strange affair, and to be honest I hoped it would never come to light again, but now you've raised it I think it's probably best if you know the full facts. I understand your concern for the man's family, and you're right justice wasn't done and the poor fellow deserved much better from us."

Adam took a short break; it was clear that the memory of events back then still troubled him, the two officers were patient knowing more was to follow. Adam didn't disappoint them.

"I don't know how or why it came about that I was given the case; I mean it should have gone to Preston for them to deal with. But someone there specifically asked for me, and as it looked a bit of a mystery I was happy to be given it. The odd thing about it I couldn't take any of my own men with me and that was something I couldn't understand. They put together a squad of men from different stations and none of them were local, not even our division. They came from the West and East Midlands and none of them knew each other or had worked together before. I didn't know what to make of it; I thought it very strange and rather weird and asked to be taken off the case, but someone up there insisted I remain in charge. Well we did our best and interviewed everyone in the village, but no-one knew who the man was or where he came from, or what he might be doing there. I started to make arrangements for an extended search of the area. I wanted to bring in forensics to search the scene of crime for evidence, and I wanted to advertise in the media and on TV for information from the public. I was hoping someone would recognise his photo and come forward. I wasn't happy with the way it had been set up, but I was still looking forward to getting things moving and trying to solve the mystery. Then all of a sudden, the very next day in fact all the plans I was going to put in place came crashing down. I arrived at our mobile incident room to find I was on my own; none of the other officers had turned up. I waited for a while and when it became obvious no-one else was coming I phoned Preston, only to be told by the Superintendent that all the officers who'd been assigned to help me with the incident had been sent back to their own stations. He gave no explanation as to why."

Adam paused again for a few moments before continuing, the two officers sat enthralled.

"As you'd expect I was shocked. He told me to come immediately to Preston and on arrival to report directly to him and no-one else; the nature of my visit was not to be discussed with anyone. I had no idea what to expect because I'd never been in a situation like that before, the whole thing was surreal from start to finish. At Preston I was taken straight in to see the Superintendent who had two other men with him in civvies. I hadn't met the Superintendent before and had no idea who the other men were either, but it wasn't long before they came to the point. It was blunt and final, the case was closed! I sat open-mouthed just staring at them. The Superintendent told me to return to my duties at Levensbridge and not discuss the incident with anyone; I was to tell them the reason for my absence was a high security course which I couldn't reveal details about. The two men sitting with him were government officials, and from what I could gather were pretty high up. One of them reminded me that I was bound under the Official Secrets Act, and if I spoke to anyone or put anything in writing about what I'd been doing the last two days I'd find myself banged up in prison for a very long time. I was ordered by the Superintendent to conclude the report, file it and forget all about it, and that was to be the end of the matter no questions asked. I was reminded again of the Official Secrets Act, so there was no excuse if I failed to comply with their instructions. The meeting only lasted a few minutes and when it was over the two men left. I was left alone with the Superintendent who told me again to forget all about it and return to my duties, the matter was closed,"

Bene and Hils were shattered.

"Bloody hell Adam," said Bene. "You've kept this to yourself all this time. What about the Official Secrets Act, does it not bother you that you've told us about it?"

"Well it was a long time ago and what would they do. It could be years before anything came of it, and how old will I be then; too old to spend much time in prison. Anyway, it depends how you use the information and whether it could be traced back to me. I can't see how it can be connected to what you're investigating now though, all this happened years ago"

Hils could sense a tension in the room and thought she knew the reason for it. The two men were wondering if she could be trusted with the information she'd just heard, and like them could she keep it to herself.

She was quick to reassure them.

"I think what we've heard here today should stay with the three of us and go no further; like you Adam, I don't think it's got anything to do with these recent murders so let's just say this conversation never happened."

She looked at Bene and noticed he looked relieved.

"I agree with you Hils, and if we have to use any of it then it'll be down to our own investigating, details that we've dug out ourselves. And don't forget Adam, we're both bound by the Official Secrets Act as well so that protects us all."

The two officers rose to shake hands and say their goodbyes, they were just about to leave when Bene suddenly remembered something.

"Sowerby said there were two deaths there in 2012, so what about the other one, nothings been mentioned about that?"

"No, well that wasn't given to us because it was suicide. One of the local farmers who lived alone had been struggling to make ends meet, so to solve his problems he took on board a load of alcohol and some tablets and went and hung himself. There was nothing suspicious about it; the coroner took accounts from people who knew him well enough and who attested to his financial situation and the fact he'd been getting more and more depressed. All that plus the fact he wasn't leaving anyone behind to mourn him. In the end it had been an easy decision for him to make and the verdict was recorded as suicide. That was clear enough for us and gave us no reason to look into it any further."

Bene and Hils left the house as it was time they went to Longbarrow village. The journey there was mostly in silence as they were reluctant to talk about their interview with Adam. As far as the report was concerned he was off the hook, and it would be put back exactly where they'd found it; with any luck it would never see daylight again.

As they drove into the village they noticed a large black saloon parked outside Willie Jameson's cottage, they pulled up behind it and walked over and looked in the window. The car was locked and there was no-one inside it. Bene was curious.

"It seems to fit the description of the car that's been seen around here lately so let's just wait a minute or two and see who comes back to it."

While they were waiting Alison Dawes came out and beckoned them over, they followed her into the house.

"Have you come to see who it is that's been pestering the villagers the last few days?"

"Yes, is that their car out there?"

"That's the one, but I don't know where they are at the moment; they've been here a good hour so they shouldn't be long in coming back; no-one knows who they are and they never tell us anything; it's very strange. Anyway, I was going to ask you about our Stephen, I know he told you about what he saw back then?"

"Yes he did, I hope he didn't get into trouble?"

"No, he told his dad, and Matthew was pleased in a way because he always thought there was something wrong with that. I think he'd like to speak to you about it."

"We'd be pleased to do that; we'd like to know a bit more about it ourselves and maybe together we'll find out what really happened."

Hils grabbed his arm.

"Bene the car's gone; they must have come back while we've been in here, now they've disappeared."

"Damn it, let's get after them; sorry Alison we'll have to go but we'll be back soon."

The two officers ran back to their car.

"There's only one road out of here, but which direction did they go?" asked Bene.

"They were facing the same way as us, so let's go that way."

Bene started up the car and they shot off along the narrow country road driving as fast as he dared, the car sped along but there was no sign of the large black saloon. Each corner they rounded they were hoping to see the back of the black car ahead of them, but each time they were disappointed. After four miles they came to the next village and saw a man tending his garden. Bene slammed the brakes on, opened the window and asked him if he'd seen the black car.

"Nothing's come through here for the last ten minutes lad, sorry."

"Damn we've lost them. It's pointless turning round and going back they'll be miles away by now, they either went off in the other direction, or they've turned off onto one of the side roads we passed on the way. Anyway we'll not see them again today."

Bene was cursing himself for letting the men get away, but Hils had some encouraging news.

"Good job I wrote down their registration eh?"

"Hils you're a godsend, what is it, let me see?"

Hils showed Bene her notebook with the number written down and he immediately phoned the station to run a check on the vehicle. He had to wait several minutes for the reply, and when it came it was not the one he wanted.

"I've put the number on the database Bene but I can't get access to it, access can only be gained through the Home Office and it would need authorisation from the commander himself to do that. You'll have to take this to him, sorry."

Bene looked at Hils.

"This is getting serious, if the Home Office is involved in this we'll have to be careful, they're not going to take kindly to us meddling in their affairs. If we keep sticking our noses in we could end up in serious trouble. Inspector Sowerby will have to be informed about it and it'll be up to him to make a decision on what happens next."

With that they headed back to Levensbridge.

Chapter 19

Gary's story

The interview with Gary Maitland was about to start, Inspector Sowerby suggested that after the lad had been cautioned ET should begin the questioning. He was keen to let the DC take the lead; he would sit back, but ready to come in and support him if needed.

ET opened the interview.

"Just so you understand Gary, you're aware that you're under caution and that this interview will be recorded, OK?"

"Yes."

"And you know why you're here, don't you?" He looked at Gary.

"Yes."

"That's good, what I want you to do Gary is to tell us everything you know about what happened at the car wash last Friday, what your involvement in it was, and why you ran away? So take your time, and in your own words tell us exactly what you know about it."

Gary was fidgeting in his chair and his hands were shaking, he was taking a long time in deciding what to tell them. Several thoughts were running through his mind. He could deny everything and say he was never there, and tell them the reason he ran away was because he was scared of being accused of the murder all because he'd taken the day off. Then there was his pal in Kendal, what if they found him; he'd told him things which when questioned would put him under pressure and he might grass on him. Could he take that chance, he wasn't sure. ET was getting impatient.

"If you're innocent Gary you've nothing to fear, but if you do know something then tell us about it. There've been two murders now and if the killer isn't caught soon there may be others, and you wouldn't want those on your conscience would you?"

ET leaned forward to make it more personal.

"You know what I think Gary, I think that if you had anything to do with this you wouldn't have given yourself up would you; you'd still be out there somewhere hiding from us. So the fact that you've come forward is a sign to me that you didn't commit these crimes. But at the same time you do know something about them, and you need to tell us what it is to help us catch the person responsible."

Gary drew a long breath but remained silent, his head bent over the table covering his shaking hands. There was no easy way out of it; whichever way he chose there were consequences. If he denied everything, and someone else was killed could he live with that, probably not. On the other hand if he told them what really happened he could end up dead himself? So if he did tell the truth he'd need assurances that he'd get police protection. Finally he spoke.

"Ok, but if I tell you what happened I'll be putting myself in danger of becoming the next victim, so I'll need protection until this man's caught, and if you can't guarantee that then I'm sorry but I can't help you."

He looked up to see their response.

ET looked to the Inspector for support and the Inspector leaned forward on the table.

"You'll have to tell us what you know first Gary and then we'll decide if protection is needed. I can't promise you anything without knowing what it is you know, or who you're afraid of. If you can give us a name that would be a good start, tell us that and we should be able to give you some form of protection, but we need something from you first. At least you've told us he's a man, you're sure about that?"

"Yes I think so, it's all a bit blurred you see, I never actually met him."

"OK Gary" said ET "let's try and put some of your fears to rest. Do you think he's local and do you think he's working alone?"

"I think it was personal so he probably is local, and I didn't see anyone else there so he's most likely on his own."

"That's a start Gary, but if you've never met the fellow why are you afraid of him?"

"Because he knows who I am and where I live that's why."

"So he's threatened you, is that it?"

"He said he'd kill me if I told anyone about what happened, and I can't take that chance unless you protect me."

ET looked to his Inspector again who came forward to make a suggestion.

"Gary I believe you live with your auntie Pat, but that's not your real home is it?"

"No."

"So where is your real home?"

"We lived in Manchester originally and then moved to Preston."

"So could you go back there until all this blows over?"

"Not really, I don't get on with my father-in-law, that's why I left."

"How about other family then, any other aunts, uncles or friends you could stay with?"

"There's my brother's house in Sale, that's empty; he's working over in Bahrain on a two-year contract so I could stay there. Nobody knows about his place, and as long as no-one knows I'm there it should be OK."

"You'll be safe there?"

"Yeah, it's a nice house and I can tell the neighbours I'm looking after it for him, but you'll have to take me there, I'm not taking the chance of him following me."

"Good that's settled then, when we've finished here we'll take you over to your aunties in a plain car and you can pick up your clothes and whatever else you need and we'll take you down to Sale, how would that be?"

"Yeah, I'd feel much safer there."

Sowerby asked the officer behind him to bring in coffees, and then indicated to ET to continue the interview.

"Now that's settled Gary let's hear your story. Start from the beginning and try not to leave anything out however trivial it may seem, whether you think it important or not just tell us everything." He leaned back and waited for Gary to speak.

"OK, well I got a phone call from this fellow on Thursday night; it was a bit weird because his voice was distorted and I couldn't tell at first if it was a man or a woman, but as it went on I thought it must be a man."

"And what did he say?"

"He asked if I'd like to make some easy money, I didn't have to do anything, just help him identify someone as they came into the car wash the next day. He said he'd be there and all I had to do was give him the signal when this person was going into the wash. I told him I wasn't going to work the next day and he said that would be better; all I had to do was be in a place where I could see who was going into the wash and point the man out to him."

"Did he give you a name then?

"Yes, he said the man's name was Arnold Bainbridge which didn't mean anything to me, but when he gave me a description of him and said it would be late afternoon I knew who he meant, and I knew the make and colour of his car. He said he wanted to give him a surprise as he hadn't seen him for a long time. He didn't know where he was living now and this was his only chance of getting in touch with him again. Anyway I believed him and it all seemed innocent enough so I asked him how much it was worth, he said he'd leave £50 in an envelope through my door later that night."

"So what happened when you got there?"

"There was no need to go until three o'clock because it was always later than that when this guy came to the wash. I got there just before three and waited a little further up the road, I didn't want Sean to see me because I was supposed to be working and he'd want to know what I was playing at. I could see someone else further up the road and thought that must be the man who phoned. I wanted to go over and see him but he waved me back, so I didn't get a good look at him. Half an hour later I saw this car going into the wash and I recognised the driver as the one he wanted to surprise, I pointed it out to him and when the car went into the wash he rushed over and stood outside the exit. I thought I'd wait and see the surprise, but when it came I was shocked. I heard a noise but it wasn't very loud and I didn't think much about it, I thought it was part of the joke. Then the man came out from the wash and walked over to the car park. I waved to him and he waved back but he was signalling me to stay away; it was quite clear he didn't want me anyway near him. A minute later I heard all the commotion and saw Sean come round to the front; he looked in the car and then went and threw up at the side, I knew then something bad had happened. I didn't want to stay there any longer so I ran away as fast as I could, and I kept looking behind to make sure I wasn't being followed."

"Go on then, what happened next?"

"I went back home and up to my room wondering what the hell had happened. It was later that night that Auntie Pat told me a man had been shot at the car wash and I was scared. The next day when that policeman came to see me I kind of blocked it out of my mind and denied everything. He seemed satisfied so I thought that was the end of it."

"But then something else happened did it?"

"Yes, when I was at home there was another phone call from this man. He told me that he knew who I was and where I lived. And if he ever suspected I'd told anyone he'd come after me. He didn't have to say any more I knew exactly what he'd do and that's why I took off."

"Can you give us any more information about this man Gary, I mean was he young, old, white, black, short or tall, and what was he wearing?"

"At a guess I'd say he was middle-aged maybe a bit older; he was wearing a tracksuit with a hood so I didn't get a good look at his face, but he was definitely white. I'd say he was average build and height. He didn't run away after he'd shot the man though, he just walked casually over the road and into the car park, he must have had a car there but I didn't stop to look. I was off man; I wasn't hanging about there any longer."

"You didn't see him get into a car then?"

"No."

There was a brief halt in the interview while Gary drank his coffee and the two officers considered how best to continue. ET led again.

"So is that all you can tell us Gary, you haven't left anything out?"

"No that's the lot, I've had plenty of time to think about it and I can't remember anything else that could help you."

"OK then, how about Sunday night, where were you then?"

"I was still over at my pal's house in Kendal; I didn't leave there until Monday morning when he chucked me out."

"So if we talk to him he'll verify that will he?"

"Yeah, he'll tell you I was with him; we stayed up until midnight and then went to bed, he gave me a bed up in the attic. The next morning when he saw the news on TV he asked me to leave, so I had no choice but to go."

"I'll need a name and address for your pal Gary?"

"Yeah sure I'll write it down, but he'll vouch for me alright."

There was nothing more they could get out of Gary so the attending officer took him back to the cells. The two officers returned to Sowerby's office to discuss what little information Gary had told them. Sowerby was disappointed; he didn't think they'd learned anything useful; all it had done was confirm that it was Gary who was seen running away from the car wash, but as for the identity of the murderer they were no nearer finding out who it was. The phone rang and Sowerby picked up the receiver. He listened in silence with his face showing more disappointment; clearly the news he was hearing wasn't good. A few grunts later the phone was placed down very slowly on the receiver. The Inspector sat quiet and motionless for a few moments before giving up the gist of the one-sided conversation.

"It's bloody well happened again and in that same damned village, another one of the villagers in Longbarrow has been found dead. It looks as though he was killed the same night as that other fellow. So why the hell wasn't it picked up when they did the house-to-house calls on Monday."

Like the Inspector ET was stunned by this latest piece of news, and like his superior he could barely believe it either, when was this ever going to end. They'd just finished interviewing their only suspect and had ruled him out, so where did that leave them? Back to square one, and on top of that another murder on their hands. Inspector Sowerby was trying to keep calm. He couldn't afford to let his feelings show or affect his duty, but the strain on his face was telling; this was fast becoming his own personal nightmare. "I think you'll have to get over there and find out who it is E T, when Bene and Hils get back I'll send them over as well."

Chapter 20

Freddie makes a discovery

The day was warm and bright and promised to be a good one for Freddie as he awoke and stretched out in his bed. Yesterday for him had been a good and a bad day. Like today it had started out alright with him planning to go back to the river and find out what the man had thrown into it, and then it all changed when his mam and dad took him away to see that rotten old boring solicitor. That had been the really bad bit; money, money, money that's all grown-ups think about. It did put his mam and dad in a good mood though, and the promise of a holiday by the sea with his pal Darren was something to look forward to; maybe the day hadn't been too bad after all. He didn't get the chance to go back to the river, but it might have been nothing anyway; maybe just some rubbish the man had in his car and wanted to get rid of. Most likely it wouldn't even be there now, probably washed away down the river, or maybe someone else had found it. Suddenly it didn't seem as important as it had done the day before. He might go down later just to check, but he wasn't going to tell Darren about it just in case it was something good.

He looked at his bedside clock; it was getting late and he really should have been up earlier. He hadn't washed or dressed and there was still his breakfast to gulp down before catching the school bus. His mam had been shouting up the stairs repeatedly for him to hurry. Quickly he donned his school uniform and shot downstairs.

"Are you sure you've washed Freddie?" his mam asked.

"Yes, of course" lied Freddie "Didn't you hear the water running?"

"Let me check behind your ears."

"Gerroff!!" Freddie waved his mother's arms away

"Right, hurry up with your breakfast the bus will be here soon, and don't forget your lunch box and schoolbag." His mother was running late as well and needed to get off to work as soon as Freddie had left for school.

He only just made the bus and was annoyed to find there were only a few seats left; his pals were sitting together at the back and there wasn't an empty seat anywhere near them.

"You'll have to sit with the girls Freddie," they scoffed. Freddie didn't see the funny side of that and plonked himself down beside Lillie and her sister Maisie.

"Hiya Freddie," they shouted in unison, both pleased to see him.

"What are you doing after school? Do you want to come and play with us? We could have a treasure hunt or something." Both girls gazed adoringly at him.

"Ooh," mimicked one of the boys at the back of the bus sarcastically. "Can we come as well or does Freddie want to play with the girls all by himself?"

He was getting very annoyed with how things were turning out, even his best friend Darren was laughing at him. Right thought Freddie you can find yourself another best friend pal, and Ha! Ha! I'm not going to tell you about the seaside holiday now because you're not going with me, so there you are clever clogs.

The school day passed as normal and when the final bell went the kids came out and walked over to the waiting bus, Freddie was the last one out because someone had hidden his maths book and he needed that for his homework. When at last he found it he rushed out to the bus, only to be greeted once more with laughter from the back seats.

"It's OK Freddie," one of the boys shouted.

"Lillie's saved you a seat beside her." More hilarity came from the back of the bus. The journey home was no better with many jibes coming his way from the back seats. Lillie asked if she and Maisie could meet up with him later and Freddie was so annoyed with his so-called pals he agreed. They could meet at the river as soon as homework was done.

It wasn't often that he attended his homework with such gusto, but the lure of the river and what it might reveal was the spur he needed to get it done as quickly as possible. His mother was most impressed; she only worked part-time so was always home to greet her son when he came home from school.

"I expect you'll want to go out and play do you?"

"Yes, as soon as I've finished this, is that alright?"

"Yes it's nice out there and the fresh air will do you good; you can go as soon as you've finished your homework, but make sure you're back for when your dad gets home for his dinner at half past six."

Quickly wrapping up his homework Freddie raced off to the river, it wasn't far from his house, no more than a leisurely five minutes' walk usually. When he got there he was surprised to see the girls already waiting for him. He hadn't planned for this; surely they should still be at home doing their homework. In truth he wasn't expecting them to come at all; he'd agreed to meet them but he didn't actually believe they would take him seriously.

"Why are you here so early, didn't you have any homework?"

"Yes, of course we have," said Maisie, "but our mam said we could do it later if we wanted to come out and play for a bit first, she's let us out for an hour, and as long as we're back for six o'clock it'll be alright. But why're you wearing your wellies?"

"Oh, I thought I'd maybe go for a bit of a paddle."

"Well we haven't got ours so we can't go in the water; we've got our trainers on. You should have said we needed wellies and we would have brought them."

Freddie had to think fast, he didn't want them hanging around when he was in the river looking for something.

"OK never mind about the river for now let's have a game of hide and seek, that'll be good fun and it should take about an hour."

The girls said that would be great; they were pleased as punch to be with him and would have agreed to anything he suggested. Freddie was chuffed, that's my extra special power over girls he chuckled. I can get them to do anything.

The next hour passed pleasantly enough, and at the end the girls went home for their dinner and to do their homework. “Ah, at long last” thought Freddie, “that’s got rid of them, now for the good bit.”

Looking around to check he was alone he carefully stepped into the river, the current wasn’t too strong but he still took his time wading out to the middle. Slowly but surely and careful not to let the water run over the top of his wellies he arrived at the place where he thought the package should be. The water was clear and slow moving, and bending forward he could easily see the bottom. His eyes scanned the river bed but he couldn’t see anything unusual, nothing but stones and sand. Side-stepping carefully around the area he at last caught sight of something waving around in the current. “This must be it” he thought, and keeping his legs straight to prevent the water getting into his wellies he reached down and picked up the sodden package. He’d been right, for when the man threw it into the river it made a big splash, and the package he brought to the surface was certainly very heavy.

Careful not to drop it he made his way back to the edge of the river and climbed out and up onto the bank. Sitting down he stared at the soaking material wondering what it contained. Now he had hold of it he was a bit scared of what he might find inside; it could be a bomb or anything. He knew if he stayed there much longer he’d be late for his dinner and that would be another telling off, so using his fingertips he slowly unravelled the material and gaped hard and unbelieving at what he'd uncovered. He was unable to move for several seconds just staring at it, and then a loud shout brought him back to reality.

"What are you doing down there boy? Get up here at once, and bring whatever that is you're gawking at with you."

CHAPTER 21

Like buses they come in threes

Bene and Hils had almost reached the station when Bene took the phone call from his Inspector; he listened intently to the news about the latest development. They'd only left the village a couple of hours ago and had spent most of that time chasing a phantom car; they must have just missed this latest discovery.

"I want you to go back there and see who the victim is, and find out why he wasn't discovered when the house-to-house calls were done the last time we were there. And when you're there have a look around to see if that car's still hanging around, maybe they have something to do with this. I need them identified and brought back here to tell us why they keep going back to that village."

Bene had to explain to his boss that they'd seen the car and taken down the registration, and the response they'd got when they requested ownership from the DVLA.

"That means there's something going on in our patch we know nothing about, I'll have to speak to division and see what they know, but I doubt I'll get anything out of them. It looks like this is coming right from the top, and if it is we'll never get to know. If you do manage to get hold of them see what you can get out of them, tell them we've had complaints and they need to give us an explanation and tell us what it is they're looking for. You never know they could tell you something, it's worth a try. On the other hand, with a bit of luck you might have scared them off and they'll stay away for a while. But your main objective is to find out who this latest victim is. When you get there you'll meet up with ET, I've already sent him over there and he'll fill you in about our interview with Gary Maitland."

On arrival at the village they saw ET waiting outside the Globe Inn. Matthew Dawes was standing beside him looking pale and distressed. Bene thought it must have been Matthew who'd found the latest victim. The poor fellow, it wasn't fair on him or his family to have to deal with this so soon after the last murder.

ET came over to the car and Bene wound down the window to speak to him.

"Matthew looks upset, was it him who found the body?"

"Yeah, it's really shaken him up; it was him who found Willie Jameson as well wasn't it? I think you should come and have a word with him. I've only been here a few minutes and I thought I'd wait until you two came before hearing what he has to tell us."

Bene and Hils got out of the car and walked over to see Matthew.

"Hiya Matthew. I'm sorry buddy you're having a rough time of it aren't you, first Willie now another one, can you tell us who it is and where we can find the body?"

Matthew wasn't up to talking but led them away to a house fifty yards away. The local policeman was standing outside who said Matthew had called him as soon as he'd found the body. He'd come over straight away and notified Inspector Sowerby of the death. He hadn't gone into the house to ensure the crime scene wasn't compromised. Matthew had told him what he'd seen in the house and there was no doubt in his mind that whoever it was, they were certainly not alive.

"There's an ambulance on the way and the Inspector has notified the pathologist, so I'm just waiting here to make sure no-one entered the house until you and the others got here."

Satisfied that the local bobby had followed the correct procedure he thanked the officer for his diligence, and along with his two colleagues put on protective SOCO equipment.

"Can you stay out here with the policeman Matthew and we'll have a look inside. Which room is it, can you tell us that?"

"In the bedroom, it's only a small house, there's only the one bedroom and a bathroom upstairs." The three officers entered the house, checking the ground floor rooms just as a precaution before climbing the narrow staircase to the first floor. The house had a deathly quietness about it and Hils especially was a little nervous; this was her first experience of entering a murder scene where the body was still in situ. On entering the bedroom they found the body of a male person lying on his side in bed with the covers still around him. ET was relieved to see very little blood at the scene; a gory mess would have done nothing for Hils confidence or her stomach. He remembered he'd vomited heavily at the sight of his first corpse. He walked round to the side of the bed and pointed out the small hole and blood mark in the centre of the man's forehead.

"That's the killers trademark alright the same as the other two victims, shot right in the centre of the forehead. It looks as if he was shot while he slept, there doesn't seem to be any sign of a struggle; he was probably fast asleep and knew nothing about it which is a blessing I suppose."

Bene offered another theory.

"I suppose whoever did shoot him could have woken him up first just to let him see who it was, and then shot the poor fellow before he had a chance to defend himself."

"Yes that's possible, maybe whoever's doing this wants the victim to know who he is and the reason he's doing it, but doesn't give them the chance to live and tell."

He looked round at Hils.

"Are you OK there?"

She'd been standing in the doorway while her colleagues explored the victims wound and had listened to their comments on the method of execution.

"Well it's only a small room and as far as I can see it's fairly tidy. Nothing seems to have been disturbed or taken, and it doesn't look like the killers left anything incriminating behind. But if there is anything then forensics will find it when they get here. We should check to see if the house was locked, and if it was we need to find out how the intruder got in."

ET and Bene were impressed with the way she'd conducted herself on her first murder. She hadn't been scared, and most importantly she hadn't frozen as first timers often did. Added to this was her contribution to the scene, checking the room for signs of anything unusual, misplaced or broken articles or other clues that might have been left behind by the killer. And then her mind had moved to the question of how the killer had entered the house.

"That's it," said Bene, "nothing more we can do here, let's leave it to the pathologist and forensics and see what they come up with, we need to go and speak to Matthew."

The three officers went back downstairs and were on their way out of the house when the pathologist and the forensics team arrived.

"My God!" said the man from the path lab, a larger than life character with a thunderous voice and a wonderful sense of humour, which in his profession served him well.

"Dead bodies seem to follow you around don't they, no chance of me being out of work as long as you lot are around."

He gave a loud guffaw, slapped Bene on the back and led the team into the house.

They walked over to meet Matthew; Bene thought it would be better if they did the interview in his house. He'd feel a bit more at ease in his own surroundings and better prepared to answer their questions.

"Do you think we could go to your place Matthew and you can tell us about it there, if Alison is in maybe she'll make us a nice hot cup of tea, I think that might help."

Matthew nodded in agreement and the four of them went over to Smithy Cottage where Alison was waiting. She took them through to the lounge and after helping Matthew sit down she left them and went to the kitchen. Once settled Bene wanted to know who the victim was and why Matthew had gone to his house.

"Take your time Matthew and tell us exactly what happened; you can start by telling us who the man was and why you went into his house. Did you know or suspect there was something wrong?" Matthew was still a bit shaken but he was able to tell them what had happened. He'd been through all this before with the murder of Willie Jameson, so in a way he knew what the detectives expected from him.

"It was after Willie's murder that I got to thinking about other folk in the village and wondered if any of them could be in trouble. I thought about Willie's pal big Robin and how I hadn't seen him this last day or two, so I thought I'd pop over and see if he was OK. He's usually in the back in his workshop so I didn't bother with the front door, I just went around the back to check on him and have a crack. I didn't hear any noise from his shed and that was odd because he's always banging about with something or other. He mends bikes and lawnmowers and things like that so it was unusual that it was quiet. I couldn't see him in the workshop so I went to the back door and noticed it was open. I didn't take much notice to see if it was naturally open or whether it had been forced because it's always open during the day. I went into the kitchen and shouted for him but I didn't get an answer, it was obvious he wasn't there. Then I noticed his dinner plates were still in the sink, and I thought that's odd because he only washes up once a day and it's always after he's had his breakfast. So I got to thinking if he hasn't had breakfast maybe he's not well and he's still in bed, I went upstairs to check and that's when I found him. Just like Willie he was laying there in bed with a bullet in his forehead. I couldn't move for a second or two because I was scared in case whoever had done it was still there, and when I got my courage up a bit I ran down the stairs, shot out of the back door and came straight home. I rang the local bobby and stood outside the house waiting until he came."

With his story told Matthews' head sank to his knees, he sobbed quietly before giving out a loud anguished cry. "It's just too much to bear, first Willie and now big Robin, what the hell's happening to this village?" Alison came into the room with the teas and put the tray down on the table. She sat down beside her husband to comfort him. The detectives had to wait until he recovered before asking any more questions. Meanwhile Hils served the teas and that seemed to help Matthew's recovery.

Bene waited for a minute or two before pressing him for more information. It wouldn't be easy but there were things about the man and the murder that he needed to know.

"His name was Robin then? We need to know his full name Matthew and everything you can tell us about him. I know it's so soon after his death and you're still upset, but anything you can tell us will help us find out who killed him, and who killed Willie as well because it has to be the same person. Do you know if there was any connection between the two of them, I mean living this close together they obviously knew each other, but was there anything else?"

"His full name was Robin Mitchell, but everyone called him big Robin, not that he was very big you understand, but we have another Robin in the village and he's a wee small fellow, so it's just our way of telling one from the other, big Robin and wee Robin. Well big Robin and Willie were good pals and they did lots of things together. They were both widowers and had been for many years. They both lived alone and neither had any close family so it was only natural they'd spend time together. Their main hobby was bowls and they were both members of the club over in Levensbridge, they'd take turns driving over there and that way they could share the cost. Like Willie, Robin was well liked by everyone in the village and I can't think of anyone who'd want to harm either of them, I just can't believe they'd have any enemies."

He looked up quizzically at Bene and shrugged his shoulders which seemed to suggest that was all he could give them. His brief description of Robin just about summed the man up; like the other victims he was just a normal bloke who enjoyed his hobbies, played bowls and was well liked.

Just as before Bene had to leave the village with no answers as to why the victim had been killed, and with no leads to take back and follow up. The local bobby who was still on guard outside the house had some information for them.

"When enquiries were made in the village after the first murder Robin's house had been checked, but it appeared to be empty as no-one answered the door."

"That's because the poor bugger was already dead." said Bene as he stormed off to phone the Inspector and inform him of the murder, and what little they had found out. They began the drive back to Levensbridge which was done mostly in silence, Bene was the only one to speak and that was only once.

"Murders are like buses, you wait for hours for one to turn up then three come along at once."

The car pulled into the station yard, and as they were reversing into a parking bay Bene's phone rang, it was Inspector Sowerby again.

"Bene, when you get here bring the other two in with you, we've got a gun."

CHAPTER 22

A lead at last?

Bene and Hils joined ET who had pulled into the car park behind them, and together they went into the station to see Inspector Sowerby. With him in the office was another man and a young boy. The Inspectors office had always been on the small side and with the extra three officers squeezed into it, it felt somewhat overcrowded. The Inspector introduced the two people with him.

"This is Frank Pearson and his son Freddie, and young Freddie here has given us a rather interesting story about this gun here."

The Inspector pointed to the handgun sitting on his desk inside a clear plastic evidence bag.

"Freddie was playing down by the river at Stainbeck where he lives, and when he was there the other day he saw someone come down to the river and throw this gun into the river. He didn't know it was a gun at that point because it was wrapped up in some woollen material. Then today, he went back after school and pulled it out of the river just as his dad was passing on his way home from work. And not only that, Freddie caught a glimpse of the man's face who'd thrown it in the river, even though he was dressed in a tracksuit with the hood up. Luckily he was behind a bush so the man didn't see him. When the man left Freddie followed him up the bank, and when he looked over the top he saw the man drive away in a silver car; it might have been a saloon or a hatchback, he's not sure."

All this time Freddie had been grinning broadly at the three officers. He was a hero, and although his dad had been mad with him at first, he'd soon realised the importance of the gun his son had found and driven Freddie and the gun straight over to Levensbridge police station to hand it in. Freddie was feeling really special because everyone was looking at him and smiling, and the Inspector had been really pleased with him. He thought he might be in for some sort of reward, maybe his picture would be on TV and the front page of the papers. That would make Darren and his other pals sit up.

"I bet they've never been involved in catching a murderer before."

Inspector Sowerby expressed his thanks to father and son. "Thanks for bringing this in Mr Pearson and well done young Freddie, I'll get the gun off to forensics right away and have it checked for fingerprints if the water hasn't washed them off, and then we'll see if it matches any of the three bullets we have. And thank you for your statement and description of the man Freddie that could be valuable, I'll let you go home now, well done both of you."

With that he asked Hils to show them out of the station.

"Looking at the gun I'd say it's more like the Walther than a Glock, although I admit I haven't come across either of them before, and the silencer looks to have been converted to fit it because these old guns never had silencers on. Run it over to forensics for me ET and tell them I need answers ASAP, if not sooner. Ask them to give us the make, model and serial number as well if they can find them and we'll see if we can trace the owner. If it's a gun that was used in the war it could be difficult but we have to try, and check that silencer as well it must have come from another gun."

ET left with the gun just as Hils was coming back into the office. The Inspector had a job for them.

"I took a call from the Inspector up in Perth earlier and he had some interesting news. You remember that chap in prison up there who we thought could be connected to our murders?"

"Yes." the officers agreed.

"Well the prison was correct in saying he didn't have much time left and wouldn't see out his full sentence; he was going to die in prison. But what he told me might have given us another lead. In all the years this fellows been in prison no-one has ever been to visit him, not even his family. Since day one he's persistently protested his innocence, but it seems that his family and his friends were all convinced of his guilt. Once the trial was over they wanted him out of their lives so they could get on with their own. The prison governor went on to say that in the last month he's had two visits from his son. When the prisoner found out he didn't have long to live he asked to see his son for one last time. The son agreed and visited him twice over the next two weeks, and the governor said that after these visits the boy believed his father was innocent. He caused a right carry on in the prison, threatening to sue the authorities and seek revenge for his dad. He said he knew who was responsible for the crime his dad was serving time for and he'd seek them out and avenge him. So it seems your trip up to Scotland and the statements you took from the village folk were well worth the journey."

"So where is the boy now?" asked Bene

"That's what I want you and Hils to find out, I have his mother's address, and as far as I know he still lives with her and his stepfather. She moved away from Levensbridge soon after her husband was convicted and now lives in Fleetwood with her new husband James Anderson."

"You want us to bring him in then?"

"Let's find him first and see what he has to say; see if he has alibi's for the two dates we're interested in and be sure to check them out. If there's any doubt bring him in, whatever the outcome we either need to charge him or eliminate him from our enquiries."

"When was his last visit to the prison?"

"Two weeks ago, and that would fit in with events here. And Bene be careful, if he is our man he probably still has a gun; if you think there's going to be a problem give me a call and I'll arrange for some armed back-up. And for God's sake don't do anything foolhardy, I know what you can be like."

"When do we go?"

"Leave it until the morning it's too late now and he could be out somewhere. Best if you catch him at home or at work tomorrow; that way if he does have the gun he's not likely to be carrying it round the house, or take it to work with him. As for now, I want you to go round to the Fox & Pheasant and make some more enquiries; maybe you'll catch one or two of the bowlers in there. But mainly I want you to check up on those Brooks' brothers', they're an odd couple those two, that Alfie in particular is an evil-looking bastard and I wouldn't want to cross him. I've heard stories from when he was in business in Liverpool and he makes sure he gets his pound of flesh alright; you owe him money and you're in big trouble. Bookmakers down there are a different breed altogether Bene, they have to be to survive, and the heavies they employ are not too fussy about how much they hurt you either. If any of those bowlers have been doing business with him and tried to rip him off, it wouldn't surprise me if he had them done away with."

Bene hadn't wanted to go out again tonight. He wanted to go home and see Alex and find out how she'd got on at the bowls club that afternoon. But he couldn't leave it to Hils to go to the pub on her own; they would both have to go. With a bit of luck if none of the bowlers or the brothers were in the pub they could still get home at a reasonable hour.

Up to now lady luck had failed to shine on them and true to form she shied away again. On entering the pub the first person they saw was Alfie Brooks along with his brother and old Donald Neves. Bene's eyes scanned the room but none of the bowlers were there. Thursday was their night, but of course even that could have changed now.

The two officers went to the bar and were greeted warmly by Ebony.

"Hiya Bene, and what do we owe this pleasure; it can't be a social visit seeing you've brought your new partner along."

"I see you've let your hair down Ebony and I have to say it really suits you."

Ebony gave her hair a shake.

"Yeah, I thought I'd give it a go, Kris likes it and it saves me about twenty minutes every morning not having to comb it all up and craft it into a bun. Anyway what's the purpose of the visit, nothing wrong is there?"

"No of course not, we just came on the off chance one or two of the bowlers might be in, but it looks like we're out of luck."

"Yes, well you know Thursday is their night, but with all this going on we haven't seen them for the last week or so. I doubt they'll be in tomorrow night either; in fact it could be a while before we see them back here again. Are you any nearer to finding out who's responsible for all these murders Bene? It's affecting everyone around here, and goodness knows how the folk in that village are coping; it must be a nightmare for them having that lunatic running around."

This did nothing for Bene's confidence; everyone in the town was looking towards him and his colleagues to catch the killer. He couldn't let it be known that the police had next to nothing to go on and were still no nearer naming a suspect. He didn't want to say anything that might raise people's hopes with what little they did have; neither did he want to tell them the truth which would worry them even more; wisely he decided to evade the question.

"How about those two over there then, do you know much about them?"

He nodded over to the table where the Brooks brothers were sitting.

"Not much apart from one of them stinks, and I'm sure when he's here other people stay away just to avoid him. I should have a word with him and tell him if he doesn't clean himself up a bit we'll stop him coming in. The truth is we've been a bit reluctant to say anything so far because his brother's a nasty piece of work and we wouldn't want to upset him. Luckily they don't come in very often, but honestly I don't know how the other two can stand being anywhere near him."

Bene was trying to think of some way he could approach the three men and engage in some friendly conversation. He didn't want to appear intrusive but he was keen to find out a bit more about them, Alfie in particular, and if possible get an idea if he could be the one they were looking for. He certainly had plenty of history, but that wasn't enough to put him in the frame for murder. He would need alibis from the man, and if he couldn't get them he'd need evidence with which to charge him and that wouldn't be easy. It wasn't something he was likely to find out in a single conversation, but if he could glean anything from the man it would be a start. Then suddenly it came to him, Donald's dog of course. He ordered two soft drinks from the bar and gave one to Hils; he took his over to the table.

"Sorry for butting in folks, I just wanted a quick word with Donald about his dog."

He got Donald's attention.

"How are you Donald I'm pleased I've caught you, my wife's been telling me about that dog of yours. She's seen you out walking it and she's been pestering me to find out what kind it is, she says she'd like one just like it. He seems such a friendly sort, is he alright with children, he doesn't snap at them or bite does he?"

"Nah, he's as good as gold and soft as a kitten, but then that's what you get with mongrels you get the best of both breeds. I couldn't tell you exactly what he is, but there's a lot of terrier in him and maybe a bit of cocker spaniel or springer as well, something like that anyway."

At that point Alfie and his brother got up to leave. Alfie leaned heavily on his walking stick.

"Let you get on with that Donald, catch you again later." Bene would rather they stayed.

"No don't leave guys I'm finished now, you carry on with your conversation."

"No, it's alright we need to be somewhere else now, you stay here and talk to Donald."

Much to Bene's annoyance they finished their drinks and left the bar.

"Sorry about that Donald, I hope I didn't scare them off?"

"Nah, don't worry about them they're no great company anyway, I don't know why I get lumbered with them. That younger bugger stinks the place out, and Alfie, well the less you know about him the better. They come in here and sit with me because neither of them have any friends, and it's quite plain to see why."

He gave Bene a long and inquisitive look.

"Am I right in thinking it might not be me you wanted to talk to, maybe it was one of them you were after?"

"No, I really am looking for a dog like yours Donald, my wife would love one, so if you know anyone who has one for sale I'd be grateful if you'd let me know." He hesitated for a moment looking after the two brothers who had just left. "But yes I was wondering what those two are like. I mean I've seen them in here before but I don't know anything about them. I don't suppose anyone knows much about them, you probably know them better than anyone Donald what do you think of them?"

Donald gave him a wistful look whilst deciding how much he should tell.

"Alright lad, I can tell you a bit about them but don't let this go any further, and if any of it comes out then this conversation did not take place right?"

Bene nodded in agreement and invited Hils over to join them.

"Now the younger one is Gordon and he came up from Liverpool with Alfie a few years ago but I don't know much about him. He never gives anything away, he just sits there listening to the conversation but taking very little part in it; he nods his head a lot and gives a few grunts and that's about all you get out of him. I don't think there's any harm in him but you never know; you know what they say about the quiet ones. Now Alfie, he's a different animal altogether; he likes people to think he's an ex-bookmaker who retired up here for a bit of peace and quiet, but I know for a fact that's a lie."

He took a break and a sip of his malt whisky, Bene was hoping Donald would tell him more.

"You don't think that was the reason for them coming up here then?"

"Partly it was, but the truth was that Liverpool was getting a bit too hot for him; he's been in the business a long time you know and up until the last few years he had everything going his way. He was a major player down there and he controlled much of what was going on in the game and in the city. Then about four years ago one of the London mobs came up looking to expand their patch, and they began to show an interest in Liverpool and Manchester. They took over one or two of the smaller businesses at first then slowly began to infiltrate the bigger ones; they even took over some of Alfie's heavies. Now Alfie isn't daft and he didn't want to stay down there and watch his empire fall apart, so he decided it would be a good time to get out. But I know for a fact he's still in the game and he has his own heavies up here now. I don't know where he operates from because he doesn't have a shop for the business; maybe he's working from home using the phone or internet, but he's certainly still in business."

He took another sip of his malt before continuing.

"I know this much though, it's a big game he's playing and there's a lot of money changing hands. And on top of that I think he may have gone into the lending game as well. I wouldn't like to be the one who owed him money I've heard too much about him from my cousin in Liverpool. If you were to take my advice I wouldn't go poking around in his business too much; you don't know what the man is capable of."

Donald stopped for another sip and this time finished his whisky; rising from his chair he was preparing to leave. “He’s always been alright with me though; underneath it all he still needs someone to talk to and for some reason he seems to have singled me out. I can’t say we’re friends or anything like that, but he knows I don’t ask questions and that’s probably why he sits here. He hasn’t got anyone else.”

Donald walked over to the bar and returned his empty glass.

At least Bene had gained some insight into Alfie Brooks and he’d become very interested in the man. It was plain that Donald was scared of him and he knows the man better than most. His warning to Bene was clear, very clear indeed; Alfie Brooks was a dangerous man.

Chapter 23

Unexpected news

Alex was waiting for him as he entered the house.

"Where on earth have you been, I've been dying to tell you how I got on today?"

It had been another rubbish day for Bene but he didn't want to bother Alex with it.

"Yeah go on then, do you want to tell me while we're eating, or will it wait?"

"What do you think?" said Alex excitedly.

Bene laughed.

"Go on then, let's have it."

"First of all Simon thinks I'm going to make a great bowler, it seems I have a natural talent for the game and with a bit more coaching I could easily get into the ladies league. And in case you're thinking that was just to make me feel good both Adam and this other man agreed with him. Nicola went with me and she's a natural too, so we're both thinking of joining how about that? They want both of us to become members, and if we continue with the coaching and get in a bit more practice and playing time they think we could be good enough to play for the county.

"You're sure it's not because they want more people to join the club just to keep the membership up?"

"No, I asked Adam that because I was thinking the same, but he assured me it wasn't the case. He said we were both naturals and we could become really good players."

"That's terrific news Alex, and you're right, Adam wouldn't say that if it wasn't true. How was he by the way? I saw him this morning and he was looking forward to seeing you?"

"Yes, he said you'd called by; he was OK but like a lot of them down there he's worried about the deaths of those bowlers. I heard that you found another body, is it connected?"

"Yes I'm afraid so, he was another bowler. Anyway were you able to find out anything?"

"Not much, I didn't really get a chance; most of the time we were on the green and concentrating on the bowling. Simon was coaching the new ones, Nicola and me and two other ladies. They enjoyed it as well but they only want to play in the friendlies and jumbles; they're looking more at the social side of the club as they're both widows and would like to make some new friends. Simon is nice and he likes to talk a lot, but I didn't get much out of him when I mentioned the murders, he thinks it goes back to something that happened a long time ago and for some reason has suddenly resurfaced. But he was reluctant to expand on it and I didn't want to sound pushy so I left it at that. So no, I don't think I've achieved much, apart from the fact Nicola and me are going back on Saturday to have a bit more practice. I might get a chance to talk to some of the others then and find out a bit more. So tell me about your day?"

Alex and her mam had both eaten, so when Dot brought his meal through Bene was much more interested in that than talking about his day.

"Not great by any means, I'll tell you all about it when I've demolished this."

He dived straight into the meal and devoured it in a few minutes. After wiping the remainder of the dinner from his face he went over to the settee to rest.

"Well we certainly covered a lot of ground today. We've been that busy flying around we never found time to eat. This new murder happened in the same village as the last one and it looks as if he was shot on the same night as well. It should have been discovered the same day as the last murder, but the house-to-house checks weren't thorough enough and it was only this morning it came to light. The man's name was Robin Mitchell, another bowler and a friend of Willie Jameson the other victim in the village. There wasn't a lot we could do; there was no disturbance in the room and no clue as to who had done it, so we've left it to forensic and hope they can come up with something. We did get one bit of good news though, we've got a gun and we think it's the one used in the first shooting; it's been sent away to be checked and we're hoping to get the results back from that tomorrow. Hopefully they'll get some prints from it and with a bit of luck give us a name. Now tomorrow I'm going down to Fleetwood to see this guy whose father's in prison for that murder up in Scotland. That's the reason I went up to Perth the other day to find out a bit more about it, we think it could be connected to our murders. Hopefully I'll have more luck there and we can get this case wrapped up before there're any more fatalities."

He didn't want to tell her about the risk he could be taking in going to Fleetwood, that the man may have a gun and if he was the murderer he may not be too fussy about using it again. Neither did he want to tell her about Adam's involvement in the murder in Longbarrow village six years ago, he would keep those things to himself for now.

Dot returned to the lounge and joined the two lovebirds.

"Well it's been a long day Bene, but you look a bit more cheerful, maybe you're finally on to something and a result isn't too far away, let's hope so anyway."

It was true he did feel better, things were starting to look a bit more promising and the next day could bring them closer to making an arrest. Maybe evidence from the gun would be the key, or maybe his visit to Fleetwood would be the turning point. There was still the problem with the other gun, the Glock, but on the whole the forecast for tomorrow did seem to look a bit brighter. They were sitting back and relaxed ready to enjoy one of Bene's favourite TV programs which had been recorded earlier. His mobile rang it was Inspector Sowerby. Bene listened for almost five minutes to what the Inspector had to say, and when the call ended he put the phone away, gave a huge sigh and slumped back down onto the settee; the room went very quiet.

"Go on then." Said Alex, what's happened, not another murder for God's sake?"

Bene's face had dropped.

"No I think it's worse than that; we've been taken off the case."

"What?" Alex exclaimed "How? Why? Who's taken you off the case?"

"That was Sowerby on the phone he said division are taking over the case. They told him this last murder had been the decider. They'd given us more than enough time to crack it, but with no suspects and no definite lines of enquiry to follow up they can't afford to let us carry on with it any longer. As from tomorrow they're taking over and putting their own men onto it. They've got a lot more manpower than we have and are better equipped to deal with it; they hope to have it wrapped up in the next day or so. They're keeping ET on to bring them up to speed with what we have so far, but that's all. There's nothing for me or Hils or anyone else at the station. So I don't have to go to Fleetwood tomorrow, I'm to report to Sowerby who'll find something else for Hils and me to do."

He was naturally gutted; his feelings were a mixture of disappointment, rage and maybe a little guilt. Alex and Dot didn't know what to say, and Bene was stunned.

"Honestly I don't know what else I could have done; maybe there was something I've missed or been missing, or something I should have done or not done, but I can't think what. Maybe I just wasn't up to this one and someone else will come in and sort it right away. I know we'd have got there eventually, but now everyone will think we're failures, and that hurts."

The mood in the last few minutes had changed from what had promised to be a day to look forward to into a day which would hold nothing but shame for him, his failure to track down and arrest the murderer, and everyone knowing about it.

Chapter 24

A new direction

After a restless night with very little sleep a much subdued Bene reported to the station the next morning. The office was in a state of chaos with half a dozen police officers rushing in and out carrying computers, boxes and files and dumping them wherever they could find space. Bene's desk had been moved and there was no sign of Val or her desk. Goodness knows where they'd dumped her. ET burst in through the door with another load of files.

"Hi boss, sorry about all this but it looks as though you'll have to move somewhere else. I'm not sure where, but these guys are taking over the whole office and a porta cabin that's coming up from Preston."

"If you've been kept on to help them you'll be alright staying in here won't you?"

"Yeah, but I think it'll only be for a day or two, then they'll take over completely and I'll be out as well. We'll be left in the dark not knowing what lines of enquiry or action they're taking. It doesn't seem right to me I'm sure we were making progress, but now all our hard work will be lost and made to look worthless. And you can be sure that if they do catch the killer or killers they'll take all the credit for it."

"Yeah it's a right kick in the guts. I hope they do catch them though; I'd be interested to see if somewhere down the line we'd missed something obvious or could have done something differently. But I hope that's not the case because if it is we're going to look pretty damned stupid."

Inspector Sowerby came out from his office and waved Bene over to join him.

"Sorry about this Bene but I couldn't hold them off any longer, given another day or so and I'm sure we would have cracked it, but division decided we'd had enough time on it so that's that. I can't say I blame them because they've been put under pressure from higher up themselves. Anyway I'll bring you up-to-date and tell you what we'll be doing while all this is being cleared up. ET will be working with them initially, but as far as this office is concerned we won't be active in the case anymore; they'll take over completely. I can tell you that the gun that was handed in was the same gun that was used in the murder of Arnold Bainbridge at the car wash. There were no prints on it but there is a record of ownership, and tracing the rightful owner will be the prime objective of the new team. If it turns out to be the killer or at least one of the killers, then we can say 'we could have done that ourselves' and they were wrong to take us off the case. But we'll have to see if it turns out that way before sending them packing and crowing ourselves. In the meantime there're other things that we need to concentrate on, and as Hils is still assigned to the squad she'll be working with you in place of ET."

"So what have we got then?"

"Obviously division will be concentrating on the gun and finding out who owns it. They're also sending a couple of men down to Fleetwood to interview that lad, and if he's a likely suspect they'll be bringing him back with them. The others will be spending most of their time in Longbarrow village looking to see if we've missed anything there.

I want you and Hils out there as well, not working on the two murders, but looking at the two deaths that took place back there in 2012. I take it you've read the file and wondered about it, why for instance the investigation was stopped before it had really got started, and that Adam was the lead investigator? Well what I want you and Hils to do is speak to Adam and get him to tell you as much as he can without breaking the Official Secrets Act, and then dig into it as deeply as you can, find out who the men were and what really happened back then."

"We've already seen the file sir and we've spoken to Adam about it, and I think we got as much as we're going to get from him, but if you like I can speak to him again."

"Yes do that, it was before my time here but I've been down and had a look at the file and I've heard Adam's side of it, it's irked both of us not knowing what really happened back then. One of the men was a local farmer, but the real mystery is the other fellow; who was he and what he was doing there. Now those two men who've been nosing around the village seem to be interested in this case but I don't know why. It must be something pretty important because they're either working directly to the Home Office or for someone connected to the Home Office."

"I did get a bit of a lead when I was out there sir; something I got from one of the village boys, but it's all a bit confusing and I never had the chance to follow it up. I'll go back and speak to him again and see if I can make any sense out of it; it'll be a start anyway."

"I'll have your desk moved down into the basement for the time being, it isn't the best place to work from but division need all the floor space in here, I'm lucky I've kept my own office. If you prefer you don't need come in here every day, but remember you have Hils with you and she's still based here along with Val and the others in the basement."

"And about this case we've been working on sir, I'm supposed to forget all about that am I?"

"Not exactly, if you do turn anything up you'll have to inform me about it and I'll be obliged to hand it over to division and let them follow it up. But if you're concentrating on this older murder it shouldn't impinge on these latest ones so don't let that distract you. And make sure you keep in regular contact with me; I want a report every day to bring me up-to-date with developments. And Bene make use of Hils, she's a bright kid and she'll be a great help to you; if she does OK with this I'll recommend she joins us on a more permanent basis."

"I don't think there's much I can do from home or the station sir; I think we'll be spending most of the time running around the country. I know one of them was a local man so he should be easy, but the other one certainly wasn't and he's going to be a hard man to track down, especially after all this time. Anyway, I'll be pleased to get my teeth into something constructive and it'll help take my mind off the murders here. I'm really sorry about how it's turned out sir; I just hope we haven't let you down."

"No, I don't think there's anything more we could have done; the leads we had didn't throw up anything, and we wasted a lot of time chasing our tails. But we went about it the right way and at least we've got one of the guns and a vague description of the man. With a bit of luck and a bit more time we might have cracked it. But we've nothing to reproach ourselves for Bene, we just have to put it down to experience and carry on. So go and pick Hils up and let's see what you can dig up on this old case. If you can solve that mystery it will do Adam and me a power of good."

Hils was already waiting for him, dressed in a sky blue open necked blouse and mid length white jeggings, her hair perfectly coiffured as usual. She was standing in the centre of the office amid the frenzied activity going on all around her, seemingly unaware of the effect she was having on the influx of new officers from division. She had plainly become their object of desire and was attracting many leering and lustful looks. Unfortunately for them they were to see very little of her during their stay in Levensbridge.

Bene had to get her out of there.

"Come on, let's get out of here before Sowerby sees you dressed like that, he'll go ballistic."

Hils grinned and chuckled.

"Just thought I'd brighten the day up a bit; anyway it's worked hasn't it. I mean look at you, last night you were down in the dumps and had a face like a smacked bum, but this morning you look loads better. Something's cheered you up, what is it have we got a nice juicy case to look at?"

Bene had to smile.

"Yes OK I was down last night, but we all were, you included, but we have to forget all about that now and concentrate on this new case Inspector Sowerby has given us. I think it'll be a difficult one and there's every chance we won't get a result, but if we could crack it then it might just move someone a little further up the ladder."

Bene laughed and grinned at her, but Hils wasn't grinning, she was hopping mad.

"Oh that's alright then, so I'm going to bust my guts getting you promoted. Well that's brilliant but what's in it for me; all I'll get is thank you very much Hils, now get back in uniform and out on the streets again."

He grinned again.

"Well you never know there might be two ladders, one for me ...."

Hils brightened up immediately.

"You mean I could get to stay in the team?"

"If we do alright with this then I'll recommend you for DC. But don't say anything because you'll have to prove to Inspector Sowerby and to me that you've earned it; and if you have then I'm sure he'll rubber-stamp it. But as I said before, we might not be able to solve this case; we may find nothing at all. But I have to give it all I've got because I feel I need to prove myself all over again. They'll be a lot of hard work involved and probably a lot of travelling. We'll have disappointments and setbacks along the way and we'll hit brick walls, and all those we'll have to deal with. But what we're really going to need is a bit of luck, and luck is something that's been in short supply lately."

Hils had gone quiet and Bene looked over to try and gauge her mood before continuing.

"So before we start I need to make sure that you're with me on this. You need to know what you're letting yourself in for and the commitment you'll have to make. For a start there will only be the two of us. We'll have no support and we'll be working long hours, and a lot of those will be unsociable. You'll have to forget all about your social life until the jobs finished, however it pans out. What I need you to do is convince me that you fully understand the commitment I'm asking you to make, and that I can count on you 100%"

It was Hils turn to convince him how much she really wanted this job.

"If there's one thing I really want Boss it's to be part of this team, working with you and ET. I've loved every minute of it so far and I've been dreading going back into uniform. I know regular policing is a great job and a very worthwhile and important one. But on this side of the force you get the chance to be first on the scene and see crime as it really happens. You go looking for clues and interview people and pull all the facts together, and I know there's a lot of foot slogging as well. But it gives you the chance to get the best out of your brain. And at the end of it all, if you can say to yourself I helped put that person away for that crime then it makes all the hard work worthwhile. And you're right,

I do have a social life and a damned good one as well, but it's only a small sacrifice to make and I'm more than happy to do that. So in answer to your question, yes I'm ready for this and I'm up for it. I really want to stay in the team so you've got my full support all the way."

Bene smiled.

"Good, then let's make a start."

"Where are we going first?"

"Your house of course."

"Why would we want to go to my house?"

"So you can change out of those clothes and put on something more suitable. What you've got on is OK for a desk job or maybe city work, but where we're going you need look as if you fit in; we're going out in the country girl, not onto the catwalk."

CHAPTER 25

Testing the water

With Hils changed into a more practical and appropriate dark suit the two officers set about their new assignment. On the way to Adam's house Bene decided it would be a good idea if they were less formal.

"In case you were wondering; you only need to call me boss or sir when we're in the office or when we're talking to or interviewing people, but when we're on our own like we are now I think it's better if we're on first name terms."

"Yes, I was thinking it's a bit official when most of the time we'll be on our own, so first names if fine. I'm a bit worried about your wife though, what will she think about it; she's not the jealous type is she? I don't want her to feel uncomfortable with us working so close together?"

"Alex doesn't know yet but she'll be alright; tell you what we'll call in tonight and you can meet her. She'll be fine about it; you'll get on like a house on fire."

When he thought about it a bit more he wasn't too sure about his last statement. Alex was very trusting but he didn't want to push it. Hils was a stunner and no mistake and Alex and Dot would easily see the threat she might pose. He would have to tread carefully there, and on reflection 'house on fire' may not have been the best phrase to use.

Adam saw the car pull up outside the house and went to the door to welcome them as they came down the path.

"Come on in then, you're welcome any time you know that. Have there been any developments in the case?"

Once inside the house Bene told him about division taking over the murders and the new case they'd been given. Adam didn't seem too surprised.

"Yes I was afraid that might happen, but I wouldn't let it bother you Bene it's been a nightmare for you, maybe you should be relieved it's been handed over, and they do have a lot more resource to do it. Anyway tell me about the one you're working on now and I'll see if I can help you with that."

"We've just started on it today and you're our first call. There're a few things you might be able to help us with, is it alright to run them by you?"

"Of course, but before we start I'll get Ellen to bring us some coffee through."

While waiting for the coffee to arrive Hils opened up a conversation with Adam. She was interested to hear about the time Bene and he had worked together and how it had worked out for them both. Adam told her about some of the cases they'd worked on, and some light-hearted moments they'd shared together, including one or two of Bene's little lapses which made her laugh. Then it was Adam's turn, he wanted to know a bit more about her. She opened up quite willingly and gave Adam an insight into her life, and also threw in a few of her own hairy escapades which made him smile. Adam thought Inspector Sowerby had made a good choice with Bene's new partner. Ellen brought in coffee and biscuits and left them to talk shop.

Adam was curious. "Tell me what you want to know and I'll see if I can help you?"

Bene responded. "Well we have very little to go on, but there is something we'd like to have a look at but can't find. Do you know if there was an evidence bag with the man's clothes and possessions in? I had a look around at the station but I couldn't find anything among our stuff, have you any idea what happened to all his things?"

"Yes, I know exactly where they are; I took them down to Preston with me when I reported back there. I gave the bag a crime number which I still have written down somewhere. They'll have it stored away with their own stuff I expect. But you'll have to be a bit sneaky if you want to see it, don't ask for it by case name or date because they might not let you have it; it could still be sensitive material. Ask for the evidence bag number which I'll let you have. I wasn't happy with the way the case had been closed down and I had to cover myself. I wasn't going to take the rap for all that, even though it was my signature on the report."

Longbarrow, when they got there was overrun with police officers. As Bene and Hils drove into the village they could see at least five police cars parked around the small village square.

"Bloody hell, how many men have they got working on this." said Bene "They've been quick off the mark to get here before we did; it looks as though they've started their enquiries in the main part of the village first." Hils thought it best to be cautious.

"Maybe we should wait for a while; if we go in now and they see us it would look like sour grapes, and I'm sure they'd take great delight in telling us to get lost, and then report our interference to their boss. Let's sit here for a few minutes and find out whose houses they're in and which direction they take when they come out, they'll be following some sort of pattern to make sure they cover the whole village. Once we know which way they're going we'll know which houses we can go to." Bene agreed.

"You're right; we'll bide our time. The last thing we want is to let them think we're trying to muscle in on their case. The house I'm interested in is that one over there; that's Matthew Dawes house and I'd like to speak to him first. He's probably still at work in the joiners shop or down at the saw mill, but if I can catch his wife she might be able to help us."

They had to wait another ten minutes until the last of three policemen came out of separate houses; they had clipboards and were obviously ticking off houses as they were checked. The last one came out of the Dawes house and walked passed the two houses that had just been checked; he knocked on the door of the next house.

"It's a good job we didn't knock on her door isn't it," said Bene "with a policeman already inside. We'll give it another five minutes to make sure we don't run into any more of them and then we'll go and see Alison."

Alison was surprised to get two visits from the police within a few minutes of each other, she told Bene she'd already answered the officers' questions but couldn't help him.

"Anyway, come in Bene and bring the lass in as well. I see you've drafted in some extra men to help, you'll be pleased about that, I hope they're going to catch whoever's doing this. It's been such a shock Bene, I mean nothing ever happens here, it's such a quiet little backwater where everyone knows everyone else. I'm sure no-one in the village can be responsible for it. But you can see how it's changed people, you pass someone on the road now and you can see them thinking, 'could they be the one,' and people who've known each other for years are now looking at them in a different light. The sooner this madman is caught the better for all of us. Anyway, less of my blather what are you going to tell me?"

"Well the police you've got in the village now Alison are not from Levensbridge, the case has been taken over by division and they're running the show now."

"So are you two not involved anymore?"

"No, they've got lots more manpower than our small station so we've been put onto another case. You remember those deaths here six years ago Matthew and your Stephen were talking about; well that's what we're looking into now. I'd hoped to speak to Matthew about it but I suppose he's still at work?"

"Yes, I told that bobby to go and have a word with him; he'd be able to tell him more than I could. Matthews' still a bit down Bene; he hasn't got over the shock of finding those bodies."

"I know it must have hit him hard. Is there any way you could get a message to him Alison, and ask if he can come here after he's spoken to the other officers? Matthew and Stephen are probably the best people to help us with this case. When this lot have finished interviewing the villagers we'll probably want to talk to some of them, but I'd like to speak to Matthew and Stephen first."

"I know Matthew has his mobile with him so I'll give him a call." She rang her husband's number. "I always insist he takes the phone with him, if he's working on his own or just has the young lad with him and something happens, the phone is his only lifeline."

Matthew was already talking to the police but told her he'd come home as soon as he'd given his statement.

"What time does Stephen get home from school? I'd like to talk to him as well? After Matthew told me about the man at the saw mill it was Stephen who came forward and gave me some details about it. There might be other things he's remembered that could help us."

"Stephen won't be home until four o'clock, but if you want to come back then I'm sure he'd like to see you. It's funny you know, he'd kept it secret all these years but once he mentioned it to his dad he felt a lot better about it; he's been keen ever since to help find out who the man was so he'll be only too happy to help you."

Matthew came into the house and was looking a lot better than the last time Bene had seen him. Clearly the trauma of finding two dead bodies over the last day or so was fading a little; he seemed a bit more relaxed and eager to talk.

"So you're looking into the death of that fellow who turned up here back in 2012 are you? I'm pleased something's being done about that at long last. I don't think I can help you anymore though I told you everything I know the last time you were here, Stephen's your best bet but he won't be home until later."

"Yes I thought so, we'll come back if that's alright and maybe we can talk to you both. How about four o'clock this afternoon will you be finished by then?"

"Yes I can get back for four, there's not much to do this week and once I've put a few fence posts into the creosote tank I'll be finished for the day, they'll have to stay in overnight so there's nothing more I can do."

"Good we'll be off then; there're a few things we have to do first so we'll see you both later."

The two officers left the house to continue their enquiries.

"Let's go to Preston Hils and get that bag, we'll see if there's anything in it that can help us."

"I think you should phone first; they might not release it without authority, and if it's still sensitive they might not let us have it at all?"

"I'd thought of that, I'll phone Sowerby and ask him to contact them and to have it ready for when we get there. We should be there in an hour max. Hopefully they won't question the Inspector's motive, and with a bit of luck we might just get it."

The drive to Preston only took fifty minutes but all the time they were worried that it could turn out to be a wasted journey. But they were lucky and on arrival the bag was waiting for them, after getting a signature from Bene the duty sergeant handed it over.

"My but that was quick, your Inspector told me it was urgent so I set off right away to find it. Sometimes if we're asked for a specific case it can take ages to find, but luckily the bags are in numerical order, and as you already had the number that saved time. Make sure to bring it back as soon as you're finished with it."

"Let's get out of here fast." Said Bene as the two detectives walked briskly back to the car. "We need to have a look in this bag before anyone finds out exactly what it is we've taken. If it is still sensitive someone will get into trouble. I hope it's not Sowerby, but then he's only requested a number that he's been given so he should be alright. It's Adam I'm worried about; I don't want him to fall foul of the Official Secrets Act. But he's retired now and it was a long time ago, I don't think it would be in their interest to press charges against him."

They drove past the barriers and out of the car park without any problem and Bene gave a sigh of relief.

"Thank goodness for that; let's get back to Levensbridge and see what we have."

Levensbridge police station was a lot quieter as most of the officers were out on enquiries. Bene and Hils took the bag straight down to the basement where they'd been dumped for the duration of division's stay. Setting it down on his desk he cautiously opened it.

"There's a lot of stuff in here and it's in a bit of a state, look at all that tacky stuff on it?"

The items were individually segregated into polythene bags, he laid them all out along the desk and they looked at each one in turn.

"The trousers don't seem to have suffered any damage, but the oilskin jacket, sweater and shirt are badly stained; the underwear looks clean as are the socks; the shoes are good quality brogue although rather muddy, and lastly there's a pair of leather gloves."

This was all the clothes that had been recovered. Another bag held the contents of the jacket and trouser pockets. There were about four hundred euros in bank notes, a small amount of loose change and a key ring with five keys attached. Apart from that there was a handkerchief and a half-opened packet of mints.

No-one seemed remotely interested in the items Bene and Hils had brought in to the office. Val was sulking and making it known to everyone she wasn't happy at being moved from her prime position in the main office and dumped down in the basement. The other two officers were avoiding eye contact with her, keeping their heads down to concentrate on their own work.

"Are we going to open them up Bene?"

"Of course, and let's do it quickly in case someone finds out we shouldn't have the bag and decide to come and retrieve it. We'll do the clean stuff first that shouldn't take long."

They put on gloves before handling any of the contents. The bags containing the shoes, socks, gloves, hanky and underwear revealed nothing apart from the make of the shoes which had been made by a well-known and expensive manufacturer, the details of these were written down. Next the money was counted and the keys looked over. The trousers were next, and after noting the size and make they checked the pockets, but these contained nothing as they'd been emptied long ago. That only left the damaged items; the shirt and sweater revealed nothing, but the sizes and makes were noted. Lastly the waterproof jacket was opened, again there was nothing in the pockets but the makers' label showed the name of an Irish clothier, and although badly burned with the creosote it appeared to be of good quality. Again the details were written down. That was everything, not much for them to go on and absolutely nothing to identify the owner.

"Right," said Hils with a big grin on her face, "I've got an idea."

"Go on then."

"Let's photograph everything and put them back into the individual bags, then we'll pack everything into the evidence bag and rush it back to Preston."

"What?"

"Well you've been worried that Inspector Sowerby, Adam or ourselves could get into trouble with this, especially when they find out we have it. Look at it this way, we've seen everything that's here and we've got photos of it all, so we don't need it any more do we? If we take it back now we can say Inspector Sowerby had given them the wrong number and this isn't the bag we wanted. We'll tell them we'll come back when we have the right crime number; that way we'll be in the clear and they'll be happy to have it back. Even if they check the bag everything will be there, they won't even know it's been opened. We haven't had it long, so if we hurry back with it they won't suspect anything."

She looked to Bene for a response.

"Bloody hell Hils, Sowerby said you were a bright kid and you've just proved it, well done girl! OK let's go, and when we get back we'll go and talk to Stephen."

They sped back to Preston as fast as they could and found the same sergeant waiting to greet them at the desk; he was relieved to see them.

"Thank the Lord for that, I only realised after you'd gone that I'd logged out something that was still sensitive and should never have left here. If you hadn't brought it back I'd have been for the high jump. Anyway now it's here I'll log it back in. If you let me know the one you do want I'll get it for you. I'll change the number on the log sheet and no-one will ever know."

Hils came up with the right answer.

"You see that's our problem, we don't know the right number, I'll have to get our Inspector to check again and we'll get it the next time, but it's not that important anyway so don't hold your breath."

"Well thanks for bringing this back folks, next time we'll make sure we get the right one and you can check it here before you go."

He picked up the bag and bade them farewell, then disappeared quickly through a door to replace it before anyone noticed it was missing.

"That was brilliant Hils." Bene chuckled. "Right, let's get over to Longbarrow and see if young Stephen has anything good to tell us."

It wasn't quite four o'clock when they got back to Smithy Cottage, Alison and Matthew had been expecting them. They went into the house and waited for Stephen to come home from school. Bene noticed there was still a police presence in the village, two police cars were parked outside the Globe Inn. "They must have quizzed almost everyone by now, have they been here all day?"

"Yes," said Matthew "but I think they're about done. There're a few houses at the top end of the village they could check on, but anyone living further out won't be able to tell them anything, they wouldn't hear any shooting out there if we didn't hear it here in the village."

The school bus pulled up outside the pub, and sitting inside Stephen recognised Bene's car parked outside his house. He jumped off the bus and came rushing in to greet him.

"You came back then, I knew you would."

"You know you can't keep me away if there's a mystery to be solved, and I'm looking for you to help me with it, do you think you can do that?"

Stephen looked at Hils

"Yes of course I can, who's this then? Is she going to help as well?"

"Yes, this is Hils," Bene made the introduction. "I've told her all about you and she's looking forward to us all working together to solve the mystery."

"When can we start, right away?" said the excited lad.

"I think we should, it's been six years, so it's time we got it sorted isn't it? Have you got any homework to do?"

"Yes but it won't take long; I can have it done in half an hour."

"Right, well you get on with that and we'll wait here and talk to your mam and dad."

Stephen ran upstairs to do his homework and Bene turned to Matthew.

"We'd like to go to the saw mill first just to get a feel of the place, do you think the police will have finished down there? We don't want to bump into them or they'll think we're interfering with their investigation?"

"They'll be well away from the place by now. I was the last person to be seen down there, and the saw mill is a good way from the other houses, it'll be clear."

"I don't think it'll throw up anything, but if Stephen can show us exactly where the body was it might help. Being there again it might jog his memory and bring back something he'd forgotten about and didn't mention back then. It's just a chance, but you never know, going back there might stir something in his memory."

Stephen rushed downstairs and into the lounge; his homework was done in record time and he was raring to go. With no further loss of time the four of them left the house and walked the short distance to the saw mill. It was only a hundred and fifty yards away but isolated from the main part of the village and not overlooked. High Yard farm was the nearest property, but only the outline of the roof and the chimneys could be seen above the bushes and trees. The large tank sat in behind the main mill, and as they approached it the smell of creosote was overwhelming.

"It's easy to see how this stuff could affect you." Hils said as she peered over the top of the tank with a paper hankie clamped tightly over her nose. She looked at

Matthew. "Do you know if there was anything in here on the night the man was found?"

"It was more than half full of timber so the level of creosote would have been close to the top. The poor fellow wouldn't have to lean too far over to get his head in there. But he wouldn't have done that would he? Somebody has pushed him over head first into it and held his head down, that's the only explanation for it. I mean no-one's going to top themselves that way are they? Look at the stuff; it would be a horrible death."

Stephen had gone quiet, and Bene wondered if going back there was having a bad effect on the lad. He may just clam up and block it from his memory and that way they'd get nothing out of him, other than what they already knew.

"How are you Stephen, are you OK with this? Look, it was a long time ago and if you'd rather go back home and forget about it that's alright, we understand."

"No it's alright, I remember I did stay away from the place for a long time, but I've been back lots of times since and I'm not scared of it anymore. What is it you want to know?"

"Can you start by telling us exactly where the man was when you found him?"

Stephen pointed to a spot near the side of the tank.

"Right there; he wasn't exactly laying down when we first saw him, he was on his knees and holding on to the tank; his head and jacket were covered in creosote and it was horrible. Then he reached out to touch us and we got scared and started to run away. We only went a few yards and when we looked back we saw him slump to the ground. We knew he couldn't catch us then so we went back."

"So there were two of you here I didn't know that, who else was with you?"

"It was me and Simmy, but he left the village years ago, and anyway he didn't go near the man so he didn't hear anything. We were still scared and worried that if we told anyone we'd get into trouble because we weren't supposed to go near the tank. We agreed to say nothing about what we'd seen, and after that we never talked about it again. We thought the police would come and find out about him and then we would get to know. But they weren't here very long and nothing seemed to happen so we never found out who he was, or what it was all about."

"Will it be worthwhile me finding this Simmy and asking him about it?"

"No, he never went near the man so he won't be able to tell you anything."

"Now you told me the man said something, I know this may be hard for you, but if you can imagine he's still there and try to remember what he did and what he said?"

Stephen took a deep breath.

"I told you that when we first saw the man we ran away, but we went back and got quite close to him. I thought he wanted to tell us something, he was a bit hoarse so I went a bit nearer so I could hear him, but Simmy stayed well back." Stephen paused, as he was trying to visualise the man lying on the ground and focus on what he could remember.

"At first he said something that sounded like wollocks, but his voice was weak and croaky so I'm not sure if that was it; but he did say it again and it sounded the same, and he was pointing over there," Stephen pointed in a direction to the left of High Yard farm.

"Did he say anything else?"

"Yes he said Judge Alice has it, and I had no idea who Judge Alice was or what she had to do with it."

"And is that all, you can't remember anything else he said or did?"

"No that was it, there was nothing else."

Bene was a bit disappointed, what he'd heard was only confirmation of what the boy had told him earlier. He hadn't come up with anything new.

"Alright Stephen that was good, we'll go back to your house and think about what you've told us, and see if we can make any sense out of it."

Matthew could see the disappointment on Bene's face, but he'd learned something from his son's story, he thought it could be important and Bene would want to hear it.

"I might be able to help you with this Bene, it's nothing concrete but it could be something."

"OK, anything you can give me will be good."

"The direction in which Stephen was pointing leads to a farm about half a mile away."

"Over there?" Bene pointed in the direction that Stephen had done earlier.

"Yes"

"And what farm is that?"

"It's a farm that was left vacant for a long time and became badly run down. It's being farmed again now but it did stand empty for a few years before it was taken over again. The man who had it back then committed suicide about the same time as this fellow was found. In fact I think it could have been the same day. It didn't get talked about much because the only thing the villagers were interested in at the time was the man who was found here."

"So you think there's a connection?"

"There could be; you see the farm is called Wool Oaks, and it doesn't need a big stretch of imagination to see it could easily sound a bit like Wollocks"

Chapter 26

A good partnership

Bene and Hils left Longbarrow with a little more hope and Hils was even excited about it.

"That was lucky wasn't it? I mean lucky that Matthew went with us and not just Stephen. We wouldn't have made that connection it was down to local knowledge."

"Maybe it does clear up one part of it; it could be the two deaths back then are connected. I think we need to check up on that farmer."

As promised, Bene took Hils back home to introduce her to Alex and Dot. He was a little apprehensive about the reception he'd get but the sooner it was done the better. Alex and her mother welcomed Hils into the house and Bene made the introductions, watching Alex attentively to gauge her reaction to his new colleague. It appeared to be friendly so he was able to relax, and soon the four of them were chatting away at will. They stayed until Bene was satisfied his new colleague had been accepted by his wife and mother-in-law then drove Hils back to her flat before returning home for dinner.

"She's a good looking girl Bene I hope you're going to behave yourself with her. She could be a man-eater that one, do you think I should be worried?"

Alex had her back to him as she spoke. Bene shrunk; he'd been under the impression he'd handled the situation pretty well and not shown any feelings towards his new colleague.

"Oh come on Alex it's just a working relationship, and anyway I had no choice in the matter. ET's been taken over by this new lot and Sowerby's given me Hils, there was nothing I could do about it. And if I refused I'd have been left working on my own, and right now I need all the support I can get; I thought you'd understand that."

Alex spun round looking very angry, but as Bene shrunk away even further she suddenly smiled and burst out into uncontrollable laughter.

"Oh Bene you really are a dope, I can always get you; I cast the line out and up you come and grab the bait and I just sit back and reel you in."

She was enjoying the reaction on Bene's face enormously.

"You're the bloody limit you are; you knew I was worried didn't you? Honestly Alex what am I going to do with you."

"Too late big boy" she rubbed her stomach and continued to laugh, "You've already done it"

The next morning Bene and Hils met at the station. The suicide of the farmer was the first thing they wanted to check, and Bene needed to find all the reports relating to his death.

"I'll get Sowerby to authorise a visit to the coroner's office and we can have a look at the findings of the inquest. It'll be much quicker than having it sent over, and we should be able to get the autopsy report as well, I'll get him to phone and make an appointment. In the meantime I'd like to go over there and have a look at this Wool Oaks, maybe ask around and get some background on the farm and the farmer."

Inspector Sowerby wasn't a happy man; his police station had been taken over and he'd effectively been made redundant until the murders were cleared up.

"Do you think the suicide and the death of that man could be connected?"

"I think they could be; they seem to have happened about the same time and possibly on the same day, it's worth looking into."

He went on to tell him how the boy had described the man pointing in direction of the farm. Inspector Sowerby seemed to think it was worth following up.

"It's something I suppose, find out who he was and if his death really was suicide, I'd check his finances at the time, if he was in debt then that's probably the reason he did take his life, but if he was solvent and his death was in any way suspicious then you'll have to look into it a bit closer. I'll give you a call when you can go and see the coroner."

An hour later they pulled up outside Wool Oaks farm. Hils made her observations.

"From here it looks OK, I mean the house and buildings look in good shape, there's a newish-looking tractor over there and a few bits of modern machinery scattered around. There're cattle in that field over there, and if the fields we passed along the way belong to this farm then they seem to be well-cultivated with good crops. I think whoever has it now is running a good business."

"Yes I agree; it looks as if it's doing alright, you seem to have summed it up pretty accurately. We'll go and see if there's anyone around who can give us a bit of history about the place."

The kitchen door was slightly ajar so that was the one they knocked on. It was answered by a good-looking smartly dressed lady of slender build with blonde wavy hair aged about thirty. Not the large round faced friendly farmer's wife they were expecting to see, complete with huge hands and a grubby apron.

"Hello, you're not reps are you; my dad won't see you if you are?"

"No we're with the police." They showed their warrant cards and Bene reassured her.

"There's no problem, we'd just like to know a bit more about the farm, it might be connected to something we're looking into. It's more to do with the previous owner and we were hoping you might be able to clear a few things up for us."

"You could speak to my dad, but he's out in the fields and won't be back until lunch time. But my mum's in and you can speak to her if you like, she's Mrs Pattinson. I'll give her a shout I'm off to work now so I'll leave you with her OK?"

The daughter revved up her car and sped out of the farmyard in a cloud of dust. The two officers waited patiently in the yard for her mother to appear. When she did she didn't disappoint, here was the character they'd pictured earlier. Hils immediately noticed the hands which were expansive to say the least, more used to delivering calves and lambs and heaving bales of straw around the barn than anything more refined. The smells drifting through the open kitchen door were truly inviting; here was the perfect farmer's wife.

"Now folks what can I do for you? She picked up her apron from the bottom to wipe her hands on. It was agreed that Hils would be best placed to take the lead; woman to woman was often more effective.

"Let me begin by saying this has nothing to do with you or your family Mrs Pattinson, it's the farm we're interested in and its previous owners. There're a few things we'd like to know about the farm, so whatever you can tell us would be useful. Is it alright if I ask you a few questions?"

"If I can help you I will, but I don't know an awful lot about the past history of it."

"That's alright; let's start with how long you've been here?"

"We came here nearly three years ago, before that we farmed at Barrock Park, two miles the other side of the village."

"You've been living in the area for quite some time then."

"Yes I was born and brought up here; my husband Bryan comes from Ulverston originally but when we got married we took over Barrock Park and that was over twenty years ago."

"So what attracted you to this farm in particular?"

"Bryan and me had put a lot of hard work into Barrock Park and made some big improvements to it over the years, and at the end of that there was nothing left to do but the running of it. Well Bryan gets fed up with routine and he needs something to get his teeth into, some sort of project he says to stop him getting bored. Then one day out of the blue this fellow came up and made us an offer we couldn't refuse. Well we'd been thinking of moving on anyway as we'd gone a bit stale and needed another challenge. This place had been standing empty for a long time and it needed a lot of work done to bring it back up again. Anyway we put in a daft offer and to our surprise it was accepted, so we moved in. We've worked hard at it ever since and it's in much better shape now, we're pleased with the way it's going."

"Did you know the man who had the farm before you?"

"Only vaguely, through the farming network I suppose you'd call it. We'd met him a couple of times but he wasn't someone we called a friend. His name was Kenny Walsh and he lived here on his own, I don't think he was ever married but I can't be certain, I know he didn't have any children though."

"And he'd let the farm run down a bit had he?"

"Well standing empty for a long time didn't help and some of the outer buildings were in poor condition. We had to replace the barn and the dairy and some of the outhouses, but the house itself was sound and only needed decorating. We just left the other buildings as they were and we use them for storing machinery and other odds and ends; we might do something with them in the future. The fields were overgrown of course, but that turned out to be a good thing as nothing had been taken out of the ground and it was full of natural nutrients, so the first crops we had were really productive."

"What about the man himself, did he have any relations nearby or any friends in the area?"

"I don't think there was anyone close. I know he had a cousin in Scotland and one over in Ireland but I think that was all. He had a few friends in the village and he'd meet up with them in the pub occasionally, but you'd have to ask in there because we don't know who they were."

"Have you any idea if he was making a profit on the farm, or was it not doing so well?"

"I think if he'd been making any money out of it he'd have put some back into doing the rebuilding and repairs we've had to do. The reason they gave for his suicide was drinking and debt, but I've no idea how much he drank or how much he was in debt."

Hils looked at Bene to see if there was anything else they needed to ask, but Bene shrugged his shoulders; he couldn't think of anything. Hils suddenly found one more question to ask.

"Thank you Mrs Pattinson, you've given us a lot of information and that will be helpful. There's just one other thing before we go. Has there been anyone else here recently showing an interest in the farm?"

"Now you come to mention it there were a couple of men here last week. They said they were with Defra; they showed me their cards and said they wanted to check all our outbuildings. Gathering information they said from all the farms in Cumbria about how many buildings and barns were on each farm and what they were used for; part of a national audit they said. I told them I was going out and my husband was working the fields, but they said they weren't interested in the house, just the buildings. Anyway, I locked the house and went shopping and left them to it, but I did think it a bit strange them dressed in good suits doing a job like that. When I came back they'd gone, but nothing seemed amiss so I never mentioned it to Bryan."

"Did you notice the car they came in?"

"Some big black thing, but I don't know about cars and I didn't take much notice."

"OK, well thanks anyway, I think that's all."

Mrs Pattinson held them back, she had some information they might be interested in.

"Something a bit odd has been happening though and we couldn't figure out what it was about. Late one night about a week ago we noticed a car drive up the lonning and stop halfway up. Well Bryan and me usually go to bed early and we just thought it was a courting couple looking for somewhere a bit more private. We didn't think too much about it but the same thing happened over the next two nights. On the last night we could see lights flashing outside and that made us think they were up to no good. We called the local police, but the daft buggers, you could hear the sirens blaring miles away and by the time they got here the car had gone. It must have scared them though because the car hasn't been back since." Hils wanted to make sure the owners were taking precautions.

"Unfortunately Mrs Pattinson rural crime is on the increase, so make sure everything is locked away."

Goodbyes were said and the two left Mrs Pattinson to get back to her kitchen.

"What do you think about that last bit?" Hils said as they reached the car.

"Well, they weren't from Defra to check on the buildings that's for sure. But they were looking for something, and I'd say it was the same ones who were here at night as well. By the description she gave us it's the same two men who have been in the village the last few days, and I don't think we'll ever get to know what they're up to."

"Where are we going now?"

Bene had to answer his phone.

"That was Sowerby; we can go and see the files on the inquest and the autopsy report. We haven't found out much here so maybe we'll have more luck with the coroner."

The files were out and ready for them in the coroner's office, he stayed with them to help explain some of the wording and medical terms which were often confusing to the average man on the street. The pathologist had recorded the cause of death as asphyxiation due to suicide by hanging. The inquest heard that the police had been called to the home of Kenneth Walsh on the sixth of July 2012, after a concerned neighbour had reported not seeing him for two days. When the neighbour called at the house he found the curtains closed and the door locked; he knocked several times but couldn't get an answer so he called the police. When they arrived they had to break down the door, the house was searched but there was no sign of Mr Walsh. They went outside to search the outbuildings and barns and eventually found him hanging from a rafter in one of the barns. They cut him down but his body was cold; it was evident he'd been dead for some time. The police confirmed there were no suspicious circumstances and the pathologist was called. He examined the body and confirmed the death as suicide. Two friends of Mr Walsh, Mr William Seaton and Mr Vernon Brough said Mr Walsh had been rather depressed of late. He was struggling to pay off a loan and maybe drinking a bit more than usual, but they didn't think things were so bad he would take his own life. In fact one of his cousins had recently died, and he was expecting to inherit quite a sum of money from the sale of his farm. The coroner had no hesitation in bringing in a verdict of death by suicide.

They left the office with more questions than they had answers for. Bene was curious.

"It seemed clear enough, but if he was coming into money that would have paid his debts off, why would he hang himself? I don't buy it there's something funny about it. Let's go and see if we can find those two friends of his who gave evidence at the inquest."

The found William Seaton at home on his farm about a mile away, busy swilling down the yard. Bene introduced Hils and himself.

"We're interested in Kenneth Walsh, I believe he was a friend of yours and you gave evidence at the inquest into his death. Can you tell us any more about what sort of man he was, and what you think made him hang himself?" The man shrugged his shoulders.

"He was alright was Kenny, a few of us lads would meet up in the pub once a week for a few drinks and he was one of the gang, we were all good pals. There was no problem that you could see with Kenny, we knew he had a few debts of course but then most of us do. Farming's not what it used to be and you have to diversify a lot more now just to keep your head above water. But we were all in the same boat and we never let it bother us. It never got any of us down, not even Kenny. It was a hell of a shock when we heard about it, we could hardly believe it, and to tell you the truth I still don't believe it. I think there was something funny about the whole thing, especially when it happened the same day that other fellow turned up dead in the village. I think Kenny's death had something to do with that."

"And what about his other friends, what do they think?"

"They all think the same, we all liked Kenny he was a grand fellow and one of us. A few of us still meet up in the pub and talk about it even after all this time. None of the lads are convinced he would hang himself. It was only recently he had a cousin die up in Scotland, a Doonhamer, and Kenny would've got quite a bit from the sale of his farm. He was looking forward to that because it would have solved all his problems. And on the strength of it he was going to see his cousin over in Ireland who he hadn't seen for years, so why would he go and hang himself eh, it doesn't make sense does it?"

"What about this other man who gave evidence, will we be able to talk to him?"

"On the phone maybe; Vernon moved to Australia to help out at his son's place over there. He went over last year and he'll not be back here again. But whichever of the lads you talk to they'll all tell you the same. We all liked the man and none of us believe he hung himself. There was something sinister at work there believe me."

Bene and Hils agreed there was no point chasing up any more of Walsh's friends they were only going to get the same information. Hils had made up her mind.

"That fellow didn't hang himself did he?"

"No I don't think so either. I tend to agree with this fellow that he had everything to live for. Now if it had happened a few months earlier when he had a debt problem fair enough, but not after his cousin had died and he was going to get a pile of money from his estate. No way, but how are we going to prove it? Hils had to agree with him.

"I don't think we can. We could have a look in the barn, or ask the policeman who found him to tell us exactly what he saw. If there was a chair or stool or something that he stood on and kicked away. He might remember something that didn't look right, should we have a word with him?"

"No, I'll give ET a call and ask him to find out if he's still working at the station; if he is then ET can have a word with him and let us know what he remembers about it. I think we should be going somewhere else."

"Where's that then?"

"Scotland."

"Scotland, why would we want to go there?"

"You must have noticed the dead man's clothes were mostly manufactured in Ireland, and Mrs Pattinson said

Walsh had a cousin in Scotland and another one in Ireland. Well we know the one in Scotland is dead, but what about his cousin in Ireland. Do you think he could be our mystery man? I'm sure there's a connection with Walsh and the man found by the saw mill because Stephen was most definite about the exact place he was pointing to. So why that farm in particular, and why did they both die on the same day, one murdered and the other a suicide or maybe they were both murdered."

Chapter 27

The Scottish connection

There didn't seem much more they could do with the rest of the day, so Bene told Hils to go home and gets a few bits and pieces together in case they had to stay overnight in Scotland.

"We could be up there a long time Bene, Scotland's a big place you know."

"But his pal said he was a Doonhamer didn't he? So that narrows it down a lot."

"What on earth is a Doonhamer when it's at home?"

"It's a name given to someone who was born in Dumfries, don't you know anything?"

"Hey that's good."

"That's why I'm the boss." Hils muttered something under her breath.

"I heard that, and what you suggest is physically impossible."

They burst into laughter.

"What time do we have to leave?

"It'll take about two hours to get up there, and it's a bit late to be setting off now everything will be closed when we get there. I think we'll set off early tomorrow morning, say about six o'clock and we should get there about eight."

They drove back to Levensbridge and Bene dropped her off at home.

"Be ready for six tomorrow and let's keep our fingers crossed for a bit of luck."

Bene left her and went home himself.

"My you're back early we didn't expect you until later." Alex greeted him. "You can sit down and eat with us and tell us how it's going."

Bene told her about his day and all the running around they'd had to do, and the plans he'd made for the next day.

"So you're off to Scotland tomorrow, is Hils going with you?"

"Yes we need to find someone up there, or rather find out about someone who died up there."

"Well that won't be easy you'll need to take a spade with you."

"Oh you are funny." Bene said sarcastically. "We need to find out his name first and see if he left a wife or family behind, and if we can find them or someone else who knew him it could help us identify our mystery man."

"You'll need a bit of help then, I'll come with you."

"What, you can't do that."

"Course I can, its Saturday tomorrow and I can do some shopping while you two are snooping around. It'll be a change from all the boring shops we have here."

"This is police work not a shopping expedition, and anyway we might not find out anything tomorrow, we might have to stay overnight so you can't come."

"Yes I can, tell him mam, anyway who's going to find out, if we're going at six in the morning there won't be anybody else around to see us. And if we're going to have an early start we'd better have an early night don't you think?" Alex gave him a long and rather obvious wink, amusing her mother and causing her to laugh.

"That's another one you've lost Bene." Dot turned and went back to the kitchen.

Six sharp the next morning Bene pulled up outside Hils' flat; she was already waiting.

"Hi Alex have you joined the team then?"

"No I'm only cadging a lift. I thought I might have a look around the shops up there."

"Yes, it'll be a change from here, anything in particular you're looking for?"

"There's a couple of birthday's coming up so I might find something a bit different up there."

Hils turned to Bene.

"So how are we going to do this?"

"Well we don't know the man's name because he was only a cousin to Walsh and might not have the same surname, but we could start with that name. We'll go through all the deaths in the area over the last two or three months and see what turns up. Being a farmer will help, they're a close knit community with everyone knowing everyone else through country dances and cattle markets and such, so we should be able to track him down. When we do, hopefully he's left some family behind who can give us a name."

The journey passed pleasantly enough and the girls chatted continually all the way. The police station in Dumfries was a new build on the road into the town, replacing the old Victorian building in the centre that had served the town for over a hundred years. Bene and Hils went in to report to the Inspector and the purpose of their visit. Returning to the car they drove into the centre of town and parked.

"I believe the records office is in Buccleuch Street which is just along there. We'll go in, but you'd better wait outside Alex; when we've finished we'll see where we need to go next, you can go and do your shopping and we'll arrange to meet up later, OK?"

"Yes, alright but don't be in there too long or I'll get bored."

Bene and Hils entered the office but returned a couple of minutes later, much to the surprise of Alex.

"Well I didn't think you'd be as quick as that, did you find him right away?"

"No, the place is closed and we can't get in until Monday. There's someone working in there but he's only there for another hour and he refused to let us look through the records. He said as we were English and not Scottish police we'd need someone from Dumfries police to accompany us, and by the time it would take to arrange that the office would be closed."

"So what are you going to do now?"

"There's usually a market on so we'll go and see the farmers down there; somebody will know who the fellow was. We'll split up here Alex and meet you at the coffee house on High Street about eleven, OK?"

"Yeah no problem, and there's no rush, I've got your card so I might go a bit wild with it."

With a big grin she waved the card around in front of his face. Bene shook his head and walked off towards the market with Hils.

The two officers arrived right on eleven o'clock at the coffee house, but there was no sign of Alex in there.

"Pity about your poor card Bene, I think it's going to get a bit of an airing."

"Yeah, well never mind about that, the whole day so far has been a waste of time. We'll have to think of something else, I keep forgetting its Saturday and any information we want is locked away in offices. When Alex turns up we may as well go home and come up again on Monday."

It was eleven thirty when Alex eventually appeared, grinning like a Cheshire cat and clutching six large bags.

"Phew that was a rush, but I've got some lovely things; do you want to see them or shall we wait until we get back home?" Bene wasn't really interested.

"We've had our coffees but we'll stay and have another one with you. Then we'll head back home, there's nothing more we can do until Monday." He ordered more coffee and scones.

"Didn't you find out anything?" asked Alex.

"No it was a complete waste of time. The market was full of bits of machinery, loads of old tools and other rubbish, and there were no farmers there either. And with the office's shut until Monday there's nothing more we can do here, Hils and me will come back then."

Alex waited until the order arrived then set about eating her scone.

"Well maybe I've had more luck than you."

"By the look of all those bags you certainly have, is there any money left on that card?"

"Yeah plenty, but I didn't mean that, I meant finding out the name of the farmer who died. His name was Stuart Brennan." Without looking up for a reaction she carried on eating.

"They're lovely these aren't they?" she said munching away noisily.

Bene and Hils were flabbergasted at the way she had just given the information as if it was something she'd seen written on the wall in front of her. Bene thought she was joking.

"If you're trying to wind us up Alex it's not funny."

Still munching away at the rather large scone, she corrected him.

"Told you I was coming to help you didn't I, and that's the name you wanted wasn't it, the cousin of the man who hung himself?"

There was silence as Bene and Hils tried to take in what Alex had just said, Alex seemingly unconcerned continued heartily with the scone.

"And how did you come about that information?" Bene asked.

"From the record office of course, it's the only place that keeps that kind of stuff."

"But it was closed."

"Maybe it was to you, but not to me!"

"Go on then spit it out."

Now she had their full attention Alex was only too pleased to tell them how she'd got it.

"Well I knew you were disappointed when you couldn't get access to the office, so after you left I thought I'd have a go, so I went back there. I told the man I'd travelled a long way and didn't realise the office would be closed, and I needed to find the death of a man who my mother thought could have been a relation, and it would have broken her heart if I'd come back with nothing. I told him I probably wouldn't get the chance to come up to Dumfries for a long time and by then my dear mother may not be with us anymore. So not only did he let me in, but he did the search for me as well, and that was the name that came up. Stuart Brennan was the only farmer who'd died in this area in that three month period back in 2012, and he lived at Kilmore farm at Lochfoot about six miles out of town, so how about that."

Hils was delighted,

"As for me Alex I can't say I'm surprised, Bene told me how you'd helped him in one of his earlier cases and I knew you had it in you. Well done! That's saved us a day's work and we don't have to come back up here again." She turned to Bene.

"Are you not going to thank her Bene?"

"Yes, I should have known she didn't come up just for the ride; she always wants to help and time and time again she pulls a rabbit out of the hat for me, well done darling."

Bene leaned across and kissed her.

"Right, let's go over to Lochfoot and see what we can find out there."

Twenty minutes later they were in the small village of Lochfoot, nestling beside one of Scotland's smaller

Lochs the lovely Lochrutton. On stopping to ask directions to the farm they were told it was a mile along the old military road and clearly signed. Five minutes later they turned into the lonning running down to the farm, they could see several large buildings and a big impressive whitewashed farmhouse.

"This place must be worth a shedload of money," said Hils.

"Yes, if Walsh had only half of this to come he would have been a very rich man."

An elderly man who seemed to have difficulty walking slowly came over to the car to enquire their business. Bene got out and showed the man his warrant card.

"We're sorry to bother you, but we're trying to find any relations of Stuart Brennan who lived here back in 2012. Were you or anyone else here related to Stuart?"

"My son-in-law was and it's him who's farming the place now, why do you ask?"

"Well we know Stuart had a cousin down in Cumbria called Kenneth Walsh who died shortly after Stuart, but we also know there was another cousin who lives in Ireland and its him we're trying to track down, but we don't know where in Ireland he lives, do you think your son-in-law would know."

"I doubt it lad, but you can ask him yourself, he's here now."

A man of around thirty years of age came over and the old man explained what Bene wanted to know. The younger man shrugged his shoulders.

"To tell you the truth there was a bit of mystery about the whole thing. I was only distantly related to Stuart and although I knew of him, we were never close and I never actually met the man. I didn't even know he'd died until a few months after. Then out of the blue I received a letter from his solicitor telling me I was his next of kin and the farm would come to me. It was quite a shock believe me; the solicitor had tried to find other relations but Stuart had never married. He only had two close relations, a cousin down in Cumbria who committed suicide shortly after Stuart died, and a brother who lived over in Ireland who they couldn't trace. They let things stand for six months in case he came forward, but when that didn't happen the solicitor contacted me to say I was the nearest relation and I would inherit the farm. And that's about it, I can't tell you anymore. As far as I know his brother still hasn't turned up."

"So the one in Ireland who we thought was his cousin is actually his brother?"

"That's right, so if you want to find him then at least you now have a name, but I don't know his first name, somebody Brennan. But I expect there'll be lots of them in Ireland."

"Well that's a start anyway," said Bene. "Thanks for that, but what if we find this Brennan fellow will he still have a claim on this place?"

"No don't worry about that, it's all legal now. If he'd come forward a year or so ago there would've been a chance he could appeal, but not now, it's far too late for that."

Back in the car the mood was subdued. Brennan was a common Irish name and without an address it would be a mammoth task trying to find the right one. Alex tried to cheer them up.

"At least you do have a name so that's good isn't it, plus the fact this Brennan in Ireland has never been found. Doesn't that suggest there's every chance he could be the man who died at the saw mill, and the one you're trying to find out about." Bene agreed.

"I suppose we should be pleased that we have a surname at least, if he'd been a cousin we wouldn't even have that, so yes it has been worthwhile coming up here."

"So where do we go now?" Hils asked.

"Ireland of course!" Bene replied.

"That's a bit ambitious isn't it; do you think Inspector Sowerby will sanction it? I mean its way out of our patch Bene; it's another country?"

"Oh he'll do it alright; he's really miffed about division taking over the murders and him handing over control to them; not only that, they seem to have blocked him right out of it. I know he's desperate to have this old case sorted, and if this is what it's going to take he'll have no problem giving us anything we need. I'll get him to OK it with the Garda and he can tell them we'll report to Dublin as soon as we arrive. I don't think they'll object to us being there as we won't be sticking our noses into any of their cases. We'll only be in the country a few days looking for this fellow, and as long as Sowerby can give them a guarantee we won't cause any trouble it should be OK."

"What time will we have to leave?"

Bene had already done his calculations and knew the ferry times.

"It's a good three hour drive down to Holyhead, there's a ferry at 02.40 in the morning but we wouldn't get any sleep at all if we were going for that one, I suggest we leave here just before five on Monday morning and catch the one at 08.15. We'll be in Dublin around lunch time and we can start from there."

Bene phoned his Inspector and was in for another shock. The conversation lasted about five minutes and during this time Hils and Alex kept very quiet. When the call ended they were interested to hear what he'd been told.

"What's happened Bene?" they asked in unison.

"There's been another murder!"

"My God, when did this one happen?" Hils asked

"They found him this morning."

"So who was he and where was he found?"

"A man called Vince Downie; he was found dead in his allotment this morning. As far as they can tell he had no connection with the other three; he lived at Stainbeck not Longbarrow and he didn't play bowls either. They've decided to keep the news out of the press for the moment. They don't want to panic the public into thinking there's a serial killer on the loose, so there'll be nothing on the TV or in the papers about it, for the time being anyway."

"But there is a serial killer on the loose, isn't there?" said Alex.

"Yes, but don't tell anyone; as far as the three of us are concerned we know nothing about this latest murder, and that goes for your mam as well Alex; promise you won't say anything to her."

"Was there anything else?"

"No that was it, but he was interested in what we'd discovered and wants us to press on with our search for this Irishman; he's given us the go ahead and he'll be speaking to the Garda this afternoon. Oh, and I have to phone ET who has some news."

Bene made the call.

"Hiya Bene, I thought you'd like to know I tracked down the constable who found that fellow strung up in the barn. He told me he couldn't remember seeing anything lying around that the man could have used to stand on when hanging himself. If he did use anything he must have kicked it a long way off because there was nothing near to the spot where he was found. He said he was in shock at the time so he can't be absolutely sure, but as far as he can remember the area around the place was clear."

"OK buddy thanks for that; how's your case going? I've just had Sowerby on the phone telling me about another murder, are the team making any progress?"

"Nothing new I'm afraid, and the Inspector in charge is getting it in the neck. They thought that putting all this extra manpower into the case would get it sorted pretty quickly but it hasn't been the case. Maybe you should come back and we could have another shot at it."

"Yeah I wish, but I've got other things to concentrate on now, so you keep plugging away down there and keep me up to date. Oh, do you know if anyone tracked down that lad in Fleetwood?"

"Two of them went down there but they couldn't find him. He'd been living with his mother but she hadn't seen him for the last few days; evidently he had some holidays to take and he'd gone off on his own without telling her where, and she was worried because he was in a foul mood when he left."

"How about the gun then, did they manage to trace the owner?"

"Well they managed to find the man it was last registered to, but that was over twenty years ago and he'd lent it to someone to shoot vermin on his allotment. He can't remember the man's name and he hasn't seen him since so that's another blank. Whoever did have the gun had converted a silencer to fit it, so whoever he is he knows all about guns."

"So that's it?"

"Yeah apart from this latest murder, they can't keep that quiet for long because when it does become public knowledge the shit is really going to hit the fan. Anyway I'm off the case tomorrow and to be honest I think we're better off out of it."

"Yeah you're probably right, keep in touch buddy."

Bene brought them up to date with ET's news.

"So the farmer could have been murdered then?" Hils asked

"Yes it's possible, but I doubt we'll ever be able to prove it."

"And Stainbeck isn't that where the young lad lives who found the gun?"

"Right again, and regardless of what they say, one way or another it has to be connected to the other deaths. But that's not our problem anymore we have to concentrate on our own case." Hils had been thinking about the trip to Ireland.

"If we do find this man over there then it rules out the man at Longbarrow, so we'll be no further forward will we, it might be best if we don't find him."

"In one way maybe, but if we don't find him we still can't be sure he was our man. I don't want to think about not finding him, let's find him or at least find out if he's dead or alive. Anyway have a good night tonight and rest tomorrow, then we'll be fresh for Monday."

CHAPTER 28

An Irish adventure

Bene, Alex and Dot were relaxing in the conservatory when they heard the letter box rattle.

"No post today Dot is there?" Bene said.

"Not on a Sunday it'll be somebody touting for business and pushing flyers through the doors; I'm not getting up for it anyway I'm too comfortable here."

Alex couldn't resist, she had to find out what it was so she went to check and returned with a handwritten envelope addressed to Bene.

"It's for you, shall I open it?"

Before Bene could stop her she'd opened the envelope and read the short message inside, she stumbled back and clutched the back of the sofa letting the letter fall to the floor.

"Are you alright Alex?" her concerned mother asked.

Alex turned white and was shaking violently. Bene grabbed hold of her as she started to fall.

"What is it Alex?"

"The letter." was all she could say as she sat down heavily beside him. Dot picked it up from the floor, read it and handed it to Bene. The message was short and to the point.

"BE WARNED KEEP YOUR NOSE OUT OR YOU WILL BE NEXT."

"What the hell is all this?" He jumped up from the sofa and raced to the door and opened it, but there was no sign of whoever had posted the letter. He went back to comfort his wife who was sobbing gently.

"Is this to do with those murders Bene?" Dot asked.

"Honestly Dot I have no idea, maybe they've got me confused with someone else."

"But it had your name on the envelope Bene it's meant for you alright. Is it something to do with the case you're working on now?"

"I don't know but it could be, or maybe they think I'm still working on the recent murders."

Sunday lunch was not the jolly one it should have been. It was their favourite but the table was quiet with each one of them deep in their own private thoughts. Alex and Dot were worried; they'd taken the threat to Bene's life seriously. Bene was worried because he had no idea who had sent it. He tried to allay their fears.

"The words are handwritten so the writer hasn't gone to the trouble of cutting out text and pasting it on paper. It looks amateurish and I think it's a cruel hoax from someone who'd like us to think it's come from the killer, but the real killer will be following our investigation and will know I'm no longer on the case so it's nothing to worry about. I bet some of the other officers have got the same letter; I'll take it to the station tomorrow and have it checked for prints. I think they'll most likely find some apart from ours of course, and if it's someone known to us they'll soon be picked up."

Alex was looking and feeling a little better now that Bene had dismissed the letter as a hoax.

"Are you still going to Ireland tomorrow?"

"Yes nothing's changed there, I just hope we don't have to stay too long, but we're not coming back until we have definite proof that this brother is either alive or dead."

Bene turned to Alex, showing concern for his wife.

"Are you OK now?"

"Yes, I forgot these things happen, and you did get something like that once before. I suppose the murders have unsettled a lot of people, everyone wants to see the killer caught and put away so they can get back on with their lives again."

They started to relax again and Bene thought a bit of fresh air would be good for them. They took off to the local park where they walked for an hour, doing a full circle before returning home much more refreshed.

"Right, I'll put a few things in a bag ready for the morning and we'll have an early night, I need to be up and away by four thirty."

"It'll just be sleep then will it?" Alex was trying to embarrass him in front of her mother.

Bene looked sheepish as he couldn't find a suitable answer, and his silence only encouraged Alex and Dot to giggle at his expense.

The motorway at five o'clock in the morning was quiet and the two officers made the long journey down to Holyhead without any problems. They arrived at the ferry port in good time with half an hour to spare. Both were feeling hungry so once on board they set off to find something to eat. The restaurant was busy as everyone on board had the same idea; they were all looking forward to a good breakfast.

"You grab a seat over there Hils and I'll go and get some food; what would you like?"

"Full English with tea and toast please."

"Good, same as me."

Ten minutes later they were tucking into a good hot meal and it was doing wonders for them.

"It's the only chance I get to have one of these Bene."

"Yeah me as well, I don't have time most mornings, and anyway I always get frowned at if I have it at home. They keep telling me how unhealthy it is and try to get me to eat more of what they like, I mean I eat it, but it's bloody boring. Whenever I get a chance like this I grab it, bacon and eggs, fried bread and Cumberland sausage, beans, mushrooms and fried tomato, the full Monty, you can't beat it."

"Make the most of it then, we won't get it again until we're back at home."

"I don't see why not, I'm going to have the same tomorrow wherever we're staying."

"But you can't."

"And why can't I?"

"Tomorrow morning we'll be having a full Irish breakfast." Hils laughed.

"Anyway, what's the plan when we get there?" she asked.

"We need to find the man who bought this jacket, and we know his name was Brennan, so we check all the outlets until we find someone with that surname who bought one."

"It's a long shot though isn't it? A lot of shops wouldn't keep records going back that far."

"I know, and cash sales probably wouldn't show a name either, but it's the only clue we have and it's our only chance."

They finished the meal and Hils pulled a face and looked over at him.

"I think we should move."

"Whatever for, the place is almost full and we'll lose our seats?"

"We can go up on top, its warm enough and it won't be crowded, come on there'll be plenty of seats up there." Hils got up ready to go.

"What's wrong with right here?" said Bene.

"The smell, don't tell me you haven't noticed?" She turned her head slightly to one side.

Bene looked to the side she'd indicated and immediately understood her meaning. They left and went up onto the deck area and sat down there.

"Couldn't you smell him Bene?"

"Yes just a bit, but I didn't catch on who it was until you pointed him out."

"It was him and his brother we saw in the Fox and Pheasant that night wasn't it?"

"Yes, and they're not on their own either, there're two other men with them."

"Go on then, tell me who are they?" Bene explained who the four men were.

"You remembered two of them, the one who smells is called Gordon Brooks and the one sitting next to him is his brother Alfie, a real nasty piece of work. The other two are men I haven't seen for a long time and they're brothers as well, Eugene and Manny Reay. They own Oceans night club and the cinema next door in Levensbridge."

Bene went on to explain about the owners of Oceans, and how he'd arrested them for drug dealing and seen them both jailed.

"My, they're a real tasty bunch then; do you think they saw you?"

"I don't know they could have done, I only noticed them when you pointed them out so I can't be sure, but what the hell are the four of them doing on this boat? I didn't even know they knew each other but it looks as if they've formed some sort of alliance. With their backgrounds I suppose I shouldn't be surprised because they do have a lot in common. But why would they be going to Ireland? Whatever the reason it won't be legitimate that's for sure. When we get to Dublin we'll go straight to the Garda and I'll alert them, they can put a tail on where they go and find out what they're up to."

They managed to avoid contact with the four villains for the remainder of the journey, once in the car and off the ferry they drove straight to the Garda HQ in Phoenix Park. They reported their arrival at the desk and alerted them to the arrival in Ireland of the two sets of brothers. Then it was off to find the makers of the clothing which had been found on the body. The desk sergeant was helpful and directed them to a well-known gentleman's outfitter who may be able to help them.

The premises of Aiden Byrne were easily found and the manager was happy to assist them. Bene showed him the photos of the jacket and the label.

"Ah yes, this is one I remember well; their suits and jackets were top quality and very popular for a while, albeit rather expensive. They were a good firm to work for you know, they paid top wages to their workforce and the materials they used were very expensive, so of course their overheads were extremely high. Being quite a small business and unable to mass-produce proved in the end to be their downfall and sadly they went out of business altogether. It was a pity because I did like their clothes."

"Will we be able to find out where this was sold?" Bene showed him the photo of the label again and the one showing the jacket.

"I know it's in poor condition, but the colour and design may help to identity it."

The manager looked at the photos.

"Well, they went out of business a few years ago so no-one will have any of their stock left, but they did supply a few shops around the country. They had a shop here in Dublin back then but their biggest customer was Conrad Lynch, and they have shops in most of the major towns. You could try them I suppose, they may have kept records; their main shop is here in Dublin, not far from here." The manager handed back the photos.

"Would you be able to give us a list of addresses for Conrad Lynch; it'll save us having to look them up because I know they won't all be in the phone book."

"Of course, give me a couple of minutes I think I've got something back here."

Five minutes later he appeared with a glossy advert for the firm and listed on it were the addresses of all their branches in Ireland. Thanking the manager they left the shop and walked back to the car.

"Let's have a look at the list Hils and see how we can plan our route."

Apart from the shop in Dublin there were another seven shops scattered around the country.

"We'll start here of course, and being the largest one we could strike gold right away; come on we'll walk round, it's not far."

The manager of Conrad Lynch was busy with a customer when they entered the shop but a few minutes later he was free to speak to them. Bene showed him the photos and asked if he recognised the jacket. The manager studied the photos.

"Yes we did stock that one and it was a good seller, but finding the person who bought this particular one could be difficult. We're talking ten years ago or maybe more; this style was around from about 2002 until 2010 and people bought them in a variety of ways, some with cash, some with cheques and some by card. But maybe we could narrow it down a bit. Wait here a moment I need to check something. He left them waiting for a few minutes before returning with a small brochure.

"Now let me see that photo again." The manager put on his glasses and looked closely at the photo and the brochure looking for a match.

"Yes, have a look at this it might help you; you see the manufacturer's name on the label in your photo, it's done in a green and orange striped effect. I remember that was one of the odd things this company did. Every year they changed the colour of the name on the labels in their clothing. I think it had something to do with the guarantee; if someone returned the garment under guarantee they could check the year of manufacturer by this means to see how old it was. No-one else did that back then but it was a good idea."

"So in which year would this jacket have been sold?" The manager referred to his brochure.

"It was made in 2010 and would probably have been sold the same year or possibly the following year, but it's one of the last ones made because that's the year I think they went out of business."

The manager smiled, feeling satisfied and rather smug that he'd been able to turn detective for them. Bene smiled in return.

"Now that is good news; it narrows it down a lot. Have you any idea how many you sold in that period?" The manager kept his smile going.

"I can tell you exactly how many we sold, none, we didn't sell any. Our owner Mr Lynch did all the ordering for his shops and he stopped buying from them in 2010. He felt they were becoming too expensive and we were having difficulty selling them, there was little or no profit in them anymore. The last stock he bought from them went to some of his other shops, but not this one. But I don't know which ones you'd have to ask them yourself."

"Would Mr Lynch remember?"

"No I'm afraid not, he passed away two years ago and it's his son running the business now. He's not a great one for records and only keeps the ones relating to the last few years of business; the one's required of him by the tax and revenue people. I'm afraid you'll have a bit of running around to do if you want to find your man."

Bene and Hils thanked him and left him to serve a new customer.

"Well it's something Hils, but it looks like we're not going home early, let's have a look at that map and see where we go first."

The large map of Ireland was laid out on the bonnet of the car.

"I think we'll have to plan on going to all of them, and if we get done sooner we can cut off and go home. Wicklow isn't too far so we'll try there first, then we can go over to Kilkenny and that'll be all we'll get done today. The next one will be Cork and that's a long way down, we can start there tomorrow OK?" Hils agreed.

"Do you want to drive Hils and I'll navigate."

"It's not the Middle Ages you know, we do have satnav."

"Alright then, so you'd rather trust that thing than my directions?"

"Yes, every time."

The three o'clock news had just started when they pulled up outside the shop in Wicklow and once inside they found it devoid of customers and staff. They waited a minute or two for someone to come to the counter but no-one did. Just as Hils went to look behind it a young man burst through the door, coffee in one hand and a phone in the other. He finished his call immediately and put the coffee down on the counter.

"Sorry about that, the kettles not working and I've had nothing to drink all day. How can I help you? Is it a fitting or ready-made you're looking for sir?"

Bene showed his card and explained the reason for their call.

"2010 that's a long time ago, Mr O'Dowd isn't in today or he would have known right away, he knows all his customers, I've only been here a few months." He looked at them vacantly.

"Maybe," Hils said. "If that's the case you could phone him or give us his address, we could ask him ourselves if he's got that good a memory."

"I'll phone him, he did say I could if there was a problem, I don't think he'll mind."

The assistant went over to use the shop phone and spoke to his boss, the call didn't last long and the young man came back smiling.

"That was easy, Mr O'Dowd said we didn't sell any of those jackets that year, this wasn't one of the shops that got stock from them in 2010. He said we stopped selling them in 2009."

Hils thanked him for the information and they left and returned to the car.

"Well two down and six to go, maybe we'll have better luck with the next one; if so we can get back to Dublin and catch the overnight ferry. Do you want me to drive again Bene?"

"Yes if you want to, but it could take a couple of hours so you'd better step on it. In the meantime I'll phone ahead and see if they'll stay open a bit later in case we get held up."

Hils didn't hold back and they made good time all the way down the M11 until they reached Enniscorthy and the turn off for Kilkenny. The roads from that point were not as good and they were held up several times by tractors and an assortment of other large vehicles. Bene checked his watch and estimated it would be six o'clock when they eventually got to Kilkenny. He phoned again to explain the delay and to make sure someone would still be there. At last they pulled up in the middle of the delightful little town of Kilkenny and saw the manager standing outside his shop waiting to greet them.

"Come on in folks, and you can leave the car there it'll be alright, the wardens have finished for the day. Now let me see if I can help you, can I have a look at your photos."

He looked at them closely and breathed heavily.

"Yes, we did have a couple of those." He looked up at Bene. "And you want to know who I sold them to, is that right?"

"Would you still have a record of the sales?"

"Better than that I can tell you, but why do you want to know will the customer get into trouble over this, I mean it's a long time ago."

"No, no trouble at all. We're trying to trace the owner of this particular jacket because he was wearing it when he died over in England and we're trying to find out who he was; this is the only clue we have."

"Alright, so you say the owner of this jacket is dead?" He looked to Bene and Hils for confirmation which they gave.

"Well I only had a couple, but they were far too expensive and I couldn't sell them. I kept them for a few months but I still couldn't shift them. In the end I offloaded one to my brother-in-law at cost price just to get rid of it, the other one I returned to the manufacturer and got a refund. My brother-in-law is still here and still has the jacket so I'm afraid you haven't found your answer here. Good luck with your search though, where are you going next?

"We'll stay here tonight and go down to Cork in the morning and try there." said Bene.

"Ah Cork is it, well maybe I can help you there I know the manager very well. So if you're staying the night here in Kilkenny pop into the shop tomorrow morning before you go and I'll give him a call; you never know it might save you a long journey."

They left with a promise to call and see him in the morning.

"Right Hils that's three down and five to go and with a bit of luck maybe just four, anyway that's it for today let's go and find somewhere to stay for the night."

They booked into a small hotel near the town centre and after a quick freshen up they met for dinner downstairs in the small but comfortable dining room. They were both a bit disappointed with the day's events which hadn't given them any leads, but Hils was the more optimistic of the two.

"At least we've got some of them out of the way and we're a lot better off knowing there were only a few of these sold. The manager in Dublin was a diamond telling us about the different colour name tags on the labels. If we hadn't known that we'd have had a hell of a job checking on all the jackets sold over a ten year period. It's narrowed our search down a lot and I'm confident we're going to strike gold in one of these last shops."

Bene phoned Alex and told her all about their day in Ireland, and seeing the two sets of brothers on the ferry which surprised her as much as it had him earlier. He told her their plans for the next day and hoped he'd be back home by Thursday at the latest. Alex informed him that another letter had been put through the door; they hadn't touched it and would leave it for him when he got back, it was similar to the first one and most likely another hoax.

The two detectives met again in the dining room the following morning and happily tucked into a full Irish breakfast before leaving for the shop on High Street. The manager was already there and bursting with news for them.

"Good morning both. I've done some phoning around and come up with some good news for you. There's no need to go to Cork because the shop there never received an order from the company; the manager told me that Mr Lynch only bought a few of these particular jackets and they only went to three of his shops. Two of them came here; two went up to his shop in Athlone and another two to the shop in Dundalk."

Hils went over and kissed him on the cheek.

"I told Bene you were my hero and you've just proved it, that's brilliant news and you've saved us a lot of time and travelling, thank you so much."

The manager blushed and went rather coy.

"Well I don't know that I deserved all that, but I'm pleased I've been able help, and I hope you find what you're looking for in one of the other two shops."

They thanked him again and were extremely relieved; it had narrowed down their search even more.

Back in the car they started the long journey up to Athlone. Bene took over driving duties for the first part of the journey, and if they had time Hils would finish the trip up to Dundalk later in the day. They were a bit more relaxed knowing their tour of Ireland had been shortened. During their brief time in the country they'd been seduced by the small but lively market towns and the pretty little villages they'd driven through on their way around the island. Bene was already making holiday plans. "I'll have to come back again and bring Alex with me; it's beautiful over here isn't it?" Hils had to agree.

The journey to Athlone via the N77 took them almost two hours, but once they arrived they had no difficulty in finding the large shop on Church Street which stood out amid an assortment of smaller ones in the bustling town centre. Bene managed to find a car park within easy reach of the centre and parked there; they walked back along the main street and entered the premises of Conrad Lynch. The manager approached and the officers produced their warrant cards, much to the amusement of the manager.

"I don't think those will help you over here." He said smiling. "But anyway how can I help, it's not a suit you've come in for is it?"

Bene explained the reason for their visit and showed the manager the photo of the jacket. The manager took a quick look at it and sighed.

"Ah this takes me back seeing something like that again. They were good sellers at one time and very popular up here, but over the last year or so they became too expensive for my customers. I wasn't at all surprised when I heard the business had gone bust. But to answer your question I never managed to sell the ones Conrad sent me, I kept them for a while but in the end I had to send them both back." He handed the photo back to Bene.

"I'm sorry but I can't help you, you could try the other shops though, they may have stocked them."

"We already have and your shop here and the one in Dundalk are the last two, as we've drawn a blank here Dundalk is our last chance."

"By all means try our shop up there, but while you're in Dundalk you should check out the old factory shop as well because that's where these jackets were made."

"They were made in Dundalk?" said Bene looking surprised.

"Yes that's where the factory was, and they did sell from the factory shop so that's probably your best bet, if it's still open of course. They've been out of business for a few years mind, but it might be worth giving them a try you could be lucky."

Hils looked at her watch.

"It's almost eleven thirty so we've got time to grab something here to eat and drink on the way up, if we leave about twelve we should get there about two or just after. I think it's my turn so I'll get these, is coffee and a sandwich alright?"

"Yes but no sugar and nothing spicy, cheese and tomato or egg and cress will be fine."

Hils ran over to the sandwich bar and brought the order back.

"You want me to drive?"

"Yes, but just for the first bit while I eat this, then I'll take over and let you have yours."

There didn't appear to be a preferred route. Taking the M6 to Dublin and then up the M1 to Dundalk was a hundred and twenty five miles; the shorter route was only ninety five but meant travelling on some minor roads. They couldn't see how either would get them to Dundalk any quicker so decided to take the shorter but more picturesque route. It was a little after two o'clock when they eventually arrived in the town and luckily parking was easy to find. They walked around to find the shop which according to the address they had was in the new shopping centre. The centre was quite small and the shop wasn't difficult to find.

On entering Hils asked to see the manager and a youngish man of about thirty appeared. Hils and Bene showed their cards but he didn't seem at all impressed.

"Well it can't be police business because you've no jurisdiction over here, so what is it you're after?

"It's connected to something we're looking into back home, and what we want to know is if you sold any jackets like this back in 2010?" Hils produced the photo of the jacket and handed it to him. The manager looked at it and smiled.

"This is a joke is it?"

"No of course not, I'm deadly serious, we're trying to find out who sold this particular jacket and get the name of the customer who bought it, and you're probably our last chance. We know Mr Lynch sent two of them to this shop and we need to know who bought them. The man who was wearing this one is dead and we're trying to find out who he was."

"Hmm alright then, well you wouldn't know of course but Mr Lynch made a big mistake with those jackets and he should have known better. There was no way we could sell them because they were made right here in Dundalk and they were selling them in their own shop. No-one would buy them from us if they could get the same one a lot cheaper in the factory shop so we just sent them back, I'm sorry."

"Is the factory shop still open then?"

"No, it closed down a couple of years ago when the stock ran out, but you could have a word with old Jimmy across the road there. He worked in the shop for years and I'm sure he kept hold of all the old ledgers and such; you might find what you're looking for in there."

"Whereabouts across the road can we find him?"

"In the pub of course, he's always there in the afternoons and he's your best bet. I have to go now we have customers in, but good luck."

Sure enough Jimmy was well-known in the pub and the two had no difficulty in finding a seat near him; he was drinking with two of his pals. Bene wanted to ask for his help so he offered to buy the company a drink. Jimmy wasn't going to turn the offer down and readily accepted.

"Aye good lad, it's pints for the three of us."

Bene got up and went to the bar to order pints for the three men and a drink for Hils and himself. Hils remained at the table and found it easy to get into conversation with Jimmy.

"And what is it you want from me lass?"

"We were told that you worked over there in the factory shop and we want to know if you remember something from back then. Is there somewhere we can talk that's a bit quieter?"

"Aye, but it will cost you another pint."

He chuckled to himself as he rose from the table and moved to another one near the door.

Bene came back and left two drinks on the table for Jimmy's friends and set the other three down on the table Hils and Jimmy had moved to.

"What is it exactly you're wanting from me?"

"The manager in Conrad Lynch told us you may still have a record of clothes that were sold in the factory shop."

"Yes I do and I can recall many of them, and those I can't remember I can easily look up. Any particular garment you're interested in?"

Hils showed him the photo of the jacket and told him the story of the man who'd been wearing it.

"Aye, that shouldn't be too much of a problem but I'll need to do some checks first. If you'd like to stay here I'll be back in ten minutes or so, and if you have another pint waiting and a whiskey chaser, that will do my memory a power of good."

Old Jimmy left them in the pub while he went off to do his checks.

"Do you think he'll come back Bene?"

"If there's a chance of more free drinks it's a certainty."

Jimmy didn't disappoint and was back with them in less than ten minutes. He sat down at the table and took a draught of his beer before opening the ledger he'd brought back with him.

"I think this is what you wanted. Now 2010 was a bad year for us, the company closed down and twenty five good men lost their jobs, me included. But when I look through here it's no surprise that it did go bust. We didn't do much business at all that year and some of the lads thought it was all down to the change in the new colours they were putting on the labels. Orange and green together does not go down too well in Ireland as you well know, and they say that was the reason for the drop in sales. But that was only the half of it, I mean the stuff was getting far too expensive and folks couldn't afford to buy it and that was the real reason. Anyway, it's this particular jacket you're interested in?"

Jimmy pointed to the photo they'd shown him.

"I can tell you we didn't make many of them; we'd barely made a few dozen before the place closed down. They were a good jacket alright but they just didn't sell; we weren't having much luck with them here so most of the stock was sent over to America. According to my records we only sold four in the factory shop, and you said your man was dead didn't you. Well that makes it easy because I still see three of the men who bought this jacket from the shop, so that just leaves the other one, am I right?"

"Yes." they both replied.

"And you want to know who that fourth man was?"

"Yes we do, can you give us a name Jimmy?"

"Aye of course I can, I told you I would have it."

"Go on then tell us."

Jimmy finished his drink and put the empty glass down on the table looking up expectantly.

"Don't worry Jimmy there's another one coming up."

Bene brought another pint and a chaser back to the table and put them down in front of the old man and sat down waiting for a name.

"Come on then Jimmy let's have it?"

Jimmy took another drink and seemed happy to tell them what they wanted.

"Finnian Brennan is the man you're looking for. He has a house on Jermaine Street near the river, but he hasn't been seen for a long time and as far as I know the house is empty."

"That's great Jimmy, do you know the number?"

"Aye it's number seventeen, and if that's all you'll be wanting I'll go back and join my pals."

Jimmy left the table and took his drinks with him.

"Wow that looks like our man Bene doesn't it? He's called Brennan, so the name's right."

"Yes it does, but I'd still like to check it out first, we'll go up to the house and have a look."

They finished their drinks and left the pub. As they walked out of the door two well-dressed men who'd been sitting at the far side of the room got up from their table and took their drinks over to join Jimmy's and his pals. A few seconds later the two men and Jimmy moved to a separate table to continue their conversation.

The satnav took them up to Jermaine Street and they parked at the end of the road. Walking along they had to count the houses as most were named but not numbered until they arrived at number seventeen. Looking up at the house it had all the appearance of being lived in.

"Has that old bugger been having us on just to cadge a few drinks out of us?" Hils asked.

"It looks like it doesn't it? I'll knock and see if anyone comes."

Bene knocked on the door and a smart middle aged woman came and answered it.

"Yes, what is it now; the two of you look a bit lost?"

"I'm sorry to bother you but we were told this house was empty, we were just checking but it seems we've been misled, I'm sorry about that."

"Are you looking for a place to buy then?"

"No we're looking for someone who lives at number seventeen and we were told the house was empty, but it obviously isn't because you live here."

The lady laughed.

"Well you're right and you're wrong as well. I do live here, but number seventeen is next door love and the house is empty alright and has been for years."

"But we counted the houses up the street and this should be seventeen."

"Maybe so, but you're forgetting we don't have a number thirteen, it's unlucky isn't it?"

"Of course, can you tell us who owns the house then?"

"Well as far as I know it's not been sold, so the man who lived there up until a few years ago will still be the owner, but we haven't seen him around here for years. To be honest he never really lived in it much because he worked away and only came back for the odd week-end."

"Do you know his name?"

"Yes it's Finnian Brennan, and he was a bank manager at the Southern Irish Bank in Ballydonal. But that bank closed down a long time ago, I expect he got moved to another one somewhere and he's living there now, but I've no idea where."

"That's OK," said Bene "it's given us somewhere to start; we'll contact the bank and see if we can find him that way. Thanks for your help, goodbye."

The lady called them back as they were preparing to leave.

"I don't know why, but you're the second lot I've had here today looking for him."

Bene and Hils turned around surprised. Hils asked.

"Do you know who they were?"

"No, there were two of them and like you they were English; one of them whiffed a bit so I stood well back from them I can tell you."

"So they'll know where to find this Finnian now?"

"I expect so because I told them the same as I've told you. Anyway, good luck to you and I hope you find him first. That pair looked a bit too mean for my liking I wouldn't want them coming looking for me."

Bene and Hils left Jermaine Street rather more worried than they had been minutes earlier.

"Never mind Hils, we'll call at the bank in Dublin and make enquiries there."

Before he could finish his phone rang. It was Adam Firth.

"Bene I've just heard there's been another shooting, and I heard the name Vince Downie mentioned, is that right or is it not public knowledge yet?"

"Yes its right, but keep it under your hat Adam. If the media get hold of it they'll cause a panic and put the police under even more pressure, and to be honest I don't think they can cope with any more."

"OK will do, but there's something you should know about this Vince chap. I didn't know him myself but I've found out something about him. Now he wasn't a bowler and I know he lived out at Stainbeck, but he was a good friend of Willie Jameson and Robin Mitchell so there is a connection you see. Oh and don't forget I've got Alex again tomorrow but don't worry she'll be fine."

Bene had just finished the call and put the phone back in his pocket when it rang again, this time it was ET.

"Bene some good news at last, they've arrested someone."

"Oh great, that's a relief, who is he?"

"It's that lad David Anderson, the son of the guy in prison up in Scotland, the one you were going to look for before this lot took over. They've charged him with the murder of Arnold Bainbridge for starters and they're trying to nail him for the other murders as well. With a bit of luck we'll soon be rid of this lot, and we can get back to running our own station again."

"Yeah that's brilliant news; we should be back tomorrow so I'll see you then for a catch up."

"How's it going over there boss, are you making any progress with it?"

"We've got a good lead but we need to check it out first, I'll tell you all about it tomorrow."

Bene gave Hils the news of the arrest and told her their plans for the rest of the day.

"I think we'll have to get back to Dublin and see the Garda. If we're going into a head office bank they'll need to sanction it and make an appointment for us. We'll have to tell them what we've got so far and how it ties in with the body back home and hope they'll agree to us interviewing the manager about this Finnian Brennan. I don't think there's any chance they'll let us interview him on our own I expect they'll insist on one of their own men going in with us." Bene got out his phone. "The bank will be shut by the time we get to Dublin so I'll phone them now and see if they can arrange an interview for tomorrow morning."

Bene contacted the Garda to explain his request and didn't have long to wait for his answer. They had no objection as long as they were accompanied in the interview by one of their own officers. Ten minutes later a second call told them the interview had been scheduled for eleven o'clock the following morning and an Inspector would be there to meet them at the bank's headquarters. The manager confirmed that Finnian Brennan hadn't been seen since a month prior to the bank's closure.

"Tell you what Bene, we've nothing else to do here so on the way down to Dublin why don't we stop off at Ballydonal and see what sort of a place it is; maybe some of the folk there can tell us about this Finnian?"

"Yeah that's a good idea, get the map out and see where it is."

Minutes later Hils had found the town and the route to take them there.

"Got it, it's about thirty or forty minutes' drive, and not too far off the beaten track?"

It didn't take them long to drive down and find Ballydonal, once there they pulled up in the small town square and parked the car; the square was almost deserted.

"OK," said Bene "let's get out and see who's around that we can talk to; it's a bit quiet though there's not many people about?"

An elderly couple appeared and crossed the square towards them, Bene greeted them.

"Hi there, we're sorry to bother you but are you resident here?" The old man answered him.

"Yes all our lives we've lived here, are you interested in our little town or are you just lost?"

"No we're not lost; we're trying to find the man who managed the bank here a few years ago before it closed. I wonder if you remember him."

The old man chuckled.

"Aye we do that, Finnian Brennan's the man you want but you won't find him here, he left the town years ago barely a week or so before the bank closed down, and under a bit of a cloud I'd say?"

"How was that then?"

"He just disappeared and was never seen again; one day he was there the next gone. He left a young lad and a lassie on their own to run it until a temporary manager could be found. Finnian never came back, and when the bank closed down the two young'uns were moved to Dublin. He was a dry old stick that Finnian, no humour in him at all. Nobody ever found out what happened to him or where he went. There was no warning or anything like that; he just up and off and left those youngsters high and dry. They did find a letter he'd received from the head office telling him about the bank closing, but he hadn't passed that information on to them. Nah, it was a queer going on that and nobody around here could understand it. And that bank's a big miss you know, there's only the post office here now."

"Well thanks for that," said Bene "we'll have to try Dublin maybe they'll know where he is."

"Aye, well if you do find him don't tell him we were asking after him because he's no great miss around here." The couple turned away and continued over the square towards the shops.

"No point in staying here Bene let's crack on to Dublin and get some digs for the night."

They found a nice little hotel fairly close to the centre and met for dinner at seven o'clock.

"Nice rooms here Bene, is yours OK?"

"Yeah good enough, I'm just thinking about tomorrow at the bank, maybe we'll find out what happened to Finnian. It must have been something fishy just disappearing like that; I think we can safely say that the man found in Longbarrow was Finnian Brennan. I've phoned Sowerby and he's delighted; with us giving him a name for the body and the murders cleared up he's mightily relieved. Of course our job isn't finished yet; we still need to know why Finnian went over to England and who killed him. Hopefully tomorrow's interview will give us some indication as to why he left in such a hurry."

The following morning saw them down for the usual full Irish breakfast. Bene sighed.

"I'm going to miss these when we get back home; it'll be porridge or cornflakes tomorrow."

"Me as well, but it might just be a coffee it depends what time I get up. There's nothing to do just now is there? I think I'll go out for a walk and get some fresh air."

She left the hotel and Bene picked up one of the daily papers in the foyer and sat down in the residents lounge to read it. Hils returned an hour later and joined him.

"You know that car we tried to trace a few days ago, the one we couldn't get an owner for?"

"Yes"

"It's just driven past here."

"So, someone is following us around. I wonder what they're up to, are they onto Finnian Brennan as well? First they were in Longbarrow asking questions and now here in Dublin. I wonder if they've been up to Dundalk as well. I did notice two smartly dressed men in that pub up there and I thought they looked a bit out of place; we'll have to watch our backs Hils."

At eleven o'clock they met up with the Garda officer and went in together to see the bank manager Mr McGrath who greeted them in his office. The Garda officer introduced them.

"Right how can I help you?" asked the manager.

Bene went on to relate the full story of the body at Longbarrow and their investigation into the death and identification of the man who they now believed to be Finnian Brennan, a branch manager for the Southern Irish Bank in Ballydonal.

"What we'd like to know is why he left Ireland to go over to England, and who would have wanted him dead?"

"Well, there is a story of course," said the manager "and I know part of it but not all, but I'll tell you what I do know. Mr Brennan had been with us for many years, most of them as manager in our branch in Ballydonal as you've discovered. He left us suddenly and without warning back in June 2012 a few weeks before the branch was due to close. The reason became clear when the branch closed and all the accounts and money were transferred over here. Our auditors went through everything and discovered many discrepancies which Mr Brennan had kept from us. Cash was missing, pensions and insurances had been tampered with, and the account of his main customer had been systematically siphoned over the years on a regular basis. So it's quite plain to see why he disappeared. If he'd stayed until the closure of the bank all this would have come to light and he would now be in jail. We calculated how much he had stolen from us, but we never did find out what happened to him or where he went; he just disappeared into thin air."

"Can you tell us who the main account holder was who lost all this money?"

"Yes, just a minute."

Mr McGrath sifted through some paperwork on his desk until he found the right account.

"I remember the customer clearly because they closed the account a week later, and we were thankful that they did. It was a company called EMR UK, a flexible account with the owners based over in the UK. We never knew how much had been in the account or how much Mr Brennan had taken from it as the payments were in cash of varying amounts and paid in on an irregular basis. It was a strange arrangement which appeared to have been set up between the manager and the account holder. It wasn't one of our recognised accounts and that was why we couldn't perform an accurate audit trail on it; in fact it was not only highly irregular it was illegal." The manager closed the file.

Something that had been bothering Bene for a while suddenly became a lot clearer. He nodded to Hils, a sign that he'd explain later. The manager continued.

"There was something else rather strange about the affair because I've had two other gentlemen in here recently asking me about something concerning that particular branch."

"What was that Mr McGrath?" Bene was curious.

"For some reason the bank in Ballydonal was chosen many years ago during the last war I believe, by someone who deposited a package he wanted kept safe. He paid a good fee for this service and told the bank it may be a year or so before it was redeemed. It had clear instructions written on to say it had been paid for in Dublin and was to be held in the bank at Ballydonal, until such time as Mr J S O'Halloran would call to collect it. Now as far as I know no-one ever did collect it, but when the vaults were checked the package wasn't there."

"So you think Mr Brennan took that as well?"

"He must have done, because he was the only one who had access to the vaults on his own, the other clerks could only go down there if he was with them."

"And you say you've had people in here asking about it?"

"That's right; they were officials working for some government office in London."

"You've told them what you've just told us then?"

"That's correct, they said I should tell no-one about it, but as you're looking into a murder I thought it only right that you should know as well. But if you happen to meet them I'd be obliged if you didn't mention where you got the information from."

"No, they'll be no need for that we'll keep it to ourselves, so if that's all I think we need to get back home and continue our enquiries there."

The three officers thanked the bank manager and left the building.

The Garda officer returned to his headquarters and Bene and Hils to their hotel.

"What are you going to tell me about that company Bene?"

"I can see now why the Reay brothers are over here, EMR UK is their company and that's the account Finnian has been stealing money from. No wonder they want to find him, they want to get their money back."

"And what about the other two men who were with them, what's their interest in it?"

"I don't know, I haven't had time to figure that one out yet, but whatever it is there'll be nothing innocent about it that's for sure. That Alfie Brooks is beginning to scare me, when we get back home I'm going to speak to old Donald and press him for a bit more information about him."

"Another thing Bene, those two men who were in the bank enquiring about that package, I bet they're the same two who've been following us around. What's so important about that package that the government are involved! To tell you the truth I'm sensing danger and I'm getting bad vibes about it. I don't know about you, but I think we'll have to be careful how we handle this from now on."

"Yes I've got the same feeling, there's a dangerous game being played out here and I think we're merely the pawns in it. Those Reay brothers are no strangers to violence and what I've heard about the Brooks brothers doesn't paint them as angels either. On top of that we now have government agents involved and God knows what they're capable of. I've a horrible feeling it's all going to come together at some point and there'll be a major conflict and even more deaths, and we're right in the middle of it."

"I think you're right, but we can't give up, can we?"

Bene sat quietly with his thoughts. This latest development had changed the whole aspect of their investigation. In his estimation Hils had proved herself beyond any doubt and become a good partner as well as a good friend. But the last thing he wanted to do was expose her to any kind of real danger. He thought he might have to let her go and get ET to take over, but he'd have to be careful how he put this over.

"We've done a great job so far Hils, we've achieved an awful lot and we should be pleased with ourselves, I know Inspector Sowerby will be. But it could get really nasty now, and as ET is finished with division he'll be back with us again. So if you'd rather finish this off when we get back tomorrow it'll be alright and I'll get ET to take over. But hey, you've done a great job and I'm going to recommend you to Sowerby, I'm sure it won't be too long before we're working together again."

Hils face distorted into anger.

"What!! Are you dumping me?"

"No, I'm merely saying that we've worked well together and we make a good team. You've done a brilliant job and absolutely proved yourself, and when we get back I'm going to recommend to Sowerby that we keep you on. But as we've just agreed it's going to get a lot tougher now. I can sense danger and I don't want to put you in a situation where you could get hurt that's all."

Hils jumped up and turned on him sharply, and did she let rip.

"Well I'm not bloody going! Both you and Sowerby said I could get to stay if I did alright, and I'm not going to throw all that away just because we're coming up against some nasty villainous bastards. If you don't want me to stay and help you I'll have to go, but I'm not bloody leaving by choice so there!" She sat back down heavily with a face like thunder.

"Alright, alright, calm down I was just checking to make sure you were OK with it. To tell you the truth I'm pleased you want to stay because I know I can rely on you. So whatever it takes we're going to see it through, yes?

Bene beamed and she melted.

"Yeah great, and I'm sorry about the outburst," adding "you bastard." Then she laughed.

"Right let's get back home," said Bene "and we'll pick it up from there. And we're not going to stop until we get to the bottom of it and find out what this is all about."

Chapter 29

The chase is on

It was nine in the evening when they got back home. The long journey had been tiring and Bene wanted to rest, but Alex wasn't interested in that she wanted to tell him about her bowling that afternoon.

"It was good again, Adam and Simon coached us for the first hour and then the four of us had a game, Simon and Nicola took on Adam and me, and guess what we beat them. It was a lot nicer today there was a much better atmosphere around the place; I think catching the murderer has eased all the tension that we noticed last week. We might go down at the week-end and have a bit of practice if that's OK with you?"

"Yeah that's good, I'm pleased you're enjoying it and you seem to have found a good friend in Nicola, and as long as I don't become a bowls' widower I'm all in favour of it."

"Good, now we've got that sorted you can tell me about Ireland and Hils?"

"It was quite exhausting because we were on the go the whole time. We did an awful lot of travelling but it was well worth it with what we found out. And Hils was a godsend I couldn't have done it without her, she came up with some great ideas and saved us loads of time.

She's cheerful, good company and a reliable partner. She'll make a good detective and I'm sure Sowerby will promote her. Oh, and I have to tell you Alex Ireland is a beautiful place I think we should go there on holiday and do a grand tour, what do you think?"

"Yes, if it's as nice as you say it is I'm up for it, maybe when this case is finished eh?"

In the morning Bene met Hils at the station and together they went in to report to Inspector Sowerby, they were sure he'd be pleased with the news. Going into the main office they were surprised to see it was still under the command of division. Bene expected they might have left someone behind to clear things up, but he didn't expect anyone from division would still be working there.

"What's with this lot sir, are there a few loose ends to tie up?"

Sowerby shook his head.

"You wouldn't believe what a cock up they're making of it; they've only gone and arrested the wrong man. They kept him here for most of the day and then had to release him through lack of evidence; the guy came up with a cast iron alibi. They eventually tracked him down in Scotland trying to see his dad again in prison, but there was no way he could have shot Arnold Bainbridge because he'd been on a course down in Milton Keynes with a dozen or so others as witnesses."

"Why did they arrest him then?"

"All they had to go on was what ET had told them; that before they took over it was you who was going down to Fleetwood to check him out. We had nothing concrete on him, but because of the threats he'd made in prison to avenge his dad we needed to speak to him and that was all. At the time the lad would be in a highly emotional state and probably made the threats in the heat of the moment. There was no evidence to suggest he did know who had framed his dad or even if it was true, and nothing to say he would have carried out his threats. Division combined all that with the fact he'd left home in an angry mood, and to them that was a sign of his guilt and enough for them to arrest him. They found the lad alright and brought him back here and quizzed him for hours. With all this going on the lad became upset and too confused to remember where he'd been on that day, and because they were putting all this pressure on him his mind just went numb. He was here for hours before they let him phone home, but as soon as he spoke to his mother she provided an alibi for him straight away. She told them he'd been in Milton Keynes on a course, and when they contacted the college it was confirmed by his tutor and other members of the group who'd been there. So that was that, they had to let him go last night."

Sowerby threw his arms up in the air.

"The only redeeming factor is this fiasco is down to them and not us thank goodness. Anyway, tell me about this Brennan fellow, I know you've kept me up to date with everything in Ireland, but tell me where we are now and what comes next."

Bene briefly went over everything they'd found out in Ireland, and then proceeded to tell him their plans for the next stage of the investigation.

"Firstly, I'd like to have another chat with Donald Neves and see if there's anything else he can tell me about Alfie Brooks, and if he has any idea why he'd be going to Ireland. Then there are the Reay brothers; we now know their interest in Brennan is the money he stole from them. But there must be something fishy about the fact they were banking in Ireland and using an account that was illegal. It wasn't registered in the banks head office and only came to their attention after Brennan disappeared. The auditors couldn't make head or tail of it and the manager in Dublin has no idea how much had been in the account or how much Brennan had taken from it. Then on top of that, there're those two men from London who've been following us around, I think their interest is in the package that Brennan took from the bank vaults. Whatever it contains it must be highly confidential and damaging to someone high up to warrant the involvement of government agents. And finally of course, there's the murder of Finnian Brennan. Did someone follow him over from Ireland and kill him or was there someone waiting for him over here; that's the tricky one and something we may never find out. So to sum it up we need to find out what Alfie Brooks' interest in this is? What Finnian Brennan did with the package and the money? And who killed him?

"OK Bene thanks for that, so are you keeping Hils with you, or do I let you have ET back now he's finished here?"

This was the moment of truth for Hils.

"I think it best if Hils and I carry on with this sir. She knows as much as I do, she's proved over the last week she's capable of seeing it through, and it will be better than bringing ET in cold."

"Right, off you go then and don't forget to keep me in touch."

They rose to leave the office.

"I'd like a quick word before you go Bene. It's OK Hils you can go Bene will catch up with you." Hils left the office.

"How is she Bene will she be alright with this, she knows the risks I suppose?"

"Yes sir, she's done really well and she'll be a great asset to the team if you decide to keep her on. She's made for this job and it would be a great pity to waste all the talent she's shown me this last week. I have no doubts about her; she's proved to be a good and reliable partner."

"OK, that's good enough for me, don't waste any more time then, and don't forget to call me if you need any help."

Hils was waiting outside.

"That was about me, wasn't it?"

"Yes, and don't worry I gave you a good reference, now let's find out where the little Scotsman lives."

The found Donald at home and he looked rather puzzled as he answered the door to them.

"Aye and what's this now that you've come knocking on my door?"

Bene introduced Hils and Donald invited them into his cottage.

"If it's more on Alfie Brooks you're wanting then I haven't seen him these past days; he never turned up at the pub and I've no idea where he'll be."

"No, it's alright Donald we know where he's been; we've just come back from Ireland and who did we see on the ferry going over there and again in Ireland, none other than Alfie and Gordon Brooks. We wondered if you've any idea why they'd want to go to Ireland."

"No idea at all, the man's a mystery and I've no wish to pry into any of his affairs thank you very much."

"Do you know the Reay brothers Donald, Eugene and Manny?"

"I know of them but have never been conversant with them, why do you ask?"

"They went over there with Alfie and Gordon, so we figured that whatever it was they were doing in Ireland they were up to no good, and you've no idea what that could be?"

"No, I'm sorry lad I canna help you any more with that, what I told you the other day was all I know about Alfie Brooks and I've no desire to know any more about the man."

Bene was getting no more from Donald, but he wanted to keep him as a contact and on a friendly basis. "I remember dining up at old Andrew McLean's place one night and what a good meal you made for us?"

This seemed to throw the little man as if he didn't want to be reminded of his time there.

"You were up there were you, dining with that old bugger?" He laughed and Bene continued.

"I remember him teasing you, giving you the sack and all that nonsense, but you seem to have come out of it alright. Did Andrew keep his word about leaving you the house?"

Donald smiled and chuckled at the memory.

"I'm sorry, but my memory is not what it was, there were a lot of dinner parties up there and so many folk

I canna remember them all. But aye, Andrew was true to his word and left me the house and his money, and those two nephews of his were sorely disappointed; you should have seen their faces when the will was read out."

"Old Andrew will be laughing in his grave I expect, and from what I've heard about his nephews they never had much time for him when he was alive, so they probably got what they deserved, nothing. Oh and by the way my wife is still looking for a dog, so if you hear of one like yours that we could buy I'd be grateful if you'd let me know."

He gave Donald his card.

They left the old man alone with his dog in the comfort of his little cottage.

"Well that didn't help much Bene. Do you think it could be the Brooks brothers behind these murders?"

"I honestly don't know, but I think they're capable of it. But what would be their connection to the bowls club? I doubt they even know the place exists. In any case it's not our problem anymore. What bothers me is why they've teamed up with the Reay's. Are Eugene and Manny using them to try and find out where the money is? I would imagine Alfie has contacts all over the country and maybe they'd know something. It's a puzzle isn't it? But it would be pointless asking them, they're not going to tell us anything are they?"

"No, and as you say it's not our problem anymore we should be concentrating on our own case, but I can't help thinking we could sort out both of them if we really tried."

"What are you suggesting Hils? That we carry on with the Brennan case but keep one eye on the murders as well?"

"Well I didn't say that but .....

"You're devious you are Hils, you knew I couldn't forget about it and all the hurt that came with failing to catch the killer. Do you think we could use some of our time to look at it again?"

"As long as we're not caught out by division or Sowerby, I think we could do a bit on the quiet and maybe find out something ourselves. Just think Bene, if we could catch him it would be a feather in our caps and a kick up the arse for division."

"Alright, but we'll have to inform Sowerby if we do come across anything that could be used to help catch the killer, and it would be up to him whether he passes it on to division or not; that way our backs will be covered."

"So where are we going now?"

"Let's not get carried away, we'll concentrate on Finnian Brennan first. The whole thing revolves around Ballydonal in Ireland and here in Longbarrow Village, and we've just come back from Ireland. I think we might have to talk to those two clerks in the bank and see what they can tell us, but for the moment let's concentrate on Longbarrow. And if we see those two London guys around we'll try and have a word with them and see if they'll tell us what's so important about that package they're looking for; they obviously think it's somewhere in the village."

"Maybe we could find that as well Bene; that would be some hat-trick wouldn't it, three cases all solved by us?" Hils laughed at her little joke.

Chapter 30

A chilling reminder

"We need to go back to Longbarrow again Hils and speak to Mrs Pattinson at Wool Oaks, there's something I'd like to ask her."

"Is it something to do with those men?"

"Yes, I want to know a bit more about the place, and I'd like us to have a look through the buildings while we're there. Those men have been looking for something in or around the farm and I suspect it's the package they're after, and if it's somewhere on the farm then I'd like to find it before they do."

Mrs Pattinson had no objection to the search.

"That car was here again last night and we saw their torches flashing about, but we soon got rid of them; Bryan has set up spotlights around the yard and when we switched them on they soon scarpered."

"That's interesting, so they haven't found what they're looking for yet; it doesn't look as if they're giving up though I think they'll be back again. If it's alright with you we'd like to have a nosey round the place ourselves and see if we can find what it is they're looking for."

Mrs Pattinson said they were welcome to look through any of the outer buildings as long as they left everything as they found it. The two detectives started in the first building they came to which was a store for cattle, pigs and hen feed.

"Right," said Bene. "wherever it is, if it is here of course, it'll be well hidden in a place that hasn't been disturbed for a long time, so we needn't bother looking in among the food stuff or anything movable because those things are in constant use; it's more likely to be up in the rafters or behind a fixture, a loose brick or something like that, so concentrate on those areas."

They went from building to building using the same systematic approach, but the result was the same in each case; they pulled out a few oddments from various places but no packet or package could be found. Dusty, dirty and dishevelled they finally conceded defeat.

"I think we've covered about every possible niche nook and cranny Bene. I need to get home and get these filthy things off and have a good long hot shower."

"I know we haven't found anything but at least we've given it a try. Now what was it Stephen said; he told us that when Brennan was pointing to this farm he said Judge Alice has it, so what did he mean by that. There's no Judge of that name around here that I've heard of. Maybe we should go back and talk to Matthew and Alison to see if they know of an Alice or a Judge that lived here, and Judge could be a surname as well so maybe it's Alice Judge; let's check that out."

Neither Matthew nor Alison could remember anyone of that name. There'd been one or two Alice's in the village, one had died and the other one was a spinster and staunch church goer, it was unlikely she'd be connected with anything of this nature. Also there'd never been a Judge or anyone called Judge in the village.

Hils wanted to ask something.

"When those two men were in the village asking questions Alison did they call on you?"

"Yes, I think they spoke to everyone here why?"

"Were they just asking about the man at the saw mill and what you remembered about it?"

"Yes, that was all they were interested in. We told them what we knew, that a body had been found and the police came and investigated. The body was removed and no-one knew who he was, or where he came from, we couldn't tell them any more than that."

"So from what Stephen told us, we now know the man was still alive when he found him but dead before anyone else got there, those men don't know that do they?"

"No, there's only you two and us who know that and we haven't told anybody. No-one in the village knows about it so there's no way they could have found out from them. It wasn't until Stephen told his dad that we knew anything about him being alive, and that was after the men had left."

Bene needed to confirm something.

"Before we go, is it alright to have a quick word with Stephen?"

Stephen was called down from his homework and eager to help.

"I just want to be clear on this Stephen, the man said Judge Alice had it didn't he, it wasn't the other way round was it, Alice Judge?"

"No, it was definitely Judge Alice."

"OK that's fine thanks again Stephen."

The two officers left Smithy Cottage.

"Did you think he might have got it mixed up? Asked Hils

"I just wanted to be sure; anyway let's call it a day and get off home. Tomorrow we'll see if we can contact the bank in Dublin and have a word with the two clerks who worked for Brennan and see if they've any idea what he was up to."

Back home again and Bene was in for another shock, two more letters were waiting for him. Alex handed them over as soon as he came in.

This one came when you were over in Ireland, I forgot all about it until another one came about an hour ago. I expect they're just more hoax letters. She left him with the envelopes and went to help her mother in the kitchen. Bene opened the first one; the message read "YOUR SECOND AND LAST WARNING" It was written in a similar style to the first message. Unworried, he stuffed it back into the envelope and opened the second one. This was a small jiffy bag and again only had his name written on it, but the writing on the outer cover and the message inside was unlike the other two, this was a different author. He read the message which was short and to the point.

"The next one has your name on it."

He tipped up the packet and something small fell out and clattered on the floor as it landed beside his feet. Looking down he recognised at once what it was; putting on his regulation surgical gloves he stooped down and picked it up. Turning the bullet casing round with his fingers he read S&W.40, a bullet that was standard issued to a Glock 22 handgun; the same gun used in the shooting of the last three victims. Bene stood rooted to the spot, as calmly as he could he put the bullet in his jacket pocket and tried to stop shaking; he had to pull himself together Alex should not see him like this. He removed his gloves just as she shouted through from the kitchen.

"OK there Bene boy, you'll be ready for this." Bene tensed and un-tensed his muscles trying to relax his body; he had to focus on anything other than what had been in the packet he'd just opened.

"Ready when you are, bring it on." Alex and Dot brought the meal to the table.

"Is everything alright, nothing to worry about is there?" Alex asked.

"No, just the usual gibberish, some poor sod thinks I'm still on the case that's all."

He was noticeably subdued during the remainder of the evening but Alex and Dot put it down to all the travelling and long hours he'd been doing, there was no cause for them to worry.

He didn't mention the message when he met Hils the next morning. He didn't want to alarm her by saying he could be the next target of this madman, and being with him she could also be in danger. He was more determined than ever to find the killer and put him away before the maniac got to him.

"I think we'll give this case a rest today Hils and try and find out who this bloody murderer is. It all revolves around the bowls club. Somebody there knows something and is keeping quiet about it, it's time we put a bit more pressure on to get them talking. Come on, we'll call on Adam first and press him a bit more."

Adam was at home busy in his garden when they arrived.

"Come on over, we'll sit in the sunshine and you can tell me how you're getting on with that fellow's murder."

Bene went through everything they'd discovered, with Adam listening quietly and nodding at the significant points, chuckling when Bene told him about the incident bag and Hils idea of taking it back before it was missed.

"You've had a lot more success than I thought you would. After all this time I believed it would be a pointless exercise and nothing to show at the end of it. So what happens now? You have a name, but you don't have the money or the packet, and with all those rogues chasing around after it I think you'll have to watch your backs."

Bene remembered the bullet, but decided against mentioning it.

"These things must be in the village somewhere, the money and the package; the farm seemed the most likely place and we've had a good look around there, but there was nothing to find. Maybe it's somewhere between the saw mill and the farm so we'll check along that route. But anyway we were thinking of giving it a rest today and doing something else, my mind's all fuzzed up with it it's getting too complicated. If we give it a rest for a day or so we can come back with clearer minds and think of a way we can best proceed with it."

"So what are you doing today?"

"Well we haven't given up with those murders, and now that division have messed up and are no nearer to making an arrest we'd like to have another shot at it ourselves. That's the real reason we've come to see you Adam, have there been any rumours floating around the club these last few days that could have a bearing on the murders, or maybe you have an idea of your own?"

"No, nothing at all, I just keep thinking that maybe it has nothing to do with the club."

He held up his hand to stop them jumping in to state the obvious.

"I know what you're thinking, but the fact they were all bowlers apart from one, Vince Downie, doesn't automatically mean the murders are connected to the club; it could be a group this fellow's targeting for an entirely different reason. You've ruled out Alan Browning's son, but Alan was a very popular fellow down here until he got done for that murder. I know our president Bernard Liversedge and Alan were good pals back then. And by your own admission the evidence you came across up there didn't look too convincing did it? So maybe he is innocent and someone else is taking up a vengeance on his behalf. But not all the victims were on that tour, so maybe that's not the motive either. My advice to you is think a bit more out of the box. Don't concentrate all your thoughts and efforts on the bowls club because the answer could be something that's completely unconnected to it."

The last statement was having the desired effect as Bene and Hils considered Adam's suggestion. Maybe that's why nothing helpful was coming out of the club or from the members. Bene assumed it was because they were too frightened to speak, but maybe the simple truth was they just didn't know anything. They left Adam to tend his garden.

"What do you make of that Bene, do you think he might be right and you've been looking at the murders the wrong way, and if he's right then where do we go from here?"

Before Bene could come up with an answer his phone rang, he didn't recognise the number and was surprised to hear the voice of Donald Neves on the other end.

"You gave me your number when you asked about the dog."

"Oh yes that's right Donald, have you found one for me?"

"Nah I'm sorry lad, not yet I haven't, it's about something else."

"What is it?"

"I thought I should warn you that Alfie Brooks wants to see you, and you've to be in the pub at eight o'clock tonight."

"What does he want, do you know?"

"I know he's aware you've been asking folk about him and he doesn't like it. Now I hope you don't say that I've told you anything because I'm awful feared of the man. But he knows you've been talking to someone, maybe it was that lassie behind the bar. Anyway he's asked me to give you that message, eight o'clock tonight." The phone went dead.

He told Hils the message.

"My God, you're not thinking of going are you?

"I don't know how I can't go. I can't avoid the man forever and I'd rather go and meet him than have him come looking for me. Anyway, I want to know what it's about, it could be something that'll help us, and he can't do anything in a public place can he. And I need to ask if it was him who sent me an anonymous message."

"What message?"

"Oh, it's just that I've had a few threatening letters pushed through the door lately and I think they might have come from him. I don't know if they have or not but I'll find out tonight."

"I'll come as well."

"No there's no need I'll tell you all about it in the morning, let's go and have some dinner."

Back in the station canteen they met up with ET, and after a brief exchange of news ET asked if he could help with their case. Bene told him they were only active in the murder of Finnian Brennan but would still like to be involved in the bowling club murders, but without the knowledge of division. ET had nothing to do as division were finished with him and he was able to do much as he pleased, he was sure they could progress with the murders without drawing attention to themselves. Bene told him of Adam's suggestion.

"We need to find something else that connects these victims, apart from bowls."

"How are we going to do that?"

"I don't know, but you're pretty bright so why don't you think of something."

"How about that fellow you're meeting tonight. I'm sure Alfie Brooks is capable of doing something like that, my money's on him. I bet he's been responsible for burying a few bodies down in Liverpool."

"Yes, well it's him that wants to see me tonight, so he's either going to tell me something or he wants something from me. But whichever it is it'll give me the chance to quiz him on Ireland and a few other things as well, so one way or another I'll be a bit wiser in the morning."

A constable came in to say the Inspector would like to see them in his office, they knew better than to keep him waiting.

"Come in, yes all three of you, sit down and tell me what's happening."

Inspector Sowerby sat back in his chair and waited. ET began.

"Well to be honest sir, I'm at a bit of a loose end, division have no need of me now and all the paperwork is up-to-date so I'm looking for something to do. I thought I could give these two a hand."

"OK now you Bene, speak to me."

Bene told him much of what he already knew adding only that they were going to search the area around the village from the saw mill up to the farm in case the money and the package had been hidden somewhere along that route.

"So you're no nearer finding out who killed the man or finding the money or the package?"

"Not as yet, but I'd like to have the clothes the man was wearing tested for DNA; I'm not sure if was done at the time. I mean whoever killed him must have left some trace on the clothes and we might get a match on our database. If we're lucky it could solve part of the mystery knowing who it was that killed him, but it will probably need someone of your rank to authorise it."

"I'll have a word with Preston and they can have them tested down there and send the results up to us. So if that's all you have for me then go and do that search and make it thorough, if there was nothing on the farm there has to be a place somewhere along that track where Brennan's hidden it."

The distance from the saw mill to the farm was about half a mile. Starting at the saw mill there was a steep cobbled hill up to High Yard farm and from there the lane swept round in a slight curve past some of the estate cottages before coming out onto a B road. After that there was a small copse and then open pasture land all the way to Wool Oaks farm. They began with the area immediately around the creosote tank where there were several work buildings all within a thirty to forty yard radius. All the buildings were locked, and Bene was sure that back in 2012 they would also be locked at night to keep the workmen's tools and materials safe. They moved to the lane and separated to make a thorough search of the land outside both sides of the high sandstone walls, and to check the lane itself. Bene took one side and ET the other with Hils concentrating on the lane. They edged their way along slowly and carefully looking for any possible hiding place. "I don't think we're going to find anything here." said ET. "The walls are high and I can't see any loose stones in them, and even if he'd thrown the package over the wall it would have been found long ago." The short walk revealed nothing.

When they reached the top the search continued along the lane that led to the B road. Apart from the houses which all had front gardens, there were gaps between two of them leading to other buildings which had to be searched. A couple of residents came out to ask what they were doing; the officers explained they were looking for a missing article without giving details. This stretch of the search was time consuming and turned out to be another disappointment. The out-buildings were open to the elements and well-kept with no obvious hiding places. On reaching the road it only remained to look through the small copse which was long but very narrow and required barely a few minutes of their time to complete the search. All three were downhearted as this had looked to be their only remaining chance of finding the elusive package and the missing money. They were convinced that if the package had been there they would have found it. ET thought they should give up.

"We could go back and do it all again but I'm sure we've not missed anywhere, let's face it there's nothing here. It might have been here at some time in the past and someone else has found it, but if not then it has to be somewhere else. What do you think boss are we done here?"

"Yes, we'll pack it in for the day."

It was five after eight when Bene walked into the public bar of the Fox and Pheasant. He didn't want to be early and take the chance of getting drawn into company he may have difficulty getting away from when Alfie arrived, but he needn't have worried because Alfie was already there. Bene saw him seated at a table on his own at the far end of the room. There was little chance that Alfie would be invited to join anyone else in the bar and certainly no-one would sit down uninvited at his table. Bene went to the bar and ordered himself a pint of beer and whatever Alfie was drinking; he took his pint and a large malt whisky over to the table and sat down. He was nervous but didn't want to show it.

"Well I'm here, and we have drinks to drink, so what is it you want to see me about?"

Alfie took a sip of his malt and looked at him curiously.

"I'm a pretty good judge of character son as you have to be in my business. If you make a wrong judgement on someone it could come back and bite you on the arse, and that can be just as painful in the wallet as well as the arse. So when I'm looking at you I'm thinking 'what kind of person is this, and is he someone I can trust'?"

There was an uneasy pause before Bene realised Alfie was waiting for a response.

"Yes, I can see where you're coming from. Well sometimes you can tell right away what type of person someone is, sometimes it takes a bit longer, but there are some people that no matter how long you've known them and think you know them pretty well, suddenly you find you don't know them at all. But I think you've already made your mind up about me and by now you have your answer. As you say, in your line of business you have to make snap decisions on people and be right at least ninety per cent of the time, and in my case I think you have your ninety per cent, whichever way it went."

Bene picked up his pint and waited.

"Yeah, you're right son."

Alfie checked around the room to make sure no-one was within earshot, and leaning across the table he explained to Bene the reason for the meeting,

"I noticed you and the young lass on the Irish ferry so I had you followed, well part of the way anyway because we did lose you in Athlone, but I guessed that like us you were eventually heading up to Dundalk. I soon figured out the reason you were over there and you could say we have a mutual interest in a certain man called Finnian Brennan."

He checked again that no-one was listening.

"Well not so much me as Eugene and Manny Reay, I think you noticed Gordon and me were on the boat with them. As you'll have found out Eugene and Manny have lost a lot of money to that man, a man who'd been well-paid to look after it for them. The money was to be withdrawn shortly before the branch closed, but Brennan hadn't been satisfied with taking the bribes he got greedy and took a lot of money out of the actual account. Now the fellow didn't have the money on him when he was found so he's hidden it somewhere. What we need to do is find out is where it's hidden and return it to its rightful owners, Eugene and Manny." He looked around again to check he wasn't overheard.

"Now here's the deal."

Bene froze. He was dreading the thought of doing any deal with Alfie Brooks or the Reay brothers, was this part of the threatening messages he'd been getting. He felt the bullet in his pocket and Alfie was scaring him. Would he carry out the threat if he didn't agree to the deal? He couldn't get up and walk away even if he wanted to he was too scared. Whatever the deal was he had to sit there and listen to it. Alfie was looking at him again and Bene tried to hide the fear that was coursing through his body. When it came, it was brief and to the point.

"You get that money back for Eugene and Manny and they'll give you the name of the man who killed Finnian Brennan."

Bene was relieved, the deal wasn't as bad as he thought it would be, but there was something bothering him and he needed to know.

"OK I've heard you out, now there's something I need from you."

"Go on then?"

"I've been getting threatening letters pushed through the door at home; the last one came yesterday, and I want to know if any of them came from you or the Reay brothers. You can be honest and tell me because it won't go any further, I just need to know?"

Alfie smiled which didn't happen often, and when he did it wasn't a nice smile.

"Surely you folk get them all the time, its par for the course isn't it."

"That doesn't answer my question though does it?"

"No I suppose not. But you can rest assured son that neither Eugene, nor Manny or me would do anything so crude, so no, they haven't come from us."

"Well the last one contained a bullet, and you're telling me that didn't come from you or the Reay's either?"

Alfie looked worried.

"No it didn't. I can promise you these things have nothing to do with us; this is the first and only contact we've had with you. But hey, anything like that you have to take seriously son; bullets are not something you pick up in the supermarket, so whoever sent it means business. We'll be keeping a look out for you but remember our deal, you get us the money and we'll give you a name."

With that Alfie stood up and finished his malt, leaning heavily on his stick he left the table and walked out of the bar. Bene remained to finish his drink, feeling a little more scared knowing that the threats hadn't come from Alfie or the Reay's. They'd come from someone else, and he had no idea who.

Chapter 31

Where is Dessie?

It was Saturday morning and more than two weeks since the first murder. Bene lay half-awake in bed his eyes still closed. There would be no lie-in for him and no Saturday shopping with Alex. Every day would be the same now, work, work and more work, until such time as the killer had been caught, and the money and package Finnian Brennan had brought over from Ireland with him had been found. If he could find the place Finnian had hidden them at least he'd have the name of his killer and that would be one case closed. His meeting the night before with Alfie Brooks had been beneficial, but the bullet and whoever had sent it worried him; he couldn't think of anyone he'd upset badly enough to warrant something like that. If it came from the killer who was targeting the bowlers then why would he be a threat to them, he was no longer officially on the case? He was still mulling these questions over in his mind when his phone rang. It was Adam.

"Bene, we have another problem, Dessie Milburn has gone missing from home. I've had his wife on the phone she hasn't seen him for two days. He didn't come home on Thursday night, but she wasn't worried about that because sometimes he gets a bit too much to drink and stays over at his friend's house. But when he didn't come home again last night she phoned his friend, and he hadn't seen Dessie since Tuesday at the bowls. She's scared for him and she wants you to find him and bring him home."

"What! I can't leave all this just to go looking for a missing person, that's a job for uniform. I take it she's reported him missing?"

"Yes, she did that just before she phoned me, but they probably won't put much effort into it. You know the score Bene, the man is an adult and as far as they're concerned he may just have gone off for a few days on his own, or had a falling out with his wife or whatever. They'll tell her not to worry and he'll turn up in a day or so."

"But it's still nothing for CID to get involved in; what would Sowerby say if he knew I was out looking for a missing person when I should be concentrating on the case he's given me?"

"Yes I appreciate that Bene, but there's something else you should know."

"Go on then; if you're concerned you must have a good reason, so tell me."

"According to his wife, Dessie thinks he knows the reason for all these murders and has a good idea who's responsible for them. He's been really scared since the last two murders and she tried to find out what was wrong with him. He didn't tell her much but he thought he'd worked out the reason for the murders, and if he was right then he knew who the killer was and he could be the next victim."

"He didn't tell her who it was then?"

"No but she's scared; and she doesn't know if he'll be safe wherever he is. She wants you to go and see her."

"I knew he was hiding something when I spoke to him at the club, but he was too bloody-minded to tell me what it was; if he had done we might have prevented those last two murders. Even so, it's crucial we find him now and find out what he does know, or suspect he knows. I'll go and see her this morning."

Bene went and showered then came back to the bedroom to dress.

"Put your other suit on Bene I'll take that one to the cleaners; you got it in a right state messing about in those old buildings. Do you know what time you'll be back because mam and me are going into town and won't be back until six, we'll bring something nice back for dinner, OK?"

She slumped back into bed and pulled the duvet over her head. Bene just shook his head.

It was a quarter past eight when he pulled up outside the Milburn household. Dessie's wife was waiting at the door and invited him in.

"You still haven't heard from him then?"

"No nothing at all, I tried to call him but his phone's switched off; I've no idea where he can be and it's such a worry. He's not been himself lately and I know it's to do with these murders."

"Adam said Dessie told you something about them?"

"It was two days ago, Dessie thought he had sussed it out and if he was right he could be the next victim."

"So weren't you worried when he didn't come home on Thursday night; I mean why wait until this morning to phone?"

"Because he told me he was going to talk to one of his pals and would probably stay overnight with him. He doesn't like to drive when he's had a drink or two so that's where I thought he was. I was in bed early last night and it was only when I got up this morning I noticed he hadn't come home. I phoned his pal and he told me Dessie hadn't been with him on Thursday night and he hadn't seen him since Tuesday at bowls. I started to panic then so I phoned the police station right away, and then Adam Firth."

"Have you any idea where he might be? Staying with another friend or a member of the family?"

"I've phoned them all and no-one has seen or heard from him, wherever he is I don't think he's in the town."

"You must have some idea where he would go if he wanted to keep out of the way for a while. Is there anywhere you went on holiday together that he enjoyed or a nice day out in the country somewhere?"

"There's only one place I can think of, but it's a long way from here."

"Go on then it must be worth a try, tell me about it?"

"Well Dessie was in the army you see and he loved it when they were camping out in the open. After we got married we couldn't afford a proper holiday in a hotel or anything like that so we always went camping. Dessie was really at one with nature. He'd go off sometimes and come back with a trout he'd tickled in the river and we'd have that for our supper. We did that until the kids came along. They came with us for the first few years, but when they were older they didn't want that kind of holiday so we never got back into it. But Dessie always missed it and said he would go back one day. He couldn't bring himself to sell the camping stuff it's still lying around in the garage."

"Would you mind going to check it's still there?"

"I didn't think about that, come on it's through here."

She led him through the kitchen and out the side door into the garage.

"It's up on that rack above his workbench, I can't get up there, but you could use that old chair to stand on and have a look."

Bene climbed up and looked on the rack, but there was no sign of any camping gear.

"Nothing up here but old sacks and bits of wood, are you sure this is where it should be?"

"Yes, it's been there for years and I've never moved it. That's where he is then; he's just gone and taken himself off to the woods again."

Bene climbed back down and replaced the chair.

"To the woods you say, and which woods would they be?"

"Galloway woods, over the border in Scotland."

"Definitely those woods, he wouldn't go to any other woods?"

"No, it was always Galloway for Dessie he knows the area like the back of his hand. It's a big place as well I'd get lost within five minutes of going in there, but not Dessie. That's where he'll be alright, and if wants to hide away in there you'll have a hell of a job finding him."

Bene left and returned to the station to report to his Inspector.

"Galloway woods you say, that's going to be a job and a half flushing him out of there, are you thinking of going up there yourself?"

"It depends on you sir, or do you think we should tell division about it and leave it to them?"

"I don't think so, this fellow's obviously used to living out in the rough, and he's hiding from someone in a place he thinks they won't find him. Division are likely to send an army up there and that would only scare the fellow off. He'd probably dig in deeper and they'd never find him. Let me have a word with them and see if they want to tackle it, they're in charge of course. But I could suggest that one man going up and trying to find him without all the heavy-handedness of a squad might be the best option; give me a few minutes Bene."

Bene left the office and went to the basement where he saw Hils.

"What are you doing here on a Saturday morning?"

"Just wondered if there was anything going on I should know about."

Bene told her of his visit to Dessie Milburn's house and his disappearance.

"Are you going up there to look for him?"

"Maybe, it depends on division; they might want to do it."

"Well if you're going can I come as well?"

"I don't know, but if division do agree you'll have to ask Sowerby yourself, I mean really you should be here looking for Brennan's booty."

He got the call to return to the Inspectors office.

"I've had a word and they're happy for one of our officers to go and look for him, so do you fancy the job or should I send ET?"

Before he could answer Hils knocked on the door and came in.

"Sorry sir, I couldn't help but overhear, and if it's alright with you I'd like to go as well, I think if there are two of us we'd stand a better chance of finding him, and as I have lots of experience in outdoor camping and a wide knowledge of that particular area I could be invaluable to DS Douglas, sir."

The Inspector looked at her and then at Bene.

"What about this other case? Who'll be working on that?" Hils answered that as well.

"ET wanted to help sir and he's nothing on just now, maybe he could cover."

"Bene?"

"Well it's up to you sir, but if she has all this knowledge it would be a shame not to use it."

"OK I'll allow it, but make sure you find him and bring him back in one piece."

Outside the office Bene had a few questions to put to Hils.

"Where's all this knowledge and outdoor experience come from you've never mentioned it before?"

Hils smirked.

"I went camping once."

"Where?"

"Butlin's."

"Butlin's is that it, you're kidding me, that isn't camping!"

"Maybe not, but it was a damned good holiday, don't tell Sowerby though."

Bene had to laugh.

"My God you've got a nerve, what if he finds out you've been lying to him?"

"Well, I won't tell him if you don't"

"I don't believe you sometimes, you'll get us both chucked out of the force."

"Yeah maybe, but before that happens let's go and find this Dessie fellow."

Bene drove Hils over to her flat to change into some old clothes and grab a drink and some food and then to his house to do the same. Alex and Dot were on the point of leaving so he had to explain it would be late when they got back but he'd phone and keep in touch.

"How far is it up there Bene?" Alex asked.

"I don't know the best part of two or three hours I would think, so the sooner we get going the sooner we'll be back. It shouldn't take us that long to find him in a wood."

He pulled into a filling station to put fuel in for the long journey. As he got back into the car Hils had a shock for him.

"Won't take long to find him in a wood you said, do you know how big these woods are?"

"No, but it can't be that big can it?

"Not that big, the forest is probably the biggest in the UK it's nearly three hundred square miles; we've got no chance of finding him in that lot."

"Well, put some of that camping experience and local knowledge to work then."

"Ha, bloody ha."

"OK not to worry, get Dessie's wife on the phone and see if we can narrow it down a bit."

Hils made the call.

"Hi Mrs Milburn it's acting DC Taylor here, I'm in the car with DS Douglas and we're on our way up to Galloway. We've just found out the size of these woods and I don't think we'll have much chance of finding him without a bit of help from you. Can you give us any idea whereabouts in the woods he could be?"

"Not really it's all so long ago; the only thing I remember is we parked at a place called Glentrool. We walked from there probably about a mile into the woods until we came to a small loch, and that's where we camped. I'm sorry but that's about all I can remember."

"That's great Mrs Milburn we'll start there and hopefully we'll find him fairly quickly."

"Before you go DC Taylor, I've just had a call from someone at the police station asking about Dessie and I've given the same information to him, he said he'd pass it on to you so you should be getting a call from him shortly. Good luck and bring Dessie back home."

"Mrs Milburn who was it called you, did you get a name?"

"Yes, it was Sergeant Andrews, and he was with Levensbridge Police."

"OK, thanks again we'll get on our way."

The call had been on loudspeaker so Bene heard everything.

"Phone the station Hils and ask Sowerby if division have a Sergeant Andrews working with them?" His suspicions were confirmed when Inspector Sowerby returned their call a few minutes later to confirm that no-one of that name was working at Levensbridge, nor was there any Sergeant Andrews in the force down in Preston.

"So who will that have been?" said Hils.

"I don't know, but now they know as much as we do and I don't like it. We'll have to find Dessie before they do because it looks as if his assumption might be right, he could very well be the next victim."

This piece of news speeded up their need to get to Dessie before the killer did. Bene put his foot down harder on the accelerator and the car sped up past Carlisle and over the border into Scotland. There was little to say for the rest of the journey as their thoughts were centred on a quick search and the detection of a frightened man. Bene's phone rang, it was Alex and she didn't sound too pleased.

"Bene, tell me what the hell is going on; I've just handed your suit in at the cleaners and they gave me back an envelope you'd left in one of the pockets. It was open and I saw the message inside and the bullet, when were you going to tell me about that?"

"I'm sorry pet, I didn't want to worry you; it's probably nothing, just someone's idea of a joke."

"A joke, a bloody joke! This is serious Bene and I want you to take it seriously as well. People don't send things like that as a joke, tell me honestly, are you in any danger?"

"I don't know, I have no idea who sent it or why, but I think we're on to something at last and when I get back I think we'll have our killer, and once we do everything will be fine, so don't worry."

Hils had also listened to the call.

"You didn't tell me about that either, do you think you are in danger?"

"You heard what I told Alex, and honestly I don't know any more than that, so let's forget about it for now and concentrate on finding Dessie."

Glentrool was a small village, but with plenty of space for car parking. It appeared the area attracted a lot of summer visitors to the woodland walks and nature trails. They parked the car and spotted one of the forest rangers nearby. Bene approached him.

"We're trying to find a Loch in the woods and were told it was about a mile from here, but we don't know which direction to take would you be able to help us?"

"Well the nearest one, and it's one of the largest is over yonder in that direction. You can take that path over there and it will take you a good way in; you'll come to a stack of timber we've cut down and when you get there you'll have to head over to your right. It's a narrow track and you'll have to be careful, but if you follow that it will take you to the end of the Loch. But be careful not to leave the path or you'll get lost."

With that information the two headed off down the path the ranger had indicated. It was well maintained and fairly wide and eventually they came to a huge stack of timber waiting to be hauled out of the woods. The narrow path to the right was exactly where the ranger said it would be and they set off along this route towards the Loch. This path was more difficult to negotiate and at one point it came to a fork. They stood for a moment undecided as to which path to take. Hils went along one way while Bene stayed at the fork, but she soon came back to say it had petered out after about twenty yards, they set off again and continued along the other path. It took them over an hour before they had sight of the small Loch; they walked over to the shore and stood for a while looking around for any sign of Dessie's camp.

"It's a fair size Loch Bene I don't think I can see the far end of it, what do you think we should do, split up and take one side each or stay together?"

"I think it's best if we go together, we'll start this side and work round it, if he's camped close to the Loch we should find him alright."

They began to circle the Loch calling out for Dessie at intervals but getting no response from the surrounding trees; an hour later they reached the end and started back along the other side calling out for Dessie along the way.

"It's getting dark Hils; if we don't find him along here we'll have to give it up for the day. We'd probably lose our way going back in the dark and we don't want to be stuck out here all night. I don't think we've much further to go, another fifteen minutes should do it then we'll have to start back, what little light is left is going quickly and we need to get out of here." Bene called again, more in hope than anything else.

"It looks like we've come to the wrong Loch. I know there're other Lochs in the forest so he must have gone to one of them. We could try another one tomorrow but that means spending the night up here. Is that alright with you?"

"Yeah whatever it takes; you heard what Sowerby said, we can't go back without him. As soon as we get out of here we'll go and find some digs for the night."

They'd all but given up hope of finding the man when a muffled voice drew their attention to the trees behind them; as they turned to look the figure of a man appeared through the dusk and waved them over.

"Is that you Dessie?" Bene called.

"Keep your voice down man, and get over here quick."

Dessie was looking rough and dishevelled the result of camping out in the wilderness.

"How the hell did you know where I was?"

"Never mind that let's get you back home. It's nearly dark now and we've no intention of staying the night in here, and you're not staying either you're coming back with us. And on the way back you're going to tell us what you know about these murders before there're any more of them."

"I will but not just yet, there's someone else creeping around in the woods and I think I know who it is; I've heard him prowling about and I need to be sure he's gone before we leave."

"OK, well while we're waiting you can tell us what you know about the murders."

"Alright, well when you were asking me at the bowling club I really had no idea what it was all about; it was only after the last two murders that it suddenly hit me. Little things that had been floating round in the back of my mind for a while started to fall into place, and I kind of figured out what it was all about. It was the names you see. Arnold, Willie and Robin were always buddies and did everything together, but when I heard Vince had been killed I suddenly remembered that him and me had been with them sometimes, so I figured that if those four had been killed then I'd be next, because I was the last member of that group and I knew what had happened."

"Go on then carry on."

"Well we were all together in ....

Two shots rang out in quick succession shattering the silence in the dark forest; Dessie collapsed to the ground in front of them just as another bullet screamed past Bene's head and embedded itself in the tree behind them.

He shouted to Hils.

"Get down!" Just in time as another two bullets flew past them and thudded into the undergrowth. They lay flat on the ground beside the fallen Dessie too scared to move. A few seconds later, and without lifting his head, Bene reached over to check if Dessie was still alive. He felt a weak pulse, but there was no movement in the body.

"I think he's still alive, but we need to get him away from here and move him under the trees. It's only a few yards; do you think you can help me? And keep your head down; we don't want to give that fellow another target to shoot at."

No sooner had he spoken than another bullet smacked into the ground about three feet from them. With a great deal of effort and keeping close to the ground they managed to drag Dessie's body far enough until they were behind the bushes and under the trees in the protection of the woodland. Once there they remained prone on the ground, silently listening for any movement in the woods or out near the Loch. A further ten minutes elapsed before Bene raised himself slightly to try and scan the area around them; it was almost dark now and he hoped this would keep them safe.

"Are you OK Hils?" he whispered quietly, she nodded in return.

"We can't stay here too long because we need to get Dessie to a hospital where he can be looked after; if we leave it too late he might not make it and we'll never know what it was he was going to tell us. We'll give it another five minutes and then I think we'll have to take a chance that whoever shot him has gone." The whispering continued.

"Should I phone for help?" said Hils. "Maybe they can get a ranger in here. It's too dark to try anything ourselves and we don't want to make Dessie's condition any worse by dragging him around, we'd probably lose our way anyway. We need to get some armed backup in here as well, in case that fellow's still hanging around."

"OK, you do it."

Hils took out her phone which had been switched off for the search and switched it on.

"Bugger I've got no signal, try yours."

Bene removed his phone from an inside pocket with as little bodily movement as possible and switched it on; he was on a different network but the result was the same.

"Now we really are in trouble. We'll leave it another five minutes then one of us will have to try and find the way back out of here and get help; the other can stay and look after Dessie until help arrives. He's still alive but there's a real chance he won't make it through the night if we don't get him to a hospital. So take your pick do you want to go or do you want me to go? There could be danger either way."

"You go Bene. I'll stay here with Dessie and try and keep him warm and make him as comfortable as I can. If we keep still and quiet we should be alright until you get back."

"Right OK, here goes."

Bene slowly rose to his feet and edged his way out from the trees, if the killer was still out there he was a prime target. Although scared for his own life he felt he had no choice in the matter, not to go would probably mean certain death for Dessie and his last hope of finding out the name of the killer. He had to take a chance that the killer was convinced Dessie was dead and had left the woods. He walked slowly to the edge of the Loch and was about to enter the narrow path they'd come down earlier when a crashing sound of breaking branches stopped him dead in his tracks. There was nowhere for him to run even if he could run; his feet were fixed firmly to the ground. All he could do was wait for the gunman to burst through the undergrowth any second now and shoot him.

A man did come rushing out into the clearance and almost knocked him over. The ranger was as surprised as Bene.

"What's been happening here, I heard shots and came as fast as I could."

Bene told him of the shooting and the need to get the injured man to a hospital quickly.

"Right, you wait here and I'll go back and bring help with me. Do you think this fellow with the gun is still around, or has he gone?"

"I honestly don't know. We had to take a chance that he'd gone because the injured man is badly in need of attention. And there's something you should know about the man who shot him; he's already killed four other people so you need to be careful. When you get out of here ring for an ambulance, and get the police to send some armed men in here just in case he's still around. And can you get someone to phone Levensbridge police station in Cumbria as well and let them know what's happened, tell them it's DS Douglas."

"Right I'm off there's no time to waste, you stay here and don't move until we get back." Then as an afterthought he turned and said.

"There was someone looking for you though and he followed you into the woods. I thought he was a friend of yours, but it looks like it was this fellow with the gun."

Before Bene could question him the ranger disappeared back down the track, Bene went back to Hils and the injured Dessie.

"That was a bit of luck Bene the ranger hearing the shots and coming in."

"Yes, but at the time I didn't know who would come bursting through. I thought I was coming face to face with the killer, and in the last two seconds of my life I would know who he was, not much satisfaction in that is there. The ranger said someone followed us in here though?"

They remained under the trees and mostly in silence, occasionally checking Dessie's body heat, his pulse and his breathing whilst waiting for help to arrive. The woods were silent, no bird calls or animal noises could be heard the shooting had scared off all the creatures of the forest. The only sound was a slight breeze drifting through the leaves. Even so the two lay nervously on the ground listening for any giveaway signs of human presence. After what seemed hours but in fact was slightly less than two the sound of someone approaching heightened their senses. Not knowing whether it would be a friendly face or the face of the killer that would appear they remained silent and close to the ground. Their fears were allayed when the sight of the uniformed ranger and a policeman came into view.

The ranger thought the danger had passed.

"There are two men with a stretcher right behind me and they'll take your friend to the ambulance, and the police have men in the woods checking to see if that fellow with the gun is still around. I'll organise the transfer of your friend to the nearest hospital, and you might want a word with the officer here and tell him what this is all about." With that he turned to direct the stretcher bearers over to the injured Dessie. The police sergeant approached and Bene introduced himself and Hils and explained what it was that had led them to the woods, and what had happened when they got there and found the missing man.

"So this is all connected to the murders down in your area. Well I'd like to know why we weren't informed there was a killer roaming around in the woods up here."

"We didn't know ourselves sergeant; we only came looking for the man on the stretcher over there. His wife told us he could be hiding out here because he thought he knew the name of the killer and he was scared of being the next victim. He thought he'd be safe up here in the woods because it's a place he knows well. All we wanted to do was find him and take him back with us we didn't know the killer was here. Someone must have found out we were coming here and followed us, but how they knew where to find us in all these woods is beyond me."

"OK, but you'll have to call in at Dumfries police station on your way back because my Inspector wants a full report from you. If that man is still in the woods we're not going to find him tonight it's too dark now. I'll call the men off and we'll have a look again in the morning. But with no clue as to who he is or what he looks like it'll just be a token gesture, I can't afford to keep the armed response unit here any longer than that. Anyway let's get you out of here, we need to keep up with the ranger or we'll get lost."

They made their way slowly out of the woods, the ranger leading with the stretcher bearers and police following. It was slow progress for the first part on the narrow pathway but once on the wider track the going was much easier. An ambulance was waiting in the village and as soon as Dessie was on board it sped away to the hospital in Stranraer. Dessie's condition was not good and he was still unconscious. The time lapse in waiting for help to arrive combined with the loss of blood and the long trek out of the woods had further weakened him.

The police had called off the search and left the area, only Bene, Hils and the ranger remained. Bene was anxious to know how the gunman had found them in the woods so easily.

"After you told us the way to the Loch you said someone followed us and you thought it was a friend of ours?"

"Aye, you had just gone into the woods when a fellow came up to me and pointed to a man standing by a silver car over there. He said that man had come up with you but you hadn't told him where you were going in the woods and he wanted to catch up with you. I didn't think there was anything strange about it so I told him where you were going and gave him the same directions I gave you."

"Did you get a look at this fellow?"

"No, he was a good way off so I couldn't give you a description; he was standing beside a silver hatchback car which I presumed was his, but it's not there now so he must have gone."

"And the fellow who came and asked you about us, do you know who that was?"

"No, he was with his wife and it looked like they were just here for a walk."

Now they were out of the woods Bene's phone picked up a signal. He phoned Inspector Sowerby and informed him of the shooting, and Dessie going to hospital.

"We're on our way back now there's nothing more we can do up here. Would someone be kind enough to let Dessie's wife know what's happened, I expect she'll want to come up and stay with him. We have to call at

Dumfries on the way back and give a report on the incident so it will be late when we get back."

"I'll go and tell her myself. I've just had a call from Dumfries to tell me what happened so I've told division and they weren't happy at all. They said some of their men should have gone with you. I told them it was only a hunch we were following and there was no evidence to say the man was up there, and if he was, there was nothing to suggest he was in any danger. I suppose I was fobbing them off a bit but they had to accept it. Anyway I'll see you both sometime in the morning."

The journey back was a long and tiring one; it was midnight when they arrived at Dumfries and an hour later when they left to continue the drive back to Levensbridge. Once they were back in the town Bene dropped Hils off at her flat and finally walked through his own door at three o'clock in the morning to find Alex waiting up for him.

"Come here you, you look terrible." She gave him a big hug. "Let's not talk about this now go and get a shower and we'll get some sleep, you must be knackered we can talk in the morning."

It was down to habit that whatever time Bene went to bed he couldn't sleep after eight o'clock, and when he did wake up he found it was bang on the hour. He lay for a few minutes thinking about the events of the previous day before deciding to get up and have some breakfast. Alex on the other hand never had a problem with sleep; she could always get her eight hours no matter what. He got up and had a quick shower without disturbing her, dressed and went down to the kitchen.

Dot was already in there and he was hoping she'd treat him to a nice cooked breakfast. She hadn't heard him come home but knew it must have been late; there'd been no plates or dishes in the sink so he hadn't eaten. When she heard him in the shower it had given her time to put together a good fried breakfast with coffee and toast to follow. Bene got stuck in and finished it in record time.

"That's better Dot, I feel like a man again, better not tell Alex eh?"

Too late! Alex had woken to the smell of a fry up and against her better judgement came down and asked her mother for the same. While waiting for the breakfast to come she wanted to know all about Galloway woods. Bene went through everything that had happened up there, how the gunman had found them and how Dessie had been shot. He decided not to mention the bullets that narrowly missed him.

"How is he then, do you know?"

"No, he didn't look too good when he left in the ambulance and the only hospital was twenty odd miles away. There was one in Newton Stewart which was nearer but they don't have a surgeon or any operating facilities so they had to take him to Stranraer. I'll have to find out how he is this morning; I hope he's OK because I think he's our last chance of finding out the name of the killer. Dessie reckons he's the last one who knows the identity of the man. If he dies the killer will have got rid of his last witness and the killing spree will stop without us ever knowing who was behind it all."

"Couldn't he have told you when you found him, and before he was shot?"

"He was in the middle of telling us when the shots were fired. If the shooting had been delayed for a few seconds we would have got a name. That's what it comes down to; a few seconds either way and the difference between catching a murderer and never finding out who he was. Let's just hope Dessie survives and can tell us."

"Anyway its Sunday Bene so can we go and look at some houses, I've got details of a few?"

"I'm sorry love but I have to go in this morning, I need to find out how Dessie is and if there's anything I need to do. But I won't be too long so we can go this afternoon, will that be alright?"

"As long as it is this afternoon, don't you dare stay any longer or I'll set the Rottweiler on you."

"What Rottweiler we don't have a dog?"

"Yes we do! We've got mam." Even Dot had to laugh at this.

Bene arrived at the station and immediately asked the Inspector for an update on Dessie.

"Not too good Bene, he'd lost a lot of blood so they had to give him a transfusion before operating to remove the bullets, which incidentally look to be from the Glock. They haven't been checked yet but I'm sure they'll turn out to be from the same gun as used in the last three murders. He hasn't regained consciousness yet, he's in a stable condition but they're keeping him in intensive care, his wife is up there with him. Division have asked for an armed guard to be at his door in case that fellow finds out he's still alive and has another pot shot at him. And there'll be another man on hand for when he wakes up so he can be interviewed straight away. The hospital said it could be hours or maybe days. It's too soon to know how much damage has been done and how long it will take to heal, but the main thing is they think he'll recover. When he does come round we'll get the killer's name, and once he's picked up that will be the end of it and the case finally put to bed. So what are you doing here today, there's nothing more you can do, go home and have a day off."

He'd just left the Inspectors office when Hils arrived at the station; she was getting as bad as him, she couldn't stay away.

"There was no need to come in today Hils there's nothing to do; we'll pick up the Brennan case again tomorrow."

"I just wondered how Dessie was, have you heard?"

Bene told her what he had learned from Inspector Sowerby.

"So are we not doing anything today?"

"I'm house hunting with Alex that's all; I'm going home now so you go home as well and have a bit of free time, I'll see you in the morning, OK?"

"Alright, what are we going to do tomorrow?"

"I'm tempted to go back to Wool Oaks because I can't think of anywhere else to look. Put some old clothes on and we'll go back and have another good look around the place."

"OK boss I'll be off then, happy house hunting."

She left with a big grin on her face.

Chapter 32

The lull before the storm

Alex and Dot were surprised to see him back so early.

"Is there any news about Dessie?" Alex enquired

Bene repeated what Inspector Sowerby had told him.

"We'll have a coffee first and then make a start." said Alex. "I've got details of four houses I like the look of and now you're back early we can go and see them. The first one is still occupied and it's a private sale, so we'd be dealing with the owner-occupier a Mr Mattocks. The others are all vacant and I've arranged viewing times with the agent, she'll take us round to see them this afternoon, is that alright?"

"Yes, but don't show me any prices before we go because I don't want that to sway me into making a decision on that alone. The house needs to be exactly what we want, and if it isn't then whatever we need to spend on top of that won't have to exceed our budget."

"Oh, you and your budgets is that all you think about?" She shouted to her mam.

"Did you know I'm married to Mr Scrooge mam?"

"It's all very well for you to scoff, but if I know you it'll be the most expensive one we look at, and you'll look at me with those big sad doggy eyes of yours and

I'll end up having to take another full time job to pay for it."

"Oh you poor thing and with another mouth to feed as well, my you are going to suffer aren't you. But never mind if you're out working twenty four hours a day at least you won't have any nappies to change will you?"

Dot came into the room.

"I never mentioned this to either of you before, but when your grandma died a few months ago she left quite a bit of money, and although it comes to me she did stipulate that if and when you decided to buy a house you should have half of it. But it was only to go towards the house and nothing else and I wasn't to mention it until you'd started looking for one. So don't be put off if the one you really want is a bit more than your budget, because there is money there for you. But don't go overboard Alex it's not a fortune, but it will help."

The two of them were dumbfounded.

"Well don't tell us how much it is mam because we really do have a budget and we'd like to stick to it if possible. And anyway we don't want to take your money, you might need it yourself when we've moved out, isn't that right Bene."

"Of course, so let's not change what we'd intended to do today, we'll go off with the same plan as we agreed. So if you're both ready let's go and see the first one."

They didn't have far to go, it was within walking distance and one of the conditions Alex had laid down. She wanted a house of her own but needed to stay close to her mother. The Mattocks family were still living in the house but expecting to move within the next two weeks. They had two young children a boy of twelve and a girl two years younger, all four were pleased to see them and welcomed them into their home. Bene wondered where they were moving to.

"Are you staying in the town or moving away?"

"We're not going too far, we're taking over my mother's old house up on the edge. It's a big place with a nice garden and there's room for my uncle who's coming to stay with us. He's getting on a bit and we didn't like to put him in a home I think that would have finished him off. If he's with us he'll have a bedroom and a small lounge area to himself and a free run of the place; he loves gardening so there's plenty for him to do up there and that'll keep him busy. This house has been perfect for us, but we need the extra rooms for uncle and that's the only reason we're moving."

"You've kept it in good order and I must say I like the décor as well; usually the first thing you do when you move house is change the colours, but this is really nice."

"Come on then, you've seen the lounge, I'll show you round the rest of the house."

Mr Mattocks took them upstairs to see three good sized bedrooms and a large four piece bathroom with separate shower. Back downstairs he showed them the small cloakroom with WC and wash basin, and then led them through to a large dining room which in turn opened up and led to an extended kitchen, at the far end of the kitchen French windows looked out onto a good sized garden. There were flowered borders around the edge of the lawn and tall hedges surrounding it for privacy. Bene was well impressed and he could tell by their faces Alex and Dot were smitten as well. Alex thanked Mr Mattocks for showing them around and promised to let him know if they decided to put in an offer.

Rather than go home they chose to go to a café and discuss the house they'd just seen. It appeared to tick all the boxes, but they decided against making any rash judgment until they'd seen the other three. Once they'd done that they could sit down at home and talk everything over at leisure.

The agent met them outside the first of the three remaining properties and had the keys ready to let them in. They'd arrived in high hopes with images of the first house still imprinted on their minds and they were looking forward to seeing more of the same. The agent was full of praise for the house, but the enthusiasm she was showing was not felt by the prospective buyers. It was a house and had all the attributes they were looking for, but it was just a house and neither of them got the feeling of it being anything other than that. On to number two and this was a case of more of the same, it took them a mere ten minutes to rule it out, again it had everything they were looking for but the wow factor was definitely missing. On to number three and the last of their viewings, the earlier excitement was definitely on the wane. This house was much better but again it was missing that special something they'd sensed in the first property. Not wanting to disappoint the agent Alex thanked her for showing them the properties and promised to let her have their decision the following day. They said their goodbyes and trudged back home to deliberate.

"OK" said Alex "what did you think?"

It was an open question, but Dot shied away from it.

"I don't feel as though I should speak first because essentially it's going to be yours and Bene's home, so I think Bene should go first and tell us what he thinks."

"Yes alright, well for me that first house spoiled it for the other three because I really liked it; it had everything we were looking for and more. I had a good feeling about it as soon as I walked in, and I thought if we moved in there tomorrow it would feel like home straight away. The others were OK, but I wasn't getting a buzz from any of them, they were just houses."

"OK mam, your turn?"

"Well I think the same as Bene and I couldn't have put it any better than he did, so it's up to you Alex to tell us what you think?"

"Snap I'll go with you two, we're all agreed then, so what now, do we wait until we've seen some more houses or do we go with the first one and put an offer in?"

Bene was a little hesitant. "You didn't tell us how much they want for it?"

"Right I'll tell you what they want for all of them and you can tell me what you think.

The second and the third houses are both priced at £200K. And the fourth one £220K"

"Well that's way too much for all of them; I'd value them much lower than that. That means the first house must be well above our budget. "

"Well you might be surprised."

"Go on then tell me."

"You're sure?"

"Yes of course, go on."

"He's asking £225K, so you see it's not as bad as you thought eh?"

"Not bad at all, it's still over budget but let's sit down and work it out."

Dot came into the conversation.

"Don't forget about gran's money you can put £30k of that towards the house if that's the one you really want."

"Wow that much, I thought maybe five or ten grand but thirty, are you sure, it won't leave you short will it?"

"No you're only getting half of it so there's still thirty left for me, and I have both your dad's and my pension so don't worry I'll be fine, and if I'm not I can come and live with you."

"And you'd be more than welcome." Bene laughed.

"So what should we do Bene, put an offer in?"

"Yes I think so before anyone else jumps in, what do you think, should we offer him the full asking price or maybe start a bit lower?"

"Let's go round now and see what he would take for a quick sale; we can get a mortgage for it can't we?"

"Yes, I've got a sort of agreement with the building society, they worked it out based on my salary and part of yours and we should be OK up to £200K then we have about £10K saved ourselves and with your grans money it would be enough."

"Come on then."

Mr Mattocks didn't seem surprised to see them back again so quickly and invited them in.

"You've had a good look around at some other houses have you?" He asked.

"Yes we saw another three this afternoon but this is the one we really like." said Alex.

"I could tell that when you were here earlier, and we hoped you might be back. Have you come for a second look or are you thinking of making an offer?"

Alex looked to Bene to make the offer.

"Well we know the asking price is £225K and we wondered if that was the only offer you'd accept or if you'd consider a slightly lower offer?"

"Well it depends on what you think is slightly lower."

"Well like most people we do have a budget and this would be at the top end of that but we both really like the house and we'd like to offer you £210K, would you consider that?"

"No, I'm afraid not."

Bene and Alex looked dismayed it seemed their dream house might not be theirs after all. Mr Mattocks could see the disappointment in their faces.

"But I would accept £215K, so if you could stretch to that we could say the house was yours."

The smiles were back and Bene and Alex shook hands with Mr Mattocks, the deal was done.

"I still think I might have got the £225K but my wife warned me that if you came back with a decent offer I had to let you have it. We've had a lovely time here and when you came round earlier we could sense that it was the right house for you as well, and we're delighted that you'll be coming to live here."

Mrs Mattocks came in smiling and said how pleased she was they'd bought the house. She made them coffee and they sat and chatted for almost an hour before leaving to return home.

Dot was delighted with the news and thought they should go out and have a meal to celebrate.

Chapter 33

Wool Oaks Farm

A Monday morning had never felt so good for Bene, with a baby on the way and a new house of their own to look forward to he was in good spirits and looking forward to the day. Hils was waiting at the station and congratulated him on agreeing the house purchase. She was dressed in old jeans and a checked shirt and wearing an old pair of trainers.

"Well you said old clothes, so it doesn't matter how dirty we get because after today I can throw them out."

"Yes, I'm much the same, but I'm not sure if Sowerby will share our opinion. Maybe we should go before he sees us."

They pulled out of the station car park and headed over to Longbarrow village; a silver hatchback pulled out behind and followed them at a discreet distance all the way to Longbarrow. The driver watched as they turned into the lane leading to Wool Oaks farm and pulled up just past the entrance and switched off the engine.

Bene and Hils were greeted by Mrs Pattinson who introduced her husband.

"This is Bryan and we're pleased to see you. I was going to give you a call but now you're here we can tell you."

"Why, has something happened?" asked Bene.

"It's those two men, they were back here again yesterday and they weren't too shy this time. They came right up to the house asking us a lot of questions about Mr Walsh the previous owner. They said it was something that had been hidden on the farm when he was living here; it was valuable and it belonged to them. They knew it wasn't in the house but hidden somewhere in the outbuildings and they needed to find it and get it back. We said the farm had been vacant for a few years before we bought it and anyone could have found whatever it was they were looking for back then. And in all the time we've been here we hadn't found anything. We knew they'd been sneaking around here at nights and told them we'd called the police. We asked them to leave us alone or we would get the police again, I told them we had the number of their car and would report them. Well they weren't too happy, but my husband is a big man as you can see and after a while they thought better of it and left. But they said they'd be back, and we're a bit scared of what they might do. We're on our own out here and isolated, there's no-one to help us."

"Well they've been looking all-round the farm for it," said Bene "and we've had a good look ourselves, and neither of us has found anything. I suppose there's a chance it might still be here somewhere but I can't think where, it's also possible it was found years ago and someone else has it. What we're looking for is a package. It must be important because those two men are desperate to find it. And on top of that there are other people interested as well; they're looking for a large sum of money which went missing at the same time and that could be in the package as well. The only clue we had was a dying man pointing over to this farm saying Judge Alice has it. We've asked around and that name means nothing to anyone around here so it may have been something else. The man was Irish and his accent would be strange to the young lad who heard it so it could have been something completely different."

"Well you're the police so you should be able to find out who these men are; I've got their car number so that should help."

She showed them the number she had written down which corresponded with the one they already had.

"I'm afraid that's no good we have that number and we can't get access to the owner. We believe these people could be MI5 or some other government agency."

"You mean secret agents?"

"Yes something like that and we don't want to mess with them, they have a reputation for dealing with people in their own way."

"Now that does scare me, what can we do?"

Bene had an uneasy feeling it was going to be a difficult day and probably a very long one.

"We'll have another look around today to see if we can find it, and if we do it'll get rid of those two men. If we don't I think we'll have to come back tonight and make sure you and your husband are safe. If they do come back they won't threaten you if we're here. And if they don't find anything this time then surely they'll have to give it up. They must have gone over every square inch of the place just like we have, and none of us have found it. Personally I don't think it's here anymore, it's more likely that in the years the place stood empty someone else has found it and it'll never be seen again. Anyway we'll carry on with our search, if we don't find anything we'll be back again later tonight when it's getting dark. Is there anywhere we could hide apart from the buildings up here? We don't want to be seen, but we want to be here in case you feel threatened and if you are we'll show ourselves."

Bryan pointed somewhere out to them.

"There is an old barn over there just off the lane, the roof has partly given in and there're no sides to it but you could shelter in there, but I'd wrap up warm if I was you because it'll be draughty in there and a bit cold. If it rains you can get shelter at one end where the bales are."

"We'll have a look at it this morning because we didn't think about that place, is there anything in there, any hiding places?"

"No, there's a couple of old bits of machinery, a plough and such, and then just the six posts holding the place up, there's no shelves or cupboards or anything like that. I have a few bales of hay in there under the good part but that's all."

They walked down the lane and checked the place over. Bene wasn't impressed with it.

"He's right it could be a bit cold in here its wide open to the weather, the only dry place is at this end where the hay is, but it'll have to do. If we have to come back tonight we should bring some warm clothes and something to eat, and a flask with something hot in it."

They had a quick look around the site but found nothing that looked remotely like a hiding place so they walked back up the lane to begin a second search of the buildings. The driver of the silver hatchback which had been parked near the entrance of the lane had been watching their movements all the way; when they returned to the farm he started the engine and drove away in the direction of Levensbridge.

The search was thorough as this was the last time they wanted to do it. If nothing was found this time they had no intention of doing it again. Three hours later the result was the same, absolutely nothing!

"That's it Hils I've had enough."

"Me too, I mean for a farm it's remarkably clean but even so just look at my clothes I'll have to chuck them."

"I'd leave it until tomorrow if I were you; we might as well come back in these if we have to stay hidden in that old barn for hours"

"What time should we come back?"

"Well it doesn't get dark until after nine, so if we get here just before that we'll have time to get settled in, and then it's just a case of waiting to see what happens. It gets light again shortly after five so if no-one comes by then we can leave, look upon it as an eight hour shift and hopefully it'll be an uneventful one."

Chapter 34

Fright Night

They arrived back at Wool Oaks just before nine and drove up to the farmhouse to let the owners know they were there. Bene wanted to reassure them that they were on hand if there was any likelihood of danger.

"Any problems ring me on this number and we'll be up here in a couple of minutes, but hopefully there won't be a problem; we'll be down in the old barn and keeping watch in case they should come."

Bene drove his car back down the lane and parked it out of sight behind the barn. It was starting to get dark when a faint humming noise drew his attention.

"Was that a car Hils? I heard something, but couldn't see what it was in the dusk?"

"Yes I think so, it slowed down but it didn't stop. It won't have been those fellows though they don't come until it gets really dark. I'll have a quick look though."

Hils walked down the lane to the road, she could see a good way along in both directions but there was nothing there. She thought if it was a car it hadn't been showing lights, she walked back to the barn. Bene was busy finding somewhere for them to sit, somewhere out of sight but giving them a good view of the farmhouse and the outbuildings.

"This should do, it's the best place I can find, I've moved the bales around so we can sit on some of them and be hidden behind the others, and the roof in this part of the barn isn't too bad. We should be able to keep dry if it rains."

"Oh it sounds really cosy; remind me to book the place for a dirty week-end sometime."

They settled down and prepared for a long boring night.

"Do you think we'll ever find this package Bene? I mean its six years since all this happened, and even if it was left here someone must have found it soon after that, or in the years when the place stood empty. I think it's long gone."

"Yeah you could be right. If it was here I'm sure we'd have found it, and I think there has to come a point when we accept the fact it's not here and move on."

"We could take up those murders again couldn't we? How's Dessie by the way, have you heard any more?"

"Not since this afternoon and nothing had changed, he still hasn't regained consciousness. When he does there's a policeman by his bedside ready to talk to him. It depends how much brain damage he's sustained, the doctors are worried it could have long term affects, if that's the case I fear we'll never know."

"And what about those brothers, have they been bothering you again?"

"When I met Alfie he said they were keeping an eye on us. If we can recover the money at least we'll have someone to charge with Finnian Brennan's murder. But unless we start getting a bit of luck everything will stay the same and just out of our reach, we could end up with absolutely nothing."

"It's getting pretty dark Bene and that wind's cold, should we have a coffee?"

"Yes, are you going to be mum?"

"I've not put any sugar in, is that alright?"

"Yeah mine's the same, we'll have yours first and keep mine for later; if it stays like this I think we'll need it."

"Here I've got a couple of buns as well. I don't know about you but I'm getting hungry."

They were busy chatting away aimlessly and enjoying the hot drinks and buns, when suddenly Bene spotted a large saloon enter the farm lane. They hadn't heard it coming, the quiet engine and the absence of any lights had taken them completely by surprise. It drove silently past them as they sat there hushed not daring to move, it pulled up a few yards past their hiding place. Two men got out of the vehicle and waited alongside the car for a moment, adjusting their eyes to the darkness before moving silently up the lane towards the farm.

Once out of earshot Bene called the farm to inform them of the men's arrival and told them to make sure all the doors and windows were locked and to stay upstairs; if the men attempted to gain entrance to the house they should call him.

"Right." whispered Bene. "Let's follow them and see where they go, I'll be interested to see if they find the package this time."

They'd just risen from the hay bales when Hils put out an arm and stopped him from going further.

"Did you hear that? There's another car pulling up outside and they haven't got lights on either, who could this be?"

The two were reduced to quiet whispers.

"I've no idea, I wasn't expecting anyone else but it looks as though there're more than two people interested in this package, what the hell is in it that's so important?"

They remained in the old barn and watched as another two men emerged through the darkness and made their way up the lane towards the farm. It was too dark to see who they were, only the outline of one could be seen, but nothing to identify either of them. Hils heard something that frightened her and she grabbed his arm tightly.

"They have guns Bene. I'd recognise that sound anywhere; one of them has just taken off the safety catch, should we phone for assistance?"

"We can't just yet because it's so quiet and they'd hear us. We'll wait until they get further up the lane."

Hils who had held on to his arm squeezed it again tightly.

"There's another car here as well, I've just seen a door light come on through the hedge over there. Whoever it is must have followed that last one here. This is crazy, we'll have to wait and see who gets out of this one now. It's getting a bit scary isn't it?"

She let go of his arm and they sat back down on the hay bales waiting for the occupants of the latest car to get out. It was deathly quiet in the barn, and there was no sound coming from the roadside where another unknown person stood quietly by the side of their car. Bene knew they couldn't move from the barn as they'd be seen by whoever was waiting there.

"We'll have to stay here for now until that last lot either come in or drive off again."

"What if the farmer phones Bene? I think you should put your phone on silent, I mean if they're in any trouble we can't just sit here and do nothing."

Bene took out his phone to switch it to silent but inadvertently pressed the wrong button and the flash light came on illuminating the barn and part of the lane towards the farm.

"Switch the bloody thing off Bene and let's hope no-one saw it."

But the light had been seen and the sound of people coming back down the lane made them nervous. Bene knew their hiding place had been discovered and they had to leave quickly before the men with guns came into the barn.

"Hils we need to go."

He took her arm and they rushed out of the barn through one of the open sides, quickly scanning the area for anywhere they could get cover. They ran as fast as they could along the grass, following the line of the hedge and trying not to make any noise. After about forty yards the hedge curved to follow the bend in the road, they followed it round hoping to be out of sight of the pursuing gunmen for a few seconds at least.

"Right over here now."

He led her across to another dilapidated old building which was in worse repair than the one they'd just left. This one was cluttered with more of the old farm machinery no longer in use. He dragged her inside and they squatted down behind an old tractor and waited to see if their getaway had been successful.

Sitting quietly Hils pulled some old sackcloth from the tractor to cover them and act as camouflage, and that was when Bene saw it. He used part of the sackcloth to wipe away the dust and accumulated dirt on the side of the tractor and revealed the name Deutz Allis.

"Look at that Hils this is what Brennan was trying to say. It wasn't Judge Alice, it was Deutz Allis the name of the tractor; the package must be hidden somewhere on it."

They remained very still listening for any signs of movement, but all they could hear was the gentle patter of rain which had just started and was drumming quietly on the corrugated roof above them.

"I think they must have gone Bene. Should we have a look around and see if the package is still here?"

"Yes, if we can find it we'll take it with us and get the hell out of here while they're still busy looking for us back there."

There was little left of the original tractor as over the years parts of it had been stripped off and put to other uses. He could feel all around the engine without difficulty but found nothing, Hils went to the front and looked over and under the machine, nothing there either, Bene moved to the back of the tractor, holding onto the metal seat with one hand his other hand came into contact with a tool box fixed underneath it. Easing open the rusty lid he put his hand inside and touched something wrapped in leather. He withdrew his hand

and brought out the package. Pulling Hils arm they sat down together and cautiously he opened the package. He pulled out a small packet which was wrapped in oilskin, tied with string and sealed with red wax. He was ecstatic.

"This is it Hils we've got it."

"Great, is there anything else in there?"

Bene put his hand back into the package and brought out a passport and an envelope, he transferred these to his pocket, but held onto the packet looking at it closely. The excitement of the moment had temporarily dimmed their natural senses and it was the sound of something rustling behind that jolted them back to reality.

"Just you stay where you are laddie and don't move."

The voice sounded familiar and Bene was trying to put a name to it, the cold barrel of a gun pressing into the back of his head had him breaking out into a cold sweat.

"Is that you Donald?"

"Aye, I told you I couldn't remember you being up at Jackdaws that night, but you said you were, so I thought I'd got my numbers wrong, I thought Dessie Milburn was the last one but if you were there as well then I must have forgotten. Anyway it makes no difference now because you really are the last one, and when I've disposed of you everything can get back to normal. It's a pity about the dog though because I had a really nice one sorted out for you. Maybe your widow will take some comfort from him, I'll take it round in a few days when she's got used to not having you around it will be good company for her."

He moved the gun to the back of Hils head.

"I'm sorry about you lassie because this has nothing to do with you, but I can't afford to let anyone live who knows my secret. The secret of Jackdaws I like to call it."

Bene was scared out of his wits, he'd no idea what secret Donald was talking about, but he wanted to know because that was the reason behind all the murders.

"What the hell is this Donald? I've no connection with the others and I've never once been in their company, so what happened when they were up at the house that night that made you want to kill them all, and why do you call it Jackdaws, its Grosvenor House isn't it?"

"Aye that's its proper name right enough but everyone over there calls it Jackdaws, on account of all the bits and pieces he brought back from his trips to the Far East and Africa, the place was full of junk. Anyway I'm sorry, but you did say you were there, and the way you looked at me I thought you'd been in that same company and you knew all about it. If you hadn't mentioned it in the pub we wouldn't have found ourselves in this situation, so you only have yourself to blame. If I were to let you live I'd be going to prison for a long time and I cannot have that. I was having a good life until those damned bowlers turned up at the pub one night and saw me. I had no choice but to do what I did, or they would have had me put away."

"But what was it all about Donald? You'll have to tell me."

"If you really want to know then I'll tell you, you're not going to live to repeat it so it'll do no harm."

"Yes tell me everything about what happened that night up at Andrew's house, as you say you've got nothing to lose because we won't be telling anyone."

Bene was trying to stall the man as long as possible in the hope that someone would come in and find them, or at some point he'd get an opportunity to turn the tables on him.

"Aye that's fair enough and you probably deserve it. I didn't give the others any warning because it was a question of them or me, and I knew it had to be me."

He relaxed and squatted down behind them but kept the gun touching the back of Bene's head. Hils sat with her head down not knowing what to do. It looked like her career in detection had reached its conclusion far too early.

"Well you know the old joke Andrew would play at his dinner parties, you were at one of them even if it wasn't that particular night so I don't need explain any of that to you. Well one night we had a big argument because Andrew took the joke a bit too far. As usual he shouted at me I was sacked, and as usual I took little notice of it; it had always been his way of course and I'd always gone along with it. But on this particular night he turned really nasty and all but threw me out of the house, screaming at me that he was changing his will in favour of those two useless nephews of his. Well those bowlers were there and they were laughing at my expense, they humiliated me. I went to see him the next morning to see if he'd got over his outburst and things had returned to normal, but they hadn't. Andrew told me I was finished up there and I'd get nothing from his will; it was all going to his nephews. There was no explanation as to why he'd changed his mind, but he was adamant. I think the drink had finally got to his brain and messed it up completely, his personality had changed overnight. I asked him for old time's sake if he would allow me to make him one last meal, and I was surprised when he agreed because I knew he'd throw me out as soon as he'd eaten it. Well I got the better of him and I slipped something into his food, the old bastard was gone the same night. I phoned the police and ambulance the next morning and told them I'd found him lying dead. It was a well-known fact that Andrew badly abused his body with over eating and the booze and the stupid doctor just wrote out a death certificate to verify that. I carried on as though I was still working for him and thought no-one would ever know the truth. I knew those bowlers wouldn't be back there and I didn't think I'd ever see them again."

"Anyway I hadn't given him time to make a new will so I got all his money and his house, and to me it was exactly what I deserved. But the place was far too big for one man so I moved down here to live in peace and comfort. I didn't know those bowlers lived out here in Longbarrow and Levensbridge and it was pure chance they saw me in the pub one night. I guessed they knew the truth so they had to go. I couldn't have them spoiling my new found wealth and comfortable lifestyle. So there you are, now you know everything."

"But why did you use two different guns Donald? Was that to throw us off the track?"

"Aye it was clever that wasn't it, it had you lot running around after two killers. That old one from the war was a bit dodgy so I chucked it; this one's much better and very reliable."

He paused, suddenly realising this was taking up too much of his time.

"I think we'll have to stop now, I want to go home."

He stood up noisily and with difficulty, keeping the gun pressed into the back of Bene's head.

"No more talking, you first and then the girl."

Two shots rang out with barely a second between them.

Chapter 35

The final reckoning

It was Alfie Brooks who slapped Bene's face and brought him back to consciousness; the shock of the gun going off had numbed his brain. Slowly he began to gather his thoughts and take in his surroundings which seemed very strange to him. Hils was sitting up and crying and he was trying to think where they were and why. It took several seconds before it came back to him and then he remembered the packet. He felt around in the dark but couldn't find it anywhere. Seeing Hils' predicament he moved over and put his arm around to comfort her. The rain was still falling lightly on the roof and darkness was all around. He swept his arm around but there was no packet to be found, instead it came into contact with a warm body lying motionless on the floor behind him. He pulled his hand away, feeling around with his other hand he touched someone else sitting on his other side, it was Alfie Brooks.

"Bloody good job them city fella's came in wasn't it, it was them that saved your bacon."

"What the hell happened, I thought we were goners?"

"You very nearly were; luckily they got here just in time, and when they saw what was happening they had no hesitation in shooting old Donald there. They wanted you alive because they hoped you had what they'd been looking for."

"The packet, did they take it?"

"Yes, you've seen the last of that; those two fellows have got it now and they didn't hang about for long once it was in their possession, I doubt you'll see them around here again."

"Damn it, I didn't get the chance to see what was in it."

"And I doubt you ever will now son; anyway did you get our money?"

Bene felt in his pocket.

"The only other things in the package were an old passport and this envelope."

He opened it and was surprised to see nothing inside.

"Let me have a look?"

Bene handed it over to Alfie who shone his torch inside and saw the bank details with an alphanumeric code that Finnian Brennan had jotted down six years ago.

"That's exactly what we needed, well done son." Alfie grimaced as he struggled to get up using his stick for support. He took something from his pocket.

"Before I go I'll leave you with this from you know who."

He handed Bene an envelope, which when opened would contain the name of the man who killed Finnian Brennan.

"Funny isn't it, in all the time I've sat talking to Donald in the pub I never suspected for a minute he could be responsible for anything like this, all those killings eh. It just goes to show how right you were son."

"What's that then?"

"You can know someone for years and think you know them well, then all of a sudden you realise you don't know them at all, funny that isn't it." Alfie chuckled. He turned to face Bene and nodded as a sign of respect for the man.

He left the barn just as Mrs Pattinson and Bryan came in with a flash lamp; the light from the torch picked out the two officers sitting on the floor and the dead body of Donald Neves behind them.

"When we heard the shots we phoned the police right away." said Mrs Pattinson "They should be here anytime now, we had to wait until those men had gone before we could get over here. We never expected any shooting; it must have been a terrible ordeal for the two of you, how are you?"

She went to sit down with Hils and try to reassure her that she was safe.

"Well I hope that's the end of it and we don't get any more visits from those two. Did you ever find out what it was they were looking for?"

Bene explained as best he could about the package and where he'd found it. He went on to tell them it had been taken away and no-one would see the package or the two smartly dressed men ever again.

"Well thank goodness for that I couldn't have stood much more of them creeping around in the dark on our farm."

And then she saw the body lying on the ground behind one of the bales of hay.

"Is that the poor devil that got shot then, was he a friend of yours?"

"No, I thought he was but it turns out he's the one we've been looking for, the man responsible for all the murders around here these last few weeks. Luckily those two men who've been bothering you recently actually came to our rescue tonight; they shot him just as he was about to shoot Hils and me, so as far as I'm concerned they can keep the packet and good luck to them."

"Can I bring you a nice hot drink love until the police get here?" Mrs Pattinson asked.

"That would be lovely Mrs Pattinson; it's just what we need." Said Hils

Bene looked at Hils.

"How are you feeling now, any better?"

"Yeah I'm great." She lied smiling.

"It's not always like this in CID you know, we don't have this much fun all the time."

"Well, if you've lasted this long I can do the same, do you think I'll be kept on?"

"I think we were lucky tonight; it could have gone either way and ended up a lot worse than it did, but you didn't crack and you handled the situation really well. But you've had a hell of a shock tonight and that may have changed your mind about joining us."

"If anything I think what happened tonight has made me even more determined to get on the team, do you think the Inspector will have me?"

"If you still want to come over to our side leave it to me, I'll make sure you're in the team."

Hils beamed.

An armed response team arrived along with Inspector Sowerby but too late to be of any use. He ordered them to check over the farm, the buildings and surrounding fields to make sure there were no guns still in the area, then came over to join Bene and Hils.

"How are the two of you?"

"We'll be fine sir, and there's our man lying over there behind that bale. Donald Neves is his name and he's the fellow we've been chasing after this last two weeks; he's killed four already, and if those guys hadn't got here just in time it would have been six."

"Good God Bene, you could both have been killed. And Hils, this must have been a nightmare for you?"

"All in a day's work sir." She forced a faint smile which failed to convince the Inspector.

"Nevertheless, I want you both to go home and get some rest and I'll see you back in the office this afternoon. Any luck with this Brennan fellow Bene before you go?"

Bene told him about the package he'd found and the two men who had taken it. He told him about the passport, and the bank details where the stolen money could be found. Finally he handed over the envelope containing the name of Finnian Brennan's killer.

"Brilliant that seems to have cleared everything up. I can't say how delighted I am that the murder of that man back in 2012 has been solved and finally put to rest. I'll tell Adam, it'll be a great relief to him to know what it was all about. Right the two of you, tomorrow afternoon in my office." He turned and went out looking for the armed squad.

Hils lived on her own in a flat she had in town. Bene thought that for the rest of the night she should spend it in company and in a place where she'd feel safe; he didn't want her to go back to an empty flat.

"Right you're coming home with me for the night OK? No arguments. There's a spare bed and you can have a bath or shower and something to eat with us. You shouldn't be on your own tonight after what you've been through."

Hils didn't bother to answer.

Bene called Alex and briefly explained what had happened and to make Hils welcome when they came home. It was going on for five o'clock and just getting light when they arrived there. Dot told Hils to go and shower and come down for something to eat before going to bed. Bene waited then followed her in the shower. When he came down there was a good old fry up waiting, Dot and Alex had been busy in the kitchen.

"Right Hils," said Dot "when you've finished that you can go up and sleep in my room."

She told her where it was, and as soon as Hils finished her breakfast Dot shooed her upstairs.

"Off you go now and have a good sleep, and don't come down until you're ready."

Bene stayed to have a quick chat with Alex and Dot to reassure them everything was alright before going to bed himself.

It was twelve o'clock when he woke up, and after a quick shower he rushed downstairs looking for something more to eat. Hils was already there and tucking in to a meal of ham, eggs and chips. The strain she'd been showing the previous night had all but disappeared from her face and she looked much brighter and quite chirpy.

"Well you've had a good sleep, how was the bed?" Bene asked.

"Lovely and I feel great, I couldn't have made all this food we've been having, so it's thanks to Dot and Alex that I feel good again, how about you?"

"Yeah OK, I'm actually looking forward to going in to work to see Sowerby."

"What do you think he'll say?"

"Who Sowerby, just leave him to me."

They sat and rested after the meal and talked briefly about what they'd been through the night before; despite the terror they'd been subjected to, a hot shower, a good sleep and hot food had all but returned them to normal. Satisfied that Hils was suffering no lasting effects from her ordeal he suggested they report to the station.

Much to their embarrassment, on arrival at the station the two were cheered into the office by the officers on duty, with Inspector Sowerby leading the applause.

"Come into my office and we'll get it all sorted."

It took the best part of an hour for Bene to give Sowerby all the details of their nights' work, and when it was done the Inspector sat back and smiled.

"As you've probably noticed division have scarpered pretty quickly and we're in the process of getting back to normal, I'll have your desks and all the other stuff moved back up from the basement and we can get back to running our own show again. The news from the hospital isn't good though, the doctors think Dessie might have sustained permanent damage to his brain with internal bleeding. There's a chance he may never fully recover, and even if he does it's unlikely he'll remember anything about what happened."

"That's sad news sir." Said Bene "It's a pity Donald Neves was killed as he'll never stand trial for all those murders; it feels a bit of an anti-climax not having him to face a jury."

"Yes, well he may be dead but we're not finished with him yet, I've ordered an exhumation of Andrew McLean's body, and I think we'll find he was poisoned just like Neves told you.

He's been a real test for us that little Scotsman and he almost got away with it. He's been damned clever all along and he never once showed up on our radar"

"Well if those MI5 men hadn't put in an appearance when they did he would have got away with it. Once he'd got rid of Hils and me there'd be no-one to know what happened up at Andrew's house that night. And if I hadn't shot myself in the foot by telling him I'd been there he'd have had no reason to come after me."

"But if you hadn't told him we'd probably never have got him. With Dessie out of the way that would have been the last witness, he'd have stopped the killing and we'd never have known who it was. We'd have been left with an open case and no chance of ever closing it. Still we did get there in the end, and we did find out the secret of Jackdaws"

"Did you get the name of the man who murdered Brennan sir? According to Alfie Brooks that envelope he gave me contained the name of his killer and I wondered who it was."

"Well there was a name in there and he's definitely Irish, there's no trace of him over here so I expect he went back over to Ireland soon after the murder. I've given his name to the Garda and they'll have him picked up if they can find him. We should get some DNA back from Brennan's clothes soon and I'll have that sent over as well. If they can track this fellow down we'll see if it matches up with him."

"I was just thinking about that business up in Scotland sir, I mean most of the victims were on that last Scottish tour, and if Alan Browning was innocent as it now seems possible then maybe in a weird sort of way he's been avenged."

Inspector Sowerby considered this.

"Well I must admit I hadn't thought about that, but maybe in some way Neves has inadvertently acted as his avenging angel, I don't think it will do Browning any good though it's come far too late for that. But it may be some sort of consolation for his son."

"Is there any chance we'll find out what was in that packet sir?"

"I thought you might ask that and I do have a bit of information, but bound by the Official Secrets Act so you will not divulge this to anyone, not family, close friends or anyone. It's come from high up and it will never be released to the media, or find its way into the public domain. I need you to swear to that."

The two officers confirmed their agreement.

"Briefly it concerns something that happened back in 1940 during the early years of WW2. It was the time when Hitler was planning an invasion of England. Some high ranking commanding officers in the Air Force and Navy didn't want a war with Germany and went behind the backs of the government and their own people to try and prevent it. They put forward a proposal to Hitler that if he gave them a specific date and location of his planned invasion they'd ensure there was little or no resistance. Ships would be kept in port, and all planes would remain on the ground. By the time the army mustered a force strong enough to get there to repel them, the Germans would have established a secure beach head. Their troops and armoury would be able to invade the country in great numbers and with little resistance. The letter was signed by those officers and it was to be taken by courier up to Liverpool and flown by private plane to Berlin. Somewhere along the way it was intercepted and ended up in that Irish bank. After the war, someone was going to blackmail those traitors and make them pay heavily for it."

"But the packet was never collected from the bank and it was presumed that whoever put it there had died. At some point the government got wind of it and had to get it back to save them embarrassment, and stop it being leaked to the press and the signatories' names being made public. Somehow they found out where it had been sitting all those years but it went missing before they could retrieve it. They soon tied it down to that fellow Brennan, and when they found out about his death six years ago they put a team onto it, the one led by Adam. But it was just a token effort because there was no way they wanted us prying into it. They closed the investigation down before anything was done so they could follow it up themselves. They did an extensive search of the farm and the area around it but never found anything so they more or less gave up. When these latest murders started up it resurrected the old murder, and when they found out you were looking into the man's death they started poking their noses in again and renewed the search on the farm, but they still couldn't find it. They were following you around hoping you might lead them to it, which in the end you did. I expect by now the letter will have been destroyed, and any rumours or theories that it ever existed will be pure conjecture. The rest as you say is history."

"Wow that's some story isn't it?" said Hils.

"Remember what I said now, nothing of what I've just told you leaves' this room."

"Of course sir," said Bene "but can I ask you something?"

"Yes as long as it has nothing to do with that letter."

"I wondered if you've made a decision on Constable Taylor sir."

"Who?"

"Constable Taylor sir, she's done a terrific job working with me and I think she deserves it. I couldn't possibly have done it without her."

"Constable Taylor? Let me think now."

The Inspector seemed at a bit of a loss.

"Constable Taylor, oh you mean Detective Constable Taylor. Do you think I haven't been aware of her involvement in this? Yes that was an easy decision to make."

He stood up and shook hands with her. "Congratulations Detective Constable Taylor you are now a fully-fledged member of the team."

Hils beamed.

"Thank you sir, you don't know how much this means to me and I won't let you down."

"I know you won't, now get out both of you. Go and do some celebrating and I'll see you in the morning."

They all went out together that night. Bene, Alex and Dot met up with Hils and her boyfriend at a local Italian restaurant where they had a wonderful meal together. Back home Bene fell into his large comfy armchair and Alex flopped down on top of him.

"I've loved living here with you and your mam Alex but I'm really looking forward to being in our own house, how about you?"

"Yes it'll be great, just the three of us, you and me and our new baby, and we'll still be handy for mam, she can come round anytime she wants can't she?"

"Yes, perfect."

ABOUT THE AUTHOR

I am Cumbrian born and bred, and though widely travelled I have spent the majority of my life living and working in my home county. After leaving school I managed to work my way through a wide range of diverse occupations before finally finding my true vocation with Royal Mail. I spent many happy years there, the last three as Customer Liaison Manager.

I am married to Pat and we have a daughter Nicola, two grandchildren Kris and Alex and three great grandchildren Lillie, Frederick and Maisie. They have given me lots of pleasure over the years and many happy memories to go with them, I'm very proud of them all. My hobbies include spending time with the kids, bowling, pottering about in the garden, eating out with friends and supporting my beloved Manchester City.

Writing a novel had been a passion of mine for many years and retirement gave me the opportunity to fulfil this ambition.

Lightning Source UK Ltd.
Milton Keynes UK
UKHW010410091220
374847UK00001B/62

9 781839 753442